Blades of the Night

The Severance Trilogy

Book One

Daniel Wiebe

United States laws and regulations are public domain and not subject to copyright. Any unauthorized copying, reproduction, translation, or distribution of any part of this material without permission by the author is prohibited and against the law.

The characters, names, events, and all places, incidents, organizations, and dialog in this novel are either the products of the writer's imagination or are used fictitiously.

Copyright © 2023 Daniel Wiebe

All rights reserved.

ISBN-13: 979-8-89217-085-7

First Printing: 2023

Follow the author, Daniel Wiebe, at:

https://www.facebook.com/theseverancetrilogy

If you're expecting a happy ending then I would stop reading here. This is the only one I'll give you.

"And they lived happily ever after."

"He who fights with monsters might take care lest he thereby become a monster..."

-Friedrich Nietzsche

PROLOGUE

My son is dead. My boy is dead, and I killed him. Right in front of my wife...

The realization of his actions finally struck him after he had traveled all this distance. Made him sick to his stomach and his blood run cold. As it turned out, he had no reason to kill that boy, his boy. He was fooled.

Arms pumped furiously by his sides as he ran. His feet thudded across the hard-packed ground, and his legs thrummed as blood pulsed through his veins. He had long ago discarded the heavy-plated armor that wore him down. He needed to be able to run for as long as he possibly could, and he knew where he was going; his armor would not protect him, for he ran into the open embrace of death.

King Nuse's only thoughts were on the recent events that unfolded barely three hours ago. The horrible images of those devilish creatures that spewed from the body of the king he murdered remained at the forefront. He also thought of the terrors he had falsely blamed on his wife, Mairead, and his family. Nervous eyes darted across the darkening horizon before him, expecting one of those awful beasts to jump out at any moment. Sweat beaded down his face and poured down his back, drenching his clothes.

His last goal in life now was to lead the vicious monsters as far away as possible from his subjects and the people he loved and cared for. To give them enough time to prepare and protect themselves as best as they could. He hoped his sacrifice would be enough, but he would never know that answer.

The last item of value that he kept on him was his sword. He knew that his life would quickly come to an end, but he would be damned if he died without a fight. He heard a growl to his left. Before he realized it, his sword was in his hand, and he twisted in that direction to face whatever made the noise. Nothing stirred, however. He sucked in a shaky deep breath, sheathed his sword, and began to run again on protesting legs.

He lost track of how far or how long he had been running. It felt like weeks, but it could not have been later than midnight. Nuse stumbled to a halt. He had to catch his breath or feared his lungs would become so tired they would be unable to pull in any air. He glanced around and saw that he was in a sparsely wooded area. He was familiar with these lands, but it was dark, and he only paid attention to his surroundings now. Nuse could feel that he was not alone. The presence of something else accompanied him.

Dry leaves crunched behind him as something heavy approached. He turned around slowly, drawing his sword in the same movement. A dozen humanoid creatures stood before him, bathed in silver moonlight. He could see more movement behind them, but there was no way to tell how many creatures there were now.

Their eyes gleamed yellow from their faces. Their skin was blacker than the night surrounding them and shone with a tar-like consistency. Shivers racked Nuse's body as he saw the unnatural length of their arms and claw-like fingers that protruded from their hands. Thin, needle-like teeth jutted from their jaws in an uncoordinated jumble. They were thin, but Nuse imagined they were more durable than they looked.

He held his sword before him and slowed his breathing, trying to calm his nerves. The creatures watched him as if saying, 'Is that all?'

Almost as if they were one, the creatures surged forward. Adrenaline rushed through King Nuse's veins one last time, and his ears pounded with the surge of blood. He let out a final scream as the creatures closed the distance.

Nuse sliced one down before he was overtaken. As he felt his body tear and rip, his final thoughts shifted to his daughter, twin to his son, to attempt to block out the pain he felt as he died. They named her Elasaid. He was sorry he would never be there for her as she grew up, and he hoped she would be cared for without him.

ONE
-FRIENDS-

"Why do you always have to leave, Sainte?" Ellie asked, twirling her black curly hair around a finger. "Why can't you just stay here with me? You come here often enough. You should stay," she pouted, already knowing what he would say. Ellie's eighteenth birthday was tomorrow, and she wanted Sainte to stay for it, even though she knew he would return later. She looked at him from across the stone table cluttered with wooden puzzles and books while she waited for an answer.

"You know I can't stay, Ellie. It's how things have been since the beginning of time, I must leave to get you food and maybe..."

He paused. "A present. No, I haven't forgotten about your birthday," he said with a smirk. "You and I both know I'll be back tomorrow, I promise," Sainte replied and smiled at Ellie as she sighed at the answer she expected. He was only twenty-two years old but already had flecks of gray in his dark brown hair, and his eyes had seen more than most people double his age.

Ellie never gave Sainte much trouble when it was time for him to leave because she knew he only left to get her necessities. She would never knowingly give him a hard time or ask him to do something he would not want to do. Ellie respected him, and she knew that it was returned.

"I know you'll be back... I just like hearing you say it. It gives me something to look forward to. Also, when you return, please bring some more carrots and grapes. I finished the last batch already." She laughed as Sainte looked at her, amazed that she had eaten them so quickly. "They were just so good, I couldn't help myself," she said in response to the face he made. "Bring something sweet, too!"

"You ate them all before I could have any? I shouldn't be surprised knowing you. Thanks a lot for thinking about me, now I won't have anything to eat because of you. Think you deserve anything sweet after this?" He smirked.

"You didn't get anything to eat because you weren't here to eat with me. You should have been here," she said matter-of-factly. "And, of course I deserve it. After all, it is my birthday."

"I already said that I know it's your birthday, yet you keep bringing it up. Keep this up, and I won't bring anything," Sainte said.

Ellie scoffed. "You wouldn't dare." Sainte just raised his brow at her but she felt her playful mood slipping away. "Sainte," she began. "I know what it's like outside, but are you sure I can't go out and see for myself some time? With you, of course."

"You know it's too dangerous. There's nothing out there for you, anyway," he explained. She'd heard this many times before but let him finish as she knew it comforted him. "The only reason I go outside is for you so that I can get you food and drink. If I had my way, I'd never leave you." He finished, as he always did, with a smile.

Ellie took a breath in and let it out. "I know. Sometimes I get so, I don't know, tired of being in here." Lonely. She didn't say that, though, because she knew it would make him sad.

"I know you do, and I'm sorry. There's plenty for you to do, however. Have you read all your books yet? Maybe try to write your own? Or tend to your garden? You must stay in here. I can't risk losing you."

"It's all right, Sainte..." She knew he was only trying to raise her spirits, but she'd grown weary of reading and gardening. Still, she smiled, trying to remain upbeat. "But tomorrow is my birthday, so you better not let me down!"

Sainte laughed. "All right, fine. I'll bring you a present, but I'm not saying what it'll be."

"Thank you," she said triumphantly. "That's all I wanted to hear."

Sainte stood up and stretched. "I'm glad you think so. But it's about time I go; got to have enough time to figure out what I'm going to get you." He stepped towards the door.

"Wait!" Ellie exclaimed as she scrambled up and embraced him in a warm hug. Sainte hugged her back.

He seemed genuinely surprised. "What was that for?"

Ellie shrugged. "Just wanted to give you a hug." She blushed, suddenly embarrassed by his piercing eyes. "Don't expect them all the time," she said while looking down, wanting him to avoid seeing her flushed cheeks.

"Whatever you say, Ellie," Sainte replied looking into her eyes. "I'll see you whenever I come back."

"I'll be here. And don't be late," she scolded to his back as he walked out the door. "Wouldn't want you to miss any more meals." But really, she didn't want to miss him any more than she had to.

▼▲▼

Sainte stepped through the door from the clean room into a muggy brick-and-mortar tunnel. He had to physically tear himself away from Ellie. Her light blue eyes were crystal clear and seemed to be made of the skies themselves. She was innocence personified. Of course, that's why she had to remain within the mountain, to protect her from the evils that lay without. For her to remain pure.

Torches lined the brick walls to stave off the humidity that hung in the air like a curtain but had little effect. Sainte looked to the door at the other end of the straight tunnel, about seventy yards away, before turning to the one he just walked out of. He pulled out a key ring that only had two keys on it. Sainte pulled a bar across the door that led to Ellie and locked it. Then he walked down the tunnel to the other door and closed it similarly, but instead of one bar, this door had three. Both doors were reinforced with metal. Satisfied that all the locks were in place, Sainte walked back down the tunnel.

He took this time to clear his thoughts of Ellie. He could not afford to be distracted by any thoughts of her for the rest of the night. Instead, he occupied his mind by double-checking the traps laid out within the tunnel he was sworn to protect every night. Cauldrons of oil sat under every other torch on each side of the tunnel, and three sets of wooden swinging doors were also in the tunnel. The doors were open and flush against the sides of the walls, held there with a lock and spring. Sainte had to step on a small button on the floor to close them. The switch would release the locks on the doors, and the spring would slam the doors shut, locking automatically upon closing.

He checked every door meticulously and every cauldron to ensure it was full. Once he returned to Ellie's door, he was satisfied that everything was working as it should be. Now he turned to his armor which he had laid out before visiting Ellie. Firelight glinted off the dull metal. When he had first received the armor two years ago, it had shined with a gleam in a way that only new armor could. Now all light it reflected was distorted by hammered-out dents and buffed-out scratches.

Sainte started to put on his armored boots and caught himself sighing as he did so. Lately, it felt as if with each passing night, he disliked what he did more and more. He cinched his left boot tight with a sharp tug, then his right. Next, on to his waist and thighs. He grunted as he clasped the gear around his waist, making sure everything still fit into place perfectly, for this armor was his last line of defense between life and death. He fitted everything to his body quickly but efficiently. Sainte had little time before his work would begin. Satisfied with his legs, he grabbed his chest piece and shrugged it on with the chains rattling together slightly. It was a simple piece, yet the most important. He connected two straps over his shoulders, then slipped his gauntlets on. The last thing he needed was his helmet.

Sainte grabbed hold of his helmet and stared at the face of it. The helmet had been through countless battles but had almost nothing to show for it. After each night, the blacksmith repaired every piece of his armor. Sainte fought every night for two years and required only perfect armor. He donned the helmet, ensuring it clicked into place and connected it to his body armor. He turned his head left and right, assuring himself he had all the maneuverability he needed. Satisfied, he grabbed his sword and buckled it to his waist. His parents had given him his sword before he left for Training. They told him that it belonged to his grandfather.

Sainte drew it, revealing the dangerous naked steel. It hissed as it was pulled from the sheath, echoing down the tunnel as if promising to protect and kill for it. He took a moment to marvel at his weapon. It was old, had seen more battles than he could guess, yet the blade had never broken. It maintained its sharpness far longer than any blade he knew of. It never let him down. He sheathed the sword and took a deep breath.

He had to remind himself why he had joined the Blades of the Night many years ago. He had joined to seek adventure, learn how to fight, protect Crearia from the night's dangers, and do something more with his life than be a farmer. He strived to do something that not many people could do. He found all that and more. After the years-long Training, he was given the most esteemed position one could be in the Blades of the Night, but not necessarily the most sought after. He was chosen to be the one to protect the Barrier. He was her last defense. The last man that stood between her and Malignin that had no goal in life except to corrupt her.

Ellie was the Barrier, and Sainte was her Shield.

▼▲▼

Iris Lispin stood on top of the above-ground tunnel that led to the mountain's base that housed the Barrier's home. She strummed the string of her bow and listened to the satisfying hum of the newly strung weapon. She checked her two quivers, one on each hip, to ensure that all her arrows were in order and would not get caught on anything as she drew them. A sword was strapped to her back if she ran out of arrows or for close combat. Iris had already donned her armor except for her helmet. Before night officially settled, she always loved to watch the sunset. She soaked it in and relished the warming breaths of light as if they may be her last. For all she knew, they might be. Iris felt her helmet stifled her in the evening twilight, so she always waited to put it on.

She watched the sun sink towards the horizon across the plains spotted with guard walls and towers. Joining the Blades of the Night was not what she had in mind for her future when she was younger, yet there she stood. When she was a little girl, she had fanciful dreams of beautiful weddings. Her wedding gowns were riddled with bright flowers. Her husband-to-be stood in a suit of gleaming ceremonial armor, smiling at her as she walked closer to him. When she was young, she only wanted to start and raise a family of her own.

All her childhood friends grew up and had the weddings Iris dreamed of. She was glad for them, but each time they married, it was a harsh reminder of the life she chose for herself. It eventually got to a point where there were no more weddings. All her friends moved on to start new chapters in their lives. None of them kept in touch with her anymore, nor did she stay in touch with them.

Iris was twenty-four and was quickly growing out of the prime age for suitors, not that it mattered. Rarely did relationships in the Blades of the Night blossom into more than one-night stands, and Iris was no exception. Her duty in the Blades of the Night often stood in the way of her romantic life. Even when it may have worked out with someone, she made an excuse to break it off. Iris wanted to be with someone who would give her a sense of protection. Someone who could provide for her. So far, every man she had been with had brought nothing to the table that she could not bring herself.

She snorted to herself; now was not the time to think of these things. Iris focused on her breathing to relax her mind before night officially began. She took a deep breath, held it, and blew it out slowly. The feeling of her chest slowly rising and falling soothed her restless mind.

Iris leaned down and picked up her helmet, stretching as she stood up. She placed the helmet on snugly. She took an arrow and nocked it as the sun sank below the horizon. After all, the time was getting close when she would have to use it. It would be foolish to be caught unawares. She had one last fleeting thought about how changed her life could have been were she raised differently before she forced herself to focus on the oncoming night.

She may have successfully settled her mind, but her fingers moved of their own free will. She continuously strummed her bowstring like an instrument. She was anxiously waiting to put it to use.

▼▲▼

Miqel Russ shifted from foot to foot in front of the doorway to the tunnel leading to the Barrier. He was a full head shorter than the top of the door, but what he lacked in height, he made up for in strength. The short man was built like an ox. His arms and legs were corded with muscles. The scar on the right side of his face always made him look like he wore a permanent scowl. When he smiled, it only made it worse.

Miqel worked alongside Iris as a buffer between Sainte and the Malignin, and they became very good at what they did. He remained on the ground as she shot arrows from atop the tunnel. They were not meant to halt the flow of Malignin completely, but they were expected to lighten the load. Miqel glanced to the top of the tunnel where he knew Iris would be.

Excitement coursed through his veins as he noticed the sun was almost below the horizon. He could not wait for the night's shadow to cover him, signaling the beginning of the battle. In anticipation of the fight, he was already fully dressed in his armor. Miqel chose to join the Blades at an early age. He held the members of the Blades of the Night in high regard ever since he learned about them at a young age and vowed to become one. He went through the Training with only himself in mind.

Every sunset before fighting, he sharpened his double-bladed-axe. The schlick of the whetstone against his axe soothed his nerves. It was one of the only things that made him calm. As the last of the sun's rays disappeared, he pocketed the stone, satisfied with the sharpness of his weapon. He stood up from his kneeling position, pushing up with his axe. The axe was almost as tall as he was. When he first chose his weapon, many of his peers in the Blades of the Night laughed at him, thinking it would be too large for such a short man. Miqel quickly proved them wrong. Once he started swinging the heavy axe around, not much could stop it.

That was a long time ago, though. It had been a while since anyone had laughed at Miqel at his expense. Most people wanted to avoid reaching the end of his short temper to see what was there.

As memories of his past swirled away in his mind, he found his fingers thrumming eagerly on the shaft of his axe. Darkness was now settling across the landscape, and his eyes scanned the land before him, searching for any movement.

▼▲▼

Iris was the first to spot the hordes of Malignin that managed to make it past the first defenses. They scrambled towards the towering mountain that held the Barrier, flowing around the towers and walls like an oncoming flood. She always hoped to ease the initial wave for Miqel, so she nocked an arrow, took aim, and waited. The Malignin still had to get within range. As soon as they did, she started releasing arrows into the horde. There was no need to aim because the Malignin rushed forward in such a large tight group that an arrow would score a hit as long as it was fired in their general direction. Some Malignin fell with one blow; others kept barreling on. It hardly mattered. Each successful hit helped Miqel and Sainte that much more. So far, she could not tell if any Malignin had died, but in truth, she did not particularly care. Iris observed arrows arcing amongst the Malignin from other Blades' positions. It was always a soothing sight to see. A reminder that she and Miqel were not the only ones fighting. At times it seemed as if they were.

As the Malignin raced closer, her hands shook more. Iris had to pick her targets now, which always made her nervous. There was no room for error. The only way she knew how to cure the shakes was to get a few good shots off. A few well-aimed shots always increased her confidence.

Iris took a deep breath and held it as she nocked another arrow. She peered down the shaft, all the way to the point, aiming at a particularly savage-looking Malignin. Slobber slung from its mouth as it tore its head left and right. It was the closest one to Miqel. She let out her breath, and as the last of it left her mouth, she released the arrow. It sliced through the air, graceful and deadly, hitting the beast in the eye and crumpling it to the ground. She nocked another arrow and did not even notice that her shakes had already gone.

▼▲▼

A grin formed on Miqel's face when he saw the first wave of Malignin. Excitement eagerly coursed through his veins in anticipation of the coming battle. He felt the ground tremble familiarly beneath his feet caused by the stampede of Malignin. His heart beat in rhythm with the quaking ground, one with the earth. He wanted to rush headfirst into the maelstrom of beasts, but he knew that the best place to fight them was right where he was.

Miqel stared down a Malignin as it rushed closer, marking it as the first to feel his axe's bite. The Malignin stared right back from the sunken hollows where its yellow eyes were. Needle-like teeth glistened in the faint starlight as its jaws snapped open and closed. Miqel could hear its snorting breaths through flared nostrils as it quickly closed the distance to him. The Malignin ran on all four legs but fought on two, using their six-inch-long claws on each hand as their primary means of attack. Their claws were as sharp as swords but never seemed to dull, and their black skin glinted in the starlight.

As it almost got within reach, Miqel braced himself for his first kill of the night. His corded muscles tensed under taunt skin, ready to burst into action. However, that Malignin was not his to claim. Arrows were already falling among the endless ranks of Malignin, felling a few here and there, but Miqel's determined eyes never left that of the first Malignin.

In the blink of an eye, the Malignin was sliding face-down on the ground, the tip of an arrow sticking out from the back of its head. It only took him a second to realize Iris had taken his kill. Disappointed but unsurprised, Miqel shifted his focus to another Malignin without losing a beat. There were more to kill. There always were.

Miqel roared at the Malignin as their forces barreled toward him as one. Claws slashed, sliced, and stabbed at him. A few got by his defense, but they slid harmlessly off his armor. He was used to this, though, and he blocked the attacks easily enough. Before he knew it, his whole world was chaos.

Suddenly, his axe head was gripped by a Malignin. It grinned at him as it pressed closer, almost close enough to kiss him. Most men would not have been able to hold a Malignin at bay like this, but Miqel was not most men. His axe was the only thing that saved him, for if it was not there, the Malignin would be holding his insides instead. Miqel's back was against the tunnel door, precisely what he wanted. Using the door as leverage, he pushed back. The more he pushed, the more the metal sliced into the Malignin's hands. With a final shove, he jerked his axe down and cut through the Malignin's hands. He quickly push-kicked the Malignin back and slammed his axe into its chest. Miqel yanked out his axe, followed by a spurt of blood spraying onto him. He basked in the red shower, even tasted a few droplets that landed on his lips, and his grin grew wider. Miqel hefted his axe, ready to move on to his next kill.

He did not have to wait long. The Malignin practically offered themselves as sacrifices to him. No matter which direction he attacked, a Malignin fell with each wild swing. He felt more Malignin blood spray onto his face through the slits of his helmet. The warmth of the blood comforted him in a way nothing else could.

▼▲▼

Sainte could hear the sounds of fighting from outside the tunnel. He knew it was only a matter of time before his own battle began. As soon as the thought crossed his mind, the door that led outside rattled violently as something was slammed against it. The rattling only lasted a few seconds, but then it ceased.

After all the torches were lit and the oil was checked, all Sainte was expected to do was wait. Wait until the Malignin broke through, and they always did. They did every night for him, as they did for Julian, the Shield before him. There was no telling how long he would have to wait before they broke in. The Malignin broke through whenever, however, they could. The Blades outside could only hold them off for so long. The onslaught was endless until sunrise. Lately, the Malignin seemed more ruthless than usual. They could break through in the first few minutes of their attack, the last few minutes, or anytime between. The past week they had broken through earlier each night. There were whispers amongst the Blades of the Night that the tactics the Malignin had been using lately had never been observed before.

Sainte strained to listen to the battle outside, wondering if he could deduce how it was going based on sounds alone. He liked to think he could hear the sound of blades sinking into dark flesh, of Malignin taking their final breaths, but those were just fanciful thoughts. The Blades were beginning to wane in number and had resorted to new Training procedures, drastically decreasing training time. For every five Blades that died, they only had two replacements, making the Blades of the Night decrease in number slowly, day after day, while the Malignin never seemed to lessen.

He pushed those thoughts from his mind as his nights were already troubling enough by themselves. When he fought Malignin, it gave his mind respite as he no longer had to think about his actions. If he took the time to think about anything else, hesitated for a second, he would die. All he had to do was rely on his muscle memory, which never failed him.

He successfully pushed those first thoughts away, but as he waited with nothing else to do, another set of thoughts took their place of a time long ago when he was young and lived with his parents. Before he joined the Blades of the Night, he lived in the small town of Bethrune, nestled in the middle of the mountain range known as the Mouth of the World. It was simple back then. Farming, herding, and trading were what his life consisted of. That was not enough for him. Sainte yearned for something more. He knew that he would not be content with that lifestyle forever. He sought to do something with his life that meant something that had more purpose than farming. Before he knew it, he found what he searched for.

To settle his thoughts, Sainte recited the White Wyvern's blessing. A common blessing among the Blades of the Night. "Darkness creates night; sun creates light, White Wyverns hear my prayer, grant me light as guidance through the night." He found that saying that always seemed to soothe his anxious thoughts before the fighting began.

No sooner had he finished the blessing did the door to the tunnel splinter. Malignins' clawed hands scrabbled greedily through, searching for flesh to tear. The sounds of battle from outside multiplied ten-fold in the tunnel now. Echoes drummed against Sainte's ears, clouding his mind with the fog of war. Bringing his thoughts right to where they needed to be.

He had to remind himself that they could only get shoulder-width apart in the tunnel. All he had to do was fight one at a time. Use the doors if necessary. As the first Malignin crawled through the door and toward him, promising death, he gripped his sword parallel to the ground with both hands. A sudden calm washed over him as his instincts took over. He moved as soon as the Malignin was close enough for him to smell the sweet odor of decay from its breath. Calculated, swiftly, precisely, he sliced his sword down. The Malignin was cut from throat to groin; putrid intestines slid to the floor.

Without missing a breath, Sainte shifted the point of his sword up, neatly skewering the next Malignin onto his blade. He felt it shudder through its last breath as he pulled his sword free. The next Malignin was already leaping at him. As it soared at him, the last thing Sainte thought was that this would be a long night.

The battle raged on throughout the night, never having a lull, never a break for the men or women of the Blades of the Night. After all, the Malignin never needed a break. The Blades matched the Malignin's ferocity in battle beat for beat. All went well, or at least as well as could be expected.

As quickly as the first rays of sunlight shone over the horizon, the Malignin ceased their assault. The sunlight did not physically hurt the Malignin but effectively rendered them blind. Since the Malignin were not stupid creatures, they knew when enough was enough, and they fled when necessary. Not all of them made it, however. There were many Malignin dead, but there were also many Blades killed. There were not enough recruits to replace the number of dead Blades. As long as the Malignin never broke through, it was nothing to worry about. At least, that was the common mindset.

The three friends, Sainte, Iris, and Miqel, shared an end-of-battle ritual. The very last Malignin they fought for the night they would wound but keep alive. Then, when the Malignin fled, they would gather outside with their wounded Malignin and watch the sunrise together. After the sun had fully risen above the horizon, they would leave the Malignin to eventually go blind if they had not already, then die.

This morning was no different.

Miqel had his Malignin on the ground, quivering with each breath, arms and legs broken. Its head looked in either direction in desperation. Iris stood next to Miqel. Her Malignin was shot through the legs multiple times and skewered to the ground with her arrows. They were both waiting outside of the entrance to the tunnel for Sainte.

"Where r'yat, Sainte?" Miqel hollered down the tunnel, "Yer gonna be late." Most of the torches were burnt out, but they could both see a light source moving further down the tunnel, followed by a grunt. Shortly after that, Sainte emerged.

His helmet was already removed, and his armor was scratched and dented in multiple places, but the Malignin he dragged behind him was in worse shape. Where its arms and legs had been, there were only stumps now. Sainte dropped it unceremoniously next to the other two Malignin.

"Had to cauterize it so it wouldn't bleed out too fast," he said between breaths. Glancing at it, he shrugged and continued. "Damn thing wouldn't stay still. I wouldn't want it to miss this beautiful morning." He looked at his two friends.

Miqel shrugged in agreement while Iris shook her head with a slight smile.

And they stood, side by side, watching the sunrise. There was a mutual understanding between them to remain silent during this time and enjoy the Malignin's squeals of discomfort. Each knew that this sunrise might be the last one they watched together; words would only ruin the moment.

TWO
-FAMILY-

Sunlight streamed into the rocky room in a solid beam. Big green leaves, red flowers, ferns, and more soaked in the light greedily. Morning dew slid off tender leaves as Ellie rustled them when she gingerly stepped around them to her favorite spot. Arriving at the large rock near the center of the room, she climbed atop it and lounged back on her arms. The base of the rock was covered with moss, but the top was cleared of it because of how often Ellie used it.

She crossed her legs and made herself comfortable. Her gaze followed the rocky walls up towards the crevice at the ceiling that allowed the sunlight in and let her mind wander. "How bad could it be outside?" she wondered aloud. This was her favorite room in the house. There were many kinds of plants with her, but she wondered how many more plants there might have been outside. The plants that grew were beautiful to Ellie but did not provide very good company. She longed for more.

After a few more minutes alone in her thoughts, Ellie took out the parchment she brought with her. She needed to finish making her gift for Sainte before he came back.

▼▲▼

Miqel, Iris, and Sainte squinted their eyes as bright rays of light broke the horizon. The Malignin screeched in agony as the same light painfully pierced their eyes. Iris glanced at Sainte standing over the Malignin he dragged out, chest still heaving from adrenaline and sweat dripping from his brow. He held himself with confidence, but not so much to call it cockiness. She may have joined the Blades of the Night to please her father, but she fought tirelessly every night to catch Sainte's attention. He looked around and Iris looked away, not wanting to be caught staring at him. She knew it was unprofessional, but she had feelings for Sainte that someone who was just a friend should not have. Feelings that were born when they were in Training. She could not, or would not, find a suitor because no man she met could be held up to the standard with which she regarded Sainte.

He loved doing what he did, was addicted to it even, but the reason he worked every night was for Iris. He did not trust anyone else to watch out for her. Unbeknownst to Iris, Miqel was observing her in the same way she was Sainte. He watched her shoulders try to shrug out any soreness from the night. They looked broad in the armor, but he knew she had a slim, fit figure underneath it all. Her brown hair was matted to her face with sweat and dirt. It was times like these when she never looked more beautiful to him.

When the stablemaster approached them with their horses in tow, all three friends were broken from their reveries. "Mornin' Shield," he said to Sainte respectfully and with a nod of his head. He carefully stepped around the wounded Malignin. "How're you all doing?"

"A'right, and ya?" Miqel responded gruffly.

"Fine, just fine," he said, wiping his hands on his pants. He already dropped the reins to the horses. They were well-trained and would not wander away from their riders. "Well, I guess I'll be goin'," he said as no one else offered up any more words to him.

"A'right." Once again, Miqel was the only one to reply. The stablemaster walked away, keeping a fair distance between himself and the Malignin. Once he was out of earshot, Miqel turned to his friends. "Ya'll suddenly lose all yer manners o'er night? Makin' me talk to 'em like I'm the nice'n."

"Well, probably good for you if people think you're not as mean as you think you are," Iris told him, pushing his shoulder playfully.

"Hell it is. I don't want no more people talkin' to me'n there already is."

"No more people talking to you?" Sainte chimed in. "Shite, me and Iris are the only people that talk to you."

"I know, and ye're already too much fer me," Miqel retorted. Sainte and Iris smiled and shook their heads.

"Sun's well on its way up. We should be on our way back to Guardstin," Iris said.

"Thinking the same thing," Sainte said.

"Aye." Miqel nodded his head.

They climbed onto their saddled horses and started the ten-mile trek to town. The clean-up crews were already beginning their work for the day. They used large horse-drawn carts to carry the dead Malignin. Once the carts were full, they would get pulled to the base of another nearby mountain and burned. Repairmen had also begun any work to be done to the defensive structures. They worked quickly because all the repairs had to be finished before nightfall.

The trio rode around the workers without speaking. The combined sawing, hammering, and nailing sounds would have drowned out all their words. Finally clearing all the hustle and noise of the day crews, Iris said, "How was your night, Sainte? Any problems?"

"Nay, no more than usual. Malignin broke through, as always, and, as always, I cut them down—one by one. Seemed like a normal night to me, but I don't get to see anything outside the tunnel. What about you guys? Anything interesting?"

"I marked me first nighter. Made eye contact an' all with'it, 'til lil miss 'ere decided to steal it from me. The blade 'o my axe resents ya fer that," Miqel said.

"Trap it, you dense rock," she said, then in a mocking voice added, "The blade 'o yer axe' had plenty more work cut out for it." Miqel grinned as Iris continued. "The Malignin did seem slightly different than normal. Almost like they were holding back."

"Didn't seem like it ta me," Miqel cut in.

"You're on the ground; I'm above you. I could see them waiting to move on you instead of moving in at once like usual," Iris explained.

"Ah well, guess I was too busy killin' 'em ta notice. Possibly had too mucha their blood in me eyes. Nighters sure like ta spray blood when I cut 'em open." He grinned.

"Or maybe you just can't handle focusing on more than one thing at a time," Sainte teased.

"Keep mockin' and we'll see how well yer title holds up to th' name, Shield boy," Miqel threatened.

Their conversation dwindled as they finally approached Guardstin. The town was rather large since it housed all the Blades and their families. Anyone could live in the town, but the housing and training areas for the Blades of the Night were closed off to everyone who was not a member. A four-foot-high wooden wall surrounded the entire town to keep out any wild animals that got too curious.

They rode through the already open gates onto the hard-packed gravel streets in Guardstin. The smell of freshly baked bread wafted through the town—the sounds of hammer on metal from the blacksmith rung out like a bell tolling on the hour. People bustled to and from shops, but the streets were not so crowded that Sainte, Iris, and Miqel could not ride side by side. They rode through housing first, then through the shops, and finally to the town circle, where vendors and traders from other towns could set up and sell their goods.

One of Guardstin's priests was already out, preaching to whoever stopped to listen. His baritone voice droned over the noise of the town, "...and thus the White Wyverns blessed the child and called her 'Barrier,' for she is the barrier that keeps the Malignin from defiling Crearia, our beautiful land. Now, join me in prayer..." He waved his arms dramatically over the people gathered before him as he began the prayer; white robes billowed gracefully with his movements. His voice faded away as the trio moved further into the bustle of the town circle, trying to get through without running anyone over.

Past the town circle was where the Blade's housing and Training area started. It was fenced off with a guarded gate. Sainte, Iris, and Miqel rode through without being stopped because they were recognizable throughout Guardstin. As they passed through the gates, the sounds of the town slowly faded behind them. No one was allowed on this side of town that was not a Blade other than traveling bards and musicians.

Just inside the Blades' housing was the stable for all the horses. They stopped there first and dismounted, handing the reins of their horses over to the stable boy that met them.

"Thanks, lad," Sainte said, even though he was only a few years older than the boy who took his horse.

"Ye're welcome, Shield," he replied respectfully before scurrying off with all their horses.

"I hate being called that," Sainte told Miqel and Iris. "I wish more people would just call me by my name."

"Of all things to complain about in your position, and you pick that?" Iris said.

"It's the little things."

"Who cares? Off ta Sun's Ale?" Miqel said, changing the subject.

"Not yet. Got to meet with the Council, remember?" Iris reminded him.

"Hate doin' that," Miqel grumbled.

"Sooner we get that done, the sooner we can be at Sun's Ale. At least they're the only people we have to report to," Sainte said. They all walked briskly to the building that the Council was in. The Council was comprised of three Blades chosen by the rest of the Blades of the Night to be there. Sainte gave weekly reports to them on how his relationship with Ellie was going. Iris and Miqel went with him to tell them about differences they may have noticed about the Malignin.

They walked to the door and entered without knocking. These meetings were always informal, and the Council had an open-door policy for all Blades of the Night members. The three men were already seated in their respective chairs, side by side, facing the entrance. They were expecting them. The room was bare except for a table off to the left side with a lit candle, some parchment, and a quill and inkwell.

"Welcome, Shield," the man in the center said to Sainte. "Iris, Miqel," he said almost as an afterthought. "How are you and Ellie?"

"We're good, as always. She does like to question me about life outside of her home. It seems with each passing day she gets increasingly more curious, and it's obvious that she gets restless," Sainte explained. "Her curiosity about outside never seems quenched no matter what I tell her, but I don't think it's a problem."

"That is to be expected. No different than any previous Barriers. We trust you're answering all her questions appropriately. Dispelling any hope of hers that she'll be able to leave." Again, the man in the center spoke for all three of them.

Sainte nodded. "Aye, I only tell her what she has been taught, Crane." He paused, "As you all know, it's Ellie's birthday tomorrow. Can I get your permission to get her a pet as a gift? I was thinking of a bird."

At his question, the three men started to discuss it amongst themselves. Sainte patiently waited for an answer. After a minute, they seemed to come to an agreement.

"As long as you're prepared to answer any questions that may arise because of the bird, we see no reason why it would be a problem," Crane told him. "Do you have anything else?"

"That's all I have regarding Ellie. I would like to speak to Nadrian, though, if he is available," Sainte said.

Crane inclined his head. "We will bring word to you when he is ready for you. Iris, Miqel, do you have anything to report?"

Iris stepped up and told them what she told Sainte and Miqel earlier about what she noticed last night. The three councilmen nodded thoughtfully but did not say anything.

"Miqel, do you have anything to add?" Crane asked.

"Nay, but I do have a question fer ye. What's goin' on with th' Trainin'? It seems 'at we're runnin' on short supply o' men lately," Miqel asked. "There've been more 'n more Malignin ev'ry night. Not like it used ta be. Sainte's too good'a man ta bring it up. I'm not."

"We're doing everything we can. We have thought of a temporary solution," Crane told him.

"What kinda solution?"

"We are going to cut down Training time," Crane said.

"What? That ain't right. We need more men, so ye're gonna give us boys that had some fast trainin'? That's how people die." Miqel took a step forward.

"Anything else?" Crane said, not in the mood to discuss this.

"Aye, I've a lot more'n that…" Miqel began but was cut off.

"Anything else?" Crane asked again, more sternly. The two men on either side of Crane stared at Miqel, warning him not to push the subject. "Then that will be all. Sainte, where do you think you might be, so we can fetch you when Nadrian is ready?"

"I'll be at Sun's Ale."

Crane nodded, and Miqel stormed out of the building without another word. Sainte watched him leave, then turned back to the seated men.

"Gentlemen," he said before walking out. Iris gave them a nod and followed Sainte out. They met Miqel, who was waiting for them a short distance away.

"What was that about?" Iris asked Miqel.

"Did ya hear what they said?" Miqel asked her.

"Aye, and it's something we've expected."

"It don't sit right with me. It ain't right," he steamed.

"Come on. Let's go to the tavern. I think we've earned some ale now," Sainte said, not wanting to get into this conversation in the middle of the street. Miqel seemed like he was going to say something else but decided against it. He'd rather be drinking than arguing too.

They went to Sun's Ale and walked into the dimly lit tavern. They sat down at their usual table in the corner. A faint smell of stale beer, tobacco, and pork stew met their nostrils as was typical. Lit oil lanterns on each table cast a dim orange light around the not-yet-full room. A few Blades sat at the bar already, and some trickled in behind the friends. Three musicians were on the small stage in the room, tuning their instruments and preparing for the day.

The bartender, Wil, was already on his way with each of their favorite ales. Wil was good at what he did and remembered every one of his patron's favorite drinks.

"Will ye three be needing anything else? A meal, perhaps?" he asked as he handed out their drinks.

"No thanks, this'll do just fine," Iris answered for them all. Sainte and Miqel nodded in agreement.

"Rough night, huh?" Wil asked, sticking his hands in his pockets.

"Always is," Miqel said.

"Right, well, if ye need anything else, ye know where I'll be," he said as he walked away, preparing to tend to another person.

Iris could feel that the general mood was stressed, some nights just ended like that. The meeting with the Council did not help. "So, Miqel," Iris nudged him, "you have any news about your romantic life? There's gotta be some special girl out there for you by now?"

He shook his head and took a drink, swishing it around his mouth before swallowing. "Nay, no one special. I gave up on women when the one I loved gave up on me. Gave up on most of 'em, at least... Gotta have some options, I guess."

"Come on; it's been two years. You gotta move on."

"Once ya have a husband up'n leave ya one night with nothin' but a letter, then ya can tell me ta move on. Til then, don't tell me what ta do 'bout that," Miqel snapped, then continued with a smile. "Either way, I move on ev'ry night."

Iris looked at Sainte for some help with raised eyebrows. He just took a drink and shrugged.

Miqel turned the questions on her now. "How about ya? Find any poor lads ta beat up in bed? Bruise their pricks and their ego all inna nights work?" His sudden questions caused a bark of laughter from both Sainte and Iris.

Iris shook her head after controlling her laughter. "No, not lately. And what makes you think I'd bruise them? That's not my style."

"What is yer style?"

"I'm not telling you two. None of your business." She took a sip from her mug to hide her blushed cheeks.

"How's Ellie doin', Sainte?" Miqel asked him.

"She's fine," he answered curtly.

"Hey, y'alright? Yer not talking as much as usual. Don't think we ain't noticed, 'cause we 'ave."

"Yeah, Miqel's right, Sainte. We're always here for you if you want to talk about something. We know that being the Shield must be difficult. It's not good to keep stuff bottled up. Sometimes you ought to just let it out," Iris said, genuinely concerned.

The tavern started to slowly fill with pipe smoke as more and more people meandered in from their shifts. The musicians began to play some familiar tunes. Miqel brought out his pipe, packed it, and lit it. He took a deep puff and exhaled with a satisfied sigh.

Sainte waved his hand slowly to clear smoke from his face, but it was as if he tried to wipe away their questions. "I'm fine. It's just that the longer I do this, the more tired I get, and the more tired I get, the less I wanna talk." He shrugged his shoulders. "Nothing's wrong."

"Well, we're here for you whenever you need us," Iris said, genuinely meaning it.

Sainte nodded. "I know, and I'm here for you two if you ever need me."

"Whadda ya think 'bout the Council's idea? What with Trainin' and all?" Miqel asked.

"It's not the best thing, but I suppose it must do. Not like we didn't expect something like this to happen. I think the Training may have been a bit too long anyway. Four weapons you have to learn, two months for each weapon. Eight months learning how to fight?" Sainte shook his head. "Too long. I say they have a month of training with each weapon. Then the instructors decide which trainee trains with which weapon. No need to learn how to fight with four different ones."

A Blade in the tavern walked to their table. "S'cuse me, mind if I join in?" Sainte gestured to an empty chair. "I just overheard what you all were talking about. I'd like to know what the Council's planning on doing to help with our numbers." He paused as he got another good look at Sainte. "Shite, you're the Shield. Apologies for interrupting."

"Don't worry about it. You've a right to know. For now, the Council has said that they're going to shorten Training to push more people through it."

The Blade looked blankly at Sainte, then Iris and Miqel. "That's it?"

"Aye," Miqel grumbled between puffs of smoke.

"Without the Council, we're already doing more than that. Some Blades work their night shifts, then during the day help with repairs. And I know many day crews are pulling night shifts, repairing during sunlight and helping fight during the night. And all the Council will do is throw some rookies at us?" He scoffed. "Damn shame. Curse me if you want, but I'm going to say it. Our numbers dwindle; it's only a matter of time…" He trailed off at the looks he received from all three of the others. "Right, well, best be getting on then. Thanks for letting me in on the goings on." He stood up and went to the bar, rejoining his friends again.

"How long you think 'til there's fifty rumors spreading around about what the Council's doing, and all of them false?" Iris asked with a smile.

"Give it a day," Sainte said as he drained his drink and stood up. "I gotta get going. I have to get some things for Ellie; then I'll get some sleep. I suggest you two do the same as well."

"All right, take it easy. See you tonight." Iris gave a slight wave.

"Later," Miqel said to his back as he left the tavern. As Sainte walked outside, a man ran up to him.

"Shield? Nadrian is ready to see you," he said, relief showing that he finally found Sainte.

"Thank you, I'll head over there now." The courier nodded and went on his way. Sainte walked to Nadrian's building. He hesitated at first but told himself that it was time for this again with each step. He had only spoken to Nadrian a handful of times since becoming the Shield. Nadrian was a philosophist. Every Shield had one, and he was there for the Shield to talk to when faced with trepidations about anything related to their assignment.

Soon Sainte stood in front of the quaint building. It was a single-floor house and very nondescript. He took a breath and stepped inside the building. His nostrils were invaded with burning incense, frankincense, and cedarwood, as always when he visited. Multiple furnishings adorned the room, even though there were only at max two people in the room at once, the Shield and the philosophist. Cushioned couches lined the left wall, and four wooden chairs carved out of tree trunks lined the right. A round oak table with five matching chairs sat in the middle of the room. All the incense was on the table, and flickering candles lined the windowless walls.

Nadrian stood in front of the table facing Sainte. He was clothed in a simple brown robe. "Welcome, Sainte. It has been too long since our last meeting. Make yourself comfortable."

"Morning," Sainte grumbled. He took a seat at the oak table. Nadrian sat opposite him.

"What brings you here today?" Nadrian asked kindly. Sainte did not know his age, never cared to ask, but he would guess he was in his thirties. He had short-cropped hair and was slowly losing it.

Sainte already regretted going to him, but he was already there. With a breath, he said what first and foremost bothered him. "I don't know if I like being the Shield anymore. Most days now, I find myself wishing I could do more of what I want to do."

"I see," Nadrian said with a nod. "You are not the first Shield to think this. Indeed, all before you have, at one point or another, felt this. I must remind you that you were not chosen on a whim. Much thought was put into it. You were not selected because you were the best swordsman or the smartest scholar. It was not because of your leadership skills. Of course, each of those played a minor role, but none of them were deciding factors.

"You were chosen to be the Shield because of your humanity. Your willingness to care for another more than you care for yourself. That is what it takes. You thinking that you're not good enough, that you don't like being the Shield anymore, is proof of that."

"You say all that, but it's not like I'm some noble person. I didn't want to join the Blades for the betterment of Crearia. I joined because I wanted an exciting life."

"I know, but what makes you different than any other person is that even though you say all that, you will still be at the mountain with the Barrier tonight. And the next night, and so on, until you have a replacement. That's what makes you different. You will do what needs to be done."

Sainte was quiet as he thought about Nadrian's words. He wanted to refute them, to prove them wrong, but he knew that Nadrian spoke the truth. He would not leave, not until his duty was over. There was another thing that bothered him.

"Tomorrow... er today, is Ellie's eighteenth birthday," Sainte said. Nadrian nodded at his words. "She's entering the prime years for childbearing. Ellie and I must have a child together to have a future Barrier, and I love Ellie..."

"But..."

"But I love her like she's my family. I've cared for her for over two years now, and our relationship has grown, but how can I be expected to carry through with this if she feels like family?"

"This is another common problem with being the Shield. It is not one that has been easily solved, however. This is something that you must find out for yourself. Nothing I say can make the answer obvious. All Shields before you have done it, and I'm sure you'll be able to as well. I know she may feel like your family, but she is not. Not by blood. A wife and husband are family yet have an intimate relationship."

"It's different," Sainte snapped, tired of his preachy attitude.

"I have no doubt. There is nothing that will make me understand your issues." He paused. "You love her as I'm sure she loves you. People show they love each other physically, which you must show her when the time is right."

Sainte rubbed his temple with a finger, eyes closed. After a few moments of silence, he finally opened his eyes. "I don't have anything else. Not right now, at least."

"All right, until next time, Sainte. Try not to make the next one so far away. I am here to tell you not only what you need to hear but also to help you," Nadrian said with a sad smile.

"I'll do my best." Sainte walked out. He had to admit he did feel better than before he spoke to Nadrian, but not by enough to matter much to him.

▼▲▼

Iris and Miqel stayed at the tavern a little longer and slowly finished their drinks amongst small talk. It was beginning to get a little crowded now, but neither of them cared. Most all the Blades there kept to their own conversations.

Drinking was a daily thing for Miqel. Iris and Sainte usually joined him, but sometimes it was just him. He was beginning to think that it was kind of nice to be drinking with someone, especially Iris, when she slapped the table with the palm of her hand, pulling him from his thoughts.

"Well, that's about it for me," she said, finishing her drink. "I'm going to head home. Sainte was right; it's probably best if we both get some rest."

It was just at that time, right when she was about to leave when Miqel realized how badly he wanted her to stay. He spent many nights alone when his wife first left, wondering why. He had long since gotten over that, but he did miss the company of an honest woman. Now he realized he did not just want any woman; he wanted Iris.

Would ya stay a bit with me? If ya have the time, I've some things I'd like ta tell ya. Miqel told himself that was what he would say, but instead, it came out as. "Ya go on ahead, more fer me ta drink."

"Oh, well, all right," Iris said. Miqel thought he saw a flash of disappointment skim across her face, but he could not be sure. "Have a good time then, Miqel, and don't stay up too long; we always need you at your best." With a last smile, she turned around and left the rowdy laughter and stories behind.

"All right, thanks, mom," he called after her sarcastically. He heard a bark of laughter from her from outside. Part of him was upset that he did not ask her to stay with him, but his rational side knew it was for the best. Getting into a relationship with her would only complicate things because they fought together. He finally decided that thinking about her would solve nothing and that he should move on, and he knew the best way to do that.

He stood up, left the table, and went to the bar. "Hey Wil, get me another ale, would ya?" Wil nodded and poured him the drink.

"Thanks," Miqel said before he took a swig. "Also," Miqel called to Wil's back after he swallowed, "get me one 'o th' girls, too."

Wil smiled knowingly. "All right, one ale and one lady. For the day?"

"Of course," Miqel said, watching Wil enter a back room. "What's th' harm?" he muttered to himself.

▼▲▼

Iris left Sun's Ale, half hoping that Miqel would have called her back because she did not want to go home just yet and face her father. However, she knew Miqel liked his alone time and did not want to push him.

The day before, she and her father argued about how he treated her mother. Iris had a feeling that he would not have let it go yet. The last thing Iris wanted to do was have some disgruntled man breathing down her neck for the rest of the day. The only reason she ever went back home was for her mother's sake.

Iris loved her mother but could not understand why she stayed with that man. Her mom cleaned the house all day, cooked, and even ran their small shop, while her father just sat around and used what little income they made with the shop to get drunk. If Iris did not use her own money to pay for their food, they would have starved to death by now.

She walked through the gates that separated the Blades' living area from the common folk. She passed through the busy town center with vendors bombarding her ears for attention. Iris stayed with her father and mother near the edge of town in a small home. She offered to buy her mother a new home on the condition that she leave her father. Her mother refused.

The house finally came into her view. It was a small home having only three rooms. Iris stepped up to the door to the house, took a breath, and mentally prepared herself for her father. She could already hear him constantly griping about how dirty the place was. "Ungrateful prick," she whispered before pushing the door open and walking in. The verbal abuse spewing from his mouth switched to her almost immediately.

"So ya fine'ly came back, eh? I's beginning ta hope that ya learned t'was best fer ya and git yerself kilt by those damned Maglinin... Malnig..." He struggled over the word. "Whatever th' fook they're called." He sneered at her drunkenly, the smell of alcohol permeating from his mouth.

Iris did not give him the satisfaction of a response but instead looked at her mother and said, "You still don't want to leave him? I can get a place for us to stay. It's not too late."

"Lookit me when I'm talkin' ta ya, ya ungracious bitch," her father said as he stumbled between her and her mother. His disheveled clothes tangled his feet and he tripped, barely catching himself on the wall before his face met the floor. Her mother just looked away; she did not even like to acknowledge the arguments.

After he regained his composure, what little of it he thought he had, he stared at Iris as if nothing happened. In his drunken stupor, he continued to talk, unable to comprehend when enough was enough. "Y'ain't got nowhere ta go; th'only reason y'ave a place ta sleep is cuz o' me."

Iris openly laughed in his face. "You're losing money with your store, which will probably close before the month ends. You," she said, now stabbing a finger in his chest, "are nothing but a drunk who abuses his family. We'd be better off leaving you for the dogs, but I doubt even the dogs would have you." Her father backhanded Iris across the face at those words, but she kept her composure and just stared him down. She clenched her fists so hard her fingernails dug into the palms of her hands. Her eyes welled with tears of anger.

"I'm leaving, Mother. This is the last time I'm asking you to come with me." Her voice was steady and cold. Her mother said nothing, nor did she move. Her father still stood in front of her with a proud look on his face. "Fuck you." Those were the last words she whispered to her father before she stalked out of the house.

Tears silently flowed down her face as she walked through the late morning streets. People bustled around town now as the day wore on, and she tried to hide her distraught face from everyone. She thought she could handle her father's abuse a little longer. He hit her when she was younger before she joined the Blades, but this was the first time since, and it took her by surprise. As soon as the palm of his hand made contact, Iris knew that she would not tolerate him anymore. Her mother would not anchor her down. If she would not leave, then that was her problem.

She knew this would happen eventually but was no less surprised that it did. She wandered around Guardstin for a while, gathering her thoughts and calming her nerves. There were places for her to stay, an inn specifically for Blades or one of her few girlfriends' houses, but there was only one place she wanted to go. Only one place that she felt she would be comfortable at.

▼▲▼

Sainte just finished closing all his blinds, darkening his home so it was easier to sleep when there was a light knock at his door. He was not expecting anyone to visit, so he was curious about who it could be. He opened the door and looked at the girl in front of him. It took him a few seconds to realize that it was Iris. Her hair covered her face and she was looking down.

"Hey, Iris. What're you doing?" he asked, slightly surprised. He waited for a reply, but none came. "Are you alri-?" before he could finish, she came forwards slowly, hugging him around the waist, face buried in his chest. Taken aback, Sainte could only return the hug, confused. He looked down at her and caught a glimpse of her face. The right side was red. It was then he realized that she was crying.

"Hey, it's all right," he said, patting her back. He did not know what else to do.

After a few seconds, she seemed to calm down a bit. As she released him Iris asked, "Can I stay...?"

"Of course, you can stay as long as you need to. Come on in." They both walked in and Sainte pulled up a chair for himself as Iris sat on his bed.

Sainte did not say anything. He would not have known what to say, but Iris did not need him to say anything. She just needed someone to listen to her. So Sainte sat quietly, tentatively, and listened to her story.

Iris told him everything from arguing with her dad daily to her mother ignoring it to their shop slowly but surely going out of business, all the way to being hit by her dad. She told him it was not the first time he had beaten her, but she knew he beat her mother worse every night when she was gone. She would not leave him out of fear of what he would try to do.

Of course, Saint and Miqel knew that Iris came from an abusive home, but she did not like talking about it. This was the first time she expressed this much detail about her home life. When she was finished they sat in silence for a few minutes. Sainte broke the tension by saying, "You want to go back home? I'll hold him down for you while you take whatever shots at him you want."

Iris choked out a small laugh through her tears but shook her head.

"You're welcome to the bed. I've got some cots I can sleep on."

"You can sleep on the bed, too," Iris said. "There's room."

"No, it's fine. You probably need the space more than I do right now," Sainte replied as he laid out his extra covers. "I don't want to put you or me in that situation. What happened in

Training was one thing, but now... that was long ago, and things are different now. We both know it."

"It's... I just..." She looked down. Her eyes watered again, but she hid it from Sainte. She just wanted to be held.

"Hmm?" Sainte questioned.

"I wanted to say thank you, Sainte."

"Don't worry about it, Iris. Let's get some rest," he said as he laid down on the cot, covering himself up.

Iris covered herself up as well, bringing the sheets up to her chin. She was glad Sainte let her stay, but she wanted something else. She wanted someone she could hold. She wanted a relationship. Iris knew it was frowned upon, against the rules, but she wanted Sainte.

Similar thoughts flashed through Sainte's mind, but they were pushed aside as his duties took priority. It was his job to be with and protect Ellie. He could not afford to be distracted from his responsibility. No one could. He had desires, just like anyone else, but it was up to him to rise above them.

The two lay in darkness, listening to each other's shallow breaths as they slipped into sleep.

THREE
-LOSS-

Iris woke up before Sainte. She looked through the curtains to see how much time she had before she had to get ready to leave for the night shift. Checking the sun, she guessed she had about two hours. She decided to go by her home again to check on her mother. Slowly she slid out of bed, trying to be quiet so as not to wake Sainte. She took a few steps, then brushed against a covered cage. An angry squawking pierced through the room. Iris nearly jumped a foot at the sudden noise. Sainte sat straight up with a bewildered expression on his face.

"Since when did you get a bird?" Iris asked him loud enough to be heard over the noise.

Sainte waited until the chirping finally slowed down before replying. "Today, after I left the tavern. It's a gift for Ellie. Where're you heading to? It's still early yet to get ready for shift."

"I've got some things I have to do. I didn't remember them because of earlier. I'll see you later."

"All right, see you later, Iris," Sainte said before laying back down.

Iris left without another word, not wanting to disturb his rest more than she already had. Once she made her way onto the street, she immediately started to head to her home. She made the journey quickly, feeling regretful for leaving her mother. She had to try harder. Before she knew it, she walked up to the door, but something was different. There was no noise coming from the house. No talking, nobody moving about, complete silence.

"Hello?" she called out from just outside the door, but there was no answer. She almost turned around and walked away but decided against it. Instead, she pushed the door open and walked in.

Her father sat on a chair draped over the table, face down. A spilled mug and sour ale dripped onto him and the floor. He must have gotten so drunk that he passed out. Iris shook her head in disgust, but this was nothing new.

"Mother?" she called out. She heard her muffled reply from her room. Iris entered the room to find her mother in bed, lying on her side, facing away from her. "Are you all right?" she asked as she stepped closer.

"Yes, fine. What're ye doing here?" she asked, still not turning over.

"I'm here to check on you. Make sure father didn't do anything stupid," Iris told her, but she did not reply. "Mother?" It was then that Iris noticed her mother's shoulders were shaking. She was crying.

"Mother, look at me." She stepped even closer to her and turned her around. Iris gasped when she saw her face.

Her nose was broken and still slightly bleeding. There was blood on the sheets from it. Her eyes were bruised, and she had several cuts on her lips where Iris could only guess that she had been hit so hard she bit through them. There was no telling what other wounds her mother was hiding from her.

"He did this to you." It was not a question. "I'm going to kill him." Her mother's plea to not hurt him fell on deaf ears. She marched straight to her father and kicked the chair leg so hard she snapped it. Her father fell backward out of the chair and groggily opened his eyes.

"Piece of shite," Iris growled. She kicked him in the face once before straddling his chest. She pummeled his face relentlessly. He raised his hands to fend her away feebly, but it was useless. Iris grabbed his right hand and simultaneously broke several fingers, trying to push it away. It felt so good, feeling his bones snap. She grabbed either side of his head and slammed it into the ground. Once she stopped, her hands reached his throat and started squeezing. He looked up at her through his bloodied face, and she smiled.

"Iris," someone said. Suddenly it was not her father's face she stared into, but her mother's. Her mother shook her again, forcing her out of her thoughts. "Iris, please promise ye won't hurt him."

Her mother's words brought her back to reality, and she found herself still standing by the bedside. "How can you still ask me that? After what he's done to you?" Iris asked as she held back tears.

"He's yer father..." Before her mother could finish, Iris was already leaving. She could not listen to her anymore. She passed by her unconscious father without looking at him for fear that if she did, she would kill him.

▼▲▼

Fingers rubbing and pushing on his sore back woke Miqel up. He cracked his eyes open, and the first thing he saw were three empty bottles of ale. He moved his tongue around his mouth, trying to create some moisture to no avail. His mouth was a desert.

"Mmmm," he groaned as a particularly rough knot was massaged. As he slowly woke up, he realized he did not know what time it was. He quickly turned over, pushing the still-naked woman off him. He realized then that he was still naked as well. He scrambled to a window and threw open the blinds. He breathed a sigh of relief as he saw that he still had at least an hour before he had to leave for the night.

"What's the rush, hun?" the woman asked, still lounging in bed.

"Nothin' anymore," he said as he sauntered back into bed. He was trying to recall what happened. He knew this was one of Sun's Ale's rooms, but he was not quite sure how he ended up there. Not that it mattered to him. "Just makin' sure I wasn't late fer the night."

"You're not the Shield. You don't have to work every night. Why not skip tonight? I'll keep you company," she purred as she laid her hand on his chest.

"Whore's company ain't much as far as company goes," Miqel muttered.

"I don't have to be a whore if you don't want me to..." She trailed off.

"And what're ye suggestin'?"

"I've been the only one you've had. I may be a whore, but I'm not stupid. You keep getting me, and if that don't mean something, then nothing does."

He scoffed. "Means ya screw better'n th' others. If yer thinkin' too much into it I can't stop ye."

"I'm being serious." She crawled over and straddled him, nestling her head into his neck. "I like you... I'll be yours and yours alone if you'll have me."

"Yer just wantin' some more coin. Get off me. I ain't fallin' for yer tricks." She fought back playfully. "I said get off." He shoved her.

"What's your problem?" she asked, clearly taken aback by his harshness.

"I'm leavin'. Tired o' ya," he said as he quickly got dressed.

"Yeah? Fine, but when you come back asking for me, I won't be there," she threatened.

"Jus' like ev'ryone else," he grumbled as he left the room.

▼▲▼

Ellie held up her drawing for Sainte and compared it to the real thing staring back at her through the mirror. Some of the shading was off, and something was wrong with the eyes. She brought it back down and looked at herself with scrutiny. All she could see was all her blemishes. With a sigh, she returned to work on her self-portrait, erasing old lines and adding new ones. She sat for hours in front of the mirror, working on her present.

After Ellie was sure everything was as good as she could make it, she went to her bookshelf. She had a wide selection of journals from all the women before her and a few books Sainte brought her. He told her they were called 'fairytales.' She pulled down a diary and walked into the living room. Reading was one of her favorite things to do when she was bored. The table in the living room was cluttered with some puzzles and card games that she promised herself she would finish later. She moved the clutter from the table to the floor to make room for the diary before cracking it open.

Wholly absorbed in the diary she was reading, she jumped at the sound of the door as it closed. Ellie searched for her drawing and snatched it behind her back, not wanting Sainte to see it before she wanted him to.

"Hello? Ellie?" Sainte called out. She heard him walk around, enter the kitchen to set something down, then go into the foyer.

"I'm coming," she called out. She walked out of the living room into the entrance room with her hands behind her back and a smile on her face. Sainte smiled back.

"What? What do you have there? What're you hiding?" he asked as he leaned against a wall.

She walked closer to him, about a foot away, and then she whipped out the drawing and held it up to his face for him to see. "It's finished," she squealed, words brimming with glee. She watched his face expectantly as he took the drawing from her to get a better look at it. Ellie waited patiently for his feedback.

After studying it for a few moments, Sainte's face broke out in a smile. "It's excellent, Ellie. It looks just like you; I can tell you put your all into this. It looks better than the real thing," he quipped. She gasped, then slapped him on the arm. "I'm kidding, you know I'm kidding. You'll have to hang this up somewhere; it's something to be proud of, for sure. I think it might be your best yet. You've always been good, but each drawing keeps improving." He held it out for her to take.

Ellie blushed from all the compliments. "It's not for hanging up. It's for you. I want you to have it." She pushed the drawing back towards him. "I wouldn't want you to forget what I look like while you're out."

"Thank you, I'll always have it on me, but you needn't worry. I could never forget you," he said, folding the portrait carefully and tucking it in a chest pocket.

"You better. And you better not lose it because I won't make another one. That was hard," she threatened. "I don't think I can stare at myself that long ever again."

"I promise I will never lose it," Sainte said earnestly. "Hey, I brought you more carrots and grapes, just as promised. Wanna eat some? You can tell me what you've been up to."

"Yeah, sounds great. I was hoping you would say that." They both walked into the kitchen, Ellie in front of Sainte. Sitting on the kitchen table was the bird cage with a little blue bird in it. Ellie paused, then gasped in excitement, "Is that a bird?"

Sainte laughed. "Yes, happy birthday, Ellie. When I was out, I searched for something special for you, and this is what I got. I hope you like it. I don't think I would've remembered to get you something if you hadn't reminded me it was your birthday a thousand times yesterday."

"It's the best, Sainte! Thank you so much." Ellie turned around and hugged him quickly. Then she ran to the cage and gazed at the bird.

"I hope it can keep you a little company while I'm gone," he said.

"It will! I've only read about them, and I didn't think there were any more. There used to be hundreds of different kinds of birds. Most could fly, but some couldn't. I can't believe you managed to find one." She babbled, excited about her new pet. "I'm sure it'll be better company than you. Won't talk back to me."

Sainte laughed. "He's one of a kind. Take good care of him, Ellie." He was glad to see her happy but upset that a present had to revolve around so many lies. "How about some grapes?" She nodded in agreement. They talked about everything she had read and done while Sainte taught her how to care for the bird.

Sainte always visited a few hours before sunset to see how Ellie was doing and to just be with her. It calmed his nerves before each night. When he was with her, it seemed he did not have to worry about anything. That feeling made leaving her all the more difficult.

Sainte stood up with a groan and stretched. "Well, Ellie, I have to go now. I'll bring some more bread tomorrow."

"Okay." She seemed to think about something for a second, pausing. "Do you really like my drawing?" she asked. "I know it's not as good as a bird, but I hope you like it all the same."

Sainte smiled and nodded. "I like it a lot. Thank you, I'll never go anywhere without it. I definitely got the better present here," he said as he patted the pocket it was in. He meant what he said. "I'll see you tomorrow, Ellie. Take care." He started walking towards the door.

"Hold on; I have one more thing. Today, in Gabriella's journal, she said she had feelings for Phillipe, her own Shield. They were nice feelings, fond feelings, and she called it love. I think I have the same feelings for you," she said, slightly blushing, unsure how to put it into words.

Sainte smiled, nervous. "I love you, too." He hesitated. "I'll be back tomorrow, but I have to go now." He left her there to wonder about his words.

"I love you," Ellie said to herself, mulling the words repeatedly in her head. She liked the way they sounded.

As Sainte closed the door, he realized he was still smiling. That might have been the only truly honest thing he ever told Ellie, and it felt good. He would have to think about how to act around her now that their relationship was growing. Nadrian's words echoed in his mind, 'She is not your family.' After two years, the words have finally been exchanged. Sainte would have to report this to the Council after shift. They had to know how their relationship was progressing in order to plan for his replacement Shield.

Sainte would have to think about all that later. The night was fast approaching. He could not afford to be distracted. He could not let Ellie down. He lit the torches around him and started to prepare.

▼▲▼

When Iris arrived at the tunnel, she saw that Sainte's horse was tethered nearby, waiting for the stablemaster. He was either already inside, spending time with Ellie, or getting ready in the tunnel. Miqel was not yet there, which was expected. She was glad for it because she did not want to talk to anyone right now anyway. As usual, Iris climbed to the top of the tunnel and watched the sunset. This time, however, her thoughts still lingered on her mother.

How could she just have stood by when her father hit her daughter? Why didn't she come with her when she left? Why did she put up with an abusive husband for so long? Iris always knew that it was only a matter of time before something like this would happen, but she always expected that her mother would be by her side and that they would leave together; support each other.

She wiped her watering eyes before any tears could fall and cursed herself. She thought she got it all out of her system before her shift, but she could not get her tears under control. Iris kept telling herself to forget about what happened. At least temporarily. She would have more time to think everything over after the night. Maybe even take the next night off.

Iris glanced down towards the tunnel entrance and noticed that Miqel finally arrived. She did not even hear him. She nodded in greeting as they made eye contact but otherwise did not say anything for fear of choking up. He nodded back.

She realized that she was about to cry again. Quickly, she put her helmet on so Miqel would not be able to call her out and make fun of her for it later. The sun had not yet set so her evening ritual did not go as usual, but she figured she could make an exception this one time.

After all, sometimes change was a good thing.

▼▲▼

Miqel almost did not make it to his shift on time, even though he began getting ready with plenty of time to spare. His headache slowed him down more than normal. Someone would have replaced him for the night, but he worked more to prove a point to himself after his conversation with the woman. Also, he chose to work because he did not know how he would spend the night if he did not come in, as nothing was as appealing to him as slaying Malignin.

Miqel put his hand to his forehead, thumb and middle finger massaging his temples. He was undeniably feeling all the drinks he had before this shift. Not to mention staying up with the whore. It was good while it lasted, but he would have to take it easy after this shift. The last thing he wanted to do was put his confining helmet on. He even contemplated not wearing it this time, but it saved his ass more than once. He would just put it on later; he needed a few more moments of unstifled fresh air. He watched the sinking sun and silently begged for his headache and knotted stomach to go away, to depart with the sun, but it refused.

Of course this hangover wouldn't leave when he wanted it to. As the top of the sun got closer to dipping below the horizon, Miqel put his helmet on, inwardly groaning. He stood up from crouching and leaned on his axe. He did not feel that bad, really.

He had been through worse.

▼▲▼

Sainte paced the length of the tunnel, checking and double-checking all the defenses. He did it not so much to make sure they were in working order, but so he could occupy his restless mind with something. He stopped in the middle of the tunnel and faced the door that the Malignin would surely tear through.

He glanced back at the door that Ellie was behind, wondering what she was doing, and once again thought about the last words he spoke to her. Then he faced forward again and waited.

It was only a matter of time.

▼▲▼

Before the night started, Iris busied herself by checking the flare. Every Blade post had a flare made of a bale of hay soaked in oil. If any post needed any extra aid, they would light the flare. The bale itself was tied onto a catapult. When lit, the fire would burn the twine that held it down, and the catapult would launch it straight into the air. Once launched in the air, it was visible for miles.

Iris looked to the horizon. The sun was now three-quarters below it. She watched as the horizon engulfed the sun completely. The sky was livid with reds and oranges, turned to dark blue, then to black. The sun's natural glow was now gone, replaced by the dark cloak of night. The daylight quickly faded, signaling the beginning of the Malignin onslaught.

Iris scanned the barren land in front of her, the recognizable defensive towers and walls protruding from the landscape a constant reminder that she and Miqel were not alone. Her eyes strained as far as she could see and searched for the first signs of Malignin. She only had to look for a short time before she saw the first group. Iris' hands shook as she pulled out her first arrow. Too bad she could not shake the thoughts of what transpired between her and her father. She figured she would forget about it soon enough, however. She nocked the arrow and aimed towards the Malignin that appeared. She counted four of them as they sprinted closer—a small group.

The Malignin rushed recklessly; there was no order in their chaos. Iris drew in a deep breath as they got into range, held it, and exhaled, all while aiming at the Malignin in the front. She released the arrow at the end of her exhalation. It pierced the air, straight and true. It struck the leading Malignin in the chest, but the beast charged on.

She cursed the Malignin and cursed her father while she was at it. Iris pulled out another arrow as she asked herself, yet again, why her mother did not help her.

▼▲▼

Miqel fought four Malignin at once, which was not uncommon, but all his blocking left no room for an offense. He furiously moved his axe, successfully withstanding the onslaught, but he was being pushed back. Damnit, his head hurt, and the jarring attacks were not exactly a good cure. He was not too worried as these seemed to be the only Malignin coming for now. He knew he could outlast them; one would make a mistake and he would kill them for it.

The Malignin suddenly pulled back their attack and slowly circled him. Miqel realized this too late as he took a moment to catch his breath. He held his axe across his chest; eyes darted back and forth. He waited for them to move. Where was Iris?

Miqel heard a thud between the sound of the snarling creatures. The Malignin with an arrow in its chest fell back with another arrow in its shoulder. Another thud and another arrow. This time the arrow's feathers jutted from the top of its head. The Malignin fell to the ground, not dead yet, but now not a problem either. The remaining Malignin flinched at the sudden attack, and Miqel took this chance while the Malignin hesitated. His axe swung with all his strength. It sliced halfway through a Malignin's thick, muscled neck. A fountain of rancid blood rained on him when he jerked his axe free.

He faced the remaining two, but one was soon preoccupied with trying to rip out arrows that appeared on its back. Miqel swung his axe at the midsection of the last Malignin in this group, but it jumped back just out of reach. As soon as its feet touched the ground, it leaped forward, claws spread to greet Miqel, but Miqel expected this. Faster than most men could, Miqel swung his axe overhead and brought it down and to the left, knocking the Malignin aside to the ground. Miqel followed the body and sunk his axe in its chest as it tried to get up. He quickly glanced around to see if any more Malignin were on their way, but these were the only ones for now. The two Malignin on the ground looked like pincushions after Iris was done.

He glanced up at her. "I like the way ya work."

"They tried to get up behind you, so I just shot until they quit moving," she called back down. "Just doing what I normally do."

"Looks a bit much, if ya ask me," he said jokingly.

"Who's asking? I'm not, and I don't hear anyone else. Besides, a little overkill never hurt anyone," she said, adding a laugh at the end. She looked around for more Malignin closing in but saw none. "Seems like it's going to be a slow night tonight."

"Still just the beginnin'," Miqel said. "My guts tellin' me dif'rent though."

"You sure it's not just the hangover talking?" Iris joked.

"Nay, I know what that feels like, and this ain't it," he replied.

However, Iris was right. It was a slow night for the first five hours, at least. There would be a group of four to five Malignin about once an hour. They almost did not have to try to take them out. It was like the Malignin had lost the will to fight.

The first flare was lit when the fifth hour of the night struck.

Iris and Miqel watched the ball of flame arc gracefully through the air and explode upon hitting the ground. On impact, they could briefly see shapes and silhouettes running to and fro in the light, but they could not differentiate between Malignin and Blades. The brief light given off by the flare slowly died down until nothing was visible from their point of view anymore.

"Must be some new guys over there, huh?" Iris asked, not expecting an answer and not getting one.

Miqel did not say anything about his feeling, the slight tinge of nervousness, almost as if he could smell a foul odor riding the wind. His sweaty grip twisted around on the handle of his axe.

"What do you...? What? What is it?" Iris asked. Miqel was looking behind her in disbelief. She was just as surprised when she turned around to see what he was staring at.

Another flare was released from another post. They could hear fellow Blades' battle cries... and death cries if they listened closely. The flare fell in silence, exploding upon the ground. Iris and Miqel could not make out anything except for the flames. It had not even been five minutes since the first one. Sounds of battle were carried by the wind more steadily now, but they were not normal. The cries and shouts were of desperation and fear, not encouragement.

As they strained their eyes to see, another flare went up, and shortly after that, another. All the north Blade posts had sent flares, now all asking for reinforcements. They had friends at those posts, at every position. Iris and Miqel watched, helpless to do anything, as they could not leave their post to help. Miqel glanced up at Iris and saw that she was having similar thoughts. She wanted to help but knew they could not, at least not them both.

"Ye go help 'em. I'll stay here. I'll be fine," he yelled up to Iris. She slightly jumped at the sound of his voice, but she shook her head.

"No, I'm staying. You'll need me when the Malignin come." There was no 'if' anymore.

Miqel nodded, relieved that she chose to stay. "Thanks." Some Blades from the south posts galloped by on their horses to aid the north and add what they could to the fight. The horses were at full speed with riders bent over their necks. Flares had stopped being sent into the sky, having already been used or not having enough time to be used, Miqel could only guess.

An hour passed, and Miqel and Iris had not seen any Malignin since they took down the last group before the flares. No more Blades were seen moving to the north. They probably did not have anyone else to spare.

"Think they got it under control?" Iris asked.

"Dunno..."

Iris tapped her foot uneasily, nerves on end. Miqel stood still, stolidly watching for any advancement of Malignin. Something flickered in the corner of his eye. Miqel turned to look and saw that it was a flare to the east. In complete silence, it flew into the air. He looked up to see if Iris was seeing it too. Her open-mouthed gaze confirmed his unasked question. All that Iris and Miqel heard was the wind blowing across the desolate land. They watched it fall to the earth.

They both stared in silence, at a loss for words. Nothing like this had ever happened before. Sometimes a flare or two would be sent up at night, but never more. A few minutes later, another went up. Then another after that. They watched for more, but there were none. Either the Blades at those posts knew it was hopeless, or they had fallen before they could ask for aid. There could not be much more reinforcements if there were any left at all.

That was it. Iris and Miqel prepared themselves for anything. They could only stand their post and hope the night passed quickly. Miqel completely faced east and made sure he had sound footing. He expected Malignin to come barreling through the darkness at any moment. He could feel his heart pounding in his chest, feel his veins pulse as blood coursed through his body. One heartbeat went by, and another, but still, the Malignin did not come.

Iris also looked to the east, expecting the Malignin to come from that direction, and absentmindedly glanced behind her. As she turned to look, a Malignin leaped and was midair towards her. Instinctively she raised her bow for a feeble defense and managed to shout "Behind!" before the Malignin crashed into her. Her bow flew from her grasp, and both Iris and the creature tumbled in a heap off the tunnel and onto the ground.

The wind was knocked out of her, but Iris forced herself to stand up and draw her sword, ready to fight while her lungs spasmed for air. The Malignin had already shaken off its fall and advanced on her, mouth agape and thin, sharp, teeth glistening in the dark. With no warning, no hesitation, it jumped at her again. Iris tried to move but was not fast enough. The Malignin gripped her around the waist in its hands, and jaws locked around her left shoulder.

The ever-furious beast jerked her this way and that as if she weighed nothing. Iris punched it in the side as hard as she could, over and over, but it would not let go. Somehow, she managed to keep a hold of her sword throughout the onslaught, but there was not enough space to maneuver her sword to stab the Malignin. She could feel her armor bending, closing uncomfortably, and bruising her shoulder.

Iris felt a stinging sensation. The Malignin's teeth punched through her armor and dug into her skin. She felt it tearing in its teeth, turning to shreds. Warm, sticky blood streamed down her front and back. There was nothing she could do. The Malignin chewed on her shoulder. It tasted her blood and drove on eagerly. Iris thought she was going to die. As soon as she came to that realization, a blinding flash of light and heat covered her body.

Iris clenched her eyes shut and fell to the ground, free from the Malignin's mouth. She opened her eyes as she landed and saw Miqel standing over her. His helmet must have been torn off in the fighting. His face was bloodied, and he clearly had a broken nose. The flare made a slow descent back down behind him. The sudden fire and heat caused them both to have a moment of respite as the Malignin shielded themselves from the light. Miqel grabbed and helped her up, then handed over her sword that she thought she still gripped. He was breathing heavily.

"Go, go back to town and warn 'em. Ye'll be able ta make it, but there's not much time." He paused as they heard the flare land on the ground, sending flames everywhere. "The nighters'll attack again soon as th' fire burns down a bit. There's no time." They could already hear the Malignin tearing at the ground in anger and frustration.

"I'm staying," Iris began.

"No, don't argue. Just fucking go!" Miqel demanded and shoved her in the direction of the town. "Run! Warn th' town!" he shouted as she stumbled into a jog, then a run. Miqel watched her go, just in case the Malignin decided to attack her. They were not even interested, though. They all but ignored her passing.

Iris knew there was no other way. Someone had to warn the folk of Guardstin, but she was afraid she would never see Sainte or Miqel again.

▼▲▼

Sainte was torn from his thoughts when he heard Miqel screaming. Almost immediately after the screaming stopped, the entire tunnel trembled. Dust showered down around him as he now felt the ground shaking too. He flinched as there was a sudden pounding and scratching at the door. Seconds after the beating began, the door was shredded into pieces and Malignin crawled through.

Reacting on instincts, Sainte rushed them, sword at the ready. His blade met the flesh of Malignin, flashing left and right. He attacked relentlessly; teeth bared in a snarl. No matter where his sword swung, it sliced through dark flesh. The Malignin struck with force and tried to overwhelm Sainte with sheer numbers. However, they could not get more than two abreast in the enclosed space, which seemed to anger them even further.

In moments his world was chaos. Never before had the Malignin attacked with such ferocity and numbers. He was slowly getting pushed back. Three more shoved through the splintered door with each Malignin he killed. He tried to step on the mechanism to close the defense doors, but there were so many Malignin in the tunnel that the doors could not shut. However, he was able to tip the cauldrons. Each time one spilled, he put himself at risk by possibly getting splashed by oil, but the Malignin paid the oil no heed. They strode through the oil, covering themselves in it. There was nothing else he could do to stem the tide; there were too many. It took every ounce of power to keep swinging his sword. He quickly lost all of his energy and had to rely on adrenaline.

"Miqel! Iris!" he screamed, but no one responded. He doubted they could hear him if they were even still alive.

Dust continued to fall from the ceiling as Malignin crawled all over the outside of the tunnel, clawing and digging their way in. Sainte could see it in their ravenous eyes that they knew they would be successful. They were intent on obtaining what they fought night after night for.

Where were the reinforcements? Surely Miqel or Iris lit the flare. Something was wrong. Help should have been here by now.

Sainte was pushed back halfway to Ellie's door when there was a crashing sound behind him like a rockslide. He risked a glance back, and what he saw filled him with rage and fear. A Malignin successfully dug through the ceiling of the tunnel. It shook its head to clear it from the fall, glanced at Sainte, and then galloped to the house's entrance and started to beat at the door.

Above him, more Malignin clawed at the hole furiously. So many were trying to get through at once that they got stuck. As more Malignin clawed, the hole increased in size, and more fell in. Something hit Sainte in the side, making him stagger. His attention jerked back to his front.

He savagely sliced his assailant across the torso, revealing its muscles underneath. Sainte grabbed the closest torch, burning his hand without realizing it, and threw it on the ground, lighting the oil. Many of the Malignin went up in flame and screeched in agony. The Malignin in the front of the tunnel were stopped for now. The fire spread quickly, wounding many Malignin and making them retreat.

With those Malignin currently preoccupied, Sainte could now face the more significant threat. More Malignin were at the hole now, expanding it as more and more came through. Sainte ran under the hole, careful to keep out of reach of their claws, and narrowly dodged a Malignin that fell in. He ran to the door, which was now broken down. He was no longer worried about the Malignin. His priority was to keep Ellie safe.

He burst through the door, sword held in both hands, swimming in his own sweat in his armor. The room was a mess, books were torn from the shelves, and furniture was ripped apart. It was almost unrecognizable. Three Malignin were in the same room he was in, and he could only guess how many more made it before them.

"Ellie!" he screamed, throat dry from the fighting and the flames. "Ellie!" he shouted again. It felt like his throat was bleeding. The three Malignin faced him and moved in. With a growl, Sainte hacked at one, slicing its arm off, and quickly ducked under the claws of the second. The third Malignin struck him on his side, but his armor held. Sainte staggered to the right from the blow but regained his balance quickly. In one quick motion, he lopped the head off of the Malignin, leaving only one left. It charged at Sainte, but he spun out of the way, slicing the creature's back open. Sainte did not even finish it off. There was not enough time; he had to find Ellie.

He ran further into the room and could hear her calling for him before he almost ran into a Malignin that entered from her bedroom. It was carrying Ellie. Immediately the Malignin reacted and lowered its shoulder to push Sainte away. He fell to the ground, and more Malignin entered the room between him and Ellie.

"Sainte? What's going on?" she called out in a trembling voice. Most of the Malignin paid no attention to him. They had what they came for, and now they were not worried about anything except leaving with their prize. Her face fell with the realization that something was not right. It was the first time that Sainte saw anything reminiscent of fear on it. "Sainte, what's happening?" She cried out.

He started screaming and scrambled up to his feet. He could feel the heat of the fire as it now spread into the room, but he paid it no heed. He attacked every creature that was in between him and Ellie. He was blind with rage, screaming incoherently. His sword struck Malignin flesh over and over. The Malignin carrying Ellie tore past Sainte as the remaining ones blocked his path. Sainte's last sight of Ellie was of her being taken through the door by a Malignin as flames now caressed the inside of the Barrier's home.

He skewered the first Malignin that came at him, but his sword got stuck in its ribs and jerked out of his hand as the beast fell to the ground. He did not bother getting it; it would have been pointless. He tried to barrel his way through the Malignin to try to follow Ellie but was tackled to the ground.

A Malignin was on top of Sainte, crushing him. Drool fell from its mouth onto Sainte's face as it bellowed at him. Sainte pummeled its face relentlessly. The creature beat back. He grabbed it on either side of its head and started head-butting it ceaselessly until it stopped moving. Sainte kept going, hearing the Malignin's skull begin to crack.

Sainte threw the dead weight off and shakily stood up. Bits of his armor were falling off, having reached its limits. His helmet was dented from the Malignin's skull and pressed uncomfortably on his forehead. Blood dripped from his fingertips. Malignin blood mixed with his own. He faced another Malignin, ready to continue the fight. He raised his fists and stepped toward it, but it twisted and spiraled up. This foe was not a Malignin; it was smoke. His eyes played tricks on him. He thought Malignin surrounded him, but it was only dark smoke in the room. There were no more left. They were all gone.

Sainte tried to take another step but fell to his knees. He was suddenly aware of the warmth growing stronger by the second. The fire spread through the furniture quickly, and the books thrown about the room did nothing to impede it. It would not be long before the flames devoured everything he protected.

Everything he failed to protect.

Sainte fell face first, and his vision slowly faded. Before he blacked out, he could have sworn that he heard Ellie call for him one last time.

▼▲▼

Iris had no idea how long she was running before she dared to glance back, afraid to see the carnage the Malignin were responsible for. The only reason she forced herself to look back was that she hoped she would see Sainte and Miqel jogging to catch up with her.

What she saw instead made her stumble to her knees, breath caught in her parched throat.

She could tell from this distance that the entire tunnel was engulfed in flames; it had been for a while. The fire reached for the sky out of multiple holes in the tunnel. Some flames even spouted from channels in the mountain. She could see shapes outlined against the fire, running away from it, Malignin. She desperately searched for her friends but knew it was useless at this distance. Iris sat on the ground; her legs were unable to hold her any longer. Her armor suddenly felt heavier than ever before. It restricted her lungs from pulling in any air. Her body shook with fear, grief, and failure. What was she supposed to do now?

What would anyone be able to do? Then she was faced with the most important question; what was going to happen now?

Iris felt paralyzed as she watched everything she defended burn to the ground. She watched hopelessly as silent tears streaked down her face. The sun began to rise behind her, but she felt no comfort in its spreading light.

FOUR
-RECOVERY-

After Miqel told Iris to leave, he quickly returned to the tunnel entrance. He had to give Sainte as much time as possible before the reinforcements arrived. If they got there. As the flames greedily ate the oil and hay mixture that remained of the flare, Miqel gazed out at the Malignin at the edge of the light. He lost all hope when he saw the writhing mass of Malignin beyond. Some were already advancing, braving the dying fire. There was no end to them. Nothing he did would change the fact that they were going to get by him.

Miqel roared and swung his axe mightily, but they just darted back out of range. "I'll shite down ye nighter's throats!"

The Malignin seemed to smile in mockery at his words. The flames shrunk, fluttered, and struggled to stay alive.

They rushed in as soon as the last flames flickered out and died. Miqel let out a battle cry. Veins popped from his neck, and his eyes promised death. As the Malignin came within reach, he managed to hack one down but then was immediately swatted aside as if he was nothing but a mere nuisance. His axe was wrenched from his grasp in the stampede. To the ravenous monsters, he was nothing but a bump in the ground now. They trampled him in their haste to flow into the tunnel. All thoughts of helping Sainte, of Iris, of his duty, were dashed from his mind.

Somehow, he managed to roll onto his stomach amidst the feet and claws. He lifted his head, only to have it shoved back into the mud by a Malignin's foot. The pressure was relieved just as he thought it would crush his head. He dug his fingers into the dirt and crawled. There was constant pressure on his back as he was trampled. He growled through mud-caked teeth and pushed on. There had to be an end to the Malignin soon.

At what seemed like a turtle's pace, Miqel crawled out of the main path of Malignin. Not that there was a main path anymore, considering most of the Malignin were in or on the tunnel. He tried to stand up but could only get his right leg under him. His left leg refused to move. He rolled to his back and looked at it. A white bone jutted from his shin, starkly contrasting with the dark mud covering him. The sight of his wound made him nauseous, and he had to look away. He almost wished he just got trampled to death.

He could only watch as the tunnel went up in flames, and Malignin both fled and rushed in. Flames licked out of the tunnel entrance like a tongue; the creatures of the night gave it a wide berth. Instead, they went through holes that they clawed in the tunnel. Miqel had never seen them attack with such ferocity ever before.

Something changed, though. The Malignin stopped their attack. They started leaping from the tunnel and sprinting away. Some tore out of the mouth of the tunnel in a frenzy, trying to get away from the fire and light as quickly as possible. They were leaving, running away. Hope fluttered to life in Miqel. Maybe reinforcements had finally arrived, or perhaps they could not stand the flames anymore. As he watched them flee with grim satisfaction, he noticed one ran rather strangely. He strained his eyes and saw it carried something. No, not something. Someone. A girl. His blood ran cold despite the overwhelming heat from the fire.

It was the Barrier. There was no one else. It could not be Iris; he watched her run away. He could tell it was not Sainte. It was her. The one that they had to protect. He slowly lost focus, unable to hold onto his thoughts any longer. Miqel could feel his skin blistering due to the heat, but he could not move. His vision faded, and his last thought was that the Barrier was taken, and Sainte was dead.

▼▲▼

Sainte came to with a start, confused and disoriented. He was attacked with a fit of coughing. Smoke filled his lungs. As he got the fit under control, he realized what woke him up; the sleeve of his left arm was on fire. He quickly beat it with his free hand, snuffing the flames out before they could do much damage. The more he moved, however, the more his body burned.

His metal armor absorbed so much heat that it scorched his skin. It felt so hot that he was surprised it was not glowing red. He ripped the armor off as hastily as he could, burning his hands more than they already were. The air was scalding. Every breath he took seemed to scorch his insides. The smoke invaded his nose and mouth, contaminating what little air he sucked in. He hunched down low, looking for the exit, mind racing. He was thinking about as clearly as the smoke-filled room.

He quickly located an opening and sprinted to it, praying to the White Wyverns that it was the way out. His only hope was to make it out of the burning mountain. If this were not the right way out, he would die. Sainte breathed hard, sucking up smoke and spitting it back out. Flames danced across his body, but he moved through them. It was as if he were running through hell itself. He now recognized that he was in the tunnel, but it never seemed to end, just burn forever. Smoldering pieces of burnt wall and ceiling fell all around him, some even hitting Sainte, but nothing so large as to drop him.

Finally, he burst through the entrance with smoke trailing him. The sharp, fresh air hit him so hard it almost pushed him back into the fire. It felt similar to when he jumped into a frozen lake as a kid. The feeling of iciness quickly passed. One breath was sucked into his spasming lungs before he was on his hands and knees, coughing up black spittle followed by vomit. Tears streamed freely down his face; he had no control over it. His face was burnt red, and his hands blistered. Sainte did not even want to see the ruin the rest of his body had undoubtedly become.

After a few minutes of catching his breath and slowing his racing mind, he finally looked around. It was morning, but the sun had almost grown out of it. As far as he could see, the ground was rutted up like an open wound on the earth. From what he could tell, many of the Blade towers and walls were in shambles. Some remained standing, but all that Sainte could see were damaged. He was the only one out there then. Where was everyone else? Where were the search parties? The clean-up crews? The rest of the Blades of the Night?

Sainte lay down, unable to hold himself up any longer. He could think of nothing except the army of Malignin that attacked them last night. How could such a significant force attack with such a surprise? How was this not foreseen?

His entire body hurt, his eyes burned, and the only thing that provided him any comfort was the ground. All he wanted to do was sink into its embrace.

Something drove him, though, and told him to stand up. Laying in defeat would not solve anything. He had to find Ellie. Sainte struggled to his knees and pushed himself up to his feet. By now, the fire in the tunnel was slowly burning itself out, both the tunnel and the house a charred cadaver of what once was a symbol of defense and strength, all up in smoke.

Sainte stumbled around the field aimlessly as he sorted through his thoughts. What was he to do now? He weighed some of his options and immediately ruled out returning to Guardstin. He would not be able to face everyone after what he let happen. People would blame him, and they would have every right to. No, he would not go back. There was only one acceptable option. He would find Ellie or die trying.

He scanned the desolate horizon looking for a sign, anything that may give him a clue to where the Malignin took her. His eyes scanned everything quickly, but he could find nothing worthwhile. There was a nagging in his head, one that he would not listen to. What if they killed her already?

There were a few corpses of Malignin lying about, signs that there was at least an attempt at a fight. Sainte was filled with dread as the longer he searched, the less he knew what to do. There were no signs he could see that would point him in the right direction. Where did they take Ellie? What were they going to do with her? He suddenly remembered the drawing she gave him. He hastily checked his breast pocket to make sure it was still there. It was, to his relief, just with a few more wrinkles. With a sigh, he let it be for now and continued looking for clues about her whereabouts.

It did not take him long before his eyes landed on a prone human. From this distance, he could not tell who it was. Sainte stumbled towards them, dreading to find out if it was Ellie. It could be her. The Malignin could have just dropped her after killing her. After they figured she was no more fun to them. Anger welled up inside of him and clouded his thoughts. He stumbled closer to the body, dragging his feet over the corpses of Malignin.

The anger that appeared just as quickly dissipated when the face came into focus. "Miqel..." he croaked as he recognized his friend's broken, beaten face. Sainte dropped to his knees beside his fallen friend. At least it was not Ellie.

Immediately he felt ashamed for thinking that as he sat next to his dead friend. Miqel was killed, and the first thing he felt was relief that it wasn't her. Sainte tried to rationalize it by convincing himself he could still find her, get her back. Of course he was saddened by the death of his friend, but the fact that Ellie was missing and not dead was foremost on his mind.

He placed a hand on Miqel's chest absentmindedly as he tried to push himself back to his feet but paused when he felt it move. He looked back down at his friend and saw his chest rise. The thought had not even occurred to him to check if Miqel was alive until that moment. He just assumed he was dead.

"Hey," he said, slapping Miqel's face slightly. There was no response, so he slapped it harder. "Wake up. Get up." Sainte started shaking him by the shoulders. "Get up, get up!" he yelled now, frantic. "I saw you move! You're alive!" Miqel's eyes flickered open, but not all the way, and he groaned. His hands moved feebly to try to push Sainte away.

"Stay with me, don't close your eyes," Sainte said repeatedly, desperately. Maybe Miqel saw where Ellie was taken. He grabbed his friend on each side of his head, forced him to look him in the face, and held his eyes open with his hands. Sainte saw recognition slowly enter his friend's eyes, but then they clouded with fear.

Miqel punched Sainte in the face with newfound strength and tried to stand, to run away, but he fell back down, clutching his leg and screaming. Sainte was more surprised than hurt by the punch. He looked where Miqel held his leg and saw a bloodied bone sticking between his fingers.

"Hey, hey, calm down. It's me, Sainte," he said, staring into Miqel's now bone-white face, eyes closed tight with pain. "You'll be all right; just breathe. Listen to me." Miqel opened his eyes a crack. "Yes, breathe, relax. Help will be coming shortly. Don't look down," Sainte said, snapping his fingers to get Miqel's attention. "Don't look at it." Talking to Miqel put the pain of his own wounds at the back of his mind. "Did you see Ellie? Did you see where she went?" he asked, trying to get anything out of his friend before he passed out again.

Miqel tried to say something, but all that came out was a groan. Sainte did not understand, so he leaned closer. All he could make out was a whispered, "Iris." So quiet he barely even understood Miqel an inch away. Iris. He had not even thought about her. Sainte was so busy worrying about Ellie that no one else mattered. Could he spare time to help his friends? He decided that he could not. Ellie had to be saved as quickly as possible. Surely Miqel and Iris would understand. They had to.

"I don't know where she's at," Sainte said. "I need you to listen to me, Miqel. You have to tell me where Ellie went right now. Nothing is more important than this. Everything could be lost, I don't know what will happen, but you must tell me where she went. Did you see anything? You're the only person who may know something, don't let me down, Miqel, don't," Sainte pleaded, staring into Miqel's pained eyes.

Then, ever so slowly, Miqel nodded. He lifted his arm as if in slow motion and pointed away from the tunnel to the east. His arm dropped like lead, and he grimaced as it hit the ground with a thud.

"That's where they took her? That's where they went? You're sure?" Miqel slowly nodded again. "You did well, Miqel. You did your duty." Miqel opened his mouth as if he wanted to say something. Before any words came out, Sainte already left his side, intent on only one thing. He had to find Ellie. He had to save her. He could do nothing more for his friend without wasting much-needed time.

Miqel watched Sainte leave, wounded that he did not offer him any help. His mind was mush. It moved as slow as a snail. Why did Sainte not ask about him or Iris? Miqel tried to call out and get Sainte's attention, but his throat was too dry. He only wanted some water, but Sainte left with the last of it.

He could only do one thing: lay on the rutted ground. It felt like he would be smothered at any moment by the unyielding sun. The adrenaline rush left him long ago, and Miqel realized that a broken leg was not his biggest problem. His biggest problem was trying to get comfortable before he died. Moving was excruciatingly painful, and he doubted he could walk even if moving did not hurt. Instead of putting himself in more pain by moving, he just lay still and accepted the fact that he would die in his current position.

There was no telling when Iris would return or a party of some sort to assess the damage. People would come, he was sure of it, but he was not sure if it would be soon enough to help him. Iris, though, she stuck in his mind. He would have given anything to see her one last time, to tell her how he really felt. He regretted not asking her to stay yesterday at the tavern.

Slowly, Miqel began to lose consciousness. He faded in and out throughout the rest of the day, slowly baking in the sun. He lost track of time, unsure if he had been lying there for a few hours or a few weeks; he was not even sure if it was day or night. The only thing he held onto was an image of Iris.

Iris made it back to town before the sun reached the sky's peak. When she lurched close to Guardstin, a group ran out to help her back in. The Council of the Blades of the Night waited for her just inside the gates. A group of people already started to show up to see what the hustle was about.

"Iris, what happened?" someone asked. Iris looked up through sweat and tears and saw that it was Crane.

"Malignin broke through. I think they got to the Barrier." At her words, the gathering crowd was set with uneasy murmurs. The three Council members looked around for silence. The onlookers reluctantly shushed.

"How do you know this? Did you see them get to the Barrier?" Crane asked again. The other two Council had their heads together behind him.

"Not exactly... On my way back here, I turned around to see if anyone else was coming with me, and I saw..." She paused to catch her breath. "I saw the tunnel. It was devoured by fire."

"But you didn't see the Malignin get to the Barrier?" he asked earnestly. She shook her head. "Then perhaps..." he trailed off, looking up at the crowd. "Everyone, please go back to your own day. We will gather a party and inspect the Mountain. Do not worry, not yet. Not until we know..." The onlookers reluctantly started to disperse.

"Maybe they should worry? Maybe we should be preparing for... For something," Iris said to him, but she said it quietly because she could understand his point of view. Crane did not think there should be unnecessary panic, but he did not see what Iris saw.

"Either way, we must go and search for survivors. I said we would check, and we will. A group of Blades and I will leave within the hour. Iris, I want you to stay here. You've been through a lot and must rest," Crane said.

"I'm going with you," she told him. Before he could decline, she kept speaking, "My friends were down there last night, and I have to look for them. You can't expect me to stay here and rest while they're down there still."

Crane saw the determination in her tired eyes and knew she would go no matter what. "Fine, come with us. But at least sit down, drink water, and rest while we gather a crew. I will send for you when we are about to leave."

Iris nodded; she was not about to push her luck with him and risk him changing his mind. The Council left quickly, and the remainder of the crowd also dispersed. Iris allowed herself to be led to someone's home. She was not sure whose it was, but it did not matter. Sitting down never felt so good to her. A canteen was brought to her. She slowly sipped on the cool, refreshing water and waited for word from Crane.

She did not have to wait long before someone came and told her they were gathering the last few people before they left. As fast as she could, she met the group at the very gates she stumbled through not even an hour ago. There were about a hundred people they could spare for the search party, primarily men from the Blades. Once she joined the crew, they spent a few minutes discussing what would be looked for, and then they set off toward the tunnel.

Along with the hundred people, they brought horses and carriages to carry any survivors they found. The going was slow with the large group, but they arrived at the burnt down tunnel with plenty of daylight left. From there, the search crew was split into five teams of twenty, each with their own carriage. They all set off to different areas to begin their searches. Iris stayed with the twenty that searched the tunnel and home of the Barrier.

They discovered that the interior of the Barrier's home largely stood intact, but the furnishings were burnt or otherwise destroyed. That would not be hard to replace, but the tunnel had all but been burnt down. It would not be hard to rebuild, but it would take time. If they even needed it anymore. Iris walked around the wreckage amongst whispers of dread from the Blades, first to witness the destruction. No one guessed that it would have been this bad.

They had been searching through the remains of the house for about an hour and still found no signs of Sainte, Miqel, or the Barrier. Just as Iris was beginning to give up hope of finding her friends again, someone shouted out. They found someone. Everyone ran to the source of the call, eager to see who it was. Afraid to see if it was someone they knew.

It was Miqel, unconscious but breathing. His leg was broken, a shard of bone stuck out, he had nasty burns, and his face was swollen and bruised. There were no apparent life-threatening injuries. They carefully loaded him onto the horse-drawn carriage, not wanting to aggravate unseen wounds.

"Easy with him, bastards, he's not dead," Iris growled at the men who loaded him, even though they were trying their best. "Can't you see he's injured?" Iris climbed on the wagon and sat down by his side. She took his hand in hers, hoping to feel a squeeze of assurance from him.

Slowly, the search crews trickled back to the tunnel. Altogether, thirteen more Blades were found alive, including Miqel, but they all had life-threatening wounds. Iris could already feel her peers' accusatory glances, blaming her for running when no one else did. They all had friends who died last night, and they could not help but hold her in contempt for fleeing. She found herself thinking that as well.

Another hour passed before all the crews returned to the tunnel and regrouped. With nothing further to do, and nothing further to bring down their spirits, they began the trek back to Guardstin. The walk back was uncomfortably quiet and slightly rushed. The evening was upon them, and no one wished to be caught outside the walls of Guardstin when night began. As they approached the town gates, Iris shuddered as she remembered the feeling of the Malignin's mouth crushing her shoulder, at Miqel's shouts at her to run, at last night in general as the current night was descending. She had not changed out of her armor yet, and she felt all the worse from it. Going back out to search was the right choice, though. She was glad they found Miqel. At least she knew that one of her friends escaped death.

The open gates spurred everyone on. They wanted to get back to their friends and families and to shut the gates behind them. As they entered Guardstin, they were greeted by a party of fifty women, the town's healers. They expected many injured to return, but their expectations were too high. The few that returned brought despair with them. The faces of the healers visibly fell as they were met with sorrowed silence, confirming their worst suspicions. Many healers broke down into tears as they had family or loved ones that perished. Each of the wounded men were escorted to separate houses for privacy. One of the healers stopped Iris as she attempted to follow Miqel.

"No, take a break, Iris. You need one. Get out of that armor and get clean. When was the last time you rested? You will need your strength soon; I can feel it. There's a reason you survived. You just don't know it yet. Come, let's get you cleaned up." The nurse, Iris faintly recalled her name being Clarenda, an elderly lady in her sixties, grabbed her elbow and gently pulled her away. Iris could only follow her as the weariness finally settled on her aching shoulders.

Soon she was sitting in a tub of warm water along with her unsettling thoughts. Worry fluttered in her chest as she considered the possibilities of what might happen now. Ellie was gone and the Malignin had free roam of Crearia. What would they do? What *could* they do? This was the first time that they had ever gotten to the Barrier. How would anyone know how to prepare for what was to come? They would find out soon enough, and Iris had a feeling it was not going to be easy.

Scared, Iris hugged her knees to her chest and quietly cried.

She was startled by a tapping at the door. She blinked slowly. She must have fallen asleep in the bath. Her skin was all pruned and the water had cooled.

"Come in," she called out softly. The door creaked open a crack.

"Iris, are you all right? You had been in there for a while and I thought to check..." Clarenda said softly.

"I'm... I'm fine," Iris said. "Must have dozed off. How long have I been in here?"

"About two hours, my dear. Come now, slip on your robe. Let's get you to a proper bed so that you can sleep comfortably."

"No, I have to see Miqel. I won't sleep again until he wakes. He'll wake up soon. I know it." Iris pulled herself out of the chilled water and slipped on clean clothes, a cotton shirt, pants, and sheepskin shoes. She pulled the door open and looked at the surprised face of Clarenda. "Take me to Miqel. I left him once, and I can't do it again."

The woman sighed. "If you insist, but I really do suggest you get some rest," Clarenda replied, genuinely concerned for Iris, but Iris shook her head in protest. "Follow me, then."

Clarenda led her out of the tiny house and through town. Most everyone was asleep by now, but there was an air of gloom about. There were no dogs barking or sheep bleating. As if all living things knew something was not right. Iris looked up to the night sky as she absentmindedly followed Clarenda, hoping to see some stars at least. A thick cloud rolled in, blocking out the distant pinpricks of light and instead promised rain. With a sigh, Iris looked down and realized they were already approaching the house where Miqel was resting.

"Here we are. He's inside, still unconscious, I'm afraid. I'll be heading back home. If you have any need of me, please ask," Clarenda said, meaning every word. Iris hugged her.

"Thank you for everything. Really, I mean it," Iris said, forcing back tears. After the less than warm welcome she received when she got to Guardstin she had not expected anyone to treat her with any kindness.

"Now, now, don't you fuss about it, child. Just be sure to gather your strength. I expect you'll need it rather soon,"

Clarenda said sadly, as if she knew something Iris did not. Iris nodded in acceptance of her words, and then Clarenda turned and walked back to her house. Iris watched her leave for a moment as large raindrops started pounding onto the ground.

Iris walked inside to a deafening sound of thunder accompanied by the beginning of a downpour. It sounded like the house was set under a waterfall because of how hard the rain fell. It was only a small one-roomed house. The bed itself took up most of the room. There were four healers inside. Two squeezed on each side of the bed that Miqel laid on. One wrung a rag of water over his mouth, one on each side rubbed his skin with a salve to lessen the burns, and one was tending to his broken leg. Each of them paused and looked at Iris as she entered the room.

"I'm sorry, I didn't mean to distract you... I just wanted to be by his side when he wakes," Iris explained, nervous they would shoo her away.

"There's not much room, but..." the healer with the rag said. All the healers looked at each other and muttered their acceptance. "You can sit by the foot of the bed."

"Thank you," Iris said and sat where directed, facing Miqel. "I promise you, Miqel, I will not leave your side. I'll stay by you until you're well again. I've let you down once, but I won't do it again." After observing the nurses for a few silent hours, Iris asked the healer feeding him water if she could do it. She initially denied it, but Iris explained that the healers also needed sleep. If she took over that simple job, that would free up one more healer for something else. Finally, the healer agreed more out of annoyance than anything, but Iris did not care.

Iris took over, dripping water into Miqel's mouth, glad to be doing something instead of nothing. He had been unable to eat anything, nor would they risk trying to feed him for fear of choking him. He would have to wait for food until he woke up. Now and again, Iris would stand up and walk outside to fend off sleep, determined to stay awake until Miqel woke. The night drove on, and Iris found herself standing at the only window in the room, waiting for the sun to rise.

As she gazed out the window, she realized how tired she was. Her sleep-deprived mind could focus on nothing. Whenever she tried to think about something, to grasp it, a fogginess just invaded her mind. She was not able to think straight. But even her clouded thoughts could not fight off the two emotions that plagued her body. Those two things, however, were the worst feelings in the world.

She felt pity, pity for herself, pity for Sainte and Miqel, pity for everyone that had to endure the terror that was sure to come. No one could possibly know how this would turn out. The only thing left to do was wait and hope that they would be able to react accordingly to whatever happened. If the Malignin attacked with the force they had before, they could not be stopped. Before the Malignin broke through, the Blades of the Night's numbers already dwindled. If she had thought their numbers were low before, she shuddered to think about how few remained now. No one deserved to live during a time like this.

The second feeling she had was fear. Iris was afraid. She did not want to admit it to anyone, but it was a fact. She was afraid she would never see Miqel wake. She was afraid of how she would die. She was scared because Sainte was missing, most likely dead.

Those two emotions intertwined within her as she stood at the window, watching, waiting for the sun to rise. The sun never rose. The blinding light never broke the horizon.

But the downpour continued.

▼▲▼

Sainte had been on the move ever since he left Miqel, moving on into the night, into the rain, and into the forest. The rain was relentless and made the night even darker. His legs were tired of wrenching themselves out of the mud he sank into with each step. Before long, he was surrounded by pale white, wraith-like trees. He knew he was in Whitweir Forest, but he long since lost which direction he was traveling without the sun's guidance. It should have been mid-morning, but the sun had not risen. Instead, the rain persisted. This had to be a consequence of not having a Barrier to protect Crearia. His journey was miserable, trekking through the soggy ground. His boots were filled with muck; trying to clean them out would have been useless.

Sainte stopped walking and stood in the rain. He was lost in every sense of the word. He did not know where he was. He did not know what he was going to do. Usually, if one headed north through Whitweir Forest, they would come out to the town of Elion after about four days of walking. Ever since he began his journey, the dire situation weighed heavy on his mind, burdening his thoughts with what may happen rather than keeping track of direction. He stumbled near the closest tree while mud greedily pulled at his feet. He slumped down in the muck, back against the bark. His arms laid in puddles, limp. His head leaned back in defeat, getting dripped on by the rain falling off the leaves. He was finished.

This is not how it was supposed to happen, he was not even sure what 'it' was, but he knew it was not this.

The last few bits of armor he had left were mere annoyances to him now and seemed to smother him. Sainte ripped them off and tossed them into the darkness. He was now only clad in leathers. Each piece of armor reminded him of all the lies, of all the empty and now broken promises he made to Ellie. Out of everything he did and fought for, there was nothing left to show for it.

He unclipped his belt that held his empty sheath, a sharp reminder that he forgot to grab his grandfather's sword from one of the Malignin's bodies. He shoved it away, not able to muster the strength even to throw it. All this movement opened his fresh burns and popped blisters. His hands were sticky with blood, puss, and mud. Sainte thought he could smell the infection setting in, nauseating him and turning his stomach over. Bile rolled down the front of his shirt.

If he did not die of exposure or Malignin, his wounds would see to it. It was only a matter of time; a short amount of time, at that. Regret stabbed him in the heart as he knew that he would not be able to find Ellie.

Sainte felt like all the problems in the world were thrust unto him. There were too many things he felt he had to do that he could not keep track of them. Not that he could do anything now. He was too tired. All he wanted to do was to sleep. Close his eyes and drift away. His wounds were slowly losing feeling, going numb.

When he rested, his mind slowed down, and he remembered the drawing. The drawing Ellie gave him. He frantically searched through his pockets, hoping it was not ruined. He suddenly remembered that it was in his chest pocket. Carefully, he took it out. It was not wet, which he was thankful for. With shaking, blood-soaked hands, he slowly unfolded it. Rain speckled the drawing.

I will not die with bad thoughts. I will not die with bad thoughts. I will not die with bad thoughts. The words circled in his mind as he held the picture until a shorter, similar sentence replaced it.

I will not die.

He held the drawing to his chest, staining it, but only thoughts of his last time with Ellie were in his mind when he told her he loved her. That strengthened his resolve. Slowly, the numbness faded away, and pain once again took over. But it was good. He held on to the pain. It cleared his tired mind.

That was when he noticed the noise, a sloshing step. Something moved in the darkness; he could hear the squelching movement through the rain. Whatever it was, there was more than one. He could not see what moved, but he had a good idea. Sainte hastily stuffed the drawing back into his pocket.

A Malignin's face slowly came into focus in Sainte's dark-adjusted vision. The creature just stared at him, yellow eyes unblinking. The head hovered as if bodiless; teeth jutted out of its jaw. It was studying him, waiting and watching the strength seep out of his body. It knew he was severely hurt. Another two heads materialized beside the first one, one on each side.

Sainte did not even bother to go for his dagger. He knew if he did, they would attack. He would not have enough time even to reach it. He held his hands up, though, getting as ready as he could. He stared right back at them, daring them to attack him, wanting them to. At least one of them was going to go down with him.

Calculatingly, the trio started moving around Sainte, surrounding him. They were wary as they had fought humans before and knew that his kind were not to be taken lightly. They also knew that there was no reason to rush this attack. Muscles rippled under their tar-like skin as their clawed limbs dug into the mud, fanged mouths parted slightly in anticipation of ripping flesh. The Malignins' backs were arched like a cat. Their heads slowly dipped up and down with each step. Yet the similarities between their limbs and humans were uncanny.

They all stopped simultaneously, and Sainte knew that it was almost time—his last fight.

As one, they leaped at him, and Sainte let out a final battle cry. There was nothing else he could do. He accepted his fate.

Over his own cry, a female voice rose from the darkness somewhere behind him. In surprise, his shout was cut short. As was the Malignin's attack.

"Leave this place, beasts of burden and wear. You will not have victory in this fight. Nuse protects me," she demanded. The Malignin paused in their advance on Sainte, snapping their jaws viciously at the newcomer. So close to Sainte their drool spattered onto his face. The one in the middle stood on its hind legs as if challenging the woman behind Sainte.

It stepped forward, splashing Sainte with mud and water as its foot sunk into the ground.

There was a bright flash of light, followed by a sound much like mud being slapped and a crack like a tree branch snapping. Two clumps of flesh fell to the ground in front of Sainte, and as his eyes adjusted to the darkness once more, he saw that it was the Malignin ripped in half.

The other two Malignin fled as soon as the light flared into existence. There was no sign of life anymore until the woman walked in front of Sainte. She knelt before him and gently grabbed his face in her hands. She turned his head so they looked at each other, and he looked upon the face of Ellie.

▼▲▼

The sun had not risen for many hours. The town Elders and the Council gathered in the city hall to discuss this endless night. Iris was invited as she was the only Blade both present during the recent attack and well enough to walk on her own. She attended, grudgingly, only on the promise that if anything new happened with Miqel, she would be notified immediately.

The building was large but was only composed of one room. A fireplace was built onto one side of the building, which was lit. A table was the centerpiece of the room, able to seat fifteen people on each side. The Elders took seven of the chairs on one side of the table, and Iris sat with the Council on the opposite side. As the meeting droned on, she heard the Elders talk but was too distracted to listen to their words.

"Someone must be held accountable. This should not go unpunished," one of the female Elders said.

"Who would you suggest we punish, Deanna? Who is at fault?" Crane asked her. In an answer, Deanna glanced at Iris, who was not paying attention. Crane scoffed. "Of course. Punishing her would get us nowhere. Punishing anyone, for that matter, would get us nowhere. We must focus less on punishment and more on what is next for us." There were murmurs of agreement around the table.

"I agree," a balding man that sat on Deanna's left said. "No one is to blame..."

"She left her post," Deanna interjected.

"It doesn't matter. What difference would it have made had she stayed? She left only to warn us. We're lucky she did. After all, she may have seen something that could be helpful," he said. Iris perked up as she realized they were talking about her.

"Thank you, Mathen," Iris said. Then to Deanna, "I assure you, I would have changed nothing if I stayed. I would've been another body."

"It's all right, Iris, you needn't defend yourself. If I recall correctly, this meeting was called to talk about the future, about what needs to be done. Not for Iris to defend herself," Crane said.

"Then what do we do?" another man asked, irritated. Iris could not remember his name. "Why hasn't the sun come up? Where have the Malignin gone? Why haven't we been attacked yet? What're they waiting for?" At his questions, everyone present was silent. No one had any answers.

"The way I see it," Crane began, "we have two options. We either get the Barrier back, or we prepare to change how we live drastically."

What he said sparked an argument about what would be best for everyone. It seemed no one could come to an agreement. Iris sat in silence. She did not partake in the conversation. What more could she add? The only thing that was on her mind was when, or if, Miqel would wake up.

With impatience riddled across her face, she sat and waited for the discussion to end so she could return to Miqel's side. The meeting was interrupted just as they had begun speaking about food and how they would grow crops. The door slammed open, and a red-faced, soaked to the bone, out-of-breath boy in his teens stood panting in the open door as rain spattered in behind him.

"Speak, boy, and quickly; you're letting the rain in," one of the Elders blurted out, clearly agitated at this interruption.

"He's awake. Miqel has woken up, and he has news about that night. Come, all of you. You should hear this in person."

Iris ran out of the building upon hearing his first two words. She cursed herself as she ran through the pouring rain; she should have stayed with Miqel. She had to reach him before the Elders did. She had to be one of the first people he saw when he woke up. Thankfully, the building where Miqel was at was not far from where the meeting was.

She burst through the door and pushed her way through the healers that were now there. Iris forced her way through people who tried to hold her back; that told her to wait. She was not waiting anymore. Finally, she came to the front of the crowd and saw Miqel looking at her. His eyes were half closed, but he was awake.

"Iris," he breathed out, quiet and weak, but it was the best sound Iris heard since she could remember. "Never thought I'd see ya again," Miqel said with a slight smile, followed by a grimace because even that small movement pained him.

Before Iris could say anything else, the Elders solemnly entered the room. Iris glanced at them, then back to Miqel, slowly filling with dread as she knew this would not be a happy reunion between friends. She took a deep breath and mentally prepared herself for the words she was about to speak. He had to hear it from her.

"Ellie and Sainte, they're... they're both missing, probably dead," she paused. What she heard next was not what she anticipated.

"Nay, they aren't," he said as he slowly shook his head. "I seen 'em. I seen 'em both."

FIVE
-DECISIONS-

Flames surrounded Sainte, the fire ate his skin away, and his eyes popped in the heat but always grew back to pop again and make him relive the agony. He screamed; the fire invaded his mouth and burned his insides, boiling his stomach. There was only suffering, but he knew he would not die. He would only live in constant, excruciating torment.

There was suddenly a cool sensation on his forehead, something he could now describe only as not pain. He expected that it was a tease. Whatever force was keeping him here was toying with him. But the coldness remained. It felt good, cooled him down a little, and expanded further on his face. The fire burned low and continued receding until it was no longer around him. Sainte was surrounded in darkness now, peaceful darkness.

And he slipped thankfully into it.

Sainte woke with a start, sweating, confused, scared, and hurt. He could feel a thin sheet that stuck to him, made him uncomfortable, but it would hurt too much to remove. His eyes slowly adjusted to the light of a small fire as he looked around. He could tell he was in a little hut or cabin, but other than that, he was at a loss as to his whereabouts.

His head ached and he was groggy. His vision was blurry as well. He could see that the room was round, with a bookshelf across from him and a table at the foot of the bed cluttered with glass jars. The fire was in the center of the room. Something moved in the corner of his eye, and fear gripped his heart as it moved closer, but it was only a woman. It had to be Ellie, he remembered now. She saved him, somehow, from the Malignin.

"Ellie, you're here. How did...?" She shushed him as she drew near. Her face came into focus, but it was not Ellie. He did not know this woman, but he had a faint feeling that he had seen her before.

"Ellie? I know not of the girl you speak of. My name is Aroc." Her voice was soft on his ears, relaxing. It reminded him of a late night's light shower, pattering upon the roof, calming and soothing but demanding attention as if it could turn into a torrential downpour at any moment. As she moved to the edge of his bed, Sainte could tell she was beautiful. She had gray eyes and hair so blonde it was almost white.

"Where... Where am I?" was all Sainte was able to mutter out. His eyes squinted in the light.

"You're safe. That's all that matters now. Don't move. I know you must have many questions, but they must wait until you regain your strength. I'm making some soup for you right now. I'll grab a bowl; we can talk after you eat."

To Sainte, Aroc seemed to float over to the pot bubbling over the fire. She grabbed a bowl from the table and scooped out a spoonful of soup. She headed back over to him, offering the bowl to him. He accepted it with weak arms, barely holding it on his own. The soup had an earthy smell as the steam rose to his nostrils. The warm clay bowl comforted his sore hands.

"I'm afraid you'll just have to drink from the bowl. I don't have any spoons," she said sheepishly, brushing a strand of hair behind her ear.

"It's fine," he said. As he took the first sip, he closed his eyes to appreciate the delicious soup fully.

Aroc helped him when she could, dabbing at the soup he spilled and cleaning it up. After the first bowl, he asked for another. Even though his body cried against every movement, the soup was so good that he could deal with the pain to feed himself. After finishing his second helping, Aroc took the empty bowl from him and dropped it in another pot that was filled only with water to soak.

"Well," Aroc said, kneeling at the side of his bed. "It seems as if my remedies are working. How are you feeling?"

"Remedies? I feel bad. I hurt. My entire body hurts," Sainte replied.

"But you are conscious of yourself, are you not? And you were able to feed yourself?" she asked, and Sainte nodded in response. "Then it is an improvement," she said with a reassuring smile.

"Where am I?" Sainte asked slowly, truly feeling better. He tried to sit up but could only get so far as to lean on his elbows.

"We're in Whitweir Forest. My family built this hut. When I found you, I was out collecting berries and herbs to restock Elion. Lucky for you, I've some decent knowledge of herbs to treat wounds, even burn wounds."

"Elion? Are we close to it? That's where I was heading," Sainte said, hoping he made it farther than he thought.

"We are only a day's travel from Elion. Two if we take it easy," she said as she laid a hand upon Sainte's brow. "Your fever is not as bad as before. Come, try to sit up all the way." She grabbed his shoulder to help him sit upright.

"How long was I out?" Sainte asked groggily, dizzy from sitting up, but he managed to hold the position with a bit of help from her.

"You've slept for three days. When I came across you, most of your burns were infected. I had feared that you would not be able to pull through. I did what I could, and now you are here," she said, motioning toward bandages that covered his arms and torso.

"Three days?" he exclaimed. He tried to stand up but quickly regretted it as pain coursed through his body. "I have to go," he said through gritted teeth.

"You're too weak. You should get more rest." She could see he did not care what she thought about his condition. "At least wait until we're done talking and see how you feel."

Sainte settled back down briefly, seeing the truth in her words. He probably did need more rest. "Wait... I saw you, though, before you got me. There were three Malignin that were about to kill me, but you ripped one in half without even touching it. How did you do that?" Sainte asked as his memory slowly came back in pieces.

Aroc only shook her head. "There was nothing around when I saved you. I found you leaning up against a tree, quite alone. The only reason I found you was because you were muttering nonsense. I heard you and came to see what was making the noise. I then managed to drag you to this hut. There was nothing else around."

After hearing this but not quite believing it, Sainte had had enough. "Thank you for helping me, truly, but I have to find Ellie. I've been down for three days, but I won't be down for anymore. Get me my armor and sword, and I'll be on my way."

Aroc let out a small breath, much like a quiet laugh. "Your armor and sword? I saw no sword, and I was not able to grab what little armor was lying around you. You have nothing except the clothes that you are wearing. If you're still planning on going to Elion, I shall travel with you. You still need more rest, but I think the trip back to town won't hurt you. If we go slowly. Once there you can get more rest. If you are still insistent on leaving to look for this Ellie, my father has many supplies that he may let you use."

Sainte could not deny that what Aroc said made sense. He was still tired, physically and mentally. He had gotten rest, but it was not enough. Maybe he should go with Aroc, get more rest, and consider his options.

"Fine, I'll head back to Elion with you. I expect we'll part ways there, but for now, thank you for the aid you've shown me." Sainte slowly, shakily, swung his legs out of bed and stood up, holding onto the edge of the bed for support. He held himself up and waited for the pain to go away. It never entirely went away, but it did recede a little.

"Sainte... You should know... The sun hasn't risen for four days. You were out of it when I found you. I'm not sure what you may or may not remember," Aroc said, somewhat reservedly, unsure how he would react to the news.

At this Sainte sighed, and thoughts of the night Ellie was taken flooded his mind. He rubbed his forehead as a headache slowly appeared. "I knew the sun hadn't risen that first day, but I didn't think it would be gone this long. I think I know the reason why. It's mostly, if not entirely, my fault. I was, am, the Shield for the Barrier, but I failed. Malignin broke through. They stole the Barrier. She's gone, and now I think we're cursed with this endless night because of it." Sainte's voice trembled as he retold the story. "This is why I must find her. I have to try to make things right," Sainte ended.

Aroc listened without interrupting and then thought to herself a moment before saying, "Well, as I said before, I'm sure my father has supplies that could aid you in your endeavors. First, let's get you out of those rags." Aroc gingerly grabbed the wrappings around his left arm and peeled them off slowly and carefully to not hurt him.

Sainte grimaced as the bandages pulled his skin slightly away, but nothing worse. The rest of the bandages were removed from his other arm and torso, much with the same results. He examined himself, surprised at the limited amount of scarring he received. It was there, of course, but not as bad as he expected. Most of his wounds were well on their way in the healing process. He would have to be careful with his movements to not reopen them again, but he was surprised with Aroc's healing abilities.

"So, do you have any clothes for me?" he asked as Aroc unwrapped the gauze. She nodded, turned around, and started rustling through a dresser. She faced him holding a leather jerkin and pants.

"This is all I have that might fit you. Try it on as fast as you dare. I think you still need rest, but I am relieved you want to leave. I don't like the idea of staying out in the forest in this dark for long, and Elion is not so far away. I have no weapons for you right now, but I'm sure my father has some spare ones." She waited patiently for Sainte to get dressed. "You ready? Everything fits?"

"Aye, let's go," he said. Aroc nodded and opened the door to the cabin, stepping out into the darkness beyond. Sainte followed her into the dark, fighting back pain with each step.

▼▲▼

Iris was by Miqel's side for three days. She brought him food and water, kept him up to date with everything the Council and Elders talked about, and, most importantly, kept him company. She replaced his bandages when they needed it and helped him go to the bathroom. He told Crane everything he knew, which was not much other than the general direction Sainte went. It had been three days of this, and Iris grew restless.

Iris returned to Miqel after a meeting with the Council and the Elders. She entered the one-roomed house and slammed the door behind her, waking Miqel. She stormed to his side, careless about waking him.

"They're stupid as ox shite!" she cursed.

"Wha? Who?" Miqel asked groggily.

"The Elders and the Council. All of them. They're not going to do anything. They're not going to look for Sainte or the Barrier. They're going to stay here and 'wait it out.' They've all got wool for brains."

"That's it? They're just stayin' 'ere?" he asked.

"Yes. They've set up shifts for Blades to watch the town's walls. Others have volunteered to build up the walls of Guardstin. The Elders selected a band to travel to other towns to find out whatever they can, whatever that means." She stopped to catch her breath.

"I'm sorry... wish I could do somethin'," Miqel said hopelessly. Iris did not reply. They did not talk for some time as they were both lost in their thoughts.

Iris slowly sat down at the edge of the bed, a thought coming to her mind. She closed her eyes and furrowed brow and, after a minute, slowly opened them.

"I'm going after Sainte," she said bluntly, emotionlessly, almost surprised at herself that she said it. Miqel looked at her open-mouthed. "I believe that you're strong enough to get better without needing me here. You have the whole town supporting you. Sainte has no one... He needs me; he needs us." She stopped as a teardrop rolled down her cheek. She did not want to look at Miqel but forced herself to. His face betrayed what he thought about her leaving.

"Goodbye, Miqel. Get better soon," she choked out. She looked away when she said that. She could feel the pain etched on his face without seeing it.

"Iris..." he managed to say, but he did not know what to follow it with.

She stood up and left the room in a hurry, afraid she would not leave if she lingered. She could feel his eyes on her as she left and closed the door behind her. Iris leaned against the closed door, letting tears flow freely down her face. Leaving Miqel again was more difficult than she imagined. She hated herself for going after saying that she would stay, but someone had to look for Sainte. If no one else would, it had to be her. She wanted to wait for Miqel to get well enough to go with her. However, she knew he would not be able to walk for some time.

Iris hoped that Miqel would have said he understood and not blamed her, but she knew that was too much to ask. She wiped the tears from her face and walked through Guardstin to gather her equipment from the Blades lodge. The rain died down to a mist which did nothing to lessen the forbidding night. Iris thought of stopping by her home and checking on her mother, but she quickly dismissed the notion. She gave her mother enough chances to leave with her. She was done trying.

She made her way through the gates into the Blades portion of town. Before she grabbed her gear, she figured she would stop by and let the Council know her plans out of courtesy. Iris walked into the Council's chamber to find all three members discussing something in hushed voices. They all stopped as they heard her enter and looked at her.

"Iris," Crane said, "what brings you here? Unannounced too."

Iris froze and looked at them all looking at her. She was suddenly struck by nerves and blurted out, "I'm sorry for interrupting, but I thought I'd tell you all that I'm going to leave to look for Sainte. I figured I'd let you know instead of just leaving. There's nothing you can say that will make me stay. Someone needs to look for Sainte, and it might as well be me. I can't just sit here and wait for change. I need to do something." When she finished, she realized she had said all that in one breath and took a sharp breath in. Crane's eyes sparkled in amusement, and a slight smile tugged at his mouth.

"This is something that we've already discussed, and we agree with you." Iris was taken aback, completely expecting to have to argue her case. "Someone should look for Sainte. We just weren't sure whom we should send. I'm glad you volunteered." He looked at the two other Council members, and they nodded in agreement. "When are you planning on leaving?"

"I was planning on going as soon as possible. In fact, I was planning on getting my gear and leaving as soon as I was done here."

"You don't mind leaving Miqel? I know you two are close," Crane said.

"I already told him of my plans. I don't really want to leave him, but I believe he's in good hands here. I can't do anything else for him, so I'm all right with leaving him," Iris explained as she tried to maintain her composure.

"Well then, I don't think we need anything else from you. You have our approval, not that it would have changed your mind if you didn't have it. Go, White Wyverns guide you," Crane finished.

"Thank you," Iris said and then briskly walked out. The Council resumed their discussion before the door closed behind her. She immediately made her way to the Blades of the Night's armory. After donning her armor and grabbing her bow, a quiver full of arrows, and her short sword, it was time for her to go. She left the lodge and stepped out into a drizzle.

Mustering her determination, she left the town without stopping to see anyone else. Iris had no desire to see her mother or father again, and she did not have any close friends other than Sainte and Miqel, and she already said goodbye to Miqel. As she walked through the familiar streets of Guardstin, she could not help but be troubled by the unfamiliar stillness that plagued them. Windows were shuttered and doors closed. The occasional flicker from a candle was the only sign of life from within any home. No one strolled along the streets, and Iris could hear no calls of vendors from the town square. She could only assume that it was empty too.

The town's gates slowly came into her view through the rain. They seemed ominous in the darkness but familiar at the same time. Two Blades stood post, barely visible with flickering torches behind them. Iris did not recognize them. She figured they were probably new trainees since they were given this post.

"Hail, what business do you have outside these walls?" one of them asked her as she walked closer.

"I'm Iris Lispin. I'm going to look for Sainte Nore," she told them. The Blades looked at each other, and then the same one spoke up again.

"Aye, we were just informed of your coming moments before you arrived. You're free to go," he told her, then looked at his partner. "Open the gates."

The other Blade nodded and set to unlocking the gates. A metal arm bar was used to keep the doors locked together. The Blade unlocked it and pushed the gate open.

"Good luck, Iris Lispin," he told her as she walked by. When she cleared the gate, it closed with a resounding thud behind her. The closing of Guardstin's gates seemed to open the gates of doubt inside her. She almost turned around and asked to be let in, but she forced herself to take a step forward. It was then she realized that she had been attacked by doubts almost her entire life. Why would she start letting them bother her now?

"Don't look back," she whispered with each step.

Iris trekked along the mud-soaked road for four hours, drenched to the bone, and stopped at the blackened, ruined House of the Barrier. The mountain loomed before her, fading away from her vision in the fog. Finding Sainte suddenly seemed like an impossible task. How could she possibly think to find Sainte from here? Miqel said he went to Whitweir Forest, but any tracks he may have left behind were surely all washed away by now. Once she reached the forest, there was no telling where he went or if he even made it to the forest. It all seemed so useless.

She stared at the remains of the tunnel and the house she and her friends once defended. Everything that was not burnt to a crisp was now waterlogged. Destroyed. The ground was a sea of mud, almost sinking to her knees. The weight of all the recent events crashed down on her, and she could not stand it anymore.

She sat down in the mud and sobbed. How could she have hoped to find Sainte? How could she have left Miqel after what she promised him before?

Stop it.

That thought came into her mind from nowhere.

That's enough crying.

Iris wiped the tears from her face for the second time that day and took a few deep breaths. She looked at the wreckage that surrounded her. Sainte was gone. He left. Miqel said that Sainte talked to him but did not offer any help. She could not blame Sainte for leaving Miqel by himself. She was sure that Sainte thought he was doing what was right. However, what troubled Iris was that she was not sure what she was doing was right.

Iris decided that she would go back to Guardstin. She would help where she was needed and ensure that Miqel healed properly. Then together, they would leave and search for Sainte. She would not leave him, not again. Her legs shook as she pushed herself up and out of the mud. She took one last look at the tunnel and shuddered at the memories it provoked, then turned around and trudged back to Guardstin.

It took her another four hours to get back to town, but it seemed to go by fast because it felt right. She knew that this was the right choice. Explaining herself to the Council would be a little awkward, but surely they would not blame her. She could not wait to see the look on Miqel's face once he saw her again. Faintly, the outline of Guardstin's walls came into her view, and she quickened her step. The rain seemed to urge her onward, and the mud that gripped her feet did not seem so strong.

As she made out more details of the walls and the gate, she slowed her pace until she completely stopped. The large wooden gates were torn to shreds, and shards of wood littered the ground. The walls were battered and portions of them were entirely torn down. She walked closer to the gates with faltering steps. There were the bodies of the two Blades that saw her out, shredded to ribbons. It was then that she smelled the smoke that had been hidden behind the curtain of rain. When she finally looked past the dead Blades, she realized the source of the smoke. Her breath was gone. Was she capable of nothing except witnessing the aftermath of the destruction of things she loved?

What remained of the buildings were embers glowing in the rain. Smoke trails led up into the darkened cloud-covered sky. The streets were littered with bodies. Her vision blurred as she fought against the tears. She stumbled throughout her ruined town, searching for any signs of life. She should never have left Miqel. She should have fought beside him, for him, died by his side. Now she was the only one who did not fight and the only one alive. The limbs of the people she lived for, fought for, seemed to reach out, asking her to join them. Some bodies had bites ripped out of their flesh, and others were torn apart.

Slowly, Iris fought back her tears and calmed her racing mind. She could still feel her heart trying to break its way out of her chest, but at least she was thinking coherently. Observing her surroundings more closely, she realized some things did not add up.

It had been raining for at least two days. How could anything catch fire? The only explanation she could think of was that the fires were started from within the buildings. Who started the fires? The Malignin would not start fires. They hated it. It was the Malignin who attacked, though, she could see all the telltale signs; the wounds on the dead were from Malignin. Even though it was raining, Iris could still make out Malignin's tracks. There was no lightning, so a lightning strike started no fires. Someone started the fires, but who?

Those had to be questions for another time. Iris found that she wandered close to her parent's home and decided to see what she could find there. She did not have high hopes for her parents, but she knew that not knowing what happened to them would eat at her for the rest of her life. Whether her father lived or died did not matter to her, she found herself hoping that he was dead, but she wanted to know what happened to her mother. She made her way through the decimated town toward her home. She arrived at the remains of it and stared with mixed feelings. The roof had collapsed, and the ashes mixed with mud. No one inside would have survived the fire, much less the collapse.

Her eyes strayed to the bodies around the street in front of the house. With grim determination, Iris began examining each one. After checking three bodies, she came across a woman face down. Her stomach dropped to her toes, and she realized she was shaking, but it was not because it was cold. Iris turned the body over, revealing the wide glass-eyed gaze of her mother. A chunk of flesh was missing from her throat. Iris shut her mother's eyelids respectfully and laid her back down emotionlessly. There was nothing more to be done for her.

With a keen numbness taking over, Iris made her way to the house that Miqel was kept in. She no longer looked at the bodies to see if they were anyone she knew. Her priority right now was to find out what happened to Miqel. She arrived at the house and found it oddly intact. A body was draped to the left of the entrance. Head bowed down. Iris paid it no heed until she saw them take a breath.

"By the Wyverns," she said, not knowing what to do. The person's head lifted slightly and Iris recognized the pale face wrought with fresh wounds. "Clarenda," she whispered, kneeling in front of the woman.

"Yes, girl, it's me," the old woman managed to croak after she cracked her eyes open.

"I'm so sorry," Iris began, a fresh waterfall of tears falling down her cheeks, mixed with rain.

"No need to be sorry," Clarenda said, attempting to pat Iris' cheek comfortingly but too weak to lift her arm. "This is what was meant to be." She paused, choking on breaths that rattled her lungs. "Fret not. None can change what has come to pass."

Iris wept, hugging Clarenda's frail frame.

"There, there, you are alive, child. You still have time..." and those were her last words. Iris could not tell that the old woman she held in her arms passed until she released her hug, and the lifeless body slumped over. Gently, Iris laid her back against the wall; she looked like she died in peace regardless of the ghastly wounds she so obviously suffered.

Iris stood up, pushing Clarenda's last words to the back of her mind. It was time to find out what happened to her friend. She walked unhesitatingly into the house, left hand never straying far from her bow, her right never far from her quiver. Water dripped through the roof and mixed with blood on the floor. Miqel's bed was empty. There were three men dead, Blades of the Night, lying sprawled out on the floor with a dead Malignin nearby, but upon quick inspection Iris found that none were Miqel. She quickly threw the bed sheets to the floor in case he hid in them. She checked every corner of the small room, finally coming to the closet.

"Miqel?" she called softly. There was no answer except for the constant drizzle of rain. She put an unsteady hand on the closet door handle, then threw it open.

Empty.

There was nothing in it. Iris knew that Miqel's armor and weapon should be there, but it was all missing. She let out a sigh. He must have escaped.

Or at least, that is what she told herself. Who else would take his gear? The armor was fitted to him, and the axe was balanced perfectly to his strength. It would be nearly impossible for anyone to match his exact body and strength for the armor or axe to be of much use to them.

Miqel had to have escaped then. There was no other option. Somehow, some way, he summoned the strength to fend off the Malignin long enough to get out of there alive.

There was always the possibility that he was eaten or his body was out in the streets with everyone else. His armor and weapon may have been strewn about in a fury by the Malignin. Anything was possible.

Iris nudged those thoughts from her mind; they would not help her now. She walked to the foot of his bed and sat down, head in her hands. What was she to do now? Clarenda's last words echoed through her mind.

'*You still have time...*'

She was alive, and now more than ever, she had to do something about it. It was clear to her that her priority was to find out what happened to Miqel and where he went. After that, she would decide when the time came. Iris thought about everything she knew, all the facts. She was thinking clearer now but still had to sort through all her thoughts. Too many were flying around at once.

Sainte was missing, possibly dead. Miqel was missing, possibly dead. Ellie was missing, possibly dead. Out of those three people, two of them would have known what to do. She was sure of it. She was probably the only one left out of them all and probably the one who was least capable of dealing with her situation.

Iris could not help but think that none of this would have happened if she did not run away that fateful night. If she stayed with Miqel, they might have been able to fight their way to help Sainte. Maybe they could have turned the tide if she remained with Miqel just a few hours ago. She would never know now.

As she stared at the floor, lost in her mind, she noticed a discoloration of mangled footprints. As she studied them, she realized they started bloody, coming from the bed, but got less so the further they went. They were of large feet, clearly not a woman's, but that did not necessarily mean they were Miqel's.

Iris followed the footprints leading to the closet, then out the door. They were accompanied by a smaller pair of muddy footprints, possibly a woman's or a child's. Whose could they be? She did not think Miqel knew any children. Maybe they were from a healer? Iris concluded that the heavy prints had to have come from Miqel. He had to have been able to get up and escape, somehow bandaging himself good enough to walk.

Miqel was alive. The footprints all but proved it. Hope sparked in her chest like a small fire, and each footprint she followed fanned the flame. She followed Miqel's trail, or what she hoped was it, out of the house and through the smoldering town. The trail was hard to follow as the chaos in Guardstin was mixed in the mud with everyone else's footprints, but Iris was sure she never strayed to the wrong trail.

She followed it to the west entrance of Guardstin, headed towards the Barrier's Mountain, where she just came from. This was the same road she had returned to town on. How had she missed him? The rain could have hidden him from view and muffled any sounds he made. She brushed her soaked hair out of her eyes and gazed into the gray darkness. She searched for any bodies outside of the walls of Guardstin but thankfully did not find any.

Iris stood at the foot of the road that led to the Barrier's house, now destroyed. The only option before her was to follow the trail as far as she could, possibly going further than ever. She would follow Miqel wherever he went. He could not have gotten far in the condition he was in.

With a determined breath, Iris set off, bow held grimly in her hand. Whatever she would come across, she would be ready. She would find her friends. Two questions bothered her, though, as she continued down the well-known path.

Where was Miqel going? And why?

SIX
-PERSEVERANCE-

Sainte's legs were sore from resting for three days, but it felt good to stretch them out. Aroc kept her pace slow for Sainte, knowing that he did not yet have his full strength back, and he was grateful for it. The rain stopped and was replaced by a misty fog that slowly rolled into the forest, making everything look blurry.

After almost running into trees several times, Sainte finally lit a torch to fend off the fog as much as possible. Firelight reflected from the pale white trees and plants, making the darkened environment seem even more surreal than it already was. Leaves rustled as the wind blew at the tree tops, but no air stirred under the canopy. Sainte felt like he and Aroc were the only living things for miles.

For all he knew, they could be.

"Do you have any guesses on why the sun hasn't been out ever since the Malignin got the Barrier?" Aroc asked Sainte.

He grunted in response, more than tired of listening to her talk. She spoke almost nonstop ever since they began their journey together.

"I think the sun actually is out. I think it's been moving across the sky like normal. Even though the Malignin are strong, I doubt they could halt the sun's movement. Instead, I believe they somehow called these thick clouds to roll in and block out the sun." She paused as she thought about her theory. "I'm willing to wager that controlling clouds is easier than the sun, no matter how many clouds it would take to block the sun this effectively. What do you think?"

"I don't know, probably." Was all he said. He was more interested in watching his feet to make sure no roots jumped out and surprised him than partaking in a guessing game.

"I wonder where the Malignin got the power to do this from... The Barrier probably did more to hinder the Malignin than we ever knew. Maybe she not only held their attention every night, but somehow her existence held their powers in check as well." This newest conclusion she came to prompted another few moments of silence as she mulled it over. Aroc glanced at Sainte and saw he was not paying attention so she figured it was time for a new topic.

"Do you know what that plant is used for?" She pointed to a plant that grew straight up from the ground. All it had were five round leaves on the stalk. Sainte groaned inwardly as she told him what it was used for without waiting for a reply. After being satisfied that she explained it correctly, she moved on to herbal remedies.

Sainte listened at first, as it could be helpful to know, but after Aroc talked about Drysdain and all the different ways it bestowed wakefulness for at least three miles, he could not take it anymore. The fog was not helping him either; it seemed to be pressing on his head from every direction. A relentless squeeze.

"Please, Aroc, stop," he said suddenly, holding a hand up just before she began talking about all the different types of mushrooms. "Thank you for trying to make time go by, but can we stop talking for a while? I just want some peace and quiet."

Aroc stopped walking and looked down. "Peace and quiet," she muttered, a twinge of hurt in her expression.

Sainte sighed quietly. "I'm sorry, Aroc, these past few days have been hard. I just, I don't know, would like some silence, you know, to sort out my thoughts." She did not immediately reply. Instead, they walked on for a few seconds before she broke the quiet between them.

"It's okay, Sainte, but what I'm telling you is useful. You could have used it to save yourself instead of me having to save you. It's good to know these things. You never know when you'll need it. But I can't make you listen or remember. That's up to you."

Sainte was not in the mood to be talked to like a child, so what she said changed his attitude from apologetic to the offensive as fast as he could snap his fingers. "Of course, it's up to me. Everything I do is up to me. You're telling me things I could figure out on my own or have no reason to know in the first place," he replied, exasperated. "I listened to you, and now all I want is silence. Then you go on acting as if you're better than me, trying to teach me a lesson, spitting shite wisdom at me after I already said sorry. I don't care about anything you have to say. None of it changes anything. All I care about is finding and saving Ellie. Everything else is a distraction." At this point, the two came to a halt.

Aroc stood still and calmly listened to Sainte's rant as he paced back and forth. "Are you finished?" she asked as he stopped talking, taking a few deep breaths.

"No, I'm not. You don't get it," he said.

"I do, Sainte, I do."

"No, you don't!" he snapped suddenly. "You weren't there. I was, I saw it all, and I couldn't do anything. I was right there, right there! So close I could almost smell her, but I lost her. They took her away from me, they could have killed me, but I was left to burn. That's how little I mattered to them. Didn't even bother to finish me off. I shouldn't have even been a part of the Blades of the Night. I shouldn't have been the Shield. It should've been someone else, anyone else. And now, just to add insult to injury, it is so damn foggy I can't see my hand in front of my face," Sainte exclaimed, throwing his hand in front of his face for effect. He brought it back down and stopped pacing.

Aroc stood patiently the entire time he ranted. "I think we should rest for a minute. We've been walking for a few hours now," she stated simply.

Sainte grudgingly followed her as she looked for an ideal tree they could both lean against and rest on. Eventually, a large oak tree revealed itself through the fog. Gnarled roots jutted out of the ground, providing decent comfort for them, so long as they found a flat spot to sit on.

They both got comfortable when Aroc said, "It wasn't your fault. You have to realize that."

Sainte just released a weary sigh in response and slid down his root a bit, tired of talking about it. He gazed up towards the sky but instead got a sight full of fog. Aroc looked over at him.

"Did you hear me?" she said lightly. Sainte thought he could hear genuine concern in her voice. "It's not your fault. It's not anyone's fault. You must stop blaming yourself. If you weren't there, it would have been some other person in your place. From how you explained it, there was nothing anyone could do. You must dig yourself out of the self-pity you've buried yourself in and focus on what must be done. You can do nothing about the past, but you can influence the future. If you want to save Ellie, you must not be so hard on yourself. Forgive yourself and move on. Your attention must be solely focused on your main task. You must not be distracted. Do you understand?" she asked.

He pondered what she said briefly before replying, "I know I can't change the past. I know there's nothing I can do about it… it's just so hard for me to accept it for what it is. If what happened isn't my fault, then whose fault is it? It's not my friends' fault, Iris and Miqel, nor is it any of the other Blades. It's just easier if I take on that burden myself. I keep going through what happened that night and think about what else I could have done to make it turn out differently," he explained somberly. "I don't know anymore. I just don't know. So much has happened, and

I've no idea what to do." He also had no idea why he was opening himself up to this woman he had only just met.

"I know what you're going through, Sainte, to an extent. I'm not sure what the future has in store for us, and I don't know what choices may come our way, but I do know that if you do not accept the past, then you have to at least forget about it for a while," Aroc said exasperated. "People need you. Ellie needs you. Your friends, Iris and Miqel, need you. You cannot be so hard on yourself." She shook her head. "What good is that to anyone?"

Sainte stared and blinked slowly, processing her words. She could tell he found the truth in what she said. He looked down finally, words echoing through his head.

Without warning, he stood up, startling Aroc slightly. He did not know what to feel, but maybe that was okay. "Well, come on. You're right; I'm worthless in this sorry state. What happened may or may not have been my fault, but I know that if I fail Ellie and can't save her, that will be my fault. I won't let her down. We've rested long enough." He reached a hand down to help Aroc to her feet. "We should keep going."

Aroc accepted his help and said, "Elion should not be much farther through the woods, though I can't say for sure because of this thick fog. It's hard to tell exactly where we're at."

Sainte did not say anything but nodded his head. In unease, he fingered the hilt of his dagger, his only weapon. Although he was resolute in leaving the past behind him, his future unsettled him. He shook himself out of these thoughts quickly, however. "What is it?" he asked when he noticed Aroc looking at him amused.

"I don't think that," she said, pointing to his dagger, "will be able to last for very long for what you have planned." A very slight smile touched her eyes.

"Mmhmm," was all she got in reply.

Aroc and Sainte continued their journey at a brisker pace than when they first started; both the rest and the talk helped their spirits.

▼▲▼

Iris stood in front of the Barrier's ruined mountain yet again. Miqel's tracks led straight to the house and continued past it into the mountains instead of going to Whitweir Forest. She never ventured into the mountains and hesitated a moment before stepping forward.

Why would he venture to the mountains alone if Sainte went to Whitweir Forest? Why would he not follow in Sainte's footsteps? Regardless of those questions, she stuck with her current plan. With a breath, Iris followed Miqel's footsteps into the mountains. Into the Broken Crags.

An hour passed as Iris sloshed through the pine forest at the foot of the mountains, feeling surprisingly better than she thought she would. Miqel's tracks were reasonably easy to follow, but the going was slow. She found it strange that his tracks were so noticeable, though. Iris was sure there would be signs of his wounds, but there was nothing. It was as if he had no wounds at all.

There were no signs of him tripping or staggering, no blood spatters. The last time she saw him he could not even sit upright without help, much less wander this far through these mountainous woods. His footprints were solid and steady as if he knew exactly where he was going, and he walked with a purpose.

It did not matter now; she would find answers as soon as she found Miqel. He needed her, and she would not let him down again, as she had so many times before. Iris did wish that someone was there to talk to, at least. She wanted to speak, to get her doubts out in the open and have her doubts proven to be naught, but no one was around. She was alone. Perhaps she needed him more than he needed her.

That thought scared her more than she cared to admit. There was not a moment in the past few years where Iris could not recall Sainte or Miqel not being there for her. No matter how often she felt alone before, she knew she always had at least one of them to talk to. Now neither of them were there for her, and the emptiness she felt was striking. Nobody was there for her now, and the fog only compounded her loneliness.

All was quiet. No wind, no birds chirping, no squirrels rustling through trees. The muddy ground had a carpet of pine needles covering it, and every step Iris took was followed by a crunch of the pine needles and a squish as her foot sank into the water-sodden ground beneath. The dense fog muffled her steps to the point where she could almost not hear them. Suddenly, a crack of a twig in the distance sliced through the mist and struck her ears. She flinched at the intrusive noise and then froze.

Her eyes strained to see through the dense fog. Her ears listened for any more signs of movement. She looked back and forth, searching for any signs of what was out there, when her gaze fell on a silhouette through the mist. Iris could not tell who or what it was, but she knew she was no longer alone. The figure did not move as if trying to hide in the concealing fog again. It was just far enough away to have its features hidden. It looked nothing more than a shadow.

Iris was not going to let it out of her sight, knowing that if she did, it would be lost, and the next time she saw it, it may be too late. She started slowly reaching for her bow, afraid her movements might startle the figure, but it remained still. She nocked an arrow with the bow still facing the ground and then ever so slowly brought it up.

As she raised the bow, she gauged the distance between her and the figure. Guessing the distance between the trees and the edge of the fog, she put the figure between fifteen to twenty yards away, an easy shot. She pulled the string back to her cheek, then released it. The arrow sped forward, unhampered by the thick fog, and struck the figure. She heard a satisfying thud as the arrow's metal tip sank into something hard. The figure did not move. Confused, Iris decided to get a closer look.

She stalked forward, and as she neared the figure, it revealed itself to be a pine tree. She found her arrow buried halfway into the trunk. At least she did not miss what she aimed at. Iris could not help but feel relieved, almost amused, that the ominous figure she thought she saw was merely a tree. The fog was no doubt causing her eyes to play tricks on her.

Just as she started to put her bow over her shoulder, something slammed into her side, sending her sprawling into the mud. Iris clenched the bow on reflex, managing to keep hold of it, but fell on it in the fall. Iris felt and heard the bow snap, her favorite weapon now rendered useless. She immediately left her bow in the mud without bothering to check it for damage. It would not serve her any purpose now.

She scrambled to her feet, drawing her sword as fast as her breathless body would allow, but the Malignin were already upon her. There were two of them that she could see, but only one attacked her. It held its mouth agape, tongue lolling between the sharp teeth. The long claws on each finger whistled through the air with the promise of death on each tip.

Iris flung herself backward, managing to escape the first onslaught of strikes. She panicked now; she knew she had no time to form an escape, much less an attack, and there was no good footing in the pine needles and slick muck.

All Iris could do was retreat, haphazardly blocking blow after blow, energy drained with each jarring hit. She could barely hold her sword anymore. Her hands cramped because of how hard she grasped the hilt. It happened then, just as she knew she could no longer keep her sword in her hand, the Malignin swatted it away. The next strike pummeled her to the ground on her back.

The Malignin wasted no time pouncing on her, crushing her beneath its weight. It started raking at her, claws squealing against her armor, denting it, slowly tearing it apart. She saw her armor weaken against the onslaught. Her skin tingled in uneasy anticipation where the Malignin's claws would meet her skin. It would not be long before her armor would give in, and the Malignin would wrench away her very life.

Iris closed her eyes, upset that she was not going to live long enough to be reunited with her friends, but there was nothing else she could do. Her arms were too weak to lift; even if she could, they would be useless against the monster atop her. She did not want to die, but everyone had to eventually.

Her helmet became dented sometime in the attack. She felt it crush against her battered face, bruising it, squeezing it painfully. It was close. She could feel it, her ears rang and through her eyelids, she saw flashes of light. She could not feel her body anymore; it was as if the Malignin was not even on her. Then she heard a voice, surely some god from the afterlife calling to her, shaking her. It felt real.

She opened her eyes and staring down at her was Miqel.

"Ah, it's you..." was all she could say before the world turned black.

Iris opened her eyes and sat up slowly, holding herself up with shaking arms. She looked around and saw that she was in a camp of sorts. A fire was started, and someone poked at it with their back to Iris. To her left was a lean-to with her sword under it and a pack that was not hers. Pine trees still surrounded them, so Iris doubted she had been taken far. Fog still clung to the ground, refusing to let go of its grasp.

The person by the fire glanced behind them and saw her moving. Almost immediately, they were by her side. When they got close Iris saw that it was Miqel, then she remembered seeing him before losing consciousness. Without a word, they moved toward the fire, towards the embrace of its heat. Miqel helped Iris get settled comfortably and then sat down next to her.

"How're ye feeling?" he finally asked.

"It feels like I shouldn't be alive," she replied, her voice cracked with pain. Almost as an afterthought, she said, "What about you? Last time I saw you, you could barely move. What happened? I went back to Guardstin and it..." She trailed off, unable to complete the sentence.

He patted her back reassuringly. "I've a lot ta explain, Iris. I've to ask ya, though, ta listen ta me with'n open mind. When I first heard this, I didn't believe it. 'Ventually I came to see that it was true. Malignin ain't evil. They're not out ta kill us. They're out ta defend 'emselves."

Iris looked at him as if he was stupid. Of all the first things to say after being reunited, he chose this. "What do you mean? They just tried to kill me," Iris said incredulously. "Or do you think they were just trying to give me directions out of the mountains?"

"Please, Iris, just listen fer now, don't ask any questions 'til I'm done. It'll just be easier that way." He looked at her disgruntled face pleadingly and took her silence as consent. "As I said before, they don't wanta hurt anyone. It's true they did wanta get ta the Barrier, but not fer any 'o the reasons we 'spected. She's th'only one who can communicate with 'em cuz she's got no pre-determined notion 'bout 'em. Ta Ellie, there's no evil. She sees everyone as good 'cause she don't know any better. This is exactly what the Malignin wanted. They needed an interpreter so they can say what they act'chly want, and what they want is fer us ta all work together in unity.

"They've so much ta bring ta the table. They can help our cities grow and prosper more'n we've ever imagined. Ellie told me what they want ta do, and it's incredible. They fixed me, Iris, which is why I can walk. I'm healed. Their powers can be used fer good. They ev'n gave me some 'o their power. It ain't much, but it'll grow stronger in time." His face lit up with hope as he told Iris this. She had never seen him so excited about something, but it unsettled her.

"Think 'bout it, Iris," he continued, "there'll be no more sickness; people'll be stronger, live longer. We won't have ta fight ta survive anymore. The Malignin'll provide fer us and us them. Ellie's convinced me. My eyes're open now. Are yers?"

Iris did not say anything for a long time, both saddened and now afraid of her friend, but she tried not to show it. "Miqel, that's crazy... Tell me you don't really believe that. If they're so friendly and all they want is to work together, then why'd they attack me? Why'd they slaughter almost all of the Blades every night? Did you not see all the death and destruction in Guardstin? They killed everyone." Iris paused then, completely at a loss for words. "They killed my mother."

Miqel looked at Iris, confused, as if he could not believe she wasn't backing him up. "I'm sorry about yer mother, Iris, I truly am, but they didn't kill everyone. The people the Malignin killed made their choice. Everyone in Guardstin was given a choice ta join us. The Malignin had ta kill anyone who wouldn't comply with their desires. It's th'only way fer true peace; everyone must want the same thing. Ellie and I explained ta the entire town what I've told ya, and the people who would not join us had ta die." He saw how she looked at him, and it made him nervous. He did not want to scare her away.

"I asked 'em ta help look fer ya, Iris," he told her as if it would make everything better. "They prob'ly attacked ya because they saw ya as a threat. They attacked the Blades ev'ry night because that's th'only way they knew how ta get ta Ellie," Miqel explained as if that was common knowledge. "Look, Iris, just come with me, and I'll show ya what kind 'o powers they gave me." But Iris cut him off before he could say anymore.

"What happened to you? You're insane," Iris told him, disgusted. She would have left if her body was physically capable of carrying her weight.

He took a few deep breaths and thought about what to say. "Ellie came ta me, Iris, in person. I could see in her eyes that what she told me was the truth. I want ya ta trust me. Believe me; I thought it was crazy at first, too, but... It's just... It ain't." Miqel was getting aggravated now with Iris. "I'll prove that they'll keep their word."

Miqel sat up straight, and Iris could see the concentration in his eyes. She felt a slight unease. Then her eyes played a trick on her; the shadows that danced around just out of reach of the flames stopped moving. Only it was not a trick. Iris realized that Miqel was forcing the shadows to do what he willed. It required great concentration on his part, however.

Miqel let out an exhalation of all his breath, and the shadows regained their movements. He looked at Iris excitedly.

"See, see what I can do now? It's only basic, but the more I practice th'easier it becomes. 'Ventually I'll be able ta move the shadows, use 'em as a tool ta do what I want. They taught me how ta do this. This is what the future holds fer us, Iris." He looked at her expectantly. "Ya could do it too."

Iris was terrified of her friend. She was afraid at how quickly he changed in only a day. "This is wrong, Miqel. This is against everything we ever fought for. This is what we were supposed to prevent." She could not say anything else; she was at a complete loss for words.

"Iris, just stay with me, understand-"

"I will not!" she exclaimed.

"All I want is fer us ta be together. Ye, Sainte, me. It'll be easier if ya just come with me now," he pleaded.

"No... Just leave me alone," was all she said.

"Fine," Miqel said as he stood up. "Since we're friends, and I love ya, then I'll leave ya fer now... I didn't want this, Iris... I can't promise I'll be as polite the next time we meet." Miqel left Iris, not bothering to grab any of his belongings.

She listened to him stomp away until she could no longer hear him. Iris sat alone, more scared than when she found her decimated town. Now she had less than what she started with; now she had no friends and no hope.

She stood up shakily and made her way to the pack that was left. Inside was a few days' worth of bread and dry, salted meats. It was not exactly packed with delicacies, but she was glad that Miqel did not think to bring it with him. She did not realize how hungry she was until she saw the food. Breaking off some bread, Iris sat under the lean-to and ate. She ensured she was close enough to her sword if anything came to investigate the fire, but otherwise, she relaxed.

She noticed that her armor was laid out nearby as well. Her chest piece and helmet were destroyed beyond any use, but her gauntlets and leg armor were still in decent shape. She mentally thanked Miqel for keeping her armor there. Her broken bow, notably not at the camp, would be a sore loss. Also missing were arrows, probably dumped on the ground when the Malignin attacked her.

She heard something through the pines, a steady sound that grew louder. The drumming of rain. Iris listened to it, finding peace in the noise as it got closer. Soon the rain fell into her camp. It was not heavy enough to douse the fire, which she was thankful for, but she did not leave the cover of the lean-to. She finished eating her bread and laid down, trying to stay dry. Exhaustion quickly overtook her body, and she fell asleep to the peaceful sound of rain.

But Iris was not as alone as she thought she was.

SEVEN
-ALLIES-

"We're further from Elion than I had figured," Aroc said while they rested for their fourth time after leaving her hut, both having completely lost track of time. Aroc did not need the rest, but she knew that Sainte did. Whenever she noticed him struggling to keep up with her, she would suggest taking a break.

"It's this damned fog clouding the senses. I'm just happy we haven't run into anything more sinister than pointless chatter," he replied as he stood up, wiping dirt off his trousers but not accomplishing much. "You about ready to head out again?" Sainte knew that Aroc was stopping for him. There was no point in bringing that up, though.

"Yeah, let's go." Aroc could not help but notice that something seemed to cloud Sainte's mood. He looked at her differently for the last few hours. "Sainte, what's the matter?" she asked as they were again on the move.

"A lot's bothering me... could you be more precise?"

"Well, about me? Is something bothering you about me?"

He did not say anything for a few steps as he thought about her words. "You aren't like me. You aren't normal," he stated. It was not a question but a fact. "I'm not an idiot, Aroc. You've been acting as if you're normal, but you're not. I don't know why I think this, but I do. I have a feeling. I've been thinking about things, and you seem to know things you shouldn't." It was Aroc's turn to be quiet and think about what he said.

"You aren't wrong," was all he got, however.

"Care to elaborate?"

"No."

"I'm not going to let this go."

"I'm not asking you to. Just leave it be for right now. There's a time and place for certain things, and right now is neither." After that exchange of words, they carried on in uncomfortable silence. The pale trees seemed to leer at the two as they stepped carefully around the uneven ground. A light, persistent rain soaked their clothes, and their skin absorbed it like a sponge. Sainte's fingertips were so water-logged they pruned.

An hour passed before Aroc started talking. "Just so you're aware, my father is a member of the Council in Elion."

"All right, am I supposed to be impressed?"

"It was just something I figured you might've liked to know before meeting him."

"Am I supposed to treat him differently? Call him your Highness or such?" Sainte asked.

"No. And his name is Isaac, so Isaac should suffice," Aroc replied as if she did not notice his sarcasm. Soon after, the trees and brush started to grow sparse.

"I think we're getting near. If I'm right, the clearing should be just past these last few trees," Aroc called back to Sainte. He could tell she was relieved to finally be close to home.

Sainte watched as Aroc broke free of the woods and stood just on the clearing that skirted the tree line. She gazed out toward the middle of the clearing, but Elion was hidden behind the fog. Sainte walked beside her.

"Come on, let's keep going," he said.

"Right, of course," she said almost absentmindedly.

"What is it?" he asked, noting her sudden change of attitude.

"Something just doesn't feel right. No matter." She shook off the feeling and headed in the direction of Elion.

As they progressed, wooden stakes and spears jutted from the ground. Archer towers soon loomed over them, and eventually, the town was revealed to them. To call it a town was an understatement.

This 'town' was powerfully built indeed. Elion was on the banks of a lake; half the town was surrounded by a menacing twenty-foot-tall wooden wall reinforced by brick at the foot of it. The lake itself guarded the back half. The top of the wall had three very long spikes jutting outward at intervals large enough for a person to fire arrows between. The bottom spike pointed down at a slight angle, the middle straight out, and the top at a slight upward angle, a solid defense against any who would try to scale the walls.

There was only one entrance to the town, and it was only large enough to let a horse and buggy in. Anything bigger would have to wait outside or come in through the lake. Once again, Sainte noted, an exceptional defensive measure, if not a little annoying for town regulars.

As Sainte was too busy admiring the town's defenses, he tripped over a matted lump. He looked down as he caught himself and saw the ground was all churned up. The air was thick with unease. A familiar metallic smell wafted through the plain. As he looked closer, he realized that the ground was littered with the bodies of Malignin. He saw a few human bodies amongst the dead, but the Malignin far outnumbered them. Where there was not a dead body, there were pools of blood. It seemed the ground was more saturated with blood than rain.

"Aroc..."

"I see," she replied grimly. "Quickly now, let us not linger out here longer than necessary." Their pace hastened and their strides lengthened until they were at the entrance. Aroc knocked three times on the door and the echoes boomed around them. They waited as patiently as they could, but no one replied.

"You think anyone stayed here after the battle?" Sainte asked her, but she only glanced at him with resoluteness set on her face.

A few more moments passed before they heard a voice call from over the wall.

"Who is it? What do you need?" The man who answered sounded exhausted.

"It is I, Aroc, daughter of Isaac. I'm returning home with a visitor in tow. Is this how Elion treats its residents and guests now?" she said impatiently, but her words were laced with apprehension. "I can't have been gone more than ten days."

"Aye, it is how we do it now, Aroc. Times change fast, so we must change faster." It sounded as if the speaker was going to say more, but there was a muffled thud and curses as if someone stubbed their toe on the corner of a wall.

The door swung open and in the way stood a barrel of a man. He was a full foot shorter than Sainte, and one could tell that he did not miss many meals. He had a tremendous round stomach as if he had drunk a few too many brews in his lifetime. However, despite all apparent appearances, Sainte was willing to bet that this man had more muscle on him than fat.

The man threw his arms out wide and bellowed out, "Aroc! I was beginning to think you'd run away and weren't ever coming back. C'mere, give your old man a hug!"

Without hesitation, Aroc embraced the man while Sainte stood to the side and looked out into the fog from where they had just come. His gaze lingered over all the dead bodies, and he shuddered at how many Malignin there were. If there were this many dead, Elion must have been attacked by a number rivaling what attacked the tunnel at night. Despite this town's notable defenses, Sainte wondered how it managed to withstand the Malignin. More troubling, though, was how much longer would it be able to withstand them?

▼▲▼

Iris woke up and stretched her weary bones. She had no idea how long she slept, nor did she suppose it mattered anymore. She stood up and her body creaked with the movement. She rolled her neck around and stretched her arms before walking over to what little armor of hers remained. She put on her gauntlets and leg armor, then strapped her sword to her waist. Finally shouldering the pack that Miqel left behind, she set off to... to nowhere. She did not know where she was going to go.

Miqel found her and made it clear what he was doing. She had no desire to continue looking for him, afraid of what she might find. Sainte could need help, but even if she wanted to find him, she doubted she could because she was lost herself. Finally, she decided to try to make it to Munich, a town beyond the mountains. The only problem was that she still needed to figure out which direction to go. There were no real roads through the mountains as the going was slow, and walking around the mountains was just as fast as going through, not to mention a lot safer. Iris closed her eyes and pictured maps she had seen of Crearia. She followed her trail as best she could until she met Miqel. She had no idea where he took her.

Clearly, she was still in the pine forest within the mountains. The ground was a little rockier, nutritious soil was sparse, and the pine trees were smaller. All signs indicated that she was deeper in the mountains than before. A flicker of light caught her eyes. It was the fire Miqel made, nothing more than a pitiful flame at this point. Something told her to pay attention to it, but she did not know why. Iris approached it, watching it spark away from her, pushed by the wind.

Wind. That was it.

Iris remembered something that was taught to her about how mountains can affect the wind. Wind flowed down mountainsides because of temperature or something. She did not memorize the specifics; she just knew that it did. All she had to do was travel into the wind.

She straightened up and set her jaw, then stepped in what she hoped was the right way. The ground was rocky and slick because of all the rain and fog. She may have been at the foot of the mountains but rocks jutting out of the ground and sheer cliffs were obstacles she had to find her way around. More often than not, she circled around these, wanting to avoid climbing and possibly falling from them. Each time she had to circumnavigate anything that increased her chances of getting thrown in the wrong direction, but that was a risk she was willing to take.

Meeting with Miqel quelled one of her fears, at least. She was no longer afraid of running into any Malignin. He also made her realize there was something much more sinister. She feared Miqel. There were so many unanswered questions she had. They all floated around in her head like gnats on a carcass. Persistent, annoying, no matter what, she could not seem to slap them away.

Of all the questions, what if what Miqel said was true? That would mean everything Iris knew about Malignin was a lie. She shook her head as she thought about that. There could be no way that was true, even if she based the answer on nothing other than how the Malignin looked. Good things did not look like the Malignin. Coming to that conclusion only brought up another question.

What did they really want? What was their end goal?

With no way to find the answer to those troubling questions, Iris aimlessly made her way through the fog, which was still as thick as ever. She knew she was deep in the mountains and still had a long way to go before being free of them. She cursed the fog. Without it, she was sure that she would be able to see the snowy peaks of the tallest mountains. If those were visible, then the sky would be, and she could use the sun or the stars to orient herself. The only way the fog would lift was if rain took its place, and that helped her as much as fog.

Iris drudged forward blindly through the forest with those disquieting thoughts. She felt lost. She doubted she'd feel different even if she could see the sky. Without any light she would not be able to make it. She kept moving, not wanting to die alone and afraid, hoping that the wind would lead her correctly.

"You're not lost. You're going in the right direction," she whispered to herself. "I have to be." She had long ago lost track of time, not that it mattered. Nothing mattered, nothing except her moving legs.

"Shite," she cursed as her legs collapsed under her. Her knees scraped against the rocky ground. She tried to stand up, but her legs no longer supported her. After nursing her knees for a few moments and ensuring the scratches were not bad, she worked up the strength to stand up and look around.

The spot she had fallen was as good as any for a camp. She then gathered what little wood she could. Eventually, a decent pile of sticks and twigs began to grow. It would be enough to warm her for a little while, but it was not as much as she hoped to get.

It did not matter; all she cared about was getting rid of her chill. Iris piled some kindling together and started a fire, slowly building it to a satisfactory strength. Who or what saw the light no longer mattered. The heat that billowed from it was a blessing to her quivering limbs.

Her eyes stared into the fire, mind blank as if it was thanking her for taking a mental and physical break. Iris took a deep breath, held it, and let it out slowly while closing her eyes. When they were shut, she stiffly laid on her side and curled up facing the fire. Iris did not bother adding any more to the fire as weariness forced her to fall into a welcome yet troubled slumber.

She woke with a start, eyes flashed open and struggled to adjust to the darkness. Her fire was nothing but embers now. How long was she out? She sat up slowly, wondering what woke her, when something grabbed her hair and yanked, snapping her head painfully back.

Her eyes immediately watered in agony, and she let out a gasp mixed equally with surprise and hurt. A knife was set against her throat and a mouth was on her ear. The bristle of a man's facial hair scratched across her cheek.

"Who're ye?" a deep, hoarse voice growled into her ear. "Another spy, are ya? Ye shoulda seen what we done to the last spy. Cut his fingers off, we did. After those we moved to his toes, didn't wanta leave anythin' out. And then, just for the fun of it, we went right 'tween his legs. Course he had'a dick, but I think we can make do with'ot one."

"Tal," another voice called out, less harsh but more commanding than the man who held Iris. "Get off the woman. She's obviously no threat to you. If she were, you'd have been dead by now. You saw what the last guy did." Iris glanced around, trying to get some grasp of the situation. She saw the other man out of the corner of her eye, but she could make out no details.

"Curse that," spat her captor. "She could be a spy or worse. I should kill 'er and be done with it." Iris could not possibly figure out what this man meant by 'worse,' but right now, she had a bigger problem. Thankfully, it was solved almost immediately.

"You'll do no such thing, Shint, other than what I say. It was agreed, by your people and mine, that I would lead this expedition. Do not test me." Iris was surprised to hear the man call him a 'Shint.' It was a derogatory term for the Shinta, a barbaric people that lived far west of Guardstin, past the Broken Crags, a day's ride from Munich. She never met one in person, only heard about them in stories. The Shinta had no reason to travel far for anything, or so she heard. They grew and hunted everything they needed.

The man called Tal spat into the sorry excuse of a fire and watched it sizzle slowly to nothing before letting her go. She stood up with as much dignity as she had left, which was not much, and straightened out her dirty wrinkled clothes. She looked around and heard before she saw the Shinta walking through the woods.

"I apologize for the actions of my companion, m'lady. Did he hurt you?" the other man asked as he walked closer to Iris to see if she was okay. He was dressed in light armor, and if Iris did not know any better, she would say he looked like a noble.

She stepped away. "Stop, don't get any closer. I've been through worse. Who are you? Why are you out here?" she asked him without trying to hide her wariness.

He respected Iris' wish and did not step any closer. "My name's Ivan, and that lively fellow that just stalked away is Tal. It is not just him and I out here, thankfully. There are three more of us, five in total. Two Shintas and three Munes." He paused, then hesitatingly asked, "Have you heard of either Munich or Shintas?"

"Of course, I've heard of Munich and Shintas. I was born and raised in Mountsville before moving to Guardstin," she answered defensively.

"I meant nothing by it. It's just that I had to ask, don't know what kind of people one might meet in these mountains," Ivan explained.

She raised her eyebrows and waited for more. He stared back. "You still haven't answered my question about why a group of five people are in this area of the Broken Crags. I haven't heard of anyone traveling straight through the mountains in a long time," she said suspiciously.

Ivan stared intently at Iris, debating whether he should tell her anything. "I could ask the same of you. Traveling alone, nonetheless." Her jaw clenched, and he knew he would not get anywhere if he continued throwing suspicions back at her. "We traveled this way to seek out aid, but I'm assuming the situation here is much direr than the one we left behind." He paused to think about what he would say next, "Why don't you come with me back to our camp? When we get there, I'll explain this in more detail. Also, it is not particularly safe for men to travel alone, much less women. We've had our fair share of troubles while on the road."

"I can handle myself, but..." Iris thought about Ivan's offer and seriously considered declining it. The only thing was that she was not sure if she could tolerate being alone much longer, even if her company was with strangers. "Fine, I'll go. Lead the way, Ivan," Iris said after she finally came to a conclusion.

"Good, I'm sure the others will understand. I know we just met, but it wouldn't sit well with me leaving you alone. This way." He turned around and walked in the same direction as Tal.

Iris followed Ivan a short distance through the woods as quietly as she could, which was not all that silent. Soon she could see a slight glow of a fire through the brush and heard hushed voices chattering, short and quiet conversations. They walked into a small clearing and Iris saw four men huddled around the fire. The Shinta were on one side, and the Munes were on the other.

Everyone's heads turned to the pair suspiciously as they entered the small clearing. It seemed Tal already told them that she was a spy and not to be trusted, and they believed him by the looks in everyone's eyes.

"What's this you've dragged back, Ivan? Tal says she's another spy. I dunno why you don't have her tied up by now, but it don't matter. She'll undoubtedly be cut just as easily as the last one," the Shinta next to Tal said, holding a dead rabbit in his hands. He drew a knife and intently examined it over the flames, then looked over the blade to lock eyes with Iris. After a few seconds of glaring, he started to skin the rabbit.

"She's not a spy, Konnick," Ivan said in a voice that was tired of dealing with him. "There's no need to make threats with that toothpick of yours. Won't be cutting anyone tonight, no one present at least." He turned to Iris, "You can take a seat, err..." He looked sheepishly at his companions. "What was your name again?" At his words, Tal and Konnick burst out in protest, voicing their concerns about having someone share their fire when they did not even know her name.

The Munes argued with the Shintas, saying she was no threat. Iris flinched at their voices, gradually getting louder with each rebuttal. She expected Malignin to crash through the trees at any moment and overrun them.

"Enough!" Ivan commanded. Immediately everyone closed their mouths and looked at him. "Let her explain herself," he said more calmly.

Iris nervously waited before speaking as Ivan shushed everyone so they could hear her. "My name is Iris. I'm from Guardstin. I was part of the Blades of the Night. I'm no spy. I'm just looking for my friends... You haven't seen anyone pass by recently, have you? They would be traveling alone. Goes by the name of Sainte," she asked somewhat hopefully. She thought it best not to ask about Miqel just yet.

"No, no one. At least not anyone that hasn't attacked us," one of the men beside Ivan said. "There was a small group that we came across, a ragged-looking bunch, but they attacked us soon as they saw us. Didn't even say nothing."

"Spies," Konnick growled.

"Iris, sit down, relax for a minute," Ivan told her because she was still standing. "Sit, and we will tell you our story." He patted the ground next to him. Iris walked closer to the fire and sat down a respectable distance from Ivan, but not that far. The Shintas made annoyed faces as she sat, and one of them groaned, but at least they did not protest any more than that.

"Now, where would be a good starting point for our story?" Ivan asked. He started talking again but was cut off by Tal.

"Ye shouldn't start. We shouldn't tell this woman anything 'fore we know her story. Sure, she's told us where she's from, but not how she got here. I still don't trust her," Tal said, glaring at Iris.

"I agree with Tal," Konnick added.

"Thank you," Tal said. Konnick nodded in response. Ivan just sighed.

"You know, Ivan, she seems nice, and I've no reason to distrust her, but we shouldn't tell her our business. You've seen what we've all seen, and much as I hate to admit it, the Shinta have good reason to be cautious. We all do." This time, it was a Mune who spoke up. He looked a little younger than Ivan and had a scar on his right cheek.

"All right, Peng, I can't deny what you say," Ivan conceded and looked at Iris. "I'm sorry you're being treated so poorly, but..."

"It's fine, Ivan. I owe you all at least my story. From what I hear, it seems like your journey has been a trying one." From there, Iris told them everything that happened to her, starting from the night the Malignin broke through and got to Ellie and ending when Tal snatched her up at knifepoint. However, she left out when she met with Miqel.

For most of the story, she looked into the fire, but when she finished and finally looked up at everyone, their faces were shadowed and troubled. Even the Shintas, who rarely cared about the problems of the more civilized people of the land, let her finish without interrupting.

"Well," Ivan said, breaking everyone's solemn thoughts. "Do we all now agree that she can be trusted? Or does anyone still not believe her?" There were grunts of reluctant approval. Everyone finally agreed to trust Iris, or at least did not think that she was an immediate threat. "Right then, now for our story. On the first Dark Day-"

"Dark Day?" Iris asked.

"Aye, that's what we at Munich have taken to calling this." He gestured towards the sky. "Figured it was easier than saying on the days the sun didn't rise," Ivan explained before continuing. "The first day, people assumed it was just a bad storm rolling in. Of course, some worried voices were heard throughout the town, but everyone carried on normally. The second Dark Day was when people started getting concerned. One of the more popular opinions was that the White Wyverns were returning. You're familiar with White Wyverns?" he asked Iris.

"Yes, but I didn't grow up in a believing household. I know that some believe the White Wyverns are actually wyverns, and they created the lands and everything in it. One day they'll return and judge us all. If we pass their judgment, they take us to live in paradise. If they don't deem us worthy, we get sent to live in agony forever. I also know others believe the White Wyverns to be nothing more than humans, albeit with powers. I personally don't believe either, so I don't know much about them besides the basics."

"Ah yes, the White Wyverns are actually wyverns. Or so the fanatics would say," Ivan said with a smile. "I don't believe that, but I do think that they are real, or at least were. I also believe they had a hand in putting us where we are." He paused momentarily. "Before we get into a debate on whether or not the White Wyverns are real, that doesn't matter. What does matter is that people are beginning to say that this is our judgment time. Others say that judgment has already passed, and we weren't found worthy. Despite the minor differences, most everyone agrees that this has something to do with the White Wyverns. A handful of people say this has nothing to do with the Wyverns, but they are few and far between."

"What do you think, Ivan?" Iris asked.

"As I said, I believe in the Wyverns. However, I haven't a clue as to the reasoning behind what's happening. Maybe they had something to do with it. After hearing your story, maybe it's just a terrible tragedy, and the Wyverns had no hand in it. To put it simply, I don't know. That's why we are out here. We're searching for answers."

"At Guardstin, before the attack, there wasn't a mention of White Wyverns, none that I heard at least... Maybe the White Wyverns existed long ago, and maybe they did have powers. Perhaps they are wyverns. To me, though, none of that matters. They're not here now. I've never seen one. As far as I know, they haven't been around for a long time, and they're not going to come back anytime soon. We will have to figure out this problem on our own," Iris said.

"I like the way she thinks. Maybe she ain't so bad after'all," Tal said.

"What of you?" Iris asked him. "Why are you out here with Munes?"

"Shinta wanna know what's goin' on as well. These 'Dark Days' affect everyone. We needa know how to fix it or live with it," he explained.

"He's right. We are out here to look for answers... and to seek help now that we know Malignin have free run of Crearia," Ivan said.

"I'm sorry," Iris started, "but there's no help to be found around here."

"Well, I dunno about anyone else, but I say we head back. There's naught to be found out here. I've to return to my family. My daughter," the other Mune said, followed by a long sigh.

"Kial!" Ivan snapped, apparently hearing enough complaining. The man promptly shut his mouth and solemnly glared into the fire. "We are not going back," he said more calmly. "Not yet. We have discovered more about the situation, but it's not enough. There must be more that we can do. Keeping our friends and families safe in Munich is our responsibility. They entrusted us with that. We cannot let them down."

"Aye, we have to push on, Kial," Peng said. "We have to. We can't go back empty-handed. The Dark Days has the entire town nervous. They expect us to return with something that can help them." Peng looked at everyone as he said this.

Iris took a breath, then decided to change the subject as no one else seemed eager to speak. "What about this 'spy' you mentioned? Why were they spying on you, and who were they spying for? Did they say?"

"I'll gladly answer this," Tal said gruffly. "He wanted to find out our purpose and why a band of five men were traversing through th' Broken Crags. It was apparent he was a spy. We could tell soon as we saw him. He walked up to our fire sayin' that he got lost and was thankful he fin'ly ran into some people.

"After some questioning, he got caught up in th' very web of lies he weaved. After a short struggle, we ended up tyin' him to a tree. Few cuts later, the truth flowed outta him much like his blood did. He said he was working with th' Malignin, that he was only doing it to survive. He said that that's the only reason people were siding with 'em. 'Fore ya told yer story, we just thought he was shittin' our ears.

"When we stopped getting more information out o' him, I killed him. We were attacked the next night and believe that he was with 'em." He stopped talking after that, and everyone waited a few seconds, expecting him to continue, but he did not.

"I think there is far more at stake than any of us realizes," Ivan said, breaking the silence. No one spoke for a while, and all that could be heard was the steady crackle of the fire. Now and again, they could hear some frantic critter let loose a small rockslide down the mountains.

In the ensuing quiet, Iris thought about everything that was said and tried to understand what it meant not only for her but everyone else. They were hopeless thoughts, and she soon gave up on them. She only needed to focus on finding Sainte and then trying to get Miqel back. As she thought of her two self-assigned missions, she came up with an idea.

"I've got an offer." As she said that, all eyes snapped to her. "Help me find my friends and fellow members of the Blades, Sainte and Miqel, and I'll do whatever I can to help you. I can't promise it'll be much, but it's got to be better than nothing." She waited a few moments before Ivan began speaking.

When Ivan spoke, he spoke for everyone. "We appreciate the offer, and we'll consider it. It will probably be the best one we're likely to hear now that we know the situation better, but it would be best if we discussed it amongst ourselves. For now, we should all get some sleep. I'll be first watch," he said as he chucked another log into the fire. After he made sure the log would not roll out, he rummaged around in his pack. He pulled out a blanket and handed it to Iris. "I'd let you use more, but this is all the extra we've got."

She graciously accepted the blanket. "It's better than I had before. Thank you, Ivan." He smiled and turned back around to pull out his sleeping arrangements. Iris laid out the blanket slightly away from the others but close enough to the fire so that she could still feel the heat.

"Hey, Ivan," Tal called out not unquietly. "Can I talk to ya fer a minute? Away from th' others."

Ivan followed Tal just out of earshot of the others into some thick brush. As Ivan walked up to him, Tal got real close to his face, real slow.

"Do ya really trust this girl so much to just let 'er sleep in our camp? We've known 'er fer two minutes!" he growled incredulously into Ivan's face.

"She's no spy, Tal. You know it. Her story's straight. If it weren't, someone would have caught on by now. No one else is uncomfortable with her but you. You just don't want to be proven wrong about her." Tal was about to reply, but Ivan put a hand on his broad shoulder and said, "Trust me."

Tal let out a breath of frustration. "We don't have much time, Ivan, if what she said is true. Ya may think that the Shinta are a barbaric people, but I care about everyone o' them, the weak and the strong. I don't want my people to die."

"I know, Tal. I fear the same for my people, but Iris is the only hope we have right now. We have to believe that she will hold true to her word," he explained. "It's all we've got."

"So ye've already decided fer us all that we will help her?"

"What do you think, Tal? Either we help her and possibly return with something, or we leave her and return with nothing." He stepped back. "We cannot return empty-handed." Ivan looked at Tal with brows raised as if waiting for a rebuttal, but the other man remained silent.

EIGHT
-INTRODUCTIONS-

Aroc told Sainte that her father was part of the Council of Elion, but he did not expect him to be the only member. Four others were on the Council, but in the time Aroc was gone, all but Isaac were killed. Malignin attacked Elion for three days now, and everyone, along with the town defenses, was worse for wear because of it. Sainte was amazed they were able to withstand the Malignin for this long, even with the remarkable fortifications.

After Aroc introduced Sainte and Isaac, Isaac took them to the Keep in the center of the town, where he resided. As they walked through the town, Sainte noticed that although a few people were walking through the streets, no one said anything to each other. The few townsfolk that were out walked quickly without so much as a nod. No one made eye contact, and their troubled faces were overcast in shadow. Their steps were muffled, and their arms were crossed across their chests. If fear had a face, it would be on the face of these people. The town itself looked like it would have been a beautiful sight to behold. Under current circumstances, however, it was dreadful.

Soon they walked up to a large three-story building. Standing in front of two oaken doors, Isaac turned around and faced Sainte and Aroc. "This is the Keep. This is where the business of the Council of Elion was had and where the Council lived. Normally there would not have been room for two extra people, but since the other Council members are no longer with us, Wyverns bless them, there's more than enough room. Welcome to the Keep." With that, he opened the doors with a flourish.

The interior of the building was dimly lit with candles every few feet on the walls. Immediately walking in, there was another door in front of Sainte, and the hall he found himself in curved to his left and right. Isaac shuffled in after Aroc and closed the doors behind him.

"Ok, go left, Sainte. This hallway we're in encircles the whole building. There are two rooms on this floor: my bedroom and the hearth room. The hearth room is straight through the doors you saw when you first entered. My room is at the end of the hallway to the right." They came to a set of stairs and climbed up. "On this floor are two more rooms and a dining room; the top floor has the same. This is where I'll leave you two. Pick any rooms you want. I'll come grab you when food is ready." He smiled at Sainte, then walked back downstairs.

"Your father seems in high spirits," Sainte observed.

"Yes, he's always like that. It takes a lot to bring him down. I'm going to grab a room and try to get some sleep. You planning on staying on this floor?" Aroc asked.

"Yes, I don't think I'd be able to make it up another flight of stairs even if I wanted," he said.

"See you in a bit," Aroc said as she walked through the door on the right and into her room.

Sainte walked through the door immediately across from it and entered the dining room. There was a sturdy-looking wooden table that would seat four easily. Lining the wall to his right were some counters and a pit built for a fire and a grate over the top. He walked through the doors across from him and entered his room. There was a bed, a cabinet, and a closet. Simple, but he did not need anything more complicated.

He could not rip his footwear off fast enough before he collapsed on the bed. Sainte closed his eyes and almost immediately fell asleep.

"Sainte, wake up. Food's ready," Aroc said, nudging him.

"Huh?" He sat up, surprised at being woken. He looked around quickly, then settled down. "How long was I asleep?"

She shrugged. "I don't know—an hour. Hurry up while the food's still hot. We're downstairs." Aroc left him to get ready.

He grabbed his shoes and put them on drowsily. His muscles protested his movements. With slow and stiff footsteps, he eventually shuffled his way downstairs into the hearth room. A stone fireplace lined an entire wall of the room. A large bookshelf was taking up the entire length of the wall opposite the fireplace. It was stocked full of ancient looking tomes, most of which had no titles on the spines. Aroc and Isaac were already eating at the table in the room. A whole roasted chicken surrounded by bowls of peas, sliced carrots, and potatoes was on the table. Sainte sat opposite Aroc, grabbed an empty plate, and started piling on food.

"Sir, I have to ask, how has everyone managed to survive this long?" Sainte asked Isaac before digging into his food. Aroc opened her mouth to scold Sainte for his rude manners, but Isaac held up a hand to stop her.

"Please, just call me Isaac. Believe me, it hasn't been easy," he started, "but somehow, we've managed to beat the devils back every time. Unfortunately, we've lost a lot of good people doing so."

"Well, I'm impressed," Sainte said after swallowing a particularly large mouthful of chicken. "I wouldn't guess that people with no formal combat training against Malignin would be able to last as long as you have, but I suppose all the defenses help."

"You can't give all the credit to the defenses. The people of Elion are a hardworking lot. Whether it be plowing a field all by yourself or fighting off creatures of the night side by side with friends and family. Everyone plays a part in keeping those monsters out of this town." Sainte shook his head in disbelief at Isaac's words, still amazed that a town primarily full of farmers could defend against the Malignin so effectively.

"Well, now that you two are well fed and have rested up a bit, care to tell me how you met? Maybe it'll shed some light on the current situation." At this, Isaac made eye contact with Aroc like he had an unspoken question for her.

153

For now, Sainte chose to ignore it.

"I'm the Shield of the Barrier and I failed my only duty." He inhaled slowly as he did not like retelling this story. Sainte spent a few minutes telling Isaac what happened, only explaining what he thought was essential and answering when Isaac had any questions. He wrapped up his story when he met Aroc.

"If Aroc hadn't found me in the woods, I would be dead. I owe her my life." Sainte paused, looked at Aroc, then at Isaac. "She healed me, and when I was well enough, we traveled together to get here."

"You are lucky indeed. It would've been a terrible thing, dying alone. As far as the Malignin stealing away the Barrier, that was bound to happen sooner or later. The world is not perfect, after all. Now, I'm not saying that it wasn't your fault or that there was nothing you could do to change it because frankly, I don't know. But I don't blame you. From what I see, you're trying to fix it, and that's the most that anybody can ask of you." Isaac spoke to Sainte like a father to his son.

"How's it been going here, father? What's happened since I left?" Aroc asked, changing the subject for Sainte's sake.

It was Isaac's turn to take a deep breath before explaining his situation more. "As I said before, it's been tough. We gathered all the crops we could to store them before they started to wither. I was surprised at how much we managed to save, but it won't last us long. The animals are confused. Some of the cows have stopped producing milk and the horses won't sleep anymore. They're all spooked because they can smell the Malignin's stench.

"They attacked us once every few hours the first day, but the attacks have been getting fewer and farther in between. I think they're just waiting for something, but I haven't the slightest idea what it could be. Maybe they're just toying with us. No matter, we've a constant watch on the walls. The rotation changes every six hours so everyone can get some rest." He took a sip out of a cup and then continued. "The very first attack was the worst because we weren't expecting it.

"We pushed them back, obviously, but we lost more people in that one fight than the others following, combined." Isaac's shoulders sagged. "It was hard dealing with each death, but soon the sadness turned to anger, the fear turned to vengeance. The entire population of Elion, four hundred of us at the time, now almost half, decided to dedicate our time to fighting rather than merely surviving.

"The next time the Malignin attacked, we expected them. Many Malignin died by our hands, but there were always more. There were many more Malignin during the second fight, but it seemed easier to push them back than the first time. I can only believe that it was because we were driven by anger.

"They attacked again before you two arrived, with the same results. We killed many of them, and they killed few of us." He shook his head sadly. "Although we keep winning the battles, each loss hurts us and it's only a matter of time before we reach our inevitable end."

"How soon do you think we have until the next attack?" Sainte asked.

"Honestly boy, I'm surprised we aren't fighting right now," came Isaac's dry reply.

"How many more do you think you can fend off?"

"I think one more," Isaac said.

"Why don't you try to leave? Find safety elsewhere, in another town?"

"This is our home. It feels wrong just leaving it, not fighting for it. Even if we did want to leave, how far do you think we'd get before the Malignin caught us out in the open? The closest town was Guardstin, but that's no longer an option. The next choice would have to be Mountsville, and that's a two-week journey." He shook his head slowly. "No, staying and fighting is our only option."

Sainte asked no more questions and instead moved the food around his plate, suddenly feeling very full. There was no sound save for the crackle and pop of the hearth.

"Father," Aroc said, and Isaac looked up at her. "Sainte lost his sword. I told him that we may have some to spare for him."

"Aye, we have plenty. We salvaged what we could from the dead, and now we have more weapons than we do people to wield them. I can take you to the armory now if you're finished eating?" he said to them both.

"Please, I would be extremely grateful," Sainte said as politely as he could. He felt sorry for the man but was also anxious to be on his way. Talking to Isaac made him realize he was perhaps the only person in Elion who wanted to leave. There was nothing to be done for these people. As Isaac said, sooner or later, they would all get slaughtered by the Malignin. He needed nothing more from the town after he got a new sword. He was thankful for Isaac's hospitality, but he had to be on his way.

Isaac stood up and prompted Aroc and Sainte to do the same. "Don't worry about the food. I've informed the workers here to use whatever we leave behind. Whether they'll eat it or give it to the animals, I don't care. Follow me." Isaac left the room with Sainte and Aroc close behind. They walked outside into the endless night.

It was not raining, but they could feel it in the air. Sainte walked behind Isaac and Aroc so they could talk privately. As they made their way through the desolate town, Sainte noticed the buildings were made of stone brick and thick timber. The streets were cobblestone, unlike Guardstin, which made walking much easier since it was not muddy. Some of the people they passed gave them greetings and welcomed Aroc back, but most passed without a word.

Elion itself did not seem like it was in bad shape. Most buildings stood with little to no wear, and Sainte could see where any holes in the street were repaired. Torches lined the streets in a poor attempt to shed some light and drive the fog away. They worked well as long as you were within two feet of the flames.

The armory was a short walk as it was near the entrance to the town. The building was long and narrow, maybe twenty feet wide. They entered the armory, and at first it looked like a straight hallway with nothing else but doors lining each side. Candles lit the way for anyone walking through.

"This building serves as both the barracks and the armory for the town guard. The armory is the middle door on the left, Sainte. You can go ahead and enter. Aroc and I will remain outside. You're free to pick whatever weapon you think would best suit your needs," Isaac told Sainte.

"Thanks, I don't think I should be too long." Sainte entered the armory and observed the vast collection of weapons. Some were old and rusty, others obviously recently used with dented blades and crusted with filth. There were pikes, maces, swords, shields, axes, bows, dirks, and much more. There was no organization to the weapons. They were all thrown about in disarray. Finding a suitable weapon might take him longer than he thought.

Even though he was not particularly interested in anything but swords, Sainte found himself testing how a variety of weapons felt in his hands. He did not like how maces were top-heavy even though they were meant to be. The spears' shafts were made out of wood which would not last very long, and he was never proficient at wielding axes. He moved on to the swords.

He overlooked the short swords altogether and searched for long swords with at least a three-foot-long blade. The first few he saw had potential, but he found faults with each one. One had too many chips in the edge, one felt good in his hands but upon closer inspection, the blade was cracked in several places. He was quickly growing frustrated because it seemed that out of all these weapons, there would not be a reliable one. He yearned for his grandfather's sword and scolded himself for losing it.

Sainte scanned the room, irritated, until he saw a small pile of swords in a corner. Most looked gaudy and more for showmanship than swordsmanship, but he saw a few that looked like they were actually meant for battle. He carefully shuffled the naked blades around until he finally found the one. The blade itself was four feet long, dark gray in color, and double-edged.

Sainte could not tell what kind of metal made the blade, but it felt strong. The balance was near perfect, and the handle fit like it was made for him.

He looked around for its sheath, which he found surprisingly quickly. He slid the sword into the sheath, attached it to his left hip, and started walking out. When he got close to the door he could hear voices echoing from the hallway, Aroc's and Isaac's voices. He could not help himself but pause and listen to what they said.

"You don't have to do this, you know. It was supposed to be me. I could still go in your stead if you want me to," Isaac said.

"No, it's fine. It isn't your responsibility anymore. You should go to Munich, find Jasmine, and buy as much time as you can, however you can. We all knew that it would come to this, one way or another." Aroc told him with a barely audible whisper. More was said, but it was hushed, and he could not make anything out.

Sainte wanted to listen more, he wanted to know what they were talking about, but if he took any longer than he already had to find a sword he was sure they would check on him. He walked out of the armory and into the hall. Aroc and Isaac stopped talking and looked toward him.

"Did you find anything?" Isaac called out.

"Yes, finally. Not a very good selection in there, but I found a sword that will hopefully be able to keep up with me," Sainte told them as he approached. He drew the sword out a few inches to show them the blade. "I'm not sure what it's made of, but it feels durable."

"You've a good eye for quality swords, Sainte," Isaac said, more than a little surprised. "That's made from bal'shene. It's a rare ore not found anywhere near here for hundreds of miles. Very sturdy blade, takes a lifetime to dull. Good eye. I didn't even realize we had a sword like that in our armory. Where did you find it?"

"It was buried under a pile of swords in the corner. It looked to have been there for some time," Sainte told him honestly.

"Aye, you don't see these blades too often anymore. So you're good, Sainte? You don't need anything else? No shield?" Aroc asked.

"No, shields are too unwieldy, they slow me down. What might be helpful is a gauntlet for my left hand. I usually used that as a shield if need be, and it's perfect for bashing," Sainte said as he slid the sword back into its sheath.

"I think I have one that might fit you. It's from my old armor back in my youth. It won't fit me now, but a gauntlet would probably be just the right size for you," Isaac told Sainte. "Sounds like it's back to the Keep from here. Let's go, time's wasting."

▼▲▼

Iris woke up a few hours later from a fitful sleep. She looked around and realized that everyone else was up, packing their things and getting ready to move. She got up and started to fold the blanket lent to her. She tried giving it back to Ivan but he said she could keep it.

"So, where do we go next?" Iris asked him.

"It sounds like Guardstin is out of the question, so I suppose we'll head to Elion to see how they're faring. Maybe they'll know something that we don't," he replied. "You do plan on staying with us, don't you?"

"It doesn't feel like I'm really wanted here. I don't blame you for not trusting me. I'm a random person you just met. I understand, believe me..." Iris did not want to split from them. She wanted to beg and plead to stay because she was scared to be alone again, but her pride would not let her. She would rather risk being by herself.

"No, that's not right at all. We'll help you look for your friends. So I guess I should be asking if Elion would also be your next choice?"

She smiled but quickly hid it, not wanting to show what a relief that was to hear. "It'll do. It makes sense. I don't know where else Sainte would go. Maybe he stopped by and someone noticed him," she said, holding back her happiness like a weight was lifted off her shoulders. Even though she had only been alone for a day, it felt like years since she last had company, even if they were not all particularly fond of her.

"Good, I'll let the others know. It'll probably be around four days before we reach Elion, three if we push ourselves." Almost as an afterthought, he said, "Since you'll be traveling with us I suggest you properly introduce yourself to everyone. They may seem rough around the edges at first, but they'll respect you for it. I'll tell you their names again to make it a little easier for you.

"Starting with the Munes, Kial is the tallest and most experienced, second only to me. I haven't seen anyone who has mastered the war hammer better than he." He nodded toward a man squatting by the dying fire. "And Peng's the youngest one amongst our group, but he's proven himself in battle. He's fast with that sword of his. I can't recall seeing anyone else faster."

"If he's so good, how'd he get that scar across his face?" Iris asked.

"Well, wouldn't be right of me to tell you his own story. You can ask him yourself." He turned around to look for the Shinta, but neither were in sight. "Well, you've met Tal. I don't think I need to explain him much to you anymore. The other one is Konnick, who really likes cutting things, particularly things that bleed. Other than his knives, he uses dual axes, more coordinated than the brute looks, I might add. Thank the Wyverns those're the only Shinta traveling with us. We would've killed each other by now if there were any more. Got them all?"

Iris nodded.

"Good, I'm going to let them know where we're heading. Talk to them while we travel. It'll help pass time. From the looks of it, we should be ready to leave soon. You're good with Elion?" he asked again.

"Aye, sounds good. I'm ready to go. Not like I've much to pack up myself," Iris replied.

"Right, well talk to you later," Ivan said and walked away, yelling out orders for everyone to hurry. Tal and Konnick walked in from through the foliage, grumbling to each other, but they shouldered their packs all the same, along with everyone else.

As everyone packed up their final things, it started to lightly drizzle again. Iris wiped her wet hair from her eyes.

"Tal, are you two ready to move out?" Ivan asked over everyone's noise.

"Been ready," was his gruff reply.

"Good, then let's go. As you all may have figured, Guardstin is no longer where we plan to head to. We're going to go to Elion. We'll want to start pushing straighter east and north now, no longer south." He was just met with murmurs of acceptance as the men started walking away. Ivan shook his head and looked at Iris helplessly.

"Just can't work with these men sometimes," he said as he adjusted his shoulder straps. Iris gave him a nod, thankful that they allowed her to travel with them. They caught up with the group and traveled with little talk.

For a while, all they heard was their feet sloshing through the mud and the constant rain. The Shintas were noticeably quieter than the Munes, mainly because they wore animal hides and leather as protection and the Munes wore chainmail and plated armor.

Ivan nudged Iris, then nodded towards the others, urging her to go talk to them, "No one here's going to go out of their way to meet you." He said so only she could hear. "You're the stranger here, not them. Go talk to them. That's the only way they'll start to warm up to you." He smiled encouragingly.

"It didn't seem to take you long to warm up to me," she said with a smile of her own.

"Well, when I looked at you I saw many things in your eyes, but ill intent was not there. Also, I've a soft spot for pretty girls."

Iris blushed and tripped over her words. "Er, I'm, uh, going to talk to Peng." Was all she managed to get out, not sure how else to respond to him. She thought about what Ivan said while she caught up to Peng, but before she could think about it too much she was already beside him.

"Peng, right?" she asked.

"Yeah, that's right."

"Nice to meet you." As soon as the words left her mouth she realized how dumb she sounded. Why was she so nervous about meeting these men? Iris thought back to her first days as a Blade of the Night, fresh out of Training. She had to put a brave face on, be one of the men. There was no time for stupidity. This situation she was in was different but nonetheless similar in its own way.

"What do you want?" Peng asked finally after several seconds of awkward silence.

Iris scrambled to say something so she would not be viewed as an empty-headed girl. She decided to go with the truth. "Just trying to meet everyone to better know who I travel with. I'd rather not travel with a band of strangers the entire time."

"So, what do you want to know?"

"How old are you?" She berated herself internally for another pointless question. He finally looked at her, but his face said the same thing she thought about the question.

"Twenty-one," he finally answered.

"What do you do? Before the Dark Days, I mean."

"I worked in the town guard. My job was mostly involved with livestock. Whenever farmers would bring their livestock, sheep, cows, what have you, out to graze, a small group of guards would go with them. The farmer herded their animals while we guarded them against wolves, panthers, or any beasts that wanted an easy lunch. It wasn't particularly exciting all the time, but when it was exciting..." He paused as he searched for the right word. Giving up, he just reaffirmed, "It was exciting."

"Sounds like it could be fun. How'd you become part of this group?"

"I met Ivan a few years back, been pretty good friends since. He asked me to join him and I couldn't tell him no. So here I am."

"How'd you get that scar?" she asked. "If you don't mind telling me, that is." She quickly added because of the way he looked at her after she asked the question.

"Happened three years ago, the first week I was a guard. I was out on my third patrol, I think it was, protecting farmer Lenran's sheep. I remember the day well. Beautiful day, sun was out, not a cloud in the sky, nice breeze rolling through the plains. We were near the forest's edge when I first heard the sound. Some large beast was stalking the sheep from the forest, I could hear its lumbering footsteps."

Iris found herself caught up in his story, almost felt herself there beside him.

"I drew my sword and instead of calling for backup, as you're supposed to, I went to check it out myself. I wanted to prove that I was better than all the other new men. I stepped forward confidently into the forest, and a bear lunged at me from the shadows. Before I could get my sword up, he slashed me across the face. I let out a cry for other guards before I fell into unconsciousness."

"How did it not take your head off?" Iris asked, entrapped in the story. "I don't know of very many men that could survive a bear attack," she said admirably.

"I had trained a lot, brutal training..." He cracked a smile, tried to continue, but then let out a held back laugh. "Well, that's because it didn't happen. That's the story I tell ladies I try to bring to my bed."

Iris let out a quick breath of air from her nose, then shook her head. "Can't believe you."

"What actually happened was it was not a bear that lunged at me, but Ivan. He thought it a good idea to prank the new guard. When he jumped at me from the shadows, I slipped and fell on my own sword, leaving this permanent scar." He traced it with a finger.

"You're not embarrassed?"

"Aye, I was. Made quite a fool of myself. Was the laughingstock for a while. I got over it with time. Now I look back in humor. Should've seen your face when I said it was a bear. Should've just stuck with that." He shook his head at his own joke.

"Aye, you should've," Iris agreed.

"Tell me, if you thought I survived a bear attack, would that have made you come to bed with me easier?"

Iris laughed at the question. "Oh, aye. I had already pictured myself with you. I could barely stop myself from throwing myself at you. Now that I know the real story, you couldn't pay me enough to sleep with you."

"Don't got to be so rude." He grimaced, bringing a hand to cover his heart. They laughed together a bit, then slowly it faded away. Peng said nothing else.

Iris could not think of much else to talk about either, so she decided this was as good a place to end the conversation as any. "Well, it was good talking to you. Thanks."

"Sure. If you ever change your mind about the bed thing, let me know," Peng said. Iris could not tell if he was being serious or not, but either way, the tone of it made her a little uncomfortable. She said nothing as they walked further apart.

Soon Iris found herself walking beside Ivan again.

"How'd it go?" he asked.

"I think he likes me. Perhaps too much," Iris told him.

"Well, he talked to you which is a good start. You've nothing to worry about with him. I know Peng, and I know that he can be a bit much at times, especially with women. I'm not so much worried about us Munes as I am the Shinta."

Iris nodded in agreement. "I'm worried about them too. How long has it been since you left Munich?"

Ivan thought about her question. "I'd say today is probably the eighth day. It's difficult to keep track of days when the sun doesn't bother to rise," Ivan told her quietly.

"No kidding," she said. "It feels like ages ago the last time I saw Sainte."

Ivan did not reply until a few steps later. "You've told us about Sainte, but what about your other friend? You mention him but haven't told us anything about him."

"Miqel... He worked with Sainte and me. I don't need to find him, but he does need help. Sainte will need to be with me for that. I can't do it by myself. I already tried."

"We can help," Ivan suggested.

"No, you can't. It's different," she said but offered no more explanation.

Ivan eyed her but saw that he would not get much more out of her about Miqel, so he dropped it. Suddenly he stopped and

Iris almost ran into him. She looked ahead of him and saw that everyone else also stopped walking. Tal held up a closed fist, the hand signal for 'stop.' He indicated that he heard something to their right, then motioned to make a defensive circle. They quietly but quickly faced outwards, backs to each other, and drew their weapons with a silent purpose. Iris moved into the interior of the circle, weaponless.

Nothing could be heard except the drizzle of the rain, but even that slowly faded. As soon as Tal began to call all clear, a twig snapped, which was heard by all. People exploded from behind trees and bushes and frantically rushed around Iris and her new companions. They were surrounded, but no one attacked. The people surrounding them looked ragged and haggard, their weapons were not well kept, but there were many of them. Iris counted twelve, and that was only what she could see. She was sure there were more hiding in the pines.

"I see ya've found new friends, Iris. Most of 'em seem quite capable, actually."

Iris looked around for the source of the voice. She did not see him, but she knew who it belonged to.

"I won't hurt any of ya if ya just hand Iris over. The rest of ya will live." Some people parted and a figure walked close to the group stopping about ten feet away. Some of the men Iris was with eyed her questionably.

Iris ignored the looks and faced her friend. "Miqel... Look at yourself. This isn't right."

"Aye, lookit me." He held his arms out. "I've never felt stronger, more alive, in my entire life. I could kill ya all." The way he said that was not a threat but a fact.

"We aren't going to give you the girl," Ivan said. "Not without a fight." Iris could feel the men around her tense in preparation and unease at his words. Ivan hefted his shield to the ready.

"Who're ya? Her protector? How sweet o' ya ta take'er on. If it's a fight ya want, ye'll get it." As he said that, he reached behind his back and pulled out his battleax. "Tell ya what. If ya beat me one-on-one, we'll leave ya alone. I beat ya, I take Iris. If any fight back, I'll kill ya all."

"Ivan..." Kial started to say.

"Quiet," he snapped at Kial. "Iris, he's your friend. What do you want to do?"

"I'm not a patient man," Miqel growled at them.

"Miqel, you don't have to do this. It's not too late for you. I don't know what you're doing or planning, but you can stop, join me and help me look for Sainte. Please." Iris' eyes teared as she said this.

"I know it's not too late fer me. It's about'a be too late fer yer friends unless ya come with me. I won't ask again." His grip tightened around his axe, and he stepped forward. Ivan walked in front of him, blocking his path and holding his shield up.

"Not another step," he demanded. The remaining four men exchanged glances but held their ground.

Miqel grinned. With an incredible amount of speed, he attacked Ivan. Miqel's axe slammed against the shield. To Ivan's credit, he accepted the blow as well as he could. He countered with a strike of his own, which Miqel stepped out of the way.

After the first round of strikes, the two men circled each other, sizing each other up. Iris watched the fight in horror, unable to do anything else.

Ivan attacked first, sword striking downwards. Miqel knocked it aside harmlessly. Without hesitation, Ivan spun to his right, quickly ending up behind Miqel. Without wasting a second, he brought his sword up, ready to skewer Miqel through the back, but suddenly a humanoid shadow appeared in front of him. His sword wavered uncertainly at the new obstacle. Instead of continuing his attack, Ivan brought his shield up. That last-second decision of defense saved his life.

Miqel's axe swung through the shadow harmlessly and would have cut Ivan's head clean off had it not been for his shield. Instead, Ivan was thrown to his back on the ground. He tried to get up quickly but only reached his knees before Miqel held his axe to his throat.

"Ya like my newest trick?" Miqel asked everyone. "Learned it only yesterday, didn't think it'd come in handy so soon. The shadowy figures're harmless because all they are's shadow. Great fer trippin' people up. Now, ya die." He lifted his axe, ready to chop the man's head off. Ivan stared him in the eyes defiantly, refusing to look elsewhere.

"No!" Iris screamed out. The four men around her jumped at the sudden noise, so intent were they on the fight that just unfolded before them. "Don't do it, Miqel. I must believe there's still a part of you that knows this is wrong. There has to be."

Miqel's axe hovered in the air as he contemplated her words, then he brought it down with all his strength. Ivan's eyes widened at his impending death. As soon as the blade touched his neck, it disappeared, along with Miqel. He was gone, as was everyone else that surrounded them. Seemed to just vanish right in front of their eyes.

The silence that followed was deafening. No one moved for an eternity, all trying to register what just happened.

"Are they all gone?" Kial asked, finally breaking the quiet.

"I think so," Iris replied in a voice not much louder than a whisper. She could hardly hear herself over her pounding heart.

Ivan stood up and sheathed his sword. He had a small cut on his neck where Miqel's axe made contact, but it was shallow. Everyone else followed suit, putting their weapons away.

"Is everyone all right?" Ivan asked.

"Aye, we're all fine. What about you?" Peng asked.

"I've had worse," Ivan murmured. Mustering himself up, he said, "Come on, let's go. What just happened changes nothing. We knew we might be met with trouble on this little expedition. We'll continue until we find suitable ground to rest. Wyverns know I need it."

Everyone nodded in agreement, even the Shintas. Soon the group was underway again without talking. Each and every one of them were troubled, not entirely sure how to process everything that just happened.

All Iris could think about was the fight. Miqel could have killed Ivan, seemed like he was going to, but he did not. Maybe there was some humanity left in him after all. No matter how horrible that last encounter was, it gave Iris a slight sense of hope that at least one of her friends could yet be saved.

NINE
-INTERRUPTIONS-

The large wooden doors to the Keep swung open smoothly on well-oiled hinges. Isaac stood to the side holding them open for Aroc and Sainte. Aroc walked in and immediately started to go to the stairs that led to her room.

"I'm going to go change out of these dirty garments. I've been wearing them since before I found Sainte," Aroc said to them as Isaac entered.

"Alright, there should be some clean clothes in the room closet," Isaac told her.

"Why don't I just go to my place, grab some clothes, and come back," she suggested.

"I don't think that's a great idea. What if something happens? What if the Malignin attack? Then we won't be together. Best to stay here," Isaac said. Aroc sighed but inclined her head, then went upstairs. "Come, follow me, Sainte. I'll take you to my room and hopefully be able to find those gauntlets. It's been some time since I last had them out."

Sainte followed Isaac down the hallway. Isaac walked with slow, deliberate steps, hands clasped behind his back. "Tell me, Sainte, how long have you been in the Blades of the Night now?"

"It's going on four years, I believe. I don't know the exact time. Once you've been in over two you start losing track of time. Days and nights blur together," Sainte said with one of his hands resting on the hilt of his new sword.

"I can imagine so," Isaac said quietly. "At least you're probably more adjusted to this ceaseless dark than most." Sainte grunted in reply. A few beats went by before Isaac spoke again, "I know this might be a sore wound for you still, but would you mind telling me a little bit about Ellie?"

"Why?" Sainte asked, immediately defensive.

Isaac shrugged. "No real reason. I just always hear her referred to as 'The Barrier.' It's almost like people forget that she's human as well. I would like to know what our Barrier, our oblivious protector, is like."

Sainte thought about how he could reply. How could he describe Ellie?

"She was kind, always wanted to know how I was doing. She could tell when I'd had a hard day or an easy one, but of course, I couldn't tell her much of anything about it. She loved grapes, they were her favorite food, and she could draw really well. She drew a portrait of herself and gave it to me... I still have it, but it's gotten a little messed up," he said as he patted the pocket it was in.

"She was so innocent... She didn't even know that she should have been upset when the Malignin came. She was just confused..." Sainte stopped talking as he got choked up, but not by sadness. By anger.

"Yes, well, she sounds like a good girl," Isaac said comfortingly as they walked down the dimly lit hall. "I'm sure she'll be all right in the end," he said unconvincingly. Nothing more was spoken until they came to a heavy-looking wooden door.

"We have come to my sleeping chambers. Consider yourself lucky. The only others who have seen this are the women who fell for my good looks and witty mind," he told Sainte with a chuckle. Sainte did not share in his laughter. Isaac finally made eye contact and realized Sainte was as grim as ever.

"Don't be so serious all the time, my boy. We have enough serious situations at hand. A little bit of humor now and then never hurts.

"Come, this way." He beckoned Sainte, not waiting for a reply. Together they walked over to an oak armoire. The room was sparsely decorated. Aside from the armoire was a dresser, desk, and bed. Isaac flung the armoire doors open with gusto, showering himself with dust. He coughed and waved a hand in front of his face. "This hasn't been used in a while."

Sainte heard some clanks and thuds as Isaac rummaged around, muttering to himself. With a shout of triumph, he held up a gauntlet.

"Here it is," he exclaimed as he handed it to Sainte. Sainte turned it around in his hands.

"This is well crafted, for sure, but..."

"But what?" he asked, eyeing Sainte sharply.

"This is for the right hand," Sainte said, slightly amused at Isaac's look of confused triumph. "I wield my sword in my right hand. My left needs the gauntlet more," he explained.

"Of course. I knew that," he harrumphed as he tried to conceal that he thought he found the right gauntlet. "I can't very well give you just one. They come in pairs. You have a pair of hands, don't you?" he snapped. "Give me a few moments more."

Sainte waited quietly and patiently and tried on the gauntlet he had, which fit surprisingly well. The armor was black, trimmed with a lighter gray metal, and covered from the bend in his elbow to his fingertips. It squeaked when Sainte moved, but he could not see any rust, so some oil would probably clear that up.

Isaac turned around with the left-hand gauntlet. "Got 'em. Aren't these the most beautiful gauntlets you've ever seen? These've smashed countless enemies in the face. They're no stranger to battles."

Sainte snorted through his nose. "What battles have these been in? Far as I can remember there haven't been any major ones in about seventy years, and you look like you could be in your fifties."

Isaac paused, then slowly shrugged. "Fighting wild animals away from my cattle counts." Sainte looked at him with raised eyebrows and an amused expression. "Well, they were battles to me, and that's what matters. Go on, try it on, make sure they fit both hands."

Sainte strapped on the remaining gauntlet and flexed his fingers. "They hardly limit my movement at all and fit like they were made for me. Thank you," Sainte said sincerely.

"Ah, don't mention it. I've no use of them anymore anyway," Isaac said as he shut the doors to the armoire.

"Well, I mean, isn't your town technically under assault right now? You may find that you wish you still had them in the near future."

"I'm no longer a man who will be standing at the front lines. Plus, like I said before, there's no way they would fit my stubby fingers. Keep them, and don't say anything more about it. I won't hear it. Come on, let's try to find Aroc and get some oil for those squeaky things."

They left his room in search of their third party, but they did not have to look long. She was in the hearth room with a fresh set of clothes on. The fire was stoked with new logs, so the room was almost uncomfortably warm. The blaze flicked toward the tall ceiling but always fell short.

Aroc was reclined on a leather chair and opened her eyes when she heard them walk in. They sat down in similar chairs on either side of her.

"I see you've found the gauntlets, good. What will our next step be? Surely the Malignin won't wait long before attacking again. You said that this was the longest break between attacks, father."

"I know what I said—no need to remind me. I suppose our next step will be to help prepare the town's defenses. Sainte, you've the most experience fighting these Malignin. If you would, I'd greatly appreciate it if you took charge of the defenses. Tell people what would work best with what we have. I know that when people realize they have someone as experienced as you on their side it would greatly improve morale. Aroc and I will help where we can," Isaac said to Sainte as if he expected he was going to stay.

Sainte knew now that leaving would not be as simple as he wanted. "Aye, that shouldn't be a problem, I suppose." He was agitated, though, and it showed.

"What's wrong?" Aroc asked him.

"Well," he began as if waiting for someone to ask him that, "I came here to get resupplied. Don't get me wrong; I appreciate everything you've done for me, Isaac, I do... But don't you think it's time I be on my way? Start looking for Ellie again? You can only fend off the Malignin for so long before Elion gets overrun, and we all know it won't last much longer as it is. I can't do anything to change that fact. I think you should stop preparing your defenses and begin fleeing. Gather your people, board them on ships, and sail across the lake. You could get a head start on the Malignin.

"Keeping me here to help with defenses is only hindering me," he paused to catch his breath. In the heat of the moment, he had not realized he stood up and was pacing around the room. "It's impossible to save everyone doing what we're doing now. I must find Ellie, I must find my friends. I'm not getting any closer to that by staying here." He looked at Isaac and Aroc.

Aroc was about to speak, but Isaac held up his hand to silence her. "I can answer this, Aroc." He looked at Sainte. "I agree with everything you've said except the last part. You're mistaken saying that you're not getting any closer by remaining here. Fact is, you're closer to Ellie now than since the last time you saw her."

▼▲▼

Iris and her new-found companions found an area that was flat enough to comfortably sleep on. Everyone was so tired, no one bothered to make a fire. They all laid down and closed their eyes, content to rest without any blankets or warmth. All of them knew that they would not rest long. There was no need to get any more comfortable than necessary.

The ground was getting less rocky, and the pine trees steadily grew larger. The edge of the mountains loomed closer with every step, but there were still a few days travel before they were completely free of them. Soon they would find themselves walking along the plains between the mountains and Whitweir Forest.

Ever since they were ambushed, Iris could feel accusatory glances from everyone. She had not told them the entire truth about Miqel, and even though she did not lie, she knew they were bitter toward her. What hurt her the most was the way Ivan treated her since. Even though she had not known him long, she quickly grew to like the man. Her intentions were not to break their trust, but it had happened.

"Alright, let's move. Think we've rested long enough," Ivan said, breaking everyone from their restless naps. Slowly the men stood up and packed what little supplies they took out. Iris was ready with her pack on before the first man was ready. She had not taken out anything and did not even sleep. Instead, her thoughts kept her awake. She waited for everyone to get prepared, and then as a group, they started off again. Iris pointedly made her way to Ivan's side.

"Hey."

"Don't really want to talk right now. Sorry," he replied.

"Ok, er, I'll just..." she stumbled over her words. "I'm sorry."

"Why didn't you tell us more about Miqel?" Ivan questioned.

"He's my friend, my problem. I didn't want you all to worry about anything more than you are already," she explained desperately.

"Well, he's our problem now. He's been our problem since we took you in. It wasn't right of you to hold that from us. You should've told us," he whispered harshly.

"I didn't know you. I wasn't sure how you would respond to that. Would you try to kill him on sight? Would you even want to bring me along? I had to trust you completely before I told you everything. I was going to tell you, but I had to know you first," she explained defensively.

Ivan sighed. "I get that, but there could've been a better way."

"Not anymore. That time has passed. You all know what I'm dealing with now."

"Aye, we do. Unless you're still holding something from us," he accused.

Iris knew that resolving this friction would take time to dissolve with Ivan. She decided that now was as good a time to try to get to know Kial as any. Even if he now had good reason to distrust her. He was not walking far from Ivan, so it did not take her long to catch up to him.

"Kial, right?" she asked, although she knew for a fact that is who he was.

"Aye, 'at's right," Kial spoke slowly, in no hurry to get the words out.

"I know I'm probably the last person you want to talk to. I just wanted to apologize," she said, hoping some of these men would accept it.

"No need for a 'pology. What's done's, done. It's the past, and we know it now. Some of these men hold grudges, hell, I do too, but way I think it wouldn't've mattered whether you told us 'bout your friend or not. Can't say I'm happy 'bout the situation, but it doesn't matter." He enunciated his words without realizing it was something he did.

"Thanks, I guess." Iris looked around at the fog surrounding them as they walked. "Have you ever fought a Malignin before?"

"Nope, can't say I 'ave. Heard stories though, none of which makes me too eager to meet one in battle. I s'pose the only thing I really need to know's they can be kill't."

"They can be killed, but I'd say there's a bit more to them than just that."

"Aye, I know it. They're 'fraid of fire, light, what 'ave you." He glanced at her sideways. "I told you I heard stories. I ain't daft." With that, he looked forward again.

Iris took the hint and fell away from his side. The group traveled on for a few hours with little conversation. Everyone was more watchful than usual, keeping eyes and ears out for any telltale sign of an attack. Their nerves were stretched taut, almost to the limits. Iris wondered how long they could travel like this before they were too mentally drained to continue.

"We should stop," Konnick said loudly enough for everyone to hear him. "Lookit here, it's a nice enough place to sleep." He glanced around him. The area was not terrible, there was a slight slant, but it was not rocky ground. It was as good as they were going to get without being picky.

"Aye, let's stay," Ivan said after he mulled over Konnick's words. His own words sounded weary. There were sighs of relief from all. "But next time we move we don't stop until we're in the plains." No one replied to him as they were too busy laying out their blankets. Tal and Konnick were already gathering wood for a fire. Iris joined them, and soon there was a large fire to warm them all.

Everyone removed their boots and let their feet air out and dry by the warming flames. The fire crackled, sending sparks up into the pine trees that towered overhead. For the first time since Miqel's ambush, the overall atmosphere was not overwhelmingly depressing. Iris did not know why, but she was not going to question it. Perhaps they were all just happy to finally be resting for once and to have an uneventful day of traveling.

"I've been saving this, but I think now is as good a time to break it out as any," Peng said as he searched his pockets. Finding what he was looking for, he pulled it out and showed it to everyone with a smug smile—a flask.

"Great minds think alike, Peng," Kial said as he brought his own flask out. "C'mon, Ivan, can't tell me 'at you didn't bring some of your own?"

"Nay, I brought no flask."

Kial and Peng looked at him, disappointed.

"I brought a canteen." He then proceeded to pull out a leather canteen from the bottom of his pack. "Filled to the brim with the finest wine I could buy."

"Must not be very good then," Peng said, nudging Kial. "Eh, what about you two?" he asked the Shintas.

"Heh, ya mean to tell me ye haven't been drinking liquor while we traveled? What 'ave ya been drinkin'? Water?" Tal asked incredulously.

"Aye, our canteens and flasks're full o' Meade. Munes," Konnick said, shaking his head in disbelief.

"Munes, what can ye 'spect?" Tal agreed.

"Iris, what've you got?" Ivan asked, bringing her into the conversation. All heads turned to her, and she expected them to shun her, but they just waited for a reply.

"I, uh, didn't bring anything." At her response, she was met with laughter. The Shintas slapped their knees in disbelief. Mutters of 'typical girl' could be heard floating her way from Peng and Kial's direction. Ivan just smiled at her expected response.

"Here, I'll share mine." He scooted closer to her. Apparently, any misgivings he held towards her for Miqel were forgiven. By this time, everyone had already started to drink what they brought.

"Alright boys, I know we deserve this, but we can't drink like we're back home. We must keep our heads about us. Mostly..." Ivan finished with a wink and a knowing smile.

"Aye," they all said in unison.

"With that out of the way," Ivan cleared his throat and held up his canteen. "Here's to the Wyverns, who'll judge us soon, and here's to our families, whom we've known for all our moons. Can't forget friends, we're never alone, but damnit I miss those whores, that we all left at home!" At the end of his toast he was met with cheers and laughter. Everyone drank, and Iris found herself laughing alongside them. After Ivan took his own drink, he thrust his canteen into her hands. She hesitated for a second, which did not go unnoticed.

"Drink up, Iris, while you can. I'm not a man prone to sharing my drinks," he said.

"Only to pretty women, I'd wager," she replied.

"No one else would deserve it." He smiled.

She felt blood flow to her cheeks. She took a drink to hide her blush as well as she could. If he noticed, he said nothing. She handed the canteen back and he took another swig.

"But I do miss th' warmth of my wife Madelaine in my bed," Kial was saying. "Ever since my first, couldn't get enough of 'em. Well, I s'pose til Madelaine came around."

"Do you even remember her name? This 'first' you're so fond of?" Peng asked him.

"Nay, I don't. You remember your first?" he retaliated.

"Course I do. Her name was Lady Illian. We were sixteen. She was from Lenshire."

"Bullshite, Lenshire's damned near across Crearia," Kial interrupted.

"Let me finish. She was from Lenshire, but it didn't happen in Lenshire. My father took me with him on a trip to Mathrik. We met there, her and her folks were on their way to Bethrune.

Shagged 'er in the back of my pa's carriage. Never knew." Peng ended with a smile.

"Sixteen, you say? What was that, three months ago?" Ivan teased.

"I may look younger than twenty-one, but at least I'm aging well. Can't say that much for any of you." Peng laughed.

"Talkin' 'bout our first times?" Tal asked. "Aye, I 'member mine. I's a lad, not more'n thirteen. My brother paid for a whore, hours' worth o' time. He finished with'er early an gave 'er to me. A gift, he said. Some gift, not just a whore, but his own used whore." He paused to drink, not noticing everyone quieted down uncomfortably. "Best damn gift I e'er got," he stated loudly with a toothy grin, causing a roar of laughter. "What 'bout ye?" he asked, nodding towards Iris.

"Tal, leave her be," Ivan said.

"No, it's fine," Iris said. She meant it. She had gotten used to this kind of talk with the men of the Blades of the Night. Ivan looked at her, surprised, but let her continue. "I don't know if you'll believe me, but my first time I was nineteen."

"Don't surprise me, you seem an uptight bi-" Konnick almost finished, but Tal elbowed him in the ribs, hard.

Iris continued as if nothing was said. "He was eighteen, though I don't know if I was his first. It happened during Training for the Blades of the Night. Just so you know, sex during Training is strictly prohibited, but he and I both were having rough weeks. We had to get steam off somehow, and we were already close. I don't remember who brought it up first, but before I knew it, there we were, naked, in the latrines," she laughed. "I remember both of us covering each other's mouths so the instructors wouldn't hear."

"What was th' lucky lad's name?" Kial asked.

"Sa-" she started, then paused. "Stephan."

"Sure? Sounded like ya were gonna say somethin' else," Tal said slyly.

"I, er, almost forgot his name. I had to remember. But aye, Stephan it was." She nodded.

"Well, how was it?" Peng asked. Ivan gave him a look. "Come off it, Ivan, I have to ask. Not often you get to hear the account of a woman's first time at screwing. Drink some more wine, maybe that'll loosen you up."

Iris smiled at the memory. "It was good. Not the best I had, but definitely wasn't the worst. Could've done without the smell of fresh shite." After a few more laughs at her story, it was Kial's turn. Time went on, each person sharing a different story. More was drunk by each, and they were all feeling better than they had in weeks by the time they decided to sleep.

All the men were curled up in their respective blankets, leaving Iris as the last one awake. She just finished tossing some fresh logs on the fire and was about to try to get comfortable with her blankets when Ivan called her over.

"If you want, you can sleep with me," he said, having drunk enough courage to ask. "Warmer that way."

She was surprised at his bluntness, yet she found herself saying, "I think I'd like that." Whether that was her or the wine talking, she was not sure. "I'll be right back." She left to grab her blanket in case they needed more. Once it was laid out, she crawled under the blankets and curled up back to Ivan.

He curled up behind her and held her close. They took refuge in each other. Feeling the warmth of another human being seemed so foreign to them. Before they knew it, sleep was upon them and they fell into it in each other's embrace, together.

▼▲▼

Sainte was taken aback by what Isaac said. "What do you mean? How can you know that?"

"There are some things about us that you do not know," Isaac said.

"Aye, no kidding," he said, clearly aggravated now. "I overheard some of your conversation in the armory, and it raised more than a few questions."

Isaac raised his eyebrows at Sainte's admission but said nothing of it. "Do you want to be informed? If so, sit down and shut your mouth," Isaac said with a surprising amount of command. Sainte slowly slid back into his seat.

"Isaac, are you sure we should be doing this?" Aroc questioned him.

"Yes, it is far too late for subtlety now. If I had it my way, we would have told him earlier. You see, Sainte, there are much larger forces at play than you, than the Blades of the Night, than the Malignin even. Aroc and I happen to be a part of one of those larger forces. We have gone by many names, but perhaps the one you are most familiar with is the White Wyverns. Our purpose is to help humanity, give them a nudge in the right direction when needed."

Sainte scoffed, unable to believe what he heard. "You expect me to believe you're White Wyverns? Don't look much like wyverns to me."

"I don't expect you to believe anything, but I do expect you to hear me out. I'm going to explain as much as I can as briefly as I can. We do not have the luxury for details right now. You see, we set this all up. The Blades of the Night, the Barrier. It was us. It was the only thing we could do. When the Malignin came, nothing we did stopped them. They spread across the land like a plague, but we noticed they went after one person: King Nuse's child. There were two kings, Nuse and Zith. Long story short, they had a deal, and while Zith didn't necessarily break it, he cheated it. They fought, and Nuse killed Zith. Are you familiar with the story?"

Sainte nodded. "I've heard it once or twice."

"Good, then I won't linger on it. Zith died in such a rage, consumed by hate, that his feelings, strong as they were, took physical form. The Malignin. They tore apart the land, but we noticed they followed the child and only came out at night. They wanted her and no one else. So, we, the White Wyverns, made this plan. We made the mountain the Barrier resided in, gave her the title 'Barrier,' and created the Blades of the Night. It evolved into what was, until recently, working well. Now that's all gone to shite, and we are trying to correct it, but there's still much to be done.

"You can tell no one what we have told you, and your questions must wait until later. Right now, we must begin setting up defenses against the Malignin. They will attack hard and fast, Ellie is with them, and they know you're here. They will not want to risk you talking to her and getting her back."

Sainte sighed, aggravated and confused. He was at an utter loss for words. Barely able to comprehend what he was told.

"Please, Sainte, understand this. We will tell you what you need to know, and the rest you must trust to us. For now, Aroc and I have much to discuss."

Sainte did not say anything. He sat back in the chair and considered what he was told. He finally gave a nod. "Alright, I won't tell anyone. But that doesn't mean I believe everything you've told me. Whether you're telling me the truth or not does not change our current situation." He had many questions he wanted to ask Aroc and Isaac now more than ever, but he agreed with Isaac. There was not enough time with the Malignin almost literally at their gates.

"Of course, I'd call you crazy if you just took me by my word. I hope now you at least understand a little more of the situation." The fire crackled violently as they sat for a moment, not saying anything. "So, you will help in the defenses?" Isaac asked. Sainte slowly nodded.

Aroc spoke up, "If I remember correctly, we have some barrels of oil unless we used that up already?" She looked at Isaac, who shook his head. "Good, you're welcome to use that if you want to, Sainte, for the defenses," she said pointedly. Sainte took that as his cue to leave.

"All right, good place to start as any," he said as he stood up. He left the room but paused at the entrance and turned around. "One quick question. Are you really Aroc's father?"

"Ha, no, I'm not. Was it that easy to tell?" Isaac asked with a small smile.

"I had my suspicions," was all he said, and then he left.

"Do you think that wise, Isaac? Telling him all that?" Aroc asked accusingly, now that Sainte was out of earshot.

"What would you have told him?" Isaac did not wait for an answer. "If I didn't tell him the truth and he found out later that I, we, lied to him, there's no way he would finish what we need him to. This is better, trust me."

"Fine..." she said with a resigned sigh. "What will you do when we leave?"

"I see that you haven't changed your mind about us swapping roles?" he sighed heavily. "I suppose I shall go on to Munich, after all. Hopefully, I'll be able to persuade the Council that we have it under control. To hold off on the Severance. Right now, you're the only hope of salvaging everything we've worked for. You can't let us down."

"You know I can't promise anything, but I'll do what I can," Aroc told him with as much hope as she could muster.

"It wasn't supposed to be you doing this..." he said quietly, more to himself than her.

"Well, it is me. And so far, I'd say I've been doing pretty well." Her words bled with self-appreciation despite the dire circumstances they were talking about.

"Right, well, we don't really have anyone to compare you to, so I wouldn't be so smug about it," Isaac said, frustrated. Her face fell at his words, and he could not help but feel a pang of guilt in his chest that he hurt her.

"I'm sorry, it's been a stressful couple of days. I know you'll be able to pull this off. If you can't do it then I sure as hell wouldn't be able to."

She smiled slightly at his words. He was the only person who could bring her down and back up with only a few sentences. Isaac may not have been Aroc's biological father, but she had no problem acting as if he was.

"What's going to happen to the people of Elion?" Aroc asked.

Isaac took a deep breath and exhaled. "They're going to flee, die, or join the Malignin. Will you be able to leave them when the time comes?"

It was Aroc's turn to sigh. "It doesn't feel right. We were put here to help them in times of need, not leave them to fend for themselves. But, I will do what must be done," she said again.

"Good, now let's discuss what plans you hold for Sainte." Isaac made himself comfortable in the chair, leather creaked as he settled into it.

Aroc was not looking forward to this conversation, but it must be had. She nestled down into her chair. This was going to take a while.

▼▲▼

"We're being attacked! Wake up!" someone yelled. Iris sat up with a jolt, Ivan not far behind her. Two people wrestled around on the ground, but Iris could not tell who was who. Stifled grunts were coming from them, and blows were being traded. More men were advancing with weapons drawn. She was jerked up suddenly by Ivan. He thrust a bow and a quiver of arrows into her hands. Before he could say anything to her, he ducked away and began fighting. Others were already up with their weapons drawn and readying themselves for the intruders.

Iris stumbled around the battle, trying not to get stabbed by stray sword thrusts. Embers were scattered as someone kicked them, and flames flared to life, briefly illuminating the battlegrounds. In the moment of light, Iris found Tal. She kept her eyes locked on the figure and made her way to him just as he cut someone down.

He turned around quickly, weapon at the ready, face bloody, and heaving at the sound of her approach. She stared up at him in surprise, not sure what to say.

"Move!" he screamed at her. She ducked and ran behind him just as he swung his axe at someone who meant to attack her from behind. After killing him, Tal turned to her yet again. "Stay with me." Then he bellowed out, "Konnick, Munes, on me!"

As if on cue, their attackers ceased and backed off a few steps, unprepared for the strong resistance. Tal and Konnick stood side by side, along with Ivan and his men. Sweat dripped from their flaming skin, weapons brandished menacingly into the dark.

"Have I got yer attention yet?" A familiar voice drawled out. "Course I do. I coulda slit all yer throats while ya slept, but I didn't. Figured I'd kill ya all while ye were awake, give ya th' chance to fight back. Not that it'll do ye any good. Do ye want'a know why?" Nobody replied, but he answered himself. "Because o' Iris. I respect 'er, and so I thought to giv'er new friends an honorable death."

"Iris," Ivan began, "Leave. Someone will go with you. Everyone who stays will hold these bastards off."

Iris was appalled. "No, I'm not going. No one would go with me any-"

"I'll go with th' girl," Tal said. "Make sure she holds up her end o' our deal."

Miqel laughed from the shadows, still not visible to the companions. "So sweet. Run, Iris. Go on, like ye left me. I'll even let ya."

"You told me to run!" she screamed back desperately.

"Aye, I did. Don't make it right. Then ye left me again and kept leavin'. But ye know what? I won't leave ye like ya left me. Go on, run. I will follow," he said.

"I'm not leaving," she told Ivan.

"Tal, take her. See to it that you finish what we started," Ivan commanded.

"Aye. Konnick, don't let 'em kill more'n you," Tal said.

"No," Iris said. "No, I'm not going."

Without warning, Tal picked up Iris and threw her over his shoulder. He took off at a slow jog away from everyone.

"Go back!" she screamed and beat at his back, but if he felt it, he paid it no heed. "Go back!" As they got further away from their friends, the sounds of battle could be heard through the pines. It was not long before they heard the screams.

Iris did not know how far they traveled before everything was quiet once more, save for the pattering rain. Tal had since let her down to walk on her own, and they spoke not a word to each other. The rain dampened their already downtrodden spirits. The sodden carpet of pine needles hushed their footsteps. There was nothing to be heard over the rain. Nothing except the screams that echoed in her head.

TEN
-REUNION-

Sainte had been helping the people of Elion for a few hours. Oil was poured over many stakes and trenches. Designated people stood by, ready to light the oil at a moment's notice. He told the residents of Elion the basics of fighting Malignin, which boiled down to fighting them near light. All the torches that could be spared were set on the wall or just inside, waiting to be lit the next time they were attacked.

Sainte knew it would not stop the Malignin but it would slow them down for a short time. He walked around the working men and women, ensuring everyone knew their place in battle. He answered any and all questions they asked as best as he could. The defenses were slowly coming together, and Sainte began to have hope for these people, but he reminded himself that the hope was pointless. The people of Elion could not know that, though.

The women and children, young and old, were tasked with making arrows and spears out of extra wood. They were going to need a lot more before the next battle was over. The additional weapons in the armory were placed in barrels. The barrels were then placed in increments along the wall for anyone who needed them.

Sainte walked up and down the battlements, advising and lending assistance when he could. By now, everyone in Elion knew his name and willingly listened to what he had to offer. He was taken aback at how readily he was accepted. Some of the men were a little disgruntled at taking orders from a stranger, but they quickly realized that if they had any hope of surviving, they would have to listen to him.

Once satisfied with the defenses and he knew that what little was left could be done without him, Sainte walked off by himself. He wanted some time alone to sort his thoughts. He meandered aimlessly through Elion and eventually found himself in the slums. The buildings here were built from uncured wood and the streets were more mud than stone. It was eerily quiet since everyone was helping around the wall.

Sainte jumped as a rat suddenly scampered across the dark street, squeaking with every hop. He shook his head sheepishly at the rodent, which had his heart pounding. His nerves already stood on end, and the lack of torches did not help, but he found the lack of people somewhat relaxing. It was easier to think without so many distractions.

He knew that the people of Elion appreciated everything he did for them. But he also knew it would not be enough, no matter how well the defenses were. These people did not have any hope of defending their town. Their only hope now was for the defenses to last long enough for them to flee. The Malignin would break through, would kill them all if they stayed. Sainte saw their fury firsthand, and if the tunnel and all the Blades could not stop them, what hope could he have for Elion?

What bothered him most was what Isaac told him. How much of that could he believe? Were they really part of the White Wyverns? If they were, then why did they hide? Why not come out in the open? It would explain when he first saw Aroc when the Malignin was torn apart midair when it leaped at him if she was a White Wyvern. She did seem to know many strange things, and he healed much faster than he should have at her hands. He saw the extent of his wounds. No medicine he knew of could have saved him. The scars from his burns were already mostly faded, which should not have been possible.

If the White Wyverns were present in Crearia, why were they not stepping in and making their presence known to all? What was their goal?

Sainte was so focused on the questions running through his head he had not realized he neared the entrance to the town again. It was not the fact that he came full circle that snapped him out of his head, but the screams. He did not hear any sounds of battle, and now that he strained to listen it sounded like only one person screaming. He quickened his steps and the wailing got louder. He rounded a corner, and the gated entrance of the town was within sight. A group gathered there, forming a half circle around the closed gates.

As he approached the back of the crowd, he tried to look over their heads, but it was impossible to tell what anything was in the flickering torchlight and from this distance. He pushed through the crowd to get to the front, gently pushing men and women out of his way. When people noticed it was him, word spread that he arrived. The closer he got, the more horrified the people looked around him. Women were crying and covering their mouths. Men looked on in stunned silence.

Soon, he found himself at the front of the crowd and beheld an awful sight.

Two men held a woman back who looked to be about thirty years old. Tears streamed down her face, and her voice was hoarse because of the yelling and screaming. Many people had their eyes averted from the scene. Sainte looked from her to the center of attention.

A man laid face up on the ground, his stomach was torn open, and his intestines glistened in the torch light. Shadows flicked across his face, making it seem like he was twisting his expression even in death. Fresh blood still oozed out of him. Upon closer inspection Sainte could see that his skin was ripped, not cut. The man presumably scooped out his own guts.

His throat was torn to shreds, and bloody hands laid close by. To his horror, Sainte realized that he must have also torn out his own throat after ripping out his intestines. All of the man's wounds seemingly were self-inflicted, there were no incisions upon his body, and his own flesh was stuck under his fingernails.

His throat and belly were ripped, not sliced. It was clear his death was not a painless one. Why would he do this to himself?

A spear was shoved into the ground, butt end first, two feet from the body. Sainte's eyes followed the spear shaft up. There was something impaled on the spearhead. The firelight made it challenging to see. A lump of flesh, part of the dead man's body? He stepped forward to get a closer look in the dim light.

Blood slowly dripped down the shaft. A baby, not more than six months old, was impaled at the tip. Its head was tilted towards the sky, and its mouth was wide open as if crying to the heavens, but there would be no sound escaping from the small lifeless body anymore.

Sainte stepped backward hastily and stumbled on his feet, bumping into those closest to him. He meant to cover his mouth but was already doubled over dry heaving. He could not stand to look at the scene any longer. It was then he realized that the woman's cries were not incoherent shrieks. She said the same things over and over.

"My baby, he killed my baby." Her cries pierced his ears. He turned his back to the scene as people dragged the poor woman away from the scene. Her screams grew fainter as she was taken further away, but her sobbing echoed through the empty streets of Elion.

"Who was this man?" he asked a man who stood close to him.

"That was her husband. He did this. To the babe, to himself," an onlooker said.

"Why did no one stop him?" Sainte asked, not expecting an answer. "Get Isaac and Aroc." At the man's hesitation, Sainte yelled at him, "Now!"

Suddenly Sainte got a peculiar feeling in his gut. At first, he thought it was because of the wretched scene, but he noticed other people looked around strangely. He slowly turned to the men who guarded the gates.

"Open the gates," he told them. They looked at him and shifted their feet uncomfortably.

"Are you sure? I don't think that's the best idea," one of the men said.

"Open them. Something is stirring. You can feel it. I can feel it. I mean to find out why. We can't stay locked in here forever, anyway. Open the gates." The men did not move. Aroc and Isaac ran up beside Saint then.

"What are you doing? What's going on?" Aroc asked breathlessly as she looked upon what lay before her.

"Who did this?" Isaac asked as he looked at the baby.

"I don't know, not for sure, but I think our answers lie just beyond the gates. I can feel something..." he searched for the right words. "Something's not right," Sainte explained.

Isaac nodded solemnly. "She's here."

"Ellie?" Sainte asked.

Isaac did not reply to him. "Open the gates."

The guardsmen shared glances, then unlocked the entrance. As soon as the gates were fully opened, Sainte strode out with Aroc and Isaac closely in tow. He had no doubt who he was walking towards.

Sainte's smile grew on his face the closer he got to her. Aroc and Isaac, however, prepared for the worst. They knew that this would not turn out how Sainte intended.

▼▲▼

Tal and Iris walked quickly, having not stopped since they left their comrades. They were at least one hundred miles from Elion when they separated from the rest of the group. Now, according to Tal's map, they traveled twenty miles and still had most of the day in front of them. The mountains were starting to shrink into small hills, signifying their end. It would not be long before they were in the plains, and they would make great time due to the flat ground and sparse trees.

For the most part, they were silent, only offering quick snaps of 'hurry up' and 'did you hear that?' Tal finally broke the silence with an entire sentence.

"We'll sleep here fer the night. We made good time, and we've reached the outskirts of th' mountains. We keep this up we'll reach Elion soon." Iris actually agreed with him. She figured that even if she disagreed, she would not have been able to change his mind.

She took off her pack and unrolled the blanket that was inside it. She laid down on it with a sigh and closed her eyes, expecting Tal to do the same. Instead, she heard him drop his pack and begin rummaging around the bushes. Twigs snapped and branches cracked.

"What're you doing?" she called out to him.

"Gettin' wood fer a fire. It'd be nice if I had someone else who could help. Oh wait..." he said in an annoyed tone.

"Don't you think that's a bad idea? Then anyone following us would be able to spot us that much easier."

"Ha, ya still think they don't already know where we are? Ye're more of a fool than I took ya fer. They know we're here, whether we make a fire or not. I fer one would like to be comfortable when I sleep." Iris stood up, irritated at herself and Tal, but she started helping him. "Not to mention we had fires this whole way."

"I get it," she said through gritted teeth. Eventually, they gathered enough twigs and wood to last about two hours. Tal broke out his flint and striker and started the fire. In a few minutes, they had a nice blaze blanketing them in comfortable heat. Iris could not deny that this was a good idea, but something Tal said bothered her.

"You know how you said they already know where we are?"

"Who? Oh yes. Aye, I said that. So?"

"If they truly know where we are, why haven't we been attacked yet? There are only two of us now, after all. What're they waiting for?"

Tal poked at the fire with a stick, sending up a shower of sparks. "I dunno. Maybe they enjoy watchin' us as our morale drops, or maybe they're waiting fer a certain moment. Maybe they want to see us reach Elion, see the hope in our eyes as we see the town, then take it all away by killing us, all within sight of it." He shrugged his large shoulders. "All just me guessin' though."

Iris struggled to bring this next topic up, but she could not leave it be. "Are we just going to forget about everyone we left? You haven't spoken about them once."

"Neither have ya," he said pointedly. "I'm not about forgettin' them. Even if Konnick was th'only one who was a Shinta, I liked them all well 'nough."

"Do you... Do you think any of them survived?"

"Prob'ly not. If any're still alive, they prob'ly are wishin' they were dead," Tal said.

"How can you say that so easily?" she questioned.

"It's the truth. Ye should be no stranger to dealin' with death. Yer a Blade, Blades die nightly, from what I 'ear."

"This is different," was all she could think to say.

"Why? Cause ye liked Ivan?"

"What? No," she scoffed.

"Aye, ya did. He liked ya too. A man don't invite a woman to sleep with'im if he ain't got no sort o' feelings for her."

Iris teared up at his words. She did indeed like Ivan. He treated her kindly, respected her, and stood up for her. And now he was dead. She wiped her face on her sleeve.

"Let it out now, girl. We won't be doin' this when we wake. I won't talk about it again," he said.

"How can you be so heartless?" Iris asked.

"What good is cryin' gonna do? Nothing. They're probably dead, and if they're not it's outta our hands now. Can't change the past, and it gets us nowhere dwellin' on it, neither. We needa move on. There'll be time to grieve when this's over or we're dead," he told her, getting frustrated with dealing with a crying girl.

Iris wiped her face again and regained her composure after some sniffles. "Of course, you're right..." She did not want to stop talking yet. It helped to calm her nerves, so she thought of another question. "What's it like? Where you're from?" Iris asked curiously.

"What do ya mean?" he asked gruffly.

"Well, I've heard stories about Shintas and wondered if they were true. Such as, if a Shinta draws their weapon it has to taste blood. If it doesn't, they have to cut one of their own fingers off using the weapon before they can sheath it." She thought she saw the side of Tal's mouth twitch into a smile, but it was gone almost as soon as she noticed it.

"Whoever told ya that must not've been a very wise person. Though, the fact that our weapons must draw blood when drawn ain't wrong. Don't start off by cuttin' off a finger. Not right away a'least. If it comes to the time when we must sheath our weapons and they've not drawn blood, we must cut the tip of one o' our fingers, a different finger fer every time it happens. If all o' yer fingers have a scar, then and only then ya must cut one of yer fingers off.

"Each scar brings more dishonor to th' individual, making it harder fer them to find a partner or even to get a job of any sort. The more scars, the less respected ya are as a person, as a Shinta, overall. If it comes to the point where ya have to lose a finger, ya are stripped of yer weapons, never allowed to hold one again, and consigned to do women's work. Planting, gardening, cleaning, and such."

"Why do that? What's the point? That's just self-harm, on a small scale, but still," Iris asked, surprised at the truth at which Tal was talking to her.

"Think 'bout it. A weapon, sword, axe, battle hammer were all made fer one thing. To be used to fight, to kill. If a Shinta draws their weapon they're expected to use it. Why else would anyone get their weapon out?" he asked her.

"I could think of a few reasons."

"Such as?"

"Clean it, sharpen it, general maintenance," she said as if he was crazy for not thinking about it.

"Of course, that's all done either immediately before or after the weapon is used." He took a deep breath. "Ya know, this is actually a relatively new thing fer us. Started when my father's father was around," Tal said as if she should have known this already.

"Why did it come about, then?" she asked.

"We Shinta are not exactly a peaceful people," he informed her as if it would come as a surprise. "We fight each other over lots o' things. It was much the same back in my grandfather's day, only they could use weapons. We hurt each other, killed each other over pointless quarrels. Our own people, we almost destroyed ourselves. Finally, th' Elders decided that enough was enough and they came up with this rule, this law. Course, it didn't stop fights, but it made those who fought think twice 'bout gettin' weapons involved.

"Permanent injuries and deaths decreased rapidly. We resorted to fist fights 'stead of using metal. Killin' a man with a weapon can happen fast. Ya almost don't have to think 'bout it. Lemme tell ya what, though, killin' a man with yer fists takes a lot o' thought. It was a good thing to pass, we started to grow again."

"Thanks for that. Telling me a little about your history," Iris said sincerely.

"Don't mention it. Maybe ya can tell others and get people's facts right about Shinta fer once."

"Do you have any scars?" she asked.

"Course."

She smiled and let out a small laugh. "I mean on your fingertips. Have you ever had to cut yourself?"

He held up his large, dirty hands toward her and wiggled his fingers. "Does it look like I 'ave any scars?" She looked at his fingers in the firelight.

"No, none that I see, at least. What if you have to cut your fingertip, but it leaves no scar after it's healed?"

"Then yer honor's safe."

"Have you ever had to cut one of your fingers?" she asked again.

"Did ya see any scars?" he retorted.

"No, but maybe the cut left no scar."

"If there's no scar, then ye've never cut yer finger. That simple," he stated bluntly. It seemed as if that would be the last of the conversation. Tal's eyes closed. He leaned slightly back but slowly opened his eyes again. "So I've told ya about me. Tell me 'bout ya."

Iris looked at him in surprise. His question caught her off guard. "Err, what do you want to know?"

"What made ya join the Blades o' the Night?"

"Well..." she paused, thinking about her answer. "My father wanted a son." She decided she would tell the truth. "But instead, I was born. He wanted a son, so he treated me like a son. He could only do that for so long, of course, because I was merely a girl. I could never live up to his standards.

"I wanted him to like me, to love me, but instead I just received abuse from him. I did the only thing that I thought might win his respect. I joined the Blades of the Night. That wasn't good enough, however. Of course, it was too late for me to get out, so I gave up trying to impress him. My mother and he, they had no more children. He used to take his anger out on me by verbally beating me, but when I left he took it out on my mother instead.

"Occasionally, he hit me, but for whatever reason, I just took it. He never hit me in the face, though, not until the last day I saw him." Her voice was overcome with anger now. "He backhanded me across the face after a night of me killing those damned Malignin. I wanted to hit back, but I knew that if I started, I wouldn't stop until he was dead. My mother didn't say anything to stop him.

"I offered to take her away, but she wouldn't leave. I did. Haven't seen him since. My mother's dead now, I found her body in my town, and my father was nowhere to be seen. I don't know if he's dead or alive. At this point, I don't even care. But if he is still alive, and I ever find him, I will kill him."

Tal nodded in understanding. "Understand that. I'd kill him too if I were ya." She did not say anything. "Well, I think it's time to get some sleep. Ya probably should too."

"Yeah, I think I will." They both laid down on opposite sides of the fire and closed their eyes. Both their minds were racing, but they were thinking about vastly different topics.

▼▲▼

"Sainte." It was a whisper carried on the wind. His name danced around his ears sent by a familiar voice. He could not see her shadow-covered face yet, but he saw her dark silhouette in front of the pale forest behind her.

He stumbled to a stop a few paces away and looked at her face. She took a step forward and slightly lifted her chin, revealing her familiar features.

"Ellie," he said as he breathed heavily, "it is you." He gazed at her face and saw the accustomed smile lines on her face. Her eyes looked at him expectantly. Her hair was pulled back over both shoulders. But there was something different about her.

Her smile lines were not as defined. Her eyes did not show as much life. The joy that usually glimmered in them was no longer there. Her hair no longer had the innocent curls but instead laid straight down her back. This was Ellie, but she was definitely not the same girl Sainte knew.

Her face broke into a smile, but Sainte could tell it was not sincere. "Yes, I found you. Come with me. Let's go back home." She held her arms out to him and waited for an embrace. Her words promised to bring comfort to him.

He almost walked to her, but he heard Isaac and Aroc run up behind him and he turned around and looked at them. They looked back with caution clearly etched across their faces.

"What about them?" Sainte asked Ellie. "What will happen to them if I leave? What will happen to Elion?"

"What must happen. They will join the Malignin and me... or die," she said the words as if they saddened her, but her eyes smiled. Her gaze flickered beyond Sainte to look at Aroc and Isaac.

Sainte looked at her in disbelief, unable to believe those words that came from Ellie's mouth. "You're with the Malignin?

Are you all right? Did they hurt you?" he asked, refusing to believe she stayed with them of her own volition. She shook her head slowly.

"No, they would never hurt me. The Malignin saved me. They showed me everything I had been missing. They took the shroud that covered my eyes and tossed it aside." She saw the hesitation on his face. "Sainte, don't worry. I know you lied to me because you thought it would save me... I forgive you, be with me again. I long for your touch. Don't you still love me?" Her voice begged him to see her way, and her words insisted he question nothing she said.

"Sainte, stop talking to her. Get behind me," Isaac said sternly, voice cutting through the thick air. He stepped forward and put a hand on Sainte's shoulder.

"Who are you going to listen to, Sainte?" Ellie asked. Her voice broke mid-sentence and her eyes began to water. "What happened to you? You're supposed to protect me, not leave me. Not again..."

"Sainte..." Aroc said cautiously.

He looked back at Isaac and Aroc. "I can't leave her again. I have to protect her." He shrugged away Isaac's hand and turned to Ellie. "I can't leave you, but I can't leave them either. Come with me. You can't trust the Malignin. I know you think you can, but you don't know everything. We'll go back to Guardstin and figure it out from there."

"You're right. I don't know everything. But I do know more than you. I'm not going with you now that I've seen all this. You cannot expect me to go back into that mountain, that prison."

Her lips curled in anger, but she quickly calmed herself. "Come with me and I'll show you the truth."

Sainte met Ellie's gaze and looked into her eyes, searching for his answers. "I'm sorry," he said over his shoulder, "but if I can go with her, I'll help her. I'll bring her back to Guardstin eventually. I can't just leave her on her own." He took a step towards Ellie. Before his foot hit the ground, he was yanked back by his collar and thrown to the ground. He looked up from his back and saw Isaac standing over him. He almost stood up in a fury of anger to push Isaac back, but he stopped cold when he caught a glimpse of Ellie's face.

It was contorted in anger, ugly with rage. He could not even recognize her.

"Aroc, pick him up and return to Elion," Isaac commanded.

"I can't just leave..." she started to say.

"Now!" he roared at her, leaving no room for argument. She bent down and quickly picked Sainte up quite easily. Sainte struggled to get his feet under him as Aroc pushed him back toward Elion. He looked back once towards Ellie. Towards the girl he was supposed to save. He was met with her shrieks.

"Yes, flee back to the people of Elion. If you won't live by my side, you'll die by theirs!" Those were the last words he heard from her.

"Cease your tongue, you witch," Isaac spouted at her, which caused her to shut her mouth abruptly. "I have heard enough of your slanderous words. Leave this place."

Her eyes followed Sainte and Aroc before snapping to Isaac. "You cannot command me. This body may look frail, but it has become anything but. Pushing poor, poor Ellie away into the deep recesses of her mind couldn't have been easier. I know what you are, Isaac, and who you belong to. You're old. You're weak. You're all weak. And I know it's already too late for you to stop me. Go back to your precious town. Try to save what you can." She turned her back on him and started to walk away.

Isaac was shaken, but he pushed through it. "You can't command me, either." He held his hands out in front of him and interlocked his fingers. A small ball of light streaked at Ellie's back but was swept harmlessly away before it hit her. She turned around slowly.

"You thought to kill me that easily?" she asked with a sneer. "You Wyrms are all the same, arrogant. You underestimated me or overestimated yourself. Either way, it doesn't matter. You are going to suffer. When I'm finished with you, Aroc will be next. You couldn't get rid of me before. What hope do you have now?"

▼▲▼

Iris woke up to Tal nudging her with the toe of his boot. For a split second, she did not know where she was. Dreams and reality blended until they were seamless, but everything rushed back at once as she sat up. Dreams faded away as reality took its rightful place. She stretched her neck, rolling it around her shoulders. The ground was not exactly the best bed to sleep on. She noticed Tal already packed up his gear.

The cloud cover lessened from a dark, ominous black to a lighter gray which allowed muffled sunlight through. It made everything dull in color. She could see now that the forest thinned out to only shorter pine trees and ferns. Instead of towering mountains surrounding them, there were smaller foothills, but the ground was still rocky. The fire was nothing but embers now, smoldering in the darkness. Tal nudged her again with his foot a little more roughly.

"Come on, get up. I know ye're a girl, but ya should be more used to this than any others. Or was I wrong in assuming that ya actually had to prove yerself to be accepted into th' Blades o' the Night? When we first set off, just ya and me, ya said that ya'd have no problems keepin' up. If ye're like this every time we wake up, it's gonna be a problem," Tal said condescendingly.

Iris immediately snapped to the defensive. "Here I thought we were beginning to get along. I guess not so much."

"Not if ya continue to take yer time," he growled back, on the verge of exploding.

"Do you not want any time to yourself? To think about your friends that you left behind? Do you care so little for them?"

"Ya bring up the past again. Pointless to dwell on it. Does no good to think about our past when our future's looking more and more shite with each moment that passes. We needa move," he said as he kicked out the embers, crushing them underfoot.

She fumed at his words and stood up in a flurry. She quickly rolled up her blanket and shoved it into her pack. She threw her bow and arrows across her back, then shouldered the pack. She turned and faced Tal.

"There, I'm ready. Happy?" she asked.

"No," he grunted, "but it's a start. It'll take more'n that to make me happy. Maybe if ya moved that fast all the time."

Iris looked down as she felt her face flush with embarrassment. She knew that Tal was right to hurry her up, but she did not want to give him the satisfaction of admitting it. She wanted to rest.

"Let's go," he said as he stomped through the brush. Iris followed a short distance behind.

"So, I know we are going to Elion, but which route are we taking?" she asked him.

"The fastest route," he stated.

"Which is...?"

"Straight."

"That's not necessarily always true. There could be obstacles in our way."

"Not through the plains. Have ya never been through them?" he asked her.

"No, not the northern plains, at least. I've traveled the southern plains between Guardstin and the Broken Crags many times. Maybe they're different."

"Doubt it... What have ya heard about 'em? Anything?"

"No, nothing particularly strange, at least. All I know is that there are no streams or lakes between here and Whitweir Forest, but I don't think that should be an issue because of all the rain we've had," she said.

Tal grunted and continued to walk. As the hours passed, the trees around them began to thin out more, and the giant hills turned into rolling slopes. As they cleared the mountains, light rain fell straight down without any wind.

"Well, now that we're out in the open, we have to make sure that we stay heading east. It'll be easy fer us to walk in circles without realizing since we have nothing to base our direction on. We just need'a make it to Whitweir Forest, find th' river that runs through it, and continue east towards th' open field. Shouldn't be too hard," he explained to Iris.

"Shouldn't be, but lately things haven't necessarily been easy." Nothing else was said for some time. Each of them were lost in their own thoughts.

Iris was caught up thinking about Sainte and Miqel. Drinking together after a night's work. The laughs they shared, the stories they told. She wanted that again. She *would* have that again. This endless night would not last forever. She would see to it. Her thoughts continued to meander among times spent with her friends, but for the first time in a long time, her thoughts never wandered to her father.

Nonetheless, she tried to push those thoughts out of her head. Tal was right. Thinking about the past did no good. It did nothing but make her miss something that was gone. Instead, she focused on the rain, steadily pattering against the ground. She focused on the sucking sound as they pulled their feet from the mud when they walked. She focused on breathing and listened to her heartbeat. Without even noticing it, her aches and strains seemed to fade away. Each footstep seemed lighter than the last.

Iris and Tal walked for a while without speaking when he finally stopped. "Let's sleep here. I'm getting tired, plus I have to shit. I'd say get a fire going, but..." he looked around at the soaked plains, "there's really not much to light anymore. I'll be back."

Iri nodded. She watched as he walked away and the darkness slowly enveloped him from view. She looked behind them, where the mountains should be, but she could not see them anymore. Gray all around. A thin fog lowered itself upon the plains, blocking the mountains from view. It was disorienting.

She dropped her pack and dug out her blanket from under the dried bread they had left over. She laid it out, sat down, and pulled her boots off to stretch her feet. She wiggled her toes, relieved that she could finally stretch them out. Her boots were full of liquid. She could not tell whether it was sweat, water, or blood but dumped it out all the same. Finally, she laid down.

She was beginning to relax when she heard someone walking, but not from the direction that Tal went. She sat up and glanced around, but there was nothing. She heard the steps again. Someone, or something, was pacing out there.

"Tal?" she called out nervously.

"What do ya want? I'm not done yet," he answered back, annoyed, but it was not from in front of her.

"Hurry, please," she called back, quieter.

"What? Ye're too quiet. I can't hear ya. Ye'll have to speak up, girl," he called back, more than a little frustrated at being interrupted.

Before she could reply, someone from beyond her said, "Shhh, don't worry. I'm not going to hurt you or your friend. Don't scream, please." The voice sounded kind and somewhat familiar.

Against her better judgment, she called out, "Who are you? What do you want?" Maybe someone needed help. She grabbed her bow and nocked an arrow, just in case.

"Don't shoot me. I'm unarmed and quite alone at the moment," the voice said as it got closer. Iris saw a shape form and get clearer as the man walked toward her. He held his arms out to his sides to show he held no weapon. As the man got closer, his features became recognizable. Iris' hands began to shake.

"Father?" she asked in an incredulous whisper.

"Aye... Before you say anything let me explain myself, please. And don't worry, I wasn't told to come here by anyone, and I told no one where I was going. I came here to talk to you, only you," he said as he glanced in the direction of Tal.

"What do you have to say to me? That you wish I was dead? Sorry to disappoint you again." Her words dripped with anger.

He shook his head. "No, quite the opposite, actually. Iris, I'm sorry. I hate myself for how I treated you and your mother. Neither of you deserved that. Come with me, and I'll try to make things right by you. As much as I can at least. That's what your mother would want." He looked at the ground as he wrung his hands together.

"You've never disappointed me. You always made me proud. I was disappointed with myself and I took it out on the wrong people. I let you down... let me try to fix that." A single tear fell from his eye.

She stared at him momentarily, unable to believe what she heard. Her mind scrambled for the appropriate response. She wanted to think that he was being honest with her, but she could not forget the torment she endured from his drunken ways. She knew that there was something off about this entire encounter.

"No, father." She spit out the word like a curse. "It's too late to be sorry. I have one question for you before I kill you..." She raised her bow and pulled back the string until it touched her cheek. She could feel her hands shake but tried to fight it off. "How did you find me?"

He faltered backward and slowly raised his hands. "Wh- what? What are you doing, Iris? Put that down. I just... I just followed your trail."

"You couldn't track down a rabbit if you held it on a leash. I've waited a long time to do this." Iris took a deep breath to try to calm her shakes down, but they persisted. She released the arrow only to watch it fly away from where she aimed. It thudded in his left forearm, and he looked at it with his mouth agape in surprise. He clutched the wound with his other hand, looked at her with astonishment scrawled across his face, and turned around and fled. He was gone before she could even try to nock another arrow.

Her hands convulsed so severely that her bow shook from her grasp. She laid down on her back and tried to slow her breathing and pounding heart. She covered her face with her hands and wept.

Tal walked back shortly after Iris' father fled. She told him everything that happened, everything that was said between her and her father. Tal wanted to chase the man down immediately, but Iris shook her head.

"No, there's no use. We wouldn't be able to find him, and we'd probably get thrown off course, lose our sense of direction. He's too far gone by now."

Tal waved his hand at her as if that dismissed what she said. "Bah, we could catch him easily. We'd follow his footprints. He's bound to've left 'em behind in this muck," he said, looking at the ground in disgust. "Where was he?"

Iris pointed to where she last saw him. Tal walked over and looked at the ground. She could tell by his face that he was confused.

"What? What is it?"

"Well, nothing... It's nothing. There're no footprints here. Are ya sure he was over here?" he asked as he walked around their small camp and looked for any telltale signs that someone else had been there, but he saw nothing.

"Pretty sure," she said, now doubtful of herself. Tal looked at her with a sadness she did not expect him to show. It was sorrow for her. "Don't worry about it. He's probably with the other traitors laughing at how much he messed with me. Let's rest and then continue to Elion." Iris did not want to talk about her dad anymore.

Tal let out a resounding sigh. "A'right. Fine with me." He unrolled his blanket and laid down as well. "I guess I'll be fine without a fire tonight."

They both looked around at their bleak surroundings. They were surrounded by tall grass, weeds, and a few flowers. The plants around them were beginning to wilt. They were getting too much water and not enough sunlight. Nothing substantial to burn.

Iris was deep in thought when Tal said something, but she did not catch it.

"Huh? What'd you say?" she asked.

"I said, ya look troubled 'bout something. Care to share?"

"Talking about fire got me thinking about the plants. They're wilting, and soon they'll all be dead. Then the animals, and then us. If the Malignin don't kill us first, then starvation will. It seems like we'll die no matter what unless the sun begins to shine again and soon. It seems so hopeless."

Tal shrugged. "Well, we're doing what we can. Ya talked as if ya and yer friends were directly involved with this before. If we can find yer friends and the girl that was taken..."

"Ellie," she filled in.

"... then everything will go back in the right order," he continued as if she had not interrupted. "If we fail, then we fail. Least we tried."

"If we fail, we die."

"Aye, goes without sayin'. But would ya rather die sitting around just waitin' for it? Or would ya rather be out here, trying to make a difference? Doing something about the situation."

Iris sat and thought about what he said, everything she had done, everything she wished she could have done, and everything that still needed to be done and, with a defeated shrug, just said, "I'm not so sure anymore."

▼▲▼

Aroc and Sainte sprinted across the clearing towards Elion, quickly getting out of earshot of Isaac and Ellie. One small flash of light flared up behind them, but neither Sainte nor Aroc dared look back. As they neared the town they saw faces peeking over the edge of the battlements.

"Open the gates!" Aroc yelled at them. The heavy wooden doors groaned and creaked as they were pulled open, the only sounds heard in the plains around Elion. They both rushed in, chests heaving and were immediately surrounded by people with many outspoken questions.

"We are being attacked. Prepare yourselves." There was silence, then the resounding thud as the doors closed behind them. Aroc looked at the people as they stood around, shifting foot from foot. Families and friends shared grave looks. No one dared stir a muscle.

"Move!" Aroc shouted. Almost at once, the group flinched as a whole and then began to go about their duties driven by fear. The gruesome scene here before Sainte, Aroc, and Isaac ran out was cleaned up, much to their relief.

Sainte was doubled over, hands on his knees, trying to catch his breath and come to terms with what happened. Aroc walked over to his side. He raised a hand to say he was ok, but she pushed it aside and violently kneed him in the face. When he looked up, mouth bleeding, she gripped his chin with one hand and forced him to look her in the eyes.

"If you ever pull a stupid stunt like that again, I will kill you. You are useful to us but don't think you're not replaceable. Never speak to Ellie again. Your mind is weak, you are weak, and you will listen to her. Now do what you were trained to do and kill Malignin," she said to him. She let go of his face with a rough push and stalked away.

He stood up, wiped his nose, and looked at everyone as they prepared themselves, thankful they were too busy to notice what transpired. Sainte meant to talk to Aroc, but she disappeared around a corner, clearly upset. His nose bled for another minute, then stopped. Sainte felt foolish for what transpired out there but was also mad that Aroc would jump to hitting him before talking about it.

The best thing to do would be to take his mind off it, so he climbed up a ladder onto the wall and looked out to the field. A vast writhing mass of Malignin covered the plains. They all stopped fifty feet from Elion's walls, where the trenches were, but it did not look like they would wait there long.

He looked around for Isaac, but he did not see him anywhere. Where did he go? What was he doing? He looked at the frightened people manning the walls. What did Aroc expect him to do against this? He could not help anyone until the Malignin decided it was time to fight. He was brought out of his disquieting thoughts by people crying out that something was happening.

He looked back out to the Malignin, and through the fog and darkness, he could tell they parted ranks. Ellie walked towards Elion alone but stopped as she reached the front ranks of Malignin. Her head moved left to right as she studied the wall and all the defenses that had been constructed. Her voice, amplified by magic, echoed through the city's alleys when she spoke. She made sure everyone would hear what she had to say.

"My purpose is not to kill or harm anyone, although you may find that hard to believe." Her voice pierced everyone to the core and sent chills through their bodies. "Right now, all I want you to do is listen to what I have to say. I know what you're all thinking. That I'm a monster, no better than these dear creatures that line the outside of your walls. But you're mistaken. We are not monsters. The monsters are you, stuck inside your little towns.

"You have refused to see how beneficial it is to side with the Malignin for too long. You refused even to give them a chance in your world. You immediately fought against them, pushed them away. You gave them no choice but to retaliate, violently. They did not want that. They didn't want it to come to this." She paused dramatically.

"All they ever wanted was to live side by side with you, with humans." People along the wall shifted uncomfortably at her words. "It is an unusual notion that I speak of, and it should make you uncomfortable. But it is a good thing. It would be a mutually beneficial relationship. Think of the possibilities, everything that could be achieved. Man and beast, together as one. Nothing could stop the successes that would undoubtedly come. If you want to join us, leave Elion. You will not be harmed. I am proof of that. I was the Barrier, the very girl Sainte was supposed to protect. The Malignin took me away, but I was not afraid. They cared for me and showed me the truth of the world.

"But if you do not accept this offer, if you fight, then you will die," Ellie stated sadly. "There can be no other way. In order for peace to exist, there cannot be any opposition to it. I speak the truth. Come out and join us. I do not enjoy death, but it will continue if it must."

While all eyes were on Ellie, the woman whose baby was killed made her way out to the courtyard. No one noticed her, but when she started to shriek back at Ellie, all heads turned to her. Her face was red and puffy from crying.

"What about my baby?" she cried in a grief-stricken voice. "He did nothing to you. He was innocent," she cried and fell to her knees. Ellie cocked her head to hear the woman. After a moment, she replied.

"You're right. Your child was guilty of no wrong, and I am saddened at his loss. However, his father, your husband, did not share that same thread of innocence. My Malignin caught him as he tried to sneak away. He was caught trying to leave you and your child to what he thought would be your deaths. When he was brought to me, I decided it would be best to show him the error of his ways.

"I let him seek out his own punishment. He made a choice. He sought a punishment that was equal to his crimes. In a way, he saved your child. By killing his son while he was still an innocent infant, he guaranteed his safe passage into the afterlife. In the end, he died a man who had the knowledge of right and wrong. In his final moments he knew more than any of you will probably know. I am truly sorry, but oft times the innocent must pay for the sins of the guilty."

At this point, three men went out to help the woman in mourning. They escorted her back to her home with her sobbing in their arms. Ellie continued to speak as if there was no interruption.

"Beginning now, you will have one hour to come out and join us. Anyone remaining in the town will be killed," she paused as she thought about something else, then said, "I have Isaac. He is alive. If he surrenders himself and the town to me, you won't be required to come out and join me, and no one else will be killed. But that choice lies solely in him. I truly hope the best for each and every one of you.

"I'll return in an hour." She walked away back towards the rear rank of Malignin. They closed in as she left them.

There were already people who rushed around Elion, trying to decide what would be best for them and theirs. Sainte looked down at the courtyard from atop the wall and saw Aroc stride to the center of it, a single point of structure amid a sea of chaos. She faced the center of the town and began to talk. Her voice moved throughout the city like a breeze. Everyone could hear it, much like Ellie's, but it was calming rather than worrying.

"Do what you think is best for you and your family. It is not up to me to decide. If you wish to leave, do so knowing that no one will try to stop you, but if you do, I pity you. If you stay, I will fight beside you and kill all who would have us dead. That woman spoke nothing but lies. The Malignin only want control. She only wants power. I will not let them take this city."

Sainte climbed down the wall and walked toward Aroc. When she was finished speaking, he could already tell that she had calmed the nerves of most of the citizens. They moved with a purpose again.

"What will you do about Isaac?" he asked her.

"Nothing... he can handle himself. She knows who and what we are, so she's trying to frighten me into making a rash decision, but it won't work. Isaac is safe, or at least he will be. He always is." Her eyes shifted to look past Sainte. He turned around to see what she was looking at.

There was a family of five who were leaving Elion. Their heads were down, and they were walking quickly—the first people to go. Sainte could not blame them. Leaving would have sounded better if he knew any less than he did. He could hear other people arguing about whether they should stay or go. They did not know what to do.

But Sainte did.

Ellie was just outside of town, the only reason he was in that situation. She was so close, but in the same aspect, she had never been more distant from him. She was with the Malignin, defended them even. For the better part of four years, he was trained to hate those creatures, to kill them.

No matter how badly he wanted Ellie back, he was not about to work alongside Malignin. He would get her back, and the Malignin would not be coming with her. He was ashamed of himself because of how easily Ellie persuaded him earlier.

With sudden inspiration, he began to bark orders at everyone running around. People looked to see who was making such a loud ruckus and stopped to listen when they saw it was Sainte. A few people began to do what he instructed, and it slowly spread through the people remaining in Elion.

Aroc looked at him from a distance and marveled at the command he demanded. Perhaps he would not let her down. Maybe they still had a chance.

Sainte cleared his mind like he used to when he fought in the tunnel. It was almost time to kill some Malignin.

ELEVEN
-ELION-

Ellie walked around Isaac slowly, enjoying the sight of him on his knees. His nose was broken and split open, eyes were bruised and red, blood ran down his face, and his arms were broken in multiple places twisting in ways that shouldn't be possible. Malignin surrounded him, waiting for Ellie's command to rip and tear his flesh.

"So, do you think you're going to give your little town hope, or are you going to destroy it?" she asked with a smile. "If you truly care for these people, care if they live or die, then you will do this one simple thing I ask of you. You'll do it for them. They won't know what happened to you but will know that you saved them. We will leave and I'll let them know you single-handedly drove me away. All you have to do is accept my offer."

"Which is?" he asked through gritted, broken teeth.

"Tell me what the White Wyverns plan to do. Join me and advise me on what they're likely to do next. If you do this, I will tell some of my human followers to go to Elion. They will say we fought, and you drove me away while saving them, but you were mortally wounded. Everyone in Elion will believe you're a hero, and the White Wyverns will believe you're dead. You wouldn't have to worry about them. Do this, and I will spare Elion. Sainte will move on, I'm sure, and I'll follow, but Elion will be safe." Her words rang true within Isaac. He knew she was not lying.

But what worried Isaac the most was not whether or not the people of Elion would survive, but what would change about their existence. If he agreed with Ellie's terms, what kind of life would they have? They would die no matter what choice he made. Either they would physically die, or their spirits would. Would it be better to live with a broken spirit or die while it was still intact?

Isaac berated himself for even considering the insane offer. He began to laugh, a wheezing, rattling sound.

"What are you laughing at?" she sneered.

"You don't know these people. Even if I accepted your incredulous offer, they would still fight you. They might even try to follow you and your 'servants' if you left. Nothing you do to me will hamper their spirits. I know you will overwhelm Elion, utterly destroy every living soul you can get your wretched hands on, but they will fight you every step of the way. And there's nothing you could say that would make me betray my brethren.

So no, I do not accept your petty offer." He tried to stand back up and push himself up from his knees, but he did not have the strength.

"I hope you're proud of yourself," Ellie said.

"Before you kill me," he paused as he spat a mouthful of blood. Ellie waited and looked at him in disgust. "Tell me, who are you? I know you're... you're not Ellie... not anymore."

"You don't already know?" she pouted. "The Wyverns aren't what they once were, are they? I'll give you a hint: I'm a lot older than you think."

She observed his face as he struggled to figure out who she was. "Still nothing? One more..."

She stepped closer.

"I was once a King." She laughed as horrible realization dawned on Isaac's face. "There it is," she whispered.

"How?" he muttered.

Ellie stepped back, allowing the Malignin to do what they did best. She shook her head. "No more questions."

▼▲▼

Sainte watched as some people fled but was relieved it wasn't more. He could count the people that left on his fingers. It hardly mattered, though, because all that mattered to him was everyone who chose to stay. All the able-bodied men were the first line of defense. They were the ones on top of the wall surrounding Elion. They were the ones who were most ready to face death in battle.

The second line of defense were the women who volunteered for it. They were just inside the town, waiting behind the wall in case any Malignin found their way through.

With the women were all the boys aged from thirteen to seventeen. They were all armed with whatever the armory had left. Sainte did not like putting children and women so close to the battle, but they had little choice. Without them, the town would fall that much easier.

Their time was about up, and after making sure the townsfolk knew what was expected of them, he wanted to talk to Aroc to find out where she would be for the battle, but she was nowhere to be found. He poked around the Keep, but she was not inside. He thought about where he could look for her next when he found himself getting close to the gates of Elion. Luckily for him, she also had it in mind to wait there.

"Hey, Aroc," Sainte said as he approached her. "How're you doing?" he asked sincerely. Those were the first words he spoke to her since she kneed him in the face, his sore nose a reminder of her vengeance. She said nothing but instead focused her gaze on someone that set up wooden spikes in the distance. Sainte hesitated to say more but knew he had to try to fix whatever was between them.

"I'm sorry about out there," he motioned towards the gate, "I don't know what happened. It wasn't what I wanted."

"It's fine," she said dismissively. "It's just... You still love her, and she knows it. She's going to use that against you because she knows she can. You can't talk to her, not without my permission, at least. You cannot let that happen again," Aroc said, ending the subject.

Sainte stood awkwardly close by because he thought she had more to say. He fidgeted around and watched the sentries atop the wall do the same as they tried to keep a watchful eye.

"What do you think happened to Isaac?" he asked.

"I don't know."

"Not even a guess?"

"No." Her answer was the end of that.

Sainte did not think pressing the issue was a good idea, so he kept his mouth shut. As he stood by her side at a loss for words, his eye caught some commotion. Someone above was waving their arms frantically.

"Movement, we have movement!" the man shouted. Sainte ran to a ladder and quickly clambered up.

"What is it? What do you see?" he asked, nervous yet excited all at once.

"I don't... I don't know. It stopped, but it looks like a Malignin. I mean, that's what we've been staring at for the past hour, but other Malignin moved out of its way. It stopped as soon as I started calling out." Sainte and the man leaned forward, trying to get a better look.

"By the Wyverns... it's carrying something... a body," he said slowly. Then he and Sainte both stepped back in surprise. "It's throwing it. Take cover!" the man screamed.

Both he and Sainte ducked under the parapet on the wall. The object soared over the heads of the guards atop it. There was a loud squelch as it thumped down into the courtyard, sounding like a sack of raw meat getting hit by a giant hammer.

As everyone scattered from it, Aroc walked towards the bloody pulp of an object. No one else dared get more than ten feet from the thing. Sainte had a sick feeling that he knew what, or rather who, it was. There were cries of dismay, women and children fled the scene.

Sainte could see the horror on Aroc's face even from atop the wall. His suspicions were confirmed. He scrambled down the ladder and ran to her side. As he got near her, he heard her choke back a sob, and tears streamed down her cheeks. She brushed by him and ran to Isaac.

Aroc fell to her knees beside the corpse and cradled him in her arms. His face was barely recognizable, riddled with gouges. His arms and legs were broken in many places. His mouth hung slack-jawed, lifeless, and his head lolled loosely from side to side with a broken neck. Claw marks covered his body, and blood oozed from fresh wounds, covering Aroc's arms and pooling around her. Isaac's glazed eyes stared at everything, yet would never see anything again.

Aroc cried over his corpse. Sainte stood slightly behind her, clueless as to what to do next. He heard her speaking, but he did not know what she said. She was talking to the corpse. Isaac was dead, Aroc was distraught, and Sainte had no idea what would happen now. Until a voice started to speak, a voice that was heard throughout Elion, a voice that sent shivers through the body.

"Do you see this? This is the last example I set for all of you. You will all end like Isaac. I hope you all clearly see the choice you made for yourselves. I gave you plenty of time to decide, and a few families have made the right choice. They will survive. None of you will. You will all die." As soon as Ellie's voice was no longer heard, multiple people began to scream from the wall.

"I will make your screams heard throughout Crearia." Those were the last harsh words that Elion heard from Ellie.

While Ellie spoke, the Malignin took that time to begin scaling the walls.

"The Malignin are coming. They're attacking!" someone screamed before being pulled down the wall. Shouts came from every direction, and most everyone stood their ground, but there was no discipline. Arrows were fired without command. Swords were drawn early before they would be of use. No one fled, which Sainte was thankful for, but no one really maintained their posts.

Sainte looked down at Aroc to find that she stared right back into his face.

"You did this," she said accusingly, seemingly unaware of the commencing battle. "Isaac's death is your fault, and now we're all going to pay for it." She stood up nose to nose with him.

He could not refute what she said, not right now. She was right, though. Finally, someone said what he knew to be true. It was his fault. Everything that was happening was his fault. He had just begun to cope with everything, but Aroc confirmed that the blame lay solely on him. Her watery eyes looked into each of his.

"Nothing to say for yourself?" she asked.

"I'm..." He shuddered as someone screamed out their last breath. "I'm sorry."

"That won't work this time. Sorry never works." He said nothing back. Aroc brushed passed him in disgust, almost knocking him to the ground.

"Aroc! Where are you going?" he shouted at her back, but she kept walking. He looked around at the chaos quickly unfolding in Elion. He took a deep breath in and breathed it out.

His mind slowed down and he focused on the battle that was quickly turning in favor of the Malignin.

Sainte turned around and beheld the people of Elion struggling to fight back. Some Malignin already crawled over the wall and into the city. Women and children fought over the dead bodies of their peers. Everyone was going to die unless he could do something about it. As he was about to run into the fray, a light so bright he closed his eyes and looked away shone forth from Aroc. Malignin in town and atop the wall scrambled away from her.

"Light the torches!" Aroc's voice boomed out. "Light the oil! Take back the walls, do not let them in!"

People shielded their eyes from her, but the panic that had overtaken them initially seemed to wash away in it. One by one, torches began to flare to life. One of the torches was dropped over the wall to light the oil that was spilled outside of it.

Flames whooshed to life, and a flash of orange lit the sky briefly. Cries of Malignin were heard as they were caught in the inferno. Aroc's light combined with the firelight bought everyone a brief respite from battle, but it would not be long before the Malignin braved the light.

"Sainte," Aroc said carefully, turning to him, attitude suddenly vastly different than it was mere moments before, "there is much more for me to do with Isaac's... with his death. There's nothing more we can do here. We must move on. There are larger things at stake than the people in this town."

Sainte's eyes slowly came to focus. The light emanating from her seemed to help him think clearly.

"No. We can't do that to them. We have to fight with them. Help them," he said as he registered what Aroc was implying. She stared at him for a second, then looked at the ruined corpse of Isaac and let out a long sigh.

"Stay on the ground. Fight where you can. I'll go atop the wall and keep watch over you. I'm not doing this for you. I'm doing this to exact as much vengeance as I can before it's too late." She left Isaac's corpse reluctantly but climbed a ladder and was on the wall before Sainte could take three steps.

Sainte drew his sword and ran to the gates, pushing through the battle-clad women and children. As he made his way to the front, he heard cries of recognition and hope because of his appearance.

The cheers were quickly silenced as the gates shuddered as Malignin pounded relentlessly at them. It sounded like a constant barrage of thunder. Sainte sucked in a shaky breath, held up his sword, and faced the people of Elion behind him.

"Weapons!" he shouted. In a moment, everyone's sword, axe, battle hammer, and spear were held above their heads. "The Malignin mean to kill you all, but we aren't going to let that happen. Fight them tooth and nail.

"They'll push at you, but you'll push harder! They will kill some of you, but we'll kill more! They are strong but fight as individuals. We fight as one, and for that we are stronger!"

Everyone cheered, and for a moment, it was louder than the beating on the gates, but another sound sliced over the cheers.

The wooden gates started to crack.

The pounding on the gates was incessant, indomitable, endless. The wooden gates began to splinter more under the onslaught. With the next thud, the gates burst to pieces, and Malignin poured in like water through a broken dam.

With Sainte at the forefront, the people of Elion surged forward and met the Malignin ferociously in battle before they could take two steps into their town. Fires fluttered in the gust of wind as people rushed by.

Sainte raised his sword as he ran at the Malignin. He sliced back and forth before him and knocked claws that sought death aside. Some Malignin were struck down, but there were already more human deaths than Malignin. From his peripherals, he could see women and teenagers fighting as best they could.

Sainte glanced up to the walls only to see that the Malignin crawled over them again, slowly pushing all the men off. No one was working together coherently.

"On me!" Sainte bellowed as he fought. "Group together, fight together!"

People began to fight their way to where he was with the women. Soon, almost the entire town was in a half circle around the gates fighting back. The Malignin had no end in sight, but they were holding them off for now.

Sainte hoped that Aroc coordinated the defenses with the men on the wall. For a few moments, it seemed like the Malignin were wavering. Step by grueling step, the beasts were pushed back. Sainte and the people of Elion stopped their advance and held them at bay.

Soon everyone was shoulder to shoulder, pushed forward and pushed back. There were times in the battle when the Malignin and people pushed so hard against each other that it was impossible to move. All they could do was bare their teeth and growl.

Sainte had to grasp his sword hilt with white-knuckled hands to keep it from getting wrenched from his grasp. The resounding cries of conflict could be heard almost throughout the entirety of Whitweir Forest.

Now and then, a particularly ferocious Malignin tore through the ranks of people, but they were almost always cut down before they could do much damage to anyone.

The battle was chaos. Black claws scratched at them from every direction. Teeth gnashed and chittered. The inexperienced fighters got in each other's way more often than not. So many people were screaming that it sounded like one never-ending scream.

All the noise combined into one jumbled, mind-filling mess. Sainte could not think about his next sword strike, much less how he and Aroc were going to survive this.

The townspeople were tiring. Desperation began to show on their faces as they realized this as well. Fear settled on their minds in a heavy blanket as their impending deaths became clearer.

Sainte stabbed a Malignin through the chest and push-kicked it off. Before he could ready his sword again, another Malignin leaped at him with its mouth wide open and claws ready to rend flesh.

He turned to the side, it was all he could do, and braced himself. From above, an arc of light sliced down and hit the fiend like a boulder. It slammed into the ground, and he heard bones crush.

"I'm here, Sainte. Fight," Aroc called down encouragingly from above.

He looked towards her voice and saw her standing on the wall. She seemed to tower above both Malignin and men alike. She battled four Malignin at once using her powers. Some magic manifested as light, but some was invisible.

She seemed to have rallied some forces on the wall and managed to retake it. Sainte tore his eyes from her to focus on the battle at hand.

That was when he noticed a wall of light where the gates used to be. Aroc must have manifested it for them. The Malignin tried to shy away from it to shield their sensitive eyes. Some Malignin could still crawl over the walls of Elion, but it was a much slower process.

Feeling oddly revitalized, Sainte corralled everyone around him. "Push them towards the light!" he commanded. "The light!" he cried out desperately, over and over.

Soon, others echoed his shouts to people too far away to hear. They pushed back towards the light. The closer they got, the more disoriented the Malignin became.

Sainte chopped through Malignin, killing one with each sword strike. His muscles no longer ached, his breathing clear and smooth, his mind as sharp as his sword.

The Malignin were all that stood between him and Ellie, and they died so easily. What chance did they have of stopping him?

The women and teenagers seemed to find their determination again as well. Each death of a friend or a family member hardened their resolve to kill as many Malignin as possible.

Instead of filling them with hopelessness and defeat, it filled them with anger. In their anger, they found courage. In their courage, they found the energy to continue the push.

The Malignin that made it into Elion were slowly being killed off. Sainte cut down a Malignin and waited for another to attack him, but none did. The main body of Malignin that entered the town had been slaughtered.

Small groups still fought a few Malignin, but many people just stood, chests heaving, as they tried to regain their composure. Some looked at the wall of light uncomfortably, but most seemed thankful.

"Take back your walls," he commanded.

Townsfolk, who stood dazed and tired after the fight, looked at him as if he was insane.

"What are you waiting for? Man the walls." Sainte pointed with his sword.

"We're tired," someone told him breathlessly. "We can't go on for much longer."

"You have no choice," Sainte said through gritted teeth. "If you give up now, you're already dead. Now get on the damn wall and fight," he told them.

They could tell that he would not allow them to argue further and realized he was right. The wall slowly started to fill with more people. The enraged monsters were getting pushed and held back.

When she realized she was no longer needed on the wall, Aroc descended and found herself to Sainte's side. She was slightly more pale than usual but looked in good shape.

"Sainte, we need to go back to Isaac's room. He had parchment that I need for the White Wyverns. Come with me. We don't have much time left." Aroc ran towards the Keep before Sainte could say anything, so he reluctantly followed close behind.

They reached the Keep quickly because the streets were cleared of everyone this far into town. Aroc burst through the doors and promptly headed to Isaac's room. She started to sort through his desk. She ripped drawers out and tore through the contents.

"Start looking, Sainte. I need those papers."

"What do they look like?" he asked as he looked through the closet. "Why are we doing this now? We should still be helping fight. We may have pushed the Malignin out for now, but they will keep attacking."

"Like regular paper," she said in frustration. "It'll be in a language you don't know. We're doing this right now because I think the people can hold the Malignin off long enough for us to leave."

Sainte stopped searching at her words.

"Leave?"

"Yes, leave. It's what you wanted, isn't it?"

"Not anymore. If we stay, I think we can actually save some of them."

"You're having a change of heart now? We don't have time for this. Just keep looking, and then we're leaving."

Sainte said nothing but continued the search. Battle sounds could be heard from the streets. The Malignin pushed in again. The fighting was getting closer.

"Aroc, they need us out there. They're going to die," Sainte said quickly.

"It doesn't matter anymore," she snapped. "We don't have the time. Do you want to save Ellie? Because helping these people won't do it. If this is hard for you, imagine how it is for me. I lived here. I know these people." She continued looking, throwing items aside.

He figured he would check Isaac's bed, although he had no hopes of the papers being there. He was wrong. He moved a pillow, and sure enough, there were papers under it, scrawled in a language that he had never seen before, just as she said.

"Aroc, I think I found them," he said as he held them up. She snatched them out of his hand faster than he could see.

"This is it. Come, Sainte, let's go," she said as she grabbed a satchel and stuffed the papers into it.

"So that's it? We stayed and fought for nothing?" he asked.

"I don't have time to explain right now. We have to leave Elion. It's lost, or can you not hear that? I'm surprised the Malignin aren't crawling through here right now. It's time to go, we did what little we could, and now we take our leave." She sounded emotionless to Sainte about this entire situation, but there was no decent way of putting it.

"What about the speech you gave them? You'll fight alongside them, won't let the Malignin take Elion?"

"I had to say something to get them to fight back. It was the only way we would have time to find this."

He looked at her incredulously. "It doesn't feel right..."

"I thought you'd be used to that feeling by now. Let's go." Aroc left the room without seeing if Sainte followed her.

He looked around Isaac's old room one last time, took a breath, and then left the room himself.

▼▲▼

Iris woke up with a start thanks to a nightmare that quickly faded. She quietly began to roll her blanket up and got ready to move. Tal was still asleep for once. When she was ready, she nudged him.

"Hey, Tal. We should get moving soon."

He grumbled in his sleep and rolled away from her prodding finger, but she persisted. He slowly opened his eyes.

"S'it time already?" he slurred.

"Aye. How much longer until we reach Whitweir Forest, do you think?"

He sat up and stretched, then rolled up his blanket. "I'd say we'll reach it 'fore we want to stop, then most likely we'll get to Elion after our next sleep." He stood up and slid his pack on. "Alright, ya good?"

"Yeah, let's go."

"What do ya think yer dad's doing now?" Tal asked.

"He's probably going to try and follow us. I don't know why... Maybe he's giving updates on our whereabouts to Miqel. Who knows?" She shivered. "It's not fair that he's still alive and my mom isn't."

"Nay, it's not," Tal agreed.

Iris did not say anything else. Instead, she focused on their walking pace, which seemed faster than they moved yesterday.

If they did not reach the forest before stopping, they must have been turned around.

They walked for two hours when Iris heard it first.

"Go a little more left," a voice called out quietly from the fog ahead. She looked up quickly at the sound.

"Did you hear that?" she asked Tal.

"Huh? Hear what?"

"It was.... Nothing, never mind. Let's push a little left, though, I feel like we've been veering slightly," she suggested.

"Ya think?" he asked, somewhat unsure. He stopped and turned around to check their tracks, what little he could see before they disappeared into the gray. "Maybe ye're right. It's hard to tell. If ya think so, won't hurt nothing, I guess."

They veered a little left. How did Tal not hear the voice? It was quiet, but if she could hear it, surely he could too. And she knew whose it was. It was her father again.

Why did he not just leave her alone? Why was he now trying to be a part of her life? It had to be another form of torment.

Another hour passed before she heard the same voice repeat the same thing.

"A little left."

Once more, Tal did not hear it. She started to walk left but did not say anything, hoping that Tal would naturally follow her. He did not even notice the slight change in direction, for which she was relieved.

Iris was not sure how she would be able to explain how she knew where to go.

She was also not sure why she listened to his voice. Why did she decide to trust her father now when he never led her correctly any time before? Maybe she just wanted to believe that he was a better person.

Perhaps he was trying to make up for how he used to treat her. Maybe he was not working with Miqel and truly wanted to help her.

That was how they traveled. Iris' father called out to her each hour and told her which direction they should head in. She did not mention this to Tal. He would not understand why she listened.

He would most likely make them go in the opposite direction the voice suggested, so she just decided to tell him later, if at all.

It was getting close to their tenth hour of traveling when Iris could not take it anymore.

"Have you heard anything today? Anything unusual?"

He looked at her curiously. "Nay... I mean, I've heard nothin', actually, which's unusual. Why do ya ask?"

"Just wondering." She glanced around in front of them. Something moved up ahead.

She focused on where she saw it and noticed it again. She heard nothing, but her eyes did not deceive her.

"Tal, do you see that? Something's moving in front of us," she whispered.

He froze and strained his eyes. "I don't see nothing..." he said.

Her eyes were locked on to whatever it was. "It's right." She raised her arm to point at it. "There."

As soon as she said that, whatever she saw took off sprinting. Iris immediately took chase without warning.

Tal was surprised at her sudden sprint, so he ran after her but was soon far behind.

Iris heard his shouts behind her for her to slow down and wait up, but she could not let this person get away. She could see the man more clearly. She gained on him.

Just by his back, she knew that it was her father. Soon there were trees that she passed by, trees with pale white bark, but she barely noticed. She was so close she could hear him breathing. Tal's cries got quieter the further into the woods they got.

She was so close.

A few more long strides and Iris lunged at him.

She tackled him to the ground landing on top of him, and he grunted as the air was pushed from his lungs.

He tried to roll her off to get on top, but she fought back.

"Tal, I've got him!" she screamed, hoping to help her friend find them. "Hurry!"

She forced her dad onto his stomach as she straddled his back. She grabbed each of his arms and held them above his head, but he fought back nonstop. He tried to buck her off, which was a constant arm wrestle for her. Somehow, he managed to rip his right arm free and slightly roll onto his left side.

He punched her square in the jaw as hard as he could. She reeled back, dazed, and he managed to crawl out from under her.

He stood up, then bent down so his face was inches away from her own and was about to say something, but someone came running up behind Iris.

She let out a fuming scream and tried to fight back, but he was already gone. Someone grabbed her shoulders from behind, and she twisted away from the grasp.

"Iris, woah, calm down. It's just me, Tal," he said. "Turn around, lookit me."

She did, slowly.

"I had him, Tal, my dad. I had him pinned. He punched me and I let him go... Right there." She pointed to where she tackled her dad.

Tal examined the area. "I don't see..." he paused. He almost said he did not see signs of anyone else here other than Iris. There were no tracks leading to or away from the scene other than their own.

"What? What don't you see?" she asked.

He thought about lying to Iris and not bringing up the footprints, but he decided otherwise. "I don't see an extra set o' footprints, Iris. I don't see any signs of a fight, all I see are yer prints, and it looked like ya fell." Tal looked at Iris, unsure how she would react.

She looked at the ground and her eyes moved quickly left and right. She searched for their footprints. He was here. She touched him. There had to be something to prove that she was not crazy, but she found nothing.

"C'mon, Iris. It's a'right. Haven't had much to eat or drink, and we've been traveling fast. Not so strange that ya hallucinated. Least we made it into Whitweir Forest. Now let's find someplace to rest." He waited for her patiently.

"But I, he was..." She shook her head as she tried to sort her thoughts. Finally, she gave it up.

"Lead the way," she said quietly.

They found a decent area close to where their run ended. Iris laid on her blanket and stared at the canopy of white leaves.

It felt like an eternity, but she eventually fell into a fitful sleep, dreams riddled of times past with her father.

▼▲▼

When Sainte walked out of the Keep, he could barely keep himself from gasping. Dead bodies lined the streets. Smoke clouded the alleys. Blood pooled together, creating sticky red puddles. Sounds of battle still echoed throughout Elion. At least there were still some people alive fighting back.

There were bodies of Malignin scattered amongst the bodies of humans, but not nearly as many as Sainte would have liked to see. Lifeless eyes stared at him with accusatory gazes. Blaming him for their deaths.

"Ellie," he whispered. "How can you do this? Why?" He looked at the destruction that surrounded him. "What happened to you?"

The smoke got thicker, and a slight glow of fire could be seen further down the street toward the gates. The crackle of flames consuming all drifted lazily with the smoke.

Just then, a Malignin ran into his view, away from the fire. It carried a dead body that bled from the numerous wounds.

Upon noticing Sainte, the six-foot-tall beast dropped the body unceremoniously into the mud. The clawed fingers on each hand flexed as if each one had a mind of its own, eager to rend flesh. It rushed him, mouth wide open, spiny teeth smeared with saliva and blood.

Sainte drew his sword and held it at the ready. When it leaped at him, he quickly stepped to the side and slashed its face.

The Malignin stumbled slightly and glared at Sainte. Its jaw had been cut nearly off, and a flap of skin hung off its cheek.

It walked cautiously around Sainte, warier now.

As Sainte was about to finish this little fight, something heavy landed on his back and knocked him face down.

Another Malignin crawled to the roof of a nearby building and leaped on him. Sainte felt blow after blow as the Malignin clawed furiously, trying to rip through his armor to his soft skin.

Sainte struggled to escape from under the beast, but the other Malignin kept hindering him, holding and pulling on his legs.

Finally, it got tired of toying with him, and the Malignin with the cut face let go of his legs and sauntered to his head. It grabbed Sainte's head in both clawed hands, scratching him on the sides of his face.

Sainte could feel his head being pulled from his body.

As soon as he was sure he was going to die, there was a blast of white light, and the Malignin on his back was flung away. The Malignin with the cut face let go of Sainte's head in surprise.

He took this opportunity to stand up and quickly slashed its head off. The Malignin's body crumpled to the ground.

Sainte took a faltering step back. He would have fallen had Aroc not run to his side and held him up. He rolled his head around gingerly, making sure his neck still worked.

It did. It just hurt like hell.

"What are you still doing here?" she asked scoldingly. "Never mind that. Are you all right? Are you able to walk?"

Sainte stood on his own and shakily put his sword away.

"Aye, I'll be fine... I just need a moment." He looked at her for the first time and noticed that she was even paler. "What about you?"

"I'll do what needs to be done. Come on." She walked briskly away.

This time Sainte followed her. She was headed towards the docks at the back of Elion.

"Where are we going?" Sainte asked. "The entrance is the other way."

"Of course it is, but we can't very well walk through an army of Malignin with much ease. We're taking a boat out of here. If we're careful, we won't be noticed."

As they moved through the town, so did the fire, spreading quicker than they moved. The heat could soon be felt, and smoke billowed from shattered windows.

It did not feel right to Sainte to flee now, after all they had done, but looking around, he knew that Aroc was making the right choice.

"We're nearing the docks," Aroc said. "Stay close to me."

They turned a corner and stopped in their tracks. Some townspeople, about fifty, were cornered against a building by numerous Malignin.

They had children behind them, protecting them from the Malignin as best as they could. They fought with everything they had, but it was evident they were not getting away from this alive.

The scene reminded Sainte of a trapped fox he and his father had encountered years ago. The fear in that animal's eyes, how it cowered away from them but bit when they got too close. This was the same thing.

One of the men noticed Sainte and Aroc.

"They've come to help us! Don't give up!" There were several more shouts of support. Sainte could not tear his eyes away as they fought with renewed strength. Many Malignin were cut down, but he knew that no matter how many were killed, it would not matter.

Aroc saw his hesitation and pushed him away.

"Sainte, come on. We have to find a different way. There are too many here. We won't be able to leave without them noticing." She grabbed Sainte's arm and dragged him. "We can do nothing for them."

"I have to try," he said as he pulled away from her grasp. "I can't keep leaving people that need my help. I can barely live with myself for leaving Miqel and Iris. I wouldn't be able to if I leave these men, women, and children to die. I have to try," he said again, reaffirming his choice.

Before Aroc could protest or prevent him from going, he drew his sword and ran toward the fray.

"Sainte! Damnit," Aroc cursed after him. She could not very well leave him there no matter how much she wanted to. With an aggravated grunt, she ran after him.

Some of the Malignin in the back of the group turned around at the sound of Sainte's footsteps, but they were not fast enough. The sharp point of Sainte's sword pierced through muscle and tendons to reach the tender innards of the Malignin. Before it knew it was being attacked, it was dead.

Sainte ripped his sword free from the lifeless body and hacked at all the Malignin before him. The Malignin were caught by surprise for the most part and put up little to no defense to his attacks.

He managed to kill four foul beasts before a handful finally turned their attention to him. He took a few steps back to distance himself from Malignin as they slowly began to advance on him.

Trying to keep them all in his vision was a constant struggle to ensure none tried to sneak up on him as he did to them. While he tried to search for a way out of his current predicament, he heard Aroc call out his name.

"Sainte, catch!" Aroc yelled.

While Sainte foolishly rushed into the overwhelming battle, she acquired some nearby torches, one of which she threw to Sainte.

One of the Malignin took this opportunity to launch its attack. He barely had time to turn around and catch it.

Sainte fumbled with the torch but firmly grasped it at the last second. He expected the attack and deftly moved to his left, successfully dodging it.

He advanced with the torch in his left hand and his sword in his right. The Malignin shied away from the fire, and Sainte killed one before the others put distance between themselves and the torch.

Now that he was free from being held up, he continued doing what he originally planned, making his way through the Malignin.

Progress was much easier now that he held a torch. The creatures all but scrambled to get away from him. The ones that were too slow became fodder for his blade.

Finally, he reached the surrounded people after what felt like hours. They eagerly welcomed him into their ranks. Sainte turned around and was face to face with Aroc. She followed behind him without him even realizing it.

She carried four torches, two in each hand. With the Malignin hesitating in the illuminating light, Aroc took advantage of it and quickly handed out the torches to men in the front.

Returning to Sainte's side, she asked, "What's your plan now?"

"How many people are here?" Sainte asked one of the closest men to him.

"We started with about sixty, but I'd put our numbers closer to thirty," he said through heavy breaths.

"Everyone listen up!" Sainte yelled quickly over Malignin's battle sounds and growls. "Four of you now have torches—each man with a torch escorts six people through the Malignin. Stay close, stay tight, and move fast. Keep the little ones safe, keep everyone close enough to be covered by light, and fight for your lives! The Malignin will shy away from the light, but not for long. Now! Move!"

At once everyone broke into motion. Organized chaos. Sainte was surprised at how quickly they separated into groups.

One by one, the groups of people made their way through the Malignin.

Not everyone made it out alive.

Sainte watched hopelessly as a few unlucky people and children were slaughtered by Malignin bold enough to ignore the light.

How was this the best option that these people had?

Slowly, however, the Malignin's numbers dwindled as they realized that these people would not be killed as easily as they thought. That and they were growing tired of the light, both from the torches and the burning town.

Finally, only Sainte and Aroc were left. They pushed through the remaining Malignin, killing any that dared cross their path. Neither Sainte nor Aroc knew where the surviving people of Elion went. All they could hope was that they made it out alive.

"Let's go, hurry up," Aroc steamed at Sainte, to which he finally followed her without any protest. They ran down streets with burning buildings on either side. Hot ash rained down on them.

Four Malignin had taken notice of the pair and followed them, thinking they would be an easy kill.

Sainte and Aroc turned a corner and slipped through an alley, oblivious to their silent stalkers. They continued towards the docks, hoping the townspeople had yet to sail away on all the ships and boats.

The Malignin chased after them, bounding on all fours closing the distance.

They rounded a corner and the docks were in sight. To their relief, a few boats remained. They sprinted for the closest one, a small three-seater canoe, but it would do for the short journey.

The Malignin were close behind now, and their heavy steps on the wooden dock caught Sainte's ears.

He stopped running and yelled to Aroc, "Untie the boat. Get it ready. I'll hold them off."

He drew his sword and turned around, immediately met by a Malignin.

He parried the claws and smashed the Malignin in the face with his left arm, protected by Isaac's gauntlet.

The next Malignin he stabbed through the chest, but the momentum of it blew Sainte to the dock with a thud.

The third Malignin was upon him when there was a blinding flash.

The third and fourth Malignin scrambled to a halt, blinded by the sudden brightness.

Aroc stood over Sainte and helped him to his feet. He violently pulled his sword from the Malignin and sheathed it, ready to move.

"Get in the boat, Sainte. I'll kill these last two."

At this point, Sainte was too tired to argue. The sprint to the boat drained him. He climbed in as fast as he could without tipping the canoe over.

He looked back to Aroc and saw a Malignin lunge at her braving the light, but its head just exploded before it got within three feet of her.

The remaining creature turned to run, but Aroc threw a ball of light. The light streaked through the air and hit her target.

The Malignin stopped moving, and the light shone from its eyes, ears, and mouth.

When the light died away, the creature fell lifeless.

Aroc turned to the last living Malignin on the docks, the one Sainte punched in the face. She walked towards the canoe, and as she passed it, its head snapped backward, breaking its neck.

Aroc elegantly, slowly, climbed into the canoe.

Sainte pushed them away from the docks, grabbed an oar, and started paddling away from Elion.

"Where are we going?" Sainte asked her. She was pale and glistened with sweat. Her breaths came in short and fast.

"North and west, a river meets the lake." Those were her last words before she slid to the canoe floor and passed out.

Sainte paddled in silence, more tired than he could remember being in recent memory.

Many people died, but at least it was not everyone. He could make a difference.

He *did* make a difference.

And, when possible, he told himself he would continue to make a difference.

However, those promises to himself seemed hollow when he could not even bring himself to look at the burning city of Elion.

Instead, he forced his eyes downward to the water and watched it burn in the reflection.

Upside down.

Exactly how his world had turned.

TWELVE
-TRICKERY-

Iris and Tal woke up at about the same time. They packed up without speaking to each other and started to walk the final distance toward Elion in silence. The only noise either made was snapped twigs and crushed brush underfoot.

Iris kept her eyes down, afraid that she would see something not really there. She made sure to keep the back of Tal's feet in her vision so she knew where to go. Tal, on the other hand, kept his eyes up and alert. Iris may have just imagined seeing her father, but he could not be too careful. There were strange things that happened to him these last few weeks, and it would not surprise him if there was something out there that did not leave footprints.

The color of the trees and plants made Tal feel uncomfortable. It did not seem natural. He was used to the typical green and browns of vegetation, and the pale white trees made the atmosphere seem gloomier than it already was. He noted that Whitweir Forest had a faintly sweeter smell than normal woods, honey-like almost. But it was another smell that made him stop in his tracks.

Iris bumped into his back. "What're you...?" she began to say, but he cut her off.

"Do ya smell that?" He sniffed the air deeply. "I smell smoke." He looked around curiously.

Iris smelled the air too. She had not noticed it before, but Tal was right. She smelled smoke as well. Tal started to walk again, slowly, and tried to keep as quiet as he could.

Iris followed, trying to stay quiet too. Where there was a fire, there were usually people, where there were people, there was the potential for danger.

Neither of them could see the fire, but the smell of smoke got stronger. Regardless, they continued to walk. The trees thinned around them. Tal stopped again and peered ahead.

"Iris, I think we found th' clearing that Elion's in. C'mon." He waved her forward. He gave up trying to be quiet.

She tromped to his side, having to push her way past a thick bush. They stood at the edge of the clearing. At the far end was an orange glow similar to the rising sun but much more sinister.

"Is that..." Tal began.

"Elion," Iris finished for him.

Elion was about half a mile across the flat plain and looked like a glowing ember on the horizon. The heat from the fire drove away the fog from the plain and covered it instead with a thick blanket of black smoke.

Iris' knees got weak, but she caught herself before she fell.

Tal slowly stepped from the tree line, still unable to believe what he saw. "What... happened?" he asked to no one.

Iris walked to his side. It looked like the town had been burning for a while. Small flames spouted up now and again, but most of it just smoldered.

The ground surrounding Elion was churned up in a familiar way to Iris. In a way that she saw almost every day for the last four years of her life.

"They were here already. The Malignin," Iris said incredulously. "It's not fair." Her words were drenched in disbelief.

"C'mon," Tal said as he touched her shoulder, "let's get closer. Maybe there're survivors."

She did not miss the doubt in his voice.

They began the final trek of their journey to Elion, blanketed with despair. Their progress was slow and painstaking. Each of them tried not to trip over the limitless ruts and holes. They helped each other with balance. Otherwise, if they were alone, they would have fallen.

Their entire journey so far had been hindered by failure after failure. Now it was almost too much to bear.

They could both feel the oppressive heat radiating from the town now, making everything all the more real. Then Tal looked up and stopped.

"Iris," he said.

She looked up as well and saw that they stood just thirty feet from the destroyed town. They could hear the crackle of fire as it slowly began to die, the snap of wooden beams of homes and stores. If the Malignin could laugh, Iris was sure they would sound like this.

"What do we do now, Tal?" Iris asked. Any hope that she had remaining was long gone.

He said nothing for a few seconds. "We keep moving." He brushed past her as he began to walk toward the town. "After we check fer survivors."

Iris hesitated. "But what if they're still there? What if the Malignin are still around here?"

"I'll kill 'em," he said without looking back. Iris stayed still for a few moments. She was scared. Miqel was on the wrong side, and Sainte was nowhere to be found.

Sainte. Maybe he was in Elion. Maybe he was dead in Elion. Either way, Iris decided she had to know. After all, she did not want to stay out here by herself.

She ran to catch up with Tal. Together they walked towards the smoldering town and basked in its heat. They stepped through the destroyed gates, neither knowing what to expect from their search.

▼▲▼

Sainte sat silently in the small boat as it rocked back and forth. The only sound accompanying him was the splash of water against the canoe. It was hard going now as they neared the mouth of the river that fed the lake, which flowed in the opposite direction he paddled. Aroc remained asleep since they left Elion. By Sainte's count that was about two hours ago.

He looked back at the town once, then decided he would not look again. He wondered how many people survived. Was the group they came across the only survivors or did more manage to escape? Many boats were missing from the dock; perhaps there were more survivors than he expected.

Aroc began to stir, and he focused on her, thankful to give his mind something else to think about.

"Hey, you all right? You passed out nearly as soon as I started to row," he said to her.

"I'll be fine..." she said as she sat up and held her head. "In time. I don't know what you think about my..." she struggled to find a word.

"Magic?" Sainte offered.

"I suppose you could call it that," she conceded, "but whatever you might think, know that it's not limitless. It takes energy and effort. It is tiring to use. I used a lot of it in Elion and hadn't used it in a long time. It took a lot out of me." She slowly laid back down. "Just, please wake me when we hit land."

"Well," Sainte said, "that'll be in about... Now."

The wooden canoe grated across rocks and sand. With every wave, it crunched against the underwater gravel.

"How long have we traveled?" she asked without moving.

"About two hours, I'd say."

She sat up. "That long?"

He shrugged. "I was tired too, alright. Plus, I rowed out to the middle, then hooked a left so we'd hit near where the river met the lake." Obviously, the amount of time it took them to hit land irked her. It showed on her face, but she quickly cleared it.

"That's probably for the best. I got to rest, and it gave time for the Malignin to clear out. Maybe it won't be so hard getting by them now. Let's go." She stood up shakily and gingerly stepped out of the canoe.

Sainte followed, sloshing as fast as he could through knee-deep water. "Where are we going, Aroc?"

"To Munich," she replied.

"Why?"

She turned on him fast and was inches away from his face. "Because Isaac is dead. He was going to go to Munich, but he can't now. We're going in his stead. If it weren't for you we wouldn't be in this mess," she said as she fought her own tears back.

The hopelessness and guilt that Sainte felt before the battle in Elion came rushing back. "I... I didn't know," he said, truly at a loss for words.

"You left Elion to talk to her. You were going to join her. Isaac stayed behind to give you time to make it back to Elion. He didn't stay behind for me," she sneered.

"I didn't ask him to do that," he said dumbly.

"You didn't have to. To think, everything he did for you and this is how you respect him. He gave his life for yours." She turned away in disgust.

"Yeah, well, I'm not sure my life was worth that much," Sainte said under his breath.

"Neither am I," she called back coldly. "It doesn't matter. It doesn't matter how I feel about you. I still have a lot to teach you. Hurry up. We have a long journey ahead of us," she said without looking at him.

Ridden with shame, Sainte's head drooped, and he walked slowly after her.

▼▲▼

"Stay close," Tal said as they stepped over burnt debris. They left footprints in the ash. Iris heeded his words and clutched her bow in her left hand with her right hand never far from her quiver.

The wind shifted and that was when the stench hit them hard. The stench of hundreds of burnt bodies. It overpowered every other smell.

It was unforgettable.

They staggered to a halt in order to cover their noses and mouths to help keep from vomiting, but it did not help Iris. She emptied what little contents of her stomach were left. When she was finished, she straightened up again.

Now that they were closer they could see the expanse of damage done to the town. What they first took for charred buildings and rubbish was mostly bodies. They were almost unrecognizable, charred hands reached for freedom, but all they got were their fingers burnt off.

Most bodies were twisted in gruesome positions. Some looked like they had been melted together before being burnt to death.

Tal suddenly began to calmly walk away, which surprised Iris. She watched him as he returned to where they came from.

"Where are you going?" Iris asked to his back.

"I'm leavin', going back to Munich, to my village. No one's alive 'ere. Pointless to waste our time. I've had enough." He explained emotionlessly.

"You can't know that," she said desperately. "Sainte could be here, hiding. Maybe he's waiting for me," she said hopefully but realized how crazy it sounded.

"Or he left, most likely. Any sensible person wouldn't stay here... More'n likely he's dead. Ya wouldn't be able to recognize the body anyway, I'd wager. Maybe ya come across his body, but ye'd never know. Maybe he was here but he fled, ye'd never know. Or, maybe he was never here at all. Ya won't know," he told her, exasperated, his stoic façade slipping away.

"I'm looking for him. At least help me," she pleaded. "I have to try... He would do the same for me. I'm not going to give up just because you are."

Tal turned around to say something, but Iris was already busy nudging corpses to see if she recognized any faces.

He sighed at the sight. "What does he look like?" Iris gave him a brief description, then he started to do the same.

"Thank you for helping. Finish checking here. I'll go further in," she said quickly before leaving.

The smoke was dense and Tal soon lost sight of her. He shook his head at her actions, surprised even more that she convinced him to stay.

He knew that she was distraught. That much was obvious. He figured the best thing to do was follow to make sure she did not hurt herself. Tal ran into the smoke and hoped he had not already lost her.

Iris was frantic. She had no idea where to start looking for Sainte. She called out his name as she searched bodies. She could tell some of the dead were Malignin, but most were human.

None of them were recognizable. She even burst into burned buildings, risking their collapse.

She searched nonstop. Her hair was matted to her face with sweat and soot. It clumped together thickly on her head with ash. Her breathing was short and shallow, her eyes red and watery, her mouth sticky and dry. Yet she called out to Sainte continuously.

After she burst back onto what remained of the street from a building, she screamed to the smoke-filled sky in frustration. No one responded. The tears down her face left a trail through soot and ash. Sainte was missing, or worse, if he was here, he was dead. Iris gave up. She would never find him again.

"Don't cry. Everything's going to be all right."

Iris snapped her head in the direction of the voice. She tried to wipe the tears away from her eyes but only got more ash in them. She knew who the voice belonged to even though she could not see him.

"I'm here for you, baby. I'm sorry you had to see this, but I had to show you that I'm all you have left. Otherwise, you never would come with me. I'm sorry, but I've changed. I can show you."

She could not see him clearly but heard him step toward her.

"Stop," she spat out. "Don't you dare come any closer."

He stopped just as a burst of flame behind him caught something else on fire.

"If you don't leave me alone, I'm going to kill you." She grabbed her bow and an arrow, nocked it, pulled back the string, and aimed it at her father.

"I tried talking to you before, and that's all I want to do right now. You can put your bow away," he said timidly. He visibly relaxed as she let the string slack, but she did not put her bow away or take her hand off the string.

"Talk then, but quickly. I'm keeping my bow out," she said. He thought about what he was going to say, then nodded his head.

"I can't argue that. You know, when the Malignin came to our town, there was nothing anyone could do. We were overrun in seconds. There was no warning. But the Malignin didn't kill us, not at first. They gathered us all together and brought us to the town center.

"There was a... girl... there. I didn't recognize her, but after what she said and what I knew had happened earlier with you and the rest of the Blades of the Night, I had no doubts who she was. All she said was, 'Join me or die.' If you heard her, heard the way she said it, you would understand. I chose to live, Iris. I picked life." He finished with a smile that faltered off of his face.

Iris shook her head slowly. "No, father. You didn't pick life. You chose death when you let mother die alone. Nothing you could say would ever change what I think about you. You're nothing but a selfish prick."

With those final words, she quickly drew her arrow back to her cheek and let it loose. It flew true to her aim, unlike the previous arrow she shot at him, and stuck in his chest with a satisfying thud. In that brief moment before the arrow hit her father, she took complete satisfaction in the look of horror across his face.

He clutched the shivering shaft with both hands and fell to his knees. The expression on his face shifted from horror to pain. He looked at her then and she met his gaze.

"I hate you, and I'm glad I'm the one who gets to kill you."

Iris pulled out another arrow, took aim, and loosed it.

The arrow pierced his throat and poked through before stopping. The feathers on the end of the shaft vibrated with fading momentum.

His mouth opened and blood drooled out. His eyes were wide with surprise. One hand clutched weakly at the embedded shaft that slowly allowed his life to pour from his body. He fell to his back, last breaths wheezed from his mouth.

As Iris walked closer to watch him die, his features began to blur and fade. She rubbed her eyes on her sleeve to clear them of any smoke or ash. She wanted to watch his life leave his body. She brought her hands back down and looked at him again. But it was not her father that she looked at.

It was Tal.

"No..." she gasped out through a tightening throat.

Tal's hands open and closed in futile grasps.

She dropped her bow in shock and scrabbled over to his side. His eyes were already closed by the time she got there, but his chest still faintly moved. She held his head in her arms.

He opened his eyes at the movement. He could not talk, but his eyes spoke more to her than he could ever have hoped for, and she cried all the harder for it.

He knew that he would be dead soon, but he did not... He just... Could not finish the thought...

Iris sobbed harder once she noticed his hands stop moving and his eyes glazed over. His blood pooled around her knees. She held his lifeless head in her lap, safe from the staining red liquid.

"I'm s-sorry," she stuttered between tears.

She killed him. She killed the only person that made any attempt to help her, to stay with her.

"There's no point in cryin' 'bout this anymore. The deed's done." A voice droned at her through the dying flames of Elion. "Ye've nothing, now. Th'only person that ya had any trust in in these dark times is now gone. Come with me."

Miqel stepped in front of Iris. His voice was cruel yet soft. "I'm all ye have left now. I tried to warn ya," he bent down, gently grabbed her hand, and pulled it from Tal's corpse.

He lifted her slowly. "C'mon, it'll all be better soon, ye'll see."

Iris struggled futilely against him but had no strength to fight anymore.

"Don't worry," he whispered in her ear as he embraced her against her will, "everything's gonna be alright."

"No," Iris sobbed quietly into his shoulder, her arms now hung limply by her sides. She could not do anything else. Miqel's touch, his voice, repulsed her, but she was too tired to fight him. She knew she could not have got away even if she tried.

Miqel held her, smiling, as the dying flames of the dead town burnt out around them, and smoke hid them from view.

▼▲▼

Aroc and Sainte had just crossed a small creek outside Whitweir Forest and bedded down for a while. They traveled ten miles since they landed their boat from Elion. They were both tired from all they had been through and decided to stop momentarily.

Aroc pulled some bread from her bag and tossed Sainte a piece. He took a bite of it and made a face.

"What?" Aroc asked.

"It's a bit stale," he told her. He held the rest of the bread out at arm's length and examined it, then promptly stuck the rest of it in his mouth and ate it anyway.

"At least you don't seem to have a problem eating it. It's all we have left until we reach Munich," she muttered.

"You never actually answered why we're going there? Is that where Ellie's heading next? Why was Isaac going there?" Sainte asked.

"I don't know where Ellie is going," she said, annoyed, "but those papers we grabbed from Isaac's house need to go there. He was going to take them, but he can't now so it's up to me, and you have to come. The person that gets them will be surprised I'm bringing them instead of Isaac, but she'll understand. It'll be fine... I hope."

Sainte took another bite before speaking. "I'm just taking a shot in the dark here, but I'm assuming those papers have to do with me?"

"Don't think everything's about you. You're mentioned, but I wouldn't say they have to do with you... More like the many people that could have been in your position," she said nonchalantly.

He finished his bread in silence and then drew his sword. He brought out his whetstone and began sharpening the blade, deciding not to be bothered by what she said.

"Such a simple thing, swords. All they are is long, sharp metal. Yet accountable for influencing so many people's decisions, accountable for so much death."

The only response he received was not from Aroc but from the trickling of the nearby creek. Sainte slid his whetstone down the length of the blade a few times before speaking again. "Shouldn't you be, I don't know, teaching me stuff? You mentioned it earlier. You're a White Wyvern; teach me. Show me the way," he said sarcastically. He was angry that she was angry at him. If she just let him die when she found him. If she had just let him go on his own. If only she hadn't brought him to Elion. This was her fault.

"You want the lessons to start? Fine, they'll start. Here's some background, the power I use and the power Ellie now has access to are similar. What I'm going to do is prepare you for all sorts of different attacks she can press on you. She's already attacked you before, but you didn't realize it then. Manipulation with words. She used it on you outside Elion, and you easily fell to her whims. I will use the same techniques on you; you must try to resist. Are you ready?" she asked with an eager glint in her eyes.

"Aye, do your worst," Sainte dared her. "How hard can it be? You just told me what to expect."

"You getting picked to be the Shield was a mistake. You're not good enough, which is why everyone's in this mess. I don't even know if you have what it takes to see this through to the end. You let down your friends, Iris and Miqel. You let down Ellie. You let down your brothers of the Blades of the Night. The people of Elion misplaced their hope when they left it with you. Isaac's death is your fault," she said coldly.

Sainte felt her words hit him like ice, then melt into his skin. "How can I refute things of which I already believe?" he asked quietly.

Aroc sighed. "This is pointless. I'm done, you're not going to be able to learn anything in time if you don't put any effort in, and I don't want to waste my time anymore with you than I already have."

Sainte was taken aback. His self-loathing was replaced with anger instantly. "You can't just stop. Teach me what I need to know to save Ellie. I'll learn it," he said, angry at her for giving up on him so easily.

"Good, not completely useless," Aroc said as she sat up straighter.

"What? Were you doing it just then?"

"Aye, of course I was. As much as I'd like to degrade you, I wouldn't do it just for fun. The best way to defend against this is to know what you believe, do not doubt it. You may say that everything happening is not entirely your fault, but you also have a small voice inside telling you that it is. You must shut that voice out. Since you hadn't yet, I attacked you where you had doubts, as Ellie will do.

"The words of manipulation can make you feel various things from emotions to sickness. The defense is all the same; you must know what is true to yourself. You must believe in yourself," Aroc explained.

"What if I don't know what I think?" he asked, exasperated.

"You already know what you must do, which is what you should know. You're trying to save Ellie. I don't know how to go about that. I've never done this before. One of the only people that could've been any help to us is dead now. All I know is that it's my job to help you along the way. I should have just passed this off to Isaac. Maybe he'd still be alive," she said accusingly.

Sainte stood up quickly and got into her face. "I didn't kill him," he said, enunciating every syllable. He stepped back to regain his composure as soon as he realized what he did.

"Very good, denying that. The only thing that actually was your fault is the thing you're most defiant about," she said.

"I didn't..."

"Stop," she commanded, and he listened. "This will be all we're doing for now. No more lessons until our next rest."

Sainte tried to settle down, but her words roused an anger in him he had not felt in a long time.

"Can I ask some questions, at least?" Aroc said nothing so he continued to talk with more composure. "Is the only reason you're here because you were the first Wyvern to find me? I'm only here because this disaster happened while I was the Shield?" He looked at her. "If I didn't know any better, I'd say this was all pre-planned."

Aroc sighed and rolled her eyes at him. "It was planned. It was no accident that I found you when I did."

"What do you mean?" he asked suspiciously.

"I was stationed near the mountains. The Shield, all of them, were my responsibility. It was my job to make sure that they did everything correctly and that they didn't try to do anything stupid like run away with the Barrier," she explained to

Sainte. By now, he sat back down and studied her. Suddenly something dawned on him.

"Wait... Wait, I've seen you before. I thought you looked familiar... You were driving the carriage that took Julian, my mentor, the Shield before me, away with his Barrier. That was you, wasn't it?"

Aroc inclined her head. "Yes, it was me. I wondered if you would ever remember. It was my job, as well, to make sure the Shield and Barrier get taken safely to their journey's end."

"What does that mean, 'journey's end'?" Sainte asked curiously, anger forgotten.

"It's... I can't tell you. Not right now. I cannot tell you everything." She stopped talking to think about how to word what she would say next. "Just remember that no matter what you find out, the White Wyverns had nothing but the best interests in mind."

"You say you took the old Barriers and Shields away. Where do you take them? Can't you just go get one back, use an old Barrier in Ellie's place?" Sainte asked.

"They're no longer... accessible... to me. They cannot come back from where they've been taken. That's the best I can explain. You'll find out sooner or later but now is not the time. As I said, I cannot tell you everything," she said slowly as she tried to think of the best way to clarify it to him. "It's too dangerous. I can't risk it."

He furrowed his brows at her. "I don't even know how to respond to that. You lied to me about Isaac being your father; how can I trust that you're telling me the truth about things that matter more than that?"

"He was my father, or at least the closest thing to one I'd ever had," she paused. "It doesn't matter. Just go to sleep, get some rest. I'll be first watch. I'll wake you in a few hours."

He did not reply but started to lay out his blanket roughly. It began to mist while they talked. It was not thick, but it was persistent. He laid down close to the base of a tree, hoping the sparse leaves would provide some cover.

Aroc sat still and just looked into the nothingness.

She woke Sainte after some time passed, and they swapped. Aroc slept while Sainte kept watch. They each only slept two hours at a time before they started to move again.

They traveled across the plains between Whitweir Forest and the Barrier's mountains without stopping and with no incidents. Aroc's lessons with Sainte continued, each one harder than the last. Every time they halted for a brief respite, she would test him with his knowledge. While they were traveling, she would test him without his knowledge. She would never tell Sainte, but he was quickly getting better at defending against the manipulation than expected.

Their sense of urgency ushered them quickly, and before they knew it, there were mountains on either side of them.

"Alright, Sainte," Aroc began, "we don't have much longer to travel. We're looking for a river fed by melted snow from the caps of the mountains. We'll have to build a make-shift raft, but we'll take the river out for the rest of the way.

"We'll stay on the water until we see a riverside path, then take the path to Munich from there. Once we reach the river in the mountains, it should take us about two days. We should rest now."

He listened to her and nodded. "Sounds good to me. So just two more sleeps, then we'll be in Munich. If all goes well."

"Aye, if all goes well," Aroc repeated.

▼▲▼

Iris was scared. After she killed Tal, Miqel took her out of Elion. They met up with a small group of Malignin and traveled a short distance away before they stopped, Elion just out of sight. Miqel sent the Malignin away to do whatever deeds he wanted them to. Then once they were alone, he turned to Iris in the darkness.

"Finally, we're alone. I told ya that I'd get ya, 'ventually. Wish it didn't have ta be this way, Iris, but ya gave me no choice." He gently brushed her hair out of her face. She shivered from his now foreign touch but otherwise did not move. He clucked his tongue as he realized how dirty she was. "Let's get ya cleaned up, eh?"

He pulled out his canteen of water and a rag and soaked it. He started to softly wipe her face while Iris could do nothing but accept it.

"Let's get ya outta those clothes. I'll clean ya up. Ya won't have ta do anything." He took her armor off, then went to pull off her shirt, but she pulled away from him, completely repulsed by him.

"No? Ye do it yerself then." He dropped the rag at her feet and smiled. "I'll have to keep watch, y'know, so ya don't run away."

Iris removed her clothes as discreetly as possible, trying to hide her breasts from his prying eyes, but there was only so much she could do. Her skin crawled with revulsion. She slipped off her pants but kept her undergarments on.

"I'm sure ye'll need ta clean 'tween yer legs. Everything off," Miqel instructed.

She said nothing as she hesitantly took off her undergarments, now completely nude. She picked up the rag and started to wash herself, scrubbing dirt off her arms. She moved to her chest, then down her body. All the while, her gaze was averted from Miqel.

"Don't forget yer gash, wouldn't want ya gettin'n infection," he reminded her.

Her skin crawled at his tone and goosebumps covered her body, but Iris did as she was bade, not wanting to provoke Miqel to anger. She was not sure what he was capable of anymore. Finally, she finished up after wiping down her feet. Miqel walked close to her and she shied away.

"Please, don't..." she whispered, not able to finish the sentence.

"Don't what?" he said calmly. "Hurt ya? Rape ya? Don't worry, I won't. Soon ye'll see that I'm on the right side. Then ye'll want me." He bent down, picked up her shirt, and handed it to her. "Get dressed."

Iris clothed herself with as much dignity as she could gather. He then pulled her close and put a collar on her that was hooked to a metal chain.

"This is more for ya than it is fer me. I don't want ya thinking of doin' anythin' stupid and gettin' hurt. I don't want ya like this, but I can't trust ya enough to not put it on fer now.

When I can trust ya, I'll take it off," he said to her in a kind voice, as if she would understand.

She looked at him with wide, scared eyes. "Who are you?" Her mouth barely moved with the question, scarcely able to get the words out.

"I'm Miqel, Iris. I still consider ya my friend... Closer'n a friend." He kissed her cheek. She tried to move her head away, but he held it in place. "Right, well, that'll change soon. I promise ye'll come ta enjoy my kisses." She shivered at his words.

"My father...?" she questioned.

"Aye?"

"Is he..."

"He's dead. You ne'er saw him, all me playin' with ya. That shadow trick I pulled wit' Ivan, I mastered it. Did ya like it?"

Iris shuddered but did not ask anything else.

He took a step back from her and straightened his clothes. "It's 'bout time we head out. Wouldn't want Sainte and his new girlfriend ta get too far ahead of us. We've a surprise fer them. C'mon, Iris. I hope ye're ready ta move." At this point, the Malignin returned and surrounded them.

Miqel waved his hand in the air and the Malignin started quickly walking west. He caught one by the arm and held it still as he hooked the end of Iris' chain around its waist.

"Make sure ya can keep up, Iris." He turned to the Malignin. "Don't go too hard on 'er." He shot her a smile. She just stared back in disbelief until she was yanked forward. She scrambled to catch up to avoid being dragged.

They moved across the plains fast and only made a few stops. Each stop Miqel checked on Iris, gave her some water and bathroom breaks if needed, all under his supervision. Throughout the entire time Iris said nothing and made almost no noise except her sobs which she tried to keep to herself.

Miqel noticed that she cried, but he said nothing. He was glad that he finally had her to himself. He waited so long and now they were together. He stayed by her side while they traveled, pushing her when she began to lag.

Finally, they stopped moving and it seemed to be for good. Iris expected Miqel to come back and make her rewash herself or talk to her, but he did not. She gathered enough courage to look around finally.

Mountains loomed over her and pine trees could be seen through the fog, which took her by surprise. She did not realize they moved through the plains that quickly. She heard footsteps behind her, recognizing them as Miqel's.

"We're stopping here fer now, but it shouldn't be too long. Sainte and Aroc're building a raft now ta float down a river."

She tried to hide her emotions at the mention of Sainte's name, but Miqel caught it.

"Ah, I see ya still hold some feelings fer him. Well, ya should know that we are so close to him that I can see him when I walk a hunnerd yards in that direction." He pointed towards the mountains.

"Aye, we're that close, and he don't even realize it. But don't worry, I'm not gonna hurt him. I'm not even gonna let him know we're here. I'm saving a little surprise for 'em, but now ain't the time." He shook his head. "We have ta wait fer a very special person ta give him the surprise. We have ta wait fer Ellie."

THIRTEEN
-CONCEPTION-

After Aroc and Sainte woke up, they packed and moved on, both eager to reach Munich. It was a few hours of walking through the mountains silently with nothing but the sound of the wind before they found the river. Using fallen trees and driftwood, they soon had a makeshift raft.

With all the rope in her bag, Aroc tied the logs together. Soon, they had a raft that was reliable enough to sit on for both of them. It did not look like it would float very well, and they both would definitely get drenched with ice-cold water on the journey, but it did not matter as long as the raft held together.

With Aroc on the raft, Sainte pushed it into the river and climbed on. The water was even colder than expected, but they would persevere. They had to.

"How long will this take us?" Sainte asked through chattering teeth.

"Maybe an hour, no more than two," she replied. "Try to keep your blanket dry." She gestured to Sainte's bag. "It would be smart to sleep in it naked and hang your clothes up to dry as much as possible when we're through with river travel."

"Right." Sainte hoisted his pack higher onto his shoulders to try to keep it further from any water that splashed.

They floated smoothly down the river, and the raft held together surprisingly well. Sainte almost wished he had just taken the canoe with them, but that would have slowed their progress significantly.

He could tell that both he and Aroc were beyond tired and needed sleep, but Aroc insisted on continuing their lessons. Aroc began to implement more than just suggestions into the lessons. She now tried to make Sainte feel sick, dizzy, and nervous. If an emotion existed, Aroc tried to make Sainte feel and fight it.

The lessons made the time go by quickly, and soon they came to the fork in the river. Each of them grabbed their makeshift oars. They shoved the long sticks into the water and tried to steer their raft to the right at Aroc's discretion.

"Not gonna make it," Sainte said as he rowed. "Push harder."

"I am," Aroc replied sharply.

Grudgingly, the raft moved where they wanted it to. Suddenly, a current grabbed it and pulled it to the right of the fork, in the correct direction.

"It won't be long now," Aroc said, relieved and panting. Sainte did not reply. He just stared at the bank of the river as they flowed by.

The sound of the water streaming by was somewhat relaxing. Sainte blanked out for a while until Aroc moved.

She pointed to the bank. "There's the path. We'll follow it until it turns away from the river, then we'll bank there."

Another hour passed when Sainte noticed the path was no longer visible.

"Aroc, we should stop," he said.

"Shite," she cursed. They frantically pushed the raft to the bank. The raft finally ran aground, and they stood up and stretched their legs as they walked to dryer land. They found a nice flat area and set up to sleep.

"Get some rest, Sainte. I'll stay up and keep watch first. I'll wake you if anything happens," she told him.

"Alright," he said, too tired to care. He removed his outer clothes and armor but left his base layer on because it was not wet. He was just glad that he could lie down on something that was not rocking. He laid down and closed his eyes, almost immediately asleep.

▼▲▼

Miqel had a Malignin carry Iris because she could no longer keep up with the pace they set. They had to match the speed of the river in order to keep Sainte and Aroc from getting too far ahead of them.

While they moved, Miqel talked to Iris in a friendly manner as she was carried. She never responded, though. She gave up trying to speak to him. There was nothing in it for her. Miqel was stuck in his ways now, brainwashed by Ellie. The frightening part was that he actually believed that what he and Ellie did with the Malignin was for the greater good.

Iris accepted that she was his slave now. She would probably die a slave. She stared emotionless at the ground—a shell of her former self. Miqel spoke with cheer, proud of himself for finally having the girl of his dreams, utterly unaware that his words fell on deaf ears.

His group of Malignin were able to keep just behind Sainte and Aroc easily. They followed them unnoticed all the way to where they decided to rest. Miqel paced around impatiently as he waited for Ellie to arrive. Iris tried to adjust her collar so it did not chafe as much.

Soon there was a disturbance with the Malignin that were at the camp. They began to look around excitedly and clicked their teeth together. Ellie walked into their midst from the pines and mist, along with five more Malignin.

"Miqel, good to see you in one piece..." Her eyes wandered lazily up and down his body. "I see you've finally got the girl you wanted. Good for you. Where's Sainte and the wyrm?"

"They're 'bout a ten-minute walk west. They've stopped fer now, and Sainte's restin', the woman, Aroc, is stayin' up fer watch. What's the plan?" he asked.

"Not in front of her. Follow me," she said.

"But Iris's tied up. She ain't goin' nowhere," Miqel protested.

"I'll not discuss this with her near," Ellie said, more than a little sinister. Miqel followed her away without another word. Not that Iris cared, she could not do anything to stop them now, anyway.

Soon the two came walking back to camp. "What're you going to do with her?" Ellie asked as she gestured towards Iris.

"I'll just chain her ta a tree. Ya understand, right Iris? I don't want ya ta do anything that might ruin our plans. Ye'll be by yourself fer a little while, but I'll be back soon. Ya won't have ta worry 'bout me." He walked over to her and caressed her cheek. She quivered in disgust.

He grabbed her chain from a Malignin, and she followed him to a tree. He wrapped the chain around and locked it, then turned to Ellie.

"Shall we go?"

She nodded her head. When they left, the Malignin followed. Iris watched them go, then slowly laid down on the ground and curled up into the fetal position with her hands clasped tightly together at her chest.

▼▲▼

"Sainte," Aroc said as she shook him. "Sainte, wake up."

His eyes snapped open and he sat up quickly. "Huh? What?" He looked around quickly.

"Easy," she said. "I just have to go pee. When I come back, we'll switch. You've slept for three hours. I didn't want to leave you while you were still asleep."

He rubbed his face to try to wipe the sleep away. "Alright, yeah. I'll be here." He watched her as she walked away. He stood up and checked his clothes that he hung up. He found hanging them up was pointless because it began to rain while he was asleep, so they were just as wet as before.

He felt strange as he put his wet clothes back on as if he was being watched. Something felt wrong here. When Aroc returned, he would ask her if she would mind just pushing the rest of the way to Munich even though she had not had time to rest. He heard her walk back to their makeshift camp area just then.

"Hey, Aroc, I think we should continue to Munich. I know..." He turned around to face her to finish his sentence but froze.

"Hi, Sainte," Ellie said weakly. She took a faltered step towards him.

"Ellie?" He looked away, remembering what happened last time he spoke to her and all his lessons with Aroc.

"Sainte, it's me." She fell weakly to her knees. He could not help himself. He rushed over and held her.

She had bruises on her arms, a few scratches here and there, and was dirty but otherwise looked unharmed. She seemed different from the last time he talked to her outside Elion. Maybe she was better now. He hugged her.

"How did you find us? Are you okay?" he asked with genuine concern in his voice.

"I'm fine, just tired." She spoke slowly and softly. "I was consumed by this... darkness. It changed me. It was terrible, I knew what I did, but I couldn't control it. It was a constant battle. Somehow, I managed to push it out. When I did, though, the Malignin fled from me. Like they couldn't stand to be near me. Then, with my own eyes, with me controlling them, I saw you and the woman getting off the raft and coming here." She started to cry. "I killed all those people in that town, didn't I? That was my fault?"

Sainte thought her explanation was strange, but he did not question her. "It's not your fault. C'mere." He hugged her tighter as she cried on his shoulder.

"I thought I'd never see you again. I thought that I was going to kill you..." she sobbed.

"You didn't, though. I'm right here. I'm fine. I have you now. It's going to be all right," he told her.

He grabbed her head gently in his hands and pulled her face in front of him so he could look her in the eyes. She gazed back with watery eyes and bit her bottom lip.

"I love you, Sainte," she said.

He was going to reply in turn but before he could even finish saying 'I,' she kissed him, and he kissed her back. He ran his hands down through her knotted hair. He could taste the saltiness of her mouth from not being cleaned, but he did not mind. He was sure he tasted the same. It seemed like a silly thing to complain about after everything they both had been through.

He broke the kiss off before anything could go further. "Ellie, we have to go back. I have to get Aroc, and we'll go back together to..." he did not know where they would go. "To wherever Aroc says. The Malignin could know where you're at. We're not safe here."

"You're right; we aren't safe," she said, then kissed him again.

▼▲▼

Aroc pulled her britches down and squatted, making sure that she would not piss on any of her clothes. She let it out and the area around her filled with the sound of liquid hitting the ground out of sync with the rain.

She finished and stood up, then heard a sound from behind her and before she could check it out, something bashed her in the head. She lost her vision and fell to the ground, unconscious.

"Pick 'er up," Miqel commanded. A Malignin slung her over a shoulder. They walked further away from where Sainte was so it would be unlikely that he would hear anything. When they reached a distance that Miqel thought was adequate, he stopped and commanded the Malignin to drop Aroc.

They circled her, twenty of them now. Miqel knelt by her and slapped her to get her to come to.

Aroc opened her eyes slowly. Everything came into focus. The pain from where she got hit in the head made her wince as she sat up. Miqel rocked back on his heels happily.

"Ye're awake. Good," he said.

"Who are you?" she asked tentatively.

He pursed his lips. "Ya mean Sainte hasn't told ya 'bout me? I'm his old friend, Miqel. He don't know it, but ye're a bad influence on him."

"So she got into your head?" She looked him up and down. "You look strong, so it's not surprising. Stronger you are, the more senseless you are." She stood up. Miqel allowed it, but he backed up a few steps.

"Don't do any of yer power stuff here. Ellie told me ta just kill ya, but I won't... Not yet. I'm gonna torture ya. I'm sure ye've got useful information fer us. Just tell us anything that would be useful, and we won't have to hurt ya. Much," he warned her.

She smiled slightly.

"Good luck." As soon as she finished speaking, a beam of light shot from her outstretched hand at Miqel. Right before it struck him, he dove out of the way. He sent back a ball of darkness at Aroc, but she swept it away easily.

"Kill 'er!" he shouted before being blown back by a ball of light. As one, the Malignin surged towards Aroc. She immediately surrounded herself in a circle of light, but they pressed forward regardless of their stinging eyes. The light that emanated from her held some of the Malignin off for now, but she would not be able to keep it up forever.

She frantically blasted Malignin in every direction. They persisted, though, each blow they struck towards her was closer as her light slowly faded. Not all of her attacks were fatal to the Malignin. Some just fell back temporarily, only to join the frenzy again a few moments later.

Aroc could feel the precise moment when her light faded from view, and as soon as it did, she shot a continuous beam of light from each of her hands and spun in a circle with her arms outstretched to her sides. She hoped to fell them all with one last blow.

She suddenly jerked to her right and risked a glance. What she saw made her blood run cold. A Malignin latched onto her right hand; the entire thing was in its mouth up to her wrist. The beast chewed at it and she could feel her bones breaking, flesh pierced by the sharp teeth.

On impulse, she surged more power through that hand than ever before and blew through the Malignin. It flung off her hand and the Malignin behind it ran away. She was free, but her hand was shredded, useless, she dared not look at it until this was over.

She was pulled to the left violently, and without looking, she already knew that her left hand was going to share the same fate. Aroc quickly summoned all her strength and moved it through her hand, pushing out a giant shield of light. It emanated away from her and pushed the Malignin off her hand and away. The remaining Malignin fled ahead of the light. She brought her hands in front of her eyes to see the damage, and the sight made her fall to her knees.

She looked around quickly, searching for any more danger that may be present. Miqel laid a few feet away from her, unconscious. Satisfied that she was no longer in danger, her thoughts wandered to Sainte. Aroc struggled to stand up, but she managed it. She stumbled back to the camp, hoping that Sainte was still there.

▼▲▼

"Sainte, it's been so long. I love you... I want to make love with you," Ellie whispered in his ear.

Something was not right. He could feel it. Aroc should have been back by now. "We can't do that, Ellie."

Her eyes showed pain. "Why? You don't love me anymore? You love that other woman you're with?"

Sainte knew.

She was manipulating him, her words dripped with hidden agendas, but he hated to see that he hurt her. He had to try to make her feel better.

"Of course I love you. I just want to get you somewhere safe."

"I don't want to wait." She climbed on him, straddling him. "We're safe enough now."

Ellie held his head in her hands, and they stared into each other's eyes. Sainte got lost in her blue eyes speckled with green—all the promises they held. A flash of light in the distance took hold of Sainte's attention.

"Aroc," he muttered. His mind became startlingly clear at that moment, and he pushed Ellie off. "She needs help."

"No," Ellie growled, "she doesn't need any help where she's going."

Sainte stood up and grabbed his sword when he was pushed back to the ground, but he did not see what pushed him. His legs and arms were held down, and he tried to see what held him. What he saw filled him with terror.

Shadows held him down, darker than the night. They wrapped around him like any other shadow but had an unnatural weight.

"You're not going anywhere. Not until I get what is mine," Ellie said. She crawled close to him and pulled his undergarments down to his knees.

"What're you doing?" Sainte asked, a trace of panic in his voice. "Ellie, stop."

"Oh no, I won't stop now. I've come too far to stop." She grabbed his dick. "What's wrong? Are you not attracted to me anymore?" she pouted. "This won't do."

She started stroking him. Against his will, Sainte felt himself reacting to her touch.

He fought with every ounce of strength he could muster against the shadows that held him, but they did not give. "Please, don't. Stop this."

"I don't think so." Satisfied with her results, she climbed on him, legs on either side. "I wanted you to make love to me willingly, it would've been easier for both of us, but this will do just as well."

She moved her undergarments aside and rode Sainte. All the while, he protested and screamed at her to stop. She did not, not until she felt him finish inside of her.

Finally, satisfied she had everything she came for, she stood up and got off him. She leaned down close to his face and patted it.

"Thank you, Sainte. I love you so much," she said. After that, she turned around and walked away, leaving Sainte alone, naked, and scared.

▼▲▼

Iris had her eyes closed for a long time before she heard footsteps again. They were lighter than Miqel's, so she assumed they were Ellie's. She did not bother opening her eyes to see. It did not matter; whoever walked near her did not bother talking to her. After an undeterminable amount of time, Iris heard more footsteps. This time they were Miqel's.

"Where have you been?" Ellie said accusingly. "I'm assuming you were able to do what I ordered?"

"Er, not really, not all of it," he said. He sounded scared to Iris.

"What do you mean, 'not really'?"

"She fought back, and she fought back hard. I was hit by a stray, er, light and got knocked out. The Malignin attacked her, I s'pose, but when I came to, she was gone. I don't think she's dead."

Iris heard a smack and could only guess that Miqel was slapped.

Ellie took several deep, slow breaths. "These wyrms are stronger than normal humans, but you have powers. I put too much faith in you. I should have known you were too weak."

Miqel remained quiet.

"There's nothing more to be done. You failed in killing her, but at least you kept her busy enough to keep her out of my way. Let's go; there's naught else here for us."

Iris whimpered as she heard the familiar footsteps getting closer to her. Miqel knelt by her side and brushed her hair off her face.

"Ye're looking lovely today, Iris," Miqel said cheerfully despite the argument he just came from.

She opened her eyes finally and looked upon his face. Tears rolled down her cheeks, so accustomed to it that she did not even notice it anymore.

"Hey, it's okay. There's nothin' ta be upset 'bout." He wiped a tear from her cheek. "Everything's going exactly as planned." He kissed her cheek, but she pulled away slightly. He paused and just looked at her, then stood up.

He walked behind her, knelt, and unlocked the chain from the tree she was chained to like a dog. He tugged on the chain until she stood up.

"We're movin' again. Hope ya got enough rest."

Sainte woke with a start, having passed out sometime after Ellie left him. Something was sprawled across his legs. At first, he thought it was Ellie, but it did not feel right. He opened his eyes to look.

Aroc was passed out on his lap, white as snow with streaks of blood across her face. Her hands were mangled and covered in blood. He also noticed something white on her hands, spider webbing beneath her skin. He looked closer and it looked like her veins, starting at her wrists and moving into her hands, were white. There was something much more wrong with her than just her hands. Aroc was not moving and barely breathing.

"Shite." He scrambled up and dressed as fast as he could. He did not bother putting everything on, just the base layers. He thought quickly, but not clearly. He ripped up an extra shirt into strips of cloth. He doused the fabric with water and started to clean her hands to better see what wounds he had to deal with.

There were bite marks on each of her hands; they were red, swollen, and probably infected. The redness seemed to have spread from her hands almost up to her elbows already. He wrapped her hands in the moist cloth with little knowledge of first aid and almost nothing to work with. He strapped on his sword, picked her up, wrapped her arms around his neck, and held her legs around his waist. Once situated, he took off at a jog towards Munich. He left all their supplies behind in his hurry.

Sainte had a fleeting thought about Ellie but was too afraid and humiliated to think about it anymore than he had. All he knew now was that Aroc needed help and that she would not last long without it. He checked her hands and arms often to track the swelling and spread of the infection.

While he ran, he talked to her, always tried to rouse her. She would occasionally moan, which was more than he hoped for. As long as she made noises, he knew she was alive.

He made it about three miles before he stopped to take a break. He did not sit down or put Aroc down, however. There was no time. He took a few deep breaths and tried to steady his shaky legs.

As he took off running again, he worried that he may have veered off course and not be going towards Munich.

There was only one way to find out, so he kept running. He was thankful that the trees and brush were less thick in this area, so it made for fast travel in the dark.

What felt like hours later, he thought he could see a glow in the distance that usually marked a large town lit by torches. He pumped his legs faster and headed in that direction. He could feel his legs wanting to collapse, but he forced them to keep moving. Aroc ceased making sounds, but he could still feel her shallow, ragged breathing against his back. Sainte could now feel a fever from her. She was soaked through with sweat and beginning to soak him.

He began to see spots in his vision as the town loomed ever closer. He was so close when blackness crept from outside his vision and started engulfing it. He shook his head to try to clear it, which helped a little bit, but never made it completely disappear.

His head was too heavy to hold up, so he stared at the ground and looked at his feet—one in front of the other. Aroc's head bounced against his as his steps got heavier. Sainte barely noticed.

He heard some shouts from somewhere, but he could not tell where. He took another step, but his leg betrayed him and buckled. He fell to the ground, unconscious, with Aroc on top.

Sainte groggily opened his eyes. His mouth was dry as dust and his legs felt like needles were stuck through them. He laid on a cot in a small room with a fire in the middle but nothing else. He moved his head to get a better look at his surroundings when he heard movement from behind him. A young man walked into his view. He did not look older than twenty. A short sword was strapped to his waist.

"Sir, how're you feeling? Try not to move too much. You need rest," he said as Sainte tried to sit up.

Sainte lay still and tried to remember what happened. He faintly recalled seeing a town in the distance before he blacked out.

"Where am I? How long have I been here?" he croaked out. The man left without answering but returned shortly with a mug of water. He put it in Sainte's hand.

"Drink. You and your companion are in Munich. Been here for several hours."

Sainte took a drink and swallowed with a grimace. "Where is she?" he asked a bit more clearly now that he wetted his parched throat.

"Jasmine is seeing her. She lost a lot of blood and has an infection. We weren't sure if we could save her, but somehow she pulled through. We think she's gotten through the worst of it. We're expecting her to live," he said with a reassuring smile.

Sainte closed his eyes and let out a small sigh of relief. When he opened his eyes again, he said, "I feel good enough to walk. Take me to her, please."

With a bit of help, Sainte stood up. His legs still had not forgiven him for the stress he put them through just a few hours ago. He knew he would be sore, but this was nothing like he ever felt before. The boy held his arm to help keep him steady.

"I'm good. You can let go." The boy let go, and Sainte steadied himself. "Thanks... What's your name? I don't think you told me."

"I'm Peng," he said as he led Sainte down a hallway. "And yours?"

"Sainte." He paused as he noticed Peng stopped walking after he told him his name. "What is it?"

"You wouldn't happen to know a girl that goes by Iris, would you?" he asked curiously.

Now it was Sainte's turn to stop walking. He turned to the boy.

"Aye, I do. How do you know her?" he asked firmly.

"It's a story best for you to be sitting down, at least for someone in your condition. I'll show you to your friend's room, then once you're back in your own I'll tell you. More people should be present for it anyway," Peng told Sainte.

Sainte inclined his head and motioned for Peng to continue to lead the way even though he brimmed with questions. It would probably be best to see Aroc first. He owed her that much.

They walked further down the dim hallway and stopped in front of a door.

"Here we are." Peng knocked gently on the door and waited for an answer. "Jasmine? It's Peng. I'm bringing a visitor."

The door opened a crack, and there was an inaudible whisper.

"Yes, it's the man who was carrying her, Sainte."

Another muffled reply, then Peng turned to him.

"You can head in now. When you're finished, Jasmine will see you get help back to your room if I'm not here."

Sainte nodded in thanks, and Peng quickly walked away. He pushed the door open and walked into a warm room. Jasmine sat next to Aroc, who was still pale and sleeping. She looked up as he entered.

"Good to see that you're able to walk." She had dark skin and eyes with hair to match.

"Yeah, I'd say it feels good, too, but I'd be lying. How's she doing?" He gestured towards Aroc.

"I just put some fresh wraps on her hands, and she still has a fever, but I don't think it's anything to worry about. Seems like she's been through a lot. There's no telling when she'll wake up." The woman paused for a second as she looked at Aroc.

"I'm sorry." She stood and outstretched her hand. "I didn't introduce myself. I'm Jasmine."

Sainte shook her hand. "Sainte. Thanks for helping her."

"Of course. What other choice did I have? Apart from the strange white veins in her hands, I expect she'll pull through. It may be a long recovery though."

He sat at the foot of Aroc's bed and Jasmine sat back in her chair. "It's hard to even look at her. What happened to her was my fault..." He meant it.

"Don't think like that. You're the one that saved her life," Jasmine said soothingly.

"But at what cost to her?" He looked at Aroc. "Thanks again. I mean it."

"Stop with the thanks. It's not necessary. We know each other, and I know that she would do the same for me if our positions were reversed."

"You know her? How?" Sainte asked curiously.

"I used to travel with a group of merchants that brought supplies to Aroc's small town. Her family used to let me stay with them when I was there," she explained.

"But, she's from Elion. That's not a small town," he said.

"Oh, it was in that time," she said offhandedly and too carelessly for Sainte to let the topic go.

"You're like her, aren't you? You weren't a merchant." When he got no immediate reply, he looked at Jasmine. She gazed at him with scrupulous eyes and her entire demeanor seemed to change.

"What has she told you?" she asked him.

His suspicions were confirmed. "Well, she's a White Wyvern. Their job is to kind of guide humans in the right direction. And you all have special abilities, at least from what I've seen. A bit different than the tales that have been told about you. That's about it."

"Well..." she was cut off as Sainte's stomach let out a loud growl, and she could not help but chuckle. "You must be famished. Come, I could use something to eat too, and Aroc needs some peace and quiet."

They both stood up and left the room. As they passed by Sainte's room, he saw two men sitting there. One was Peng and the other he did not recognize.

"Hey, I'm still talking to Jasmine. We're going to get something to eat. I will be back," he explained to them. They looked slightly irritated but nodded in understanding and continued their conversation.

The hallway opened into a larger dining room that was dimly lit with candles on every wooden table. People spoke in hushed conversation, hunched over their tables. They found an empty one and sat across from each other.

"This is actually a decent tavern, even though it's in the medical building. Good food," she told him when she saw his expression. A man walked up to them and stopped at the head of the table.

"What'll be fer ya two?"

"Soup of the day will be fine." She looked at Sainte. "Er, if that's what you want?"

He nodded his head and muttered in affirmation.

"Thanks," she said, looking back at the waiter. He nodded his head and shuffled away towards the kitchen.

Jasmine and Sainte made idle chit-chat until their soup arrived, then Jasmine sat forward.

"So, tell me what happened to Aroc. I can guess what happened to her hands or, more accurately, what caused her to do that. But I don't know any details. Are you able to clear those up for me?" Jasmine asked in a hushed voice, but he could feel the intensity behind the question.

He sighed inwardly, knowing that this question was unavoidable, but he would not hold the truth from her. "We stopped to rest and bed down. She told me she would be first watch and would wake me up to switch. She woke me up and said she was going to take a piss, and I was supposed to stay up because she wouldn't be there. We would switch when she got back.

"I..." he hesitated. "Ellie came to me in Aroc's absence. She said that she was herself and wanted to be with me. I know about her words of manipulation, and I fought against it but almost gave in. There was a flash of light far away but so bright I noticed it and I snapped out of it. I told Ellie I had to get Aroc. She got mad," he paused. "She raped me," he muttered.

"What? I didn't catch that last part," Jasmine said.

"I said she raped me," he repeated a bit louder.

She leaned back in shock. She said nothing for a few moments as she soaked the information in and studied him.

"Afterwards, she left me there. I passed out for whatever reason, and when I awoke, Aroc was sprawled upon me."

"I'm so sorry..." she said. "For obvious reasons, I'm sorry, but this is not good."

Sainte could tell by how she said it that not good was an understatement. "What do you mean?"

"That would explain..." she said more to herself than to him. "The others must know." She made a move to stand up, but Sainte grabbed her hand.

"Please, don't go yet. Just talk to me for a bit," he pleaded, not wanting the conversation to end on that note. She looked at his face and felt pity for him, so she sat back down.

"What do you want to know?"

"Do you know how long it's been since the Malignin took Ellie?" he asked, wondering if she had the same ideas as Aroc.

"I think we are going on three weeks now, maybe a few days longer," she told him, hoping to calm him down. "It's tough to tell."

"That's it?" he said, almost unable to believe her. "It feels much longer."

Jasmine did not say anything but shook her head. She waited patiently for more questions, but he did not have any.

"Was that it?" she asked him. Sainte just showed her his empty bowl. "Right, you should get back to bed, and I should get back to Aroc. I'll help you back to your room."

"I can do it myself."

"Well, it was good chatting with you, Sainte. Take it slowly. I'll let you know if anything changes with Aroc. I'll be in touch. Let me know if you need anything."

"Thanks." They walked together for a short distance, then split up. When Sainte returned to his room the two men were still there. He walked past them without saying anything and laid down on his bed.

"So... you know Iris," he said to them as a statement more than a question. They nodded their heads in unison.

"Yes," Peng said. "I do."

Iris had much time to think while Miqel was away. At first, she hated being stuck in her head, being her only company. Over time she got used to it and even enjoyed the moments spent alone. After many conversations with herself and some deep thought, she concluded that there was one thing she wanted more than to kill herself.

To kill Miqel.

She devoted all her time thinking up ways to kill him. She did not stop imagining how great she would feel staring at his corpse.

Finally, she settled on a plan.

She prepared herself mentally because she knew it would take much time. It would not be easy for her, and she would enjoy no part of it except upon completion. Only then would she allow herself to feel any satisfaction.

After all, it included her earning Miqel's trust back. There was only one way she knew that it would work.

She heard some footsteps and cringed when she recognized them as his. She could not help it anymore. He knelt before her, grabbed her chin, and forced her to look at his smiling face.

"Ye'll be happy to know that I found the location of one of our mutual friends again." Her eyes showed no emotion, but inside she felt nothing but hatred. "I am, o' course, talking about Sainte. He's staying in Munich right now. Wonder what he's up ta? I don't think it'll be much longer 'fore we're all reunited again, just like ol' times." He continued to smile.

She wanted to spit in his face and scream that nothing would ever be like the 'old times' again.

Miqel stood back up and walked behind her, checking her chain. Since their last stop, when she was left alone, they moved north. They did not stop until they reached a cave Iris was not allowed to enter. Miqel chained her to another tree just outside the entrance.

"Miqel," she forced out. "Can we go talk somewhere? I want to know more about what you will do with Ellie. Are you going to be in charge of anything?" She heard him as he walked back around in front of her.

"What's this? Ye're finally liking my company?" He thought about his answer. "I'll be glad ta tell ya what's gonna happen. Fine, somewhere private then. Get up." He grabbed her arm and pulled her to her feet. He pulled out a key and unlocked the chain from around her neck.

"Come with me. Right after ye're going back on the chain, though."

"Of course," she replied. One small step at a time, she thought to herself. This was exactly what she wanted to accomplish.

She knew this was the beginning of the end of Miqel, but she took no pride in it. She did not want to kill him, the man who was once her friend.

She *needed* to.

FOURTEEN
-HORRIFIED-

"Aroc, are you awake? Can you hear me?" Jasmine said urgently in the dark room. The fire was smothered to give Aroc a more peaceful rest. She stirred at her voice.

"Mmmm... Yes, is that you, Jasmine?" Aroc asked with a scratchy voice. She sounded groggy, but at least she was awake.

"Yes, it's me. How're you feeling?" Flint and steel struck together as Jasmine attempted to reignite the fire. After three tries, a small flame burned furiously and grew into a full blaze.

"I feel terrible, of course. How bad is it?" she asked, looking at her wrapped hands, dreading the answer.

"Teeth went through your hands, damaged a lot of tendons and nerves beyond repair. You'll probably never have full function of your hands again. And..." Jasmine trailed off.

"And what?"

"They're seared. I don't know how much power you pushed through them, but the Light seared your veins. You'll never be able to channel your power again," Jasmine explained.

"I know what seared means," Aroc snapped, then sighed. "I didn't mean to yell at you. It's just a lot to take in."

"I understand... Also, there's something else."

"What?"

Jasmine paused, not wanting to be the bearer of more bad news. "Nothing, I already regret bringing it up. You have much to deal with already."

"Tell me."

Jasmine licked the inside of her cheek. "Fine. I talked with Sainte, and I have reason to believe that the seed has been planted," she told her reluctantly.

"Damnit, damn him, he learned nothing from the lessons," Aroc cursed, fuming.

"It wasn't his fault," Jasmine quickly said. "Ellie took him against his will. I feel bad for him. You've been through much, but so has he."

"How long have I been out? You've known about the planted seed and done nothing?"

"Just over a day," Jasmine told her. "What do you expect me to do? I haven't heard from the Council since the start of these Dark Days. Sainte has been up and walking around. I can tell he already grows restless. He needs something to do."

"He'll be fine. Has the Council at least received the letter yet?" Aroc asked earnestly. She was met with a confused look from Jasmine.

"Letter? About what?"

Aroc closed her eyes in disbelief. "He brought nothing with him?"

"Just you and the clothes on his back. That was it. Why? What should he have brought?" Jasmine asked.

"The letter with Isaac's seal on it. Asking for an extension before they implement the Sever."

"You have that? Why did Isaac not bring it himself?" she asked. Deep down, she knew the answer but did not want to admit it to herself.

"He's dead. Sainte and I found the letter before we fled from Elion. Sainte must have left it in his rush to get me here. We have to get it back," she said desperately.

"We will, but you're not going. I'll gather a small party and send them out to retrieve it. I'll send Sainte with them because he'll know where your camp is. If that's ok with you," Jasmine said as she tried to calm her.

"Send him, I don't care. Hopefully it's still there..."

"Don't worry, I'm sure it is. They'll find the letter and bring it back. From talking to Sainte, it didn't sound like you were too far from here when attacked. I'll ask him if he's willing to go and try to find other people to accompany him. I already have a couple people in mind.

"Get some more rest, Aroc. You need it." She patted her leg gently. "I'll be back in a little while to let you know how things are going and our plans from here."

"Alright. Thanks Jasmine, for everything. I don't know what I'd do without you."

Jasmine did not reply. She just smiled at her and stood up. She covered the fire with a metal lid to put it out, then walked out of the room, closing the door behind her.

▼▲▼

Peng nodded. "Aye, I know Iris. Another man, Kial, also knows her but he's been with his wife and daughter," Peng said. "He knows her just by reputation," he nodded to the other man in the room.

"Who are you?" Sainte asked.

"My name's Mitch. I'm Ivan's brother," he said as if Sainte knew who Ivan was. "Peng reported to me once he returned..." he started to say, but Peng put his hand up for him to stop.

"I think we should start at the beginning for Sainte, he doesn't know who we are, and I'm sure he would like to understand our story."

"Of course, go ahead, Peng," Mitch said.

Peng told Sainte how he and his friends met Iris and then how they were ambushed.

"Miqel attacked us, but one of our guys, Tal, took Iris and headed to Elion. I don't know if they ever made it... The rest of my comrades were killed, except for Kial and I. Miqel spared us and told us to return here and tell the people that they are coming."

Sainte was stunned by their story. "I can't believe Miqel would do that. He wouldn't. You know this because Iris recognized him? That can't be. He would never..." he said, unable to believe their story. He could not believe it unless Ellie got to Miqel and used the words of manipulation.

"All we are saying is what we experienced. She seemed pretty certain that it was him, your other friend."

"You said they went to Elion?" Sainte asked.

"Aye, I did," Peng said.

"It's destroyed, overrun by Malignin. I was there, Aroc and I managed to escape." His voice slowly quieted as realization dawned on him.

"Maybe she and Tal were there before you? Maybe you just missed them?" Peng said hopefully. Mitch looked at him with eyes that told him it was pointless to suggest that.

"No, if a Shinta had arrived in town with a girl, people would have been talking about it. I would have heard something. They had to have arrived after it was ruined... I hope she's alright." He looked at Peng and then Mitch. "You haven't heard anything from this, Tal, guy?" he asked with slight hopefulness in his voice. They both just shook their heads.

"Ah, well... Thanks for telling me all this. It's a little uplifting to know that Iris may still be alive... I hadn't thought about her for a long time..." he was somber as he said this. "I'm sorry about your friends. How long ago did you say you all separated?"

"No more than two weeks, I'd say, give or take a few days. And no worries, I would hope I would be treated the same if I were in your position," Peng said. He looked to Mitch. "Come on, we should let him get some rest."

The two men both stood up. "Hope you get to feeling better soon, Sainte," Peng told him.

"Aye," Mitch agreed.

They both turned away and prepared to walk out. When Peng opened the door, Jasmine stood there with her hand up ready to knock. She looked at them in surprise.

"I was just looking for... All of you, actually. I have an order for you two and a question for one. Mitch, Peng, ride out to Sainte and Aroc's last location outside of Munich to get a letter for me. Sainte, would you ride with them since you know the location and what the letter looks like? We need this as expediently as possible. You will be given horses to quicken the process." She looked at them expectantly.

"Of course we'll go, Jasmine. When do you need us ready?" Mitch asked without hesitation.

"As soon as Sainte is ready, if he's willing to go?" She looked past the two standing men and right at Sainte.

He was tempted to say no, but he knew he forgot the letter, which meant a lot to Aroc for whatever reason. He did not leave it on purpose but felt responsible for it now.

"I'll go. Give me an hour, and I'll be ready," he said. Mitch and Peng nodded. Jasmine moved aside to let them leave and prepare.

"Thank you, Sainte. I know that you must be tired..."

He stopped her. "Don't worry about it. I'm used to restless nights, even if they're particularly long. Also, this gives me a chance to go back and grab my armor. I even forgot a pair of gauntlets that Isaac had given me," he said as he stood up.

"Yes, you wouldn't want to leave those behind," she said strangely. "Well, I'll leave you to get ready." She left and closed the door behind her.

An hour later, Peng came to Sainte's room to make sure he was ready. Once he was, he took him to the stables. The horses were in good health despite the dwindling food supply. Mitch explained they had a lot saved up in grain stores for the livestock.

Soon they were on the horses and riding south. Sainte did not exactly remember how to return to where they stayed, but he figured it would not be too hard to find. He was not wrong. Soon, he began to recognize their surroundings. For the most part, all they had to do was follow the path.

"We're getting close. Keep an eye out for anything that may look like a campsite," he called out to Peng and Mitch. Twenty more minutes passed before they came upon it. Peng spotted it first and pointed it out to the other two.

Sainte dismounted and tied his horse up to a tree. He walked over to the site and examined it, surprised that it looked untouched.

"Everything here?" Mitch asked him.

"Looks like it." He walked over to his gear. He put his chainmail on, then his leathers over it.

Lastly, he grabbed the two gauntlets and put them on, relieved that he found all his armor. Next, he grabbed Aroc's and his satchels and hooked them to his horse's saddle. He mounted his horse after checking Aroc's satchel to make sure it still had the letter.

"Come on, I don't want to waste any more time and risk being found by any roaming Malignin," he said to Peng and Mitch. They slowly mounted, and Mitch let out a short snort of laughter.

"What's so funny about that?" Sainte asked.

"I thought you were kidding?" Mitch looked at Sainte. He returned Mitch's gaze. "Guess you're not. I thought Jasmine told you?"

"Told me what?"

"There are no Malignin down in these parts. Least not anymore. Scouts said they're in the mountains south of Bethrune, north of Litewood. They say they're ninety to a hundred miles north of us. You didn't know?" he asked.

"You know where they're at and you're doing nothing?" Sainte asked incredulously.

"What should we do?" Peng asked.

"Bring an army there and kill them all. What else would you do?" he asked angrily.

"Isn't that what the Blades are for? No, we will study them, figure out their weaknesses, and maybe find out what they plan to do next?" Mitch retorted, a little frustrated that Sainte disapproved of how they dealt with the situation.

Sainte thought quickly about this news. Why had Jasmine not told him? Probably because she knew what he would do.

What he was going to do.

"I won't ask you two to lie for me but hear me out. I must track them down. I have to go there, to the mountains. I have to find Ellie," he started to explain.

"The Barrier?" Peng asked.

"Aye, I have to do what I can to save... stop her. If I can't stop her, then I'll kill her. All I'm asking you to do is let me ride there, now, by myself. Take your time getting back to Munich. I'll give you Aroc's satchel. Make sure she or Jasmine gets it. It has the letter that Jasmine wanted. But give me time. Give me at least a day's travel before you return to Munich," he almost pleaded with them.

Peng and Mitch shared worried glances.

"Jasmine won't be happy about this. What if she asks about you? You know she will," Mitch said.

"Tell her the truth. Let her know that you accidentally told me where the Malignin were, and I forced you to let me get a head start on you or something. You're smart men. I'm sure you can figure something out."

"What if you get killed?" Peng said. "Your death would be on our hands."

"If I don't go, everyone's deaths will be on your hands," Sainte retorted, then more calmly said, "I won't get killed. Ellie wouldn't do that to me," he told them that, but he was not confident that there was truth to the statement anymore.

After a moment of thought, Mitch said, "Alright, if that's what you think is best." Sainte was surprised he gave in so quickly; apparently, so was Peng.

"Mitch," Peng exclaimed. "You can't mean to just let him go by himself?"

"Course I can. He's the Shield. He knows these Malignin and the Barrier better than anyone else. If he thinks he can fix this, then I believe him. It's about time we believe in something anyway. It might as well be him." He looked at Sainte. "I'll only give you a day. Even though I trust you, I don't trust the Malignin. You have my word that Jasmine won't know about you leaving until you've a head start. I reckon, on horseback, you could travel fifty miles in a day. You should be well into Litewood by then."

"Thank you, Mitch. This is for the best, believe me," Sainte said, relieved.

"I don't know what you're still doing here. I'd be riding by now if I were you," Mitch said as he waved his hand.

Sainte nodded, then tossed him Aroc's satchel. He galloped away as the two men watched.

Peng turned to Mitch. "Are you insane? That man's going to ride straight to his death. What chance does he have?"

"Better chance than anyone else does," Mitch said. Peng shook his head in disbelief.

"Wyverns watch over you, Sainte," Peng said.

▼▲▼

A day passed since Jasmine sent the men off to retrieve the letter, and she paced around Aroc's room impatiently muttering to herself.

"Where are they? They should have been back by now."

Aroc opened her eyes. "Sainte and the two others aren't back yet? Just give them some time. I'm sure they won't be much longer."

"They've had plenty of time," she started to say something more but was interrupted by a knock on the door. She opened it and slipped outside. She was gone for a few minutes, then came back, head bowed.

"What is it?" Aroc asked. "Did they come back?" She could feel that something was not right.

"Most of them... Sainte did not return. Mitch says he discovered that the Malignin went to the mountains north of Litewood. He means to find them and face Ellie."

"Damn... Why did they not stop him?" she asked, clearly irritated.

"I don't know. Good news is they brought your satchel back, which has the letter." Jasmine held it up.

"At least that means you can get it to the Council. Maybe they'll give us time. It might be too late now." She sat up.

"What are you doing, Aroc? You can't think I'll just let you go after Sainte?" Jasmine said, already knowing what was flowing through her friend's head. She put her hands gently on Aroc's shoulders and tried to push her back down, but she refused.

"Get off me, Jasmine. You have to let me find him. It's my duty. We both know what has to happen and I'm the best option right now. I can't channel anything out anymore. That means it's been storing up. There's only one way to release it. You are useful for many things, but this is the last thing I can do," Aroc said fiercely.

"There's got to be another way," Jasmine said, doubting her own words. She gazed at her friend with a profound sadness.

"Don't do that to me. Don't let me continue to live this way." She held up her hands, white veins riddled across her skin. "This is no way for us to live. Let me finish this."

Jasmine sighed and backed away, "How are you even going to get him?"

"Get me a horse that's been trained to steer with leg movements. I know you have them here." Aroc stood up. "Help me get dressed."

Jasmine started to help and consented, "We have horses trained on leg cues. I'm sorry it has to be like this, Aroc." She held her friend at arm's length before embracing her.

"It's too late to be sorry, Jasmine. You should know that." Once she was dressed, Jasmine led her to the stables and saddled her a horse.

After she was mounted Aroc said, "If either Sainte or I are not back in five days, come looking for us. Until then, talk to the Council, make them see the opportunity for what Isaac's letter offers. There's hope, but only a little remains." She almost rode off then, but Jasmine grabbed hold of the reins.

"I will see you again, Aroc," Jasmine promised.

"Don't get your hopes up."

She rode out of Munich as fast as she could tolerate.

▼▲▼

Ever since Iris began to talk to Miqel and tell him that she wanted to be a part of his future, he visited her much more often. She was still chained outside the cave and was not allowed inside, but she did not need to be inside for her plan to work. Whenever he came to talk to her, he would unchain her. She would follow him to an area a short distance away where the Malignin were not allowed to go.

Each time they went off by themselves, Miqel asked her if she was ready for sex, but each time she denied him. She said she wanted to take it slowly, and to her surprise, he respected her wishes. Instead, they talked about what their futures held in store, and then Miqel would hold her close, and Iris pretended to enjoy their time.

She did all this to bide her time, examine her surroundings, and plan how best to kill Miqel. After the eighth time, Iris knew what she was going to do.

"Hey, Miqel?" she said sweetly as he walked up to her, ready for their next talk.

"Yes?"

"I think I'm ready now," she said confidently.

"Ready fer what?" he asked slyly.

"For you. I want to prove that you can trust me. That I'm with you forever." She caressed his arm while he stood in front of her. He was excited but tried to keep it under control.

"Let me just unhook ya back here," he said as he walked around and removed her collar. "Yer good. Follow me." He led her away down the path that they used before. Soon they entered the familiar clearing, and he turned to face her. "So, how do ya want it?"

"Take your clothes off first, then undress me," she said as she slowly lowered herself to the ground and laid on her back. Miqel took his clothes off with contained anticipation.

He smiled at her. "I've been waitin' fer this moment fer a long time, Iris." He lowered himself over her and caressed her cheek.

Iris slowly spread her legs for him. She reached her arms above her head as he walked himself between her legs. He did not start to take her clothes off yet, but he kissed her hard, biting her lip. This entire time her hands searched for one of the potential weapons she noticed throughout their private talks. She desperately hoped it would be one of the rocks she spotted.

"Ya ready?" he whispered in her ear, his legs pushing hers farther apart.

"I can't wait," she whispered back, trying to hide the adrenaline coursing through her veins. Her hand found a rock. She grasped it with both hands slowly, quietly so as not to alert him.

He started to sink to her stomach, getting closer to her crotch when she brought the rock crashing down on his head with both hands. Iris swung it with all the strength she could muster.

Except it was not a rock as she initially thought, but a fallen branch. Her aim was true, though, and the branch broke across the top of his head.

He crumpled on her with a grunt, and she quickly shoved him off. She looked at the broken branch in her hand and tossed it to the side. She hastily stood up and watched him snivel with his bleeding head grasped by his hands.

She snatched a rock that she saw and smashed him across the head again.

Iris kicked him over with adrenaline pumping. Filled with a fury she never felt before, she smashed him in his cock with her foot. She railed him in the face again with the rock and heard a satisfying crunch as his nose broke.

Her hand was lifted to hit him once more, but she was tackled before she could finish the strike. She untangled herself from the confusion and saw that a Malignin tackled her. It stood up but did not attack her. Instead, it looked from her to Miqel as if waiting for an order. She could think of nothing else but to run. There was no way she could fight off a Malignin with a rock.

"Bitch!" she heard Miqel scream. "I'm goin' ta fucking kill ya!" His voice echoed. It followed her through the forest, rang through her head, but she did not stop running. Suddenly she burst from the trees.

She stood on a road that was overgrown with brush. No one traveled on it in a long time. She looked left and right and quickly decided that going right was the correct decision. Better than not deciding at all.

She only took five steps before Miqel burst from the tree line not twenty feet in front of her. She froze in her tracks. He was still naked and outraged. He held his axe in his right hand, and his chest heaved. An evil grin was born on his face. Blood poured from his nose like a waterfall.

"I loved ya," he growled. "I could've killed ya long ago, but I didn't. After all that I've done fer ya, all I've shown ya. We could've been great together, but still ya choose ta defy me." He took a step closer.

"Miqel," her voice quivered, "please, let me go." Tears streamed down her face, and she choked back a sob. "Please..." She begged him, hoping there was a sliver of the old Miqel inside.

"Ya know I can't do that, Iris. I can't trust ya, and ya obviously don't love me. I have ta kill ya." He ran at her, axe ready to strike her down.

Iris threw her arms up in a hopeless defense. When Miqel swung his axe, she felt a slight tugging sensation on her left arm and a sharp burning pain. The force of his attack flung her to the ground. She looked at her left arm, and her bicep was torn open. White bone shone from the wound before blood poured out from it. Her arm hung limp by her side, she tried to move it, but it refused.

Iris wailed in pain and agony. She held her grievous wound as blood poured from between her clutching fingers and managed to make it to her knees.

"I didn't wanta do this, Iris. I was gonna make it fast fer ya, but ya just had ta move." Spittle flecked from his mouth when he talked. He shoved her to the ground with his foot. "I'm sorry, fer what good it does ya. Now let me finish."

She knew she was dead no matter what. The need to cry was as strong as ever, but a sudden thought stopped her. She had spent the better part of the last few weeks crying. She was tired of it. She would not die crying. Iris calmed herself down and looked Miqel in his eyes, ready to accept her fate with all the dignity she had left.

Miqel hefted his axe like an executioner at the block.

"I never wanted it ta be like this, my love."

▼▲▼

Sainte rode fast, taking only short breaks. He stopped once to let his horse drink but quickly continued his ride through Litewood.

He was certain that Jasmine would have sent people out to search for him by now, perhaps Peng and Mitch, but he was far enough ahead that he did not worry about being discovered. Not anytime soon, at least. Sainte was cautious as he rode, concerned because he had not seen any Malignin. He figured they would be crawling around this area if Ellie was here.

He was slowly drawn out of his thoughts by a noise. It sounded like a man yelling. He came to a stop and listened.

There was a woman's scream, too. Sainte spurred his horse into a gallop towards the scream. It did not sound very far. He rounded a turn on the overgrown path and came to a surprising scene.

He expected to find some scouts for Ellie, perhaps, or someone getting ambushed, but what he saw was nothing he could have ever dreamed.

Miqel, naked, stood above Iris, ready to cut her head off. Iris was on her knees, looking up defiantly, but blood pooled around her. Sainte saw Miqel's mouth move but was not close enough to hear what he said. Then he lifted his axe, about to kill her.

"Miqel!" Sainte roared at him in a panic. This caused him to stop and look up. His eyes found Sainte, and they narrowed.

Sainte rode up slowly, cautiously. When he was twenty paces away, he dismounted and walked towards the two.

"What are you doing, Miqel?" he asked in disbelief. "I've heard stories about you, but I did not think them to be true."

"I'm killin' Iris, Sainte," he spat his name out in disgust. "After her, I'll kill ya too."

"Why? What happened to you?" Sainte nonchalantly laid his hand on the hilt of his sword.

"My eyes 'ave been opened, that's what happened. Ellie made me realize that the Malignin aren't the problem. We are, we're the problem. She's tryin' ta make the world right again, Sainte. Anyone who disagrees with what she's doing must die," he finished, hefting his axe up again to finish Iris.

Sainte sprang into motion and tackled him. Instead of drawing his sword, Sainte decided to pry Miqel's weapon from his grasp. Maybe he could get his friend back. He had to try. He wrung the axe from his fingers, but Miqel punched him in the face and sent Sainte reeling. They both scrambled to their feet, trying to beat the other.

"I'll kill ya with my bare hands," Miqel said as he sprinted towards Sainte, fists raised. Sainte dodged the punches and slapped them away when he could.

He saw that Miqel was in such a rage that he gave off tells of what his next move would be. After dodging another blow, Sainte saw his chance. He ducked under a wide punch and kicked Miqel in the leg, making him stumble. Sainte kicked him again before he could regain his composure and knocked him to the ground on his back.

Sainte clambered on top of Miqel and punched his face so hard he heard his own knuckles crack. There was so much blood that he could no longer tell who it came from. Suddenly Sainte's vision went black and he flew off of Miqel. It felt like he was just kicked in the stomach by a horse.

"Ya think ya can beat me? I 'ave powers that Ellie gave me," he heard Miqel say. "That was just a small taste of it. How much more do ya think ya can take?"

His vision slowly returned, and he saw the person who was once his friend. Miqel was naked and more horrifying because of it. Darkness smoked off Miqel's body, and his eyes were pitch black. Sainte stood up as fast as he could and drew his sword.

"Ya think that can kill me? I don't even needa axe anymore," he said with a sinister grin. "I am the weapon."

"Where's Ellie?" Sainte asked through clenched teeth.

"In the caves, that direction." He gestured to his left. "Ya can't miss it. She's been expecting ya, I'm surprised it took ya this long ta get here. I was told ta try ta keep ya alive fer Ellie, but I doubt she would care much if I killed ya."

Sainte rushed him again. He was immediately met with resistance. Tendrils of darkness snaked from Miqel and surrounded him. He could not physically feel the touch of the darkness, but the effects were tremendous.

His bones began to ache, but he forced his legs to move. He felt as if he had a sickness, bile rose in his throat, but he forced himself to swallow it. His muscles tried to go limp, but he clenched his sword harder. The darkness snaked around his waist, yet he continued his charge. His mind was filled with doubt, and his failures surfaced, yet he did not stop. All of Aroc's lessons were forgotten at the moment.

All that consumed him was rage.

Miqel's eyes widened in surprise at Sainte's resistance to the darkness, but he easily sidestepped his attack. He punched Sainte in the face again, causing him to misstep. Sainte caught his balance quickly, however, and swung his sword around for a backwards strike. Miqel could not get out of the way, so he summoned a barrier of darkness between himself and the blade, catching the blade inches before it sliced open his throat.

Sainte pushed harder against the darkness, pushed harder against Miqel's grinning visage. Something happened to the blade. Before either of the quarreling men could guess what it was, they were both thrown backward with the force of an explosion.

They hit the ground hard. Their ears rang after a loud clap of thunder that was Sainte's blade exploding into a million different pieces. The only piece remaining whole was the hilt still clasped in Sainte's hand.

Sainte moved to his feet before Miqel, who took the brunt of the blast. He laid on his back, trying to regain his composure. Sainte strode over to him with only one purpose in mind.

Miqel looked up at him. "Ye've no idea what yer doing," he grunted. "My death'll get ya nowhere."

Before he could say anything else, Sainte smashed him in the face with the hilt. He smashed him again and again, over and over. The crunch of bone slowly turned to the squish of brain with each consecutive hit. Blood sprayed across Sainte's face, but it did not deter him. Miqel was unrecognizable after Sainte stood up weakly, still feeling the effects of the darkness.

He looked down at his now deceased friend with sorrow. How had it come to this? He dropped his bloody hilt to the ground with a thump and suddenly remembered Iris.

He ran to her and felt her neck for a pulse which fluttered weakly, but it was there. He grabbed her arm to examine her wound. It was deep, but Sainte could not tell how serious it was. He held it high to try to stem the blood flow. He had some cloth in his satchel, which he ran and grabbed.

He wrapped her arm up as best and as tight as he could. It was a severe wound and she lost a lot of blood. He dragged her to the side of the path carefully. After he made sure that she was as comfortable as possible, Sainte tried to leave for the caves, but Iris' eyes opened weakly.

"Sainte?" she could barely say his name.

"Yes, Iris, it's me. Listen to me. I'm going to go find Ellie and set things straight, then I'm coming back for you, okay?" he explained, hoping she understood him.

"No... Please stay with me. Don't go," she rasped.

He was torn. After Elion, he told himself he would not leave anyone needing help. Right now, though, if he left Iris and accomplished what he intended to do, she would not need his help for the rest of her life.

"I have to, Iris. I have to go. I have to do this. I'll be back for you." He ran to his horse, pulled out some bread and water, and set it down beside her. There was also a blanket which he laid over her. "I'm coming back for you," he promised again before he left her.

Sainte looked back at her once and saw her short and shallow breaths. He hoped she was still alive when he returned... if he ever returned.

It was slow going as the vegetation grew in thickly, and the ground was uneven, so close to the mountains now. He found animal trails, some rather large, and he guessed Malignin made them rather than deer. He occasionally came across their tracks, too, so he knew he was headed in the right direction.

It was not long before his boots and clothes were soaked through and muddy. Most of his clothes were torn, and he suffered minor scratches from thorns. The effects of the darkness from Miqel were still felt, but they were lessening.

It started to rain shortly after he left Iris, which did nothing but dampen his already low spirits. Finally, he spotted the entrance to a cave. The brush was cleared away, and there was nothing to hide it from prying eyes. Not that it needed hiding.

Sainte hid behind a tree and watched the cave entrance for any activity. He waited for half an hour, and there was no movement. Nothing went in or out. Stepping from behind the tree, he decided that he would check it out. If it was the wrong cave, he would leave and continue looking for the right one, but he had a bad feeling that this was the correct one.

Sainte entered the cave slowly, his senses on high alert, and looked for any traps. Nothing happened, so he went in deeper. He was about to leave when he smelled smoke. He then came across a smoldering torch on the ground that had been recently extinguished. This had to be the right cave. He drew a dagger and held it defensively in front of him.

He continued going straight as there was no other choice. Soon what little light was shining in was no longer there, so his vision was completely gone. He lost track of time when his eyes started to adjust to the dark slowly. There was some light from the outside, but it was not a lot. He came into a large cavern; the ceiling was thirty feet high. In the ceiling was a hole, the source of the faint moonlight.

Directly under the hole stood a lone figure.

Directly under the cascading moonlight stood Ellie.

▼▲▼

Aroc rode tirelessly without stopping. Her steed was used to long rides and needed little to no breaks. With every gallop, pain sliced up her arms. At least she did not have to worry about falling asleep. The pain made sure of that.

She was into a day's worth of travel when she encountered a body lying in the path. A man, naked, and his face was shattered to the point of being unrecognizable, brains splayed around his ruined head. Upon closer inspection, she assumed that the man was Miqel.

He was the same general size and shape as him. She looked around the area for more clues about what might have happened here when her eyes lingered over another body.

Whoever it was, they were still alive. Aroc dismounted her horse and hurried to their side. It was a girl with a deep cut in her bicep, a relatively fresh wound. Someone was hospitable enough to lay a blanket over her and give her food and water, but it was untouched.

"Hey, can you hear me?" she asked and lightly shook her. The girl was unconscious, and no amount of words were going to rouse her anytime soon. Thankfully she knew of an herb, Drysdain, which would wake people from sleep, and in dangerously large quantities, from a coma.

Drysdain grew in small patches everywhere, but it was most common in Litewood. After a short search, Aroc found what she was looking for. A small two-leafed plant that looked like a clover, but the stem was red.

She picked some with a grimace, even that small task pained her hands. She put it in her mouth and chewed it up, preparing it for the girl. As she chewed, she could already feel the grasp of sleep lessening around her mind.

When she got back to the girl, she took the herb out of her mouth and forced it past the girl's lips. Aroc held her mouth closed as her tongue mulled the Drysdain around. Then she sat back and waited for the effects, but she did not have to wait long.

The woman started to cough, and Aroc was by her side, put her arm around her, and told her to breathe. The girl looked around frantically, eyes filled with terror, then her gaze settled on Aroc, confused.

"It's alright. You're okay—my name's Aroc. Who are you?" she asked soothingly. She wished she could do more to calm her, but nothing else could be done.

The woman's breathing slowed a bit as she calmed down. "Iris," she croaked out.

Sainte's friend, the other one that he looked for. "Have you seen Sainte? He's looked for you for a long time. Was he here? Did he do that to Miqel? Do you know where he went?" She did not get a verbal reply, but Iris nodded her head.

"Can you take me to him? If I help you can you walk?" Her words came out quickly. She was nervous and desperate. Again Iris responded with a slight nod.

"Here, drink some water." Aroc held up the canteen and slowly poured a little into Iris' mouth. She swallowed with a grimace.

Aroc shrugged Iris' right arm over her shoulders and slowly stood up. She had to give Iris credit. She did not cry out at the obvious pain from the movement. Aroc did not move for a few moments, letting Iris prepare herself.

"Ready?" Aroc asked her.

"Yes." came her short answer. Together they started the slow walk to the cave.

▼▲▼

"Ellie," Sainte said, not quite in a whisper. She inclined her head slowly.

Suddenly Sainte was grasped by both arms and legs. Four Malignin held onto him, one on each limb. This resulted in him being lifted from the floor. His diminutive dagger was forced from his hand and clattered to the rocky ground.

He looked around in surprise and saw movement in the cavern that he previously missed. It was filled with Malignin—lots of movement.

He was a fool to come alone. A group of twenty people would be hard pressed to kill these Malignin. How could he expect to beat them? But it was too late for him to change any of his decisions.

"It's me again. Miss me?" Ellie spoke. Her voice was dark and smoky and seductive. She walked towards him in a skin-tight black dress with a slit down the front, showing her smooth legs with each step as she got closer. "You've finally come. I was wondering if you were ever going to show up."

She stopped about two feet before him and looked at his face, "But now, here you... hang."

"Ellie," he grunted. "Why are you doing this? You must stop."

"Why?" she sneered, making her beautiful face hatefully ugly. "You lied to me. My own father lied to me about everything. My entire life, and the lives of countless women before me, have been lies. And now you are here, daring to ask me 'why?' I've been locked in a mountain for eighteen years as 'bait' for these precious Malignin," she gestured around her, "My Malignin are the only truth in my life now, they are my family. They've never lied to me."

"It was for the best. One life sacrificed for countless others. I never wanted to lie to you, Ellie, but it's just how it had to work. It was the only way. Because of you, people were safe. They're not anymore," Sainte said, trying to convince her of his words, trying to convince himself that it was indeed the best way.

She scoffed. "Listen to yourself. You don't even believe your words. How would you feel if you were the one locked away for your entire life? Not knowing that anything existed beyond the walls? Shut up," she growled as Sainte tried to say something.

"You've no idea what it's like." She looked down at the ground and softly said, "I thought you might have been the one person who would see things the way I do, support me. I really wish you were... After all, I am carrying your child. It's not noticeable now, but I can feel it," she said, caressing her stomach.

Sainte stared at her in disbelief. The Malignin lowered him until he was at eye level with her. She slithered closer, her hands crawled up from his groin and stopped on either side of his head.

Her lips brushed against his when she said, "Congratulations. You're going to be a father." Her eyes were half-lidded. She was so close he felt her eyelashes on his own.

He remained silent, but his disgust was apparent.

She backed away. "Before we move on to the main event, I feel like I should tell you a little bit about the White Wyverns you've been with. I'm not sure what Aroc has told you," Ellie spit out Aroc's name like a sour taste, "but I'm sure it wasn't all the truth. You see, you and the world you know of are trapped, much like I was in the mountain. The White Wyverns, upon discovering that they couldn't defeat the Malignin, sectioned off a portion of the world. They effectively trapped the Malignin, contained them, and everyone else along with them in a small area of the greater world.

"You're imprisoned, but did the White Wyverns ever tell you that? The Malignin told me. They proved it to me. Now that I know this, now that I have followers, we are going to break out of this prison. We were sentenced by the White Wyverns without having done anything to deserve it. Unfortunately, you will not live long enough to see the world in its entirety.

"But you will have the great honor of watching the birth of your baby," as she said that, she let her dress fall to the ground. Completely nude, Ellie laid down on a rock slab near the center of the cavern. Her legs were spread towards Sainte. He was speechless.

Her fingers beckoned forth a Malignin. It stepped in front of her, now between herself and Sainte.

"Don't... What're you...?" Sainte began to say. Vomit started to rise in his throat. The Malignin mounted Ellie and thrusted. Ellie let out a gasp and moaned, not in agony. Her hands opened and closed, grasping in pleasure.

Sainte grimaced and closed his eyes. His stomach twisted in knots. He turned his head away. He puked and felt it run down the front of his leathers. He could still hear the terrible noise. The vile creature's movement in and out of Ellie. The girl he once loved and was sworn to protect. To keep innocent.

This was it, his greatest failure. He was shattered.

"What's this? Does our guest want to look away? Tear off his eyelids, then hold his head in place. I don't want him to miss anything," Ellie ordered.

Another Malignin stepped in front of Sainte and tore his right eyelid off with surprising precision and no hesitation. Sainte tried to move his head away from it and let out a strangled

"No." The Malignin grabbed his head with one hand to prevent him from shifting, then ripped his left eyelid off. It now walked behind him and forced him to watch the procession with Ellie behind a curtain of hot blood.

Sainte could barely see as it was, with the blood running over his eyes. It felt like they were on fire.

He could not help but watch as the first Malignin shuddered over Ellie, then moved aside, finally finished. Then, with renewed horror, Sainte watched as another Malignin moved forward to replace the one that just left.

FIFTEEN
-FAILURE-

The two girls moved slowly, and by now, Aroc was unsure if she would be able to reach Sainte in time to help. She guessed that they had been looking for the cave for about an hour, and still there were no signs of it.

"Iris, are we getting close? Are we almost there?" she asked worriedly. Iris looked around and nodded.

"Just a little further," she said quietly. Iris did not seem to be doing too well, but no fever set in yet, and occasionally Aroc would check her bandaged arm, which appeared to be doing fine, considering the circumstances. At least she was not delusional.

True to her word, Aroc saw the opening to the cave a few minutes later.

"Perfect, Iris. You did well. Rest now. It won't be long until help comes, wait here," Aroc told her as she laid her down, hidden from easy view. She was tempted to lay beside her and wait this whole thing out.

It's not like it would matter. She would be dead either way.

As soon as those thoughts entered her head, Aroc pushed them out. She made it this far and would see to it that she ended it.

After ensuring Iris was as comfortable as possible, she set off into the cave.

It was a fairly straight walk, with only a few twists and turns. She was fairly deep in the cave when she came across the first torch.

She took this as an indication that this was the right cave, and she was not sure if she felt relief or fear with that knowledge. Her steps faltered as she continued, ever closer to whatever waited at the end. She had no idea what to expect, no plan of action. She would think of something when the time came. At least, she hoped she would.

In all actuality, Aroc did know what she needed to do, but she did not want to admit it to herself. There had to be another way, something else. No matter what she thought of, out of all the possibilities, the only one that was the best for everyone was the worst for her. Even then, it might not work out.

Maybe it would not even have to come to that option, perhaps it was not too late, but Aroc knew better.

She always knew. She was not going to be leaving these caves alive.

As she walked down the dark tunnel, a sound reached her ears. It was faint, an echo, but it was terrible. It sounded like a crowd roaring and one man's screams.

She quickened her steps.

▼▲▼

Sainte begged and pleaded for Ellie to stop, but she only laughed at his cries.

"Ellie, I loved you. I would have done anything for you. Stop this, please," he sobbed.

"You never loved me."

Her words were poison.

"You lied to me about everything. Be quiet. You're getting no less than what you deserve." Ellie's voice rang throughout the cavern, even above the Malignin's wails.

Sainte lost track of how many Malignin mated with Ellie, and her stomach was starting to bloat unnaturally. It was as if she was going through all the stages of pregnancy in a matter of minutes.

"Your seed and the Malignin's are mixed, Sainte. This child will be corrupt upon birth. This child will be my key to freeing everyone from our oppressors, even if they don't look at themselves that way. They will thank me later."

"Oppressors?"

"The White Wyverns, of course. They're the ones to thank for all your problems," she told him. "It doesn't matter now, not for you. The ritual is almost finished," she said. The last Malignin that was on her moved away.

Ellie's legs were pushed out of socket at her hips, ugly black veins sprawled across her belly. Her grinning visage was peering over all of that, eyes wide with ecstasy, staring at Sainte.

"And now, Sainte, watch the birth of what you created. What we created."

A black ooze that looked like oil seeped from between her legs. It poured out of her, down the rock slab to the ground and pooled there. It kept coming out, and Sainte saw through his blood-soaked eyes that it congealed as it pooled together. It slowly formed a shape. It slowly grew.

The sounds of the Malignin, of Ellie, fell on Sainte's unwilling ears. Her stomach slowly deflated as the ooze leaked out, and beyond that was her still grinning face. She had not broken eye contact with him once.

The liquid grew and slowly formed a humanoid shape. The Malignin beat everything, the floor, walls, each other, and jumped around out of pure excitement. This is what they had been trying to accomplish.

Ellie pushed one last time, and now all of it was out of her. It just had to complete forming itself and the abomination would be complete. Sainte was helpless to do anything to stop it.

The ooze formed into a wretched creature. It was all black, darker than Malignin, than even the darkness of the cave, and it looked as if its skin had the consistency of tar. The face was featureless. There were depressions where the eyes should have been and a slit for a mouth. It had arms and legs, hands and feet, much like a human, but they were unnaturally long, like a Malignin's.

It was a freak of nature, man and Malignin as one. Something that never should have existed.

Ellie cooed at it the entire time. It slowly looked around and worked its jaw up and down. It stretched all its limbs as if to get used to the movements. When finished, it finally looked down upon Ellie, who gazed at it admiringly.

It let out an earsplitting scream, and the Malignin went wild. The two Malignin that held Sainte's feet had let go at some point in their ecstatic craze to join in on the excitement, but he was still held on each arm.

When it was finished screaming, it looked again at Ellie, who did not flinch at the noise and smiled at it.

"You're so beau-" she started to say but never finished. For no apparent reason and not holding back at all, the abomination thrust its hand back into Ellie as if it tried to go back from whence it came.

Ellie cried out in pain and surprise. Her entire frame tensed up as if cramps consumed her body. She tried to claw herself away, but the abomination held her fast. Sainte would have screamed, but his throat was so raw that he was incapable of it.

The abomination pushed harder, and Sainte could now see the outline of its arm through her stomach. Ellie quivered uncontrollably as it went further into her. She was ruined now. Her eyes nearly bulged out of her head.

With one last push, there was a sickening squelching sound as some of her guts were pushed through her stretched neck and out of her mouth. The abomination lifted her, still skewered on its arm, and shook. It tried to get her off, but the shaking did not do it. It slammed her on the rock slab two times. Her bones crunched with each hit. Sainte felt the cavern shake with the power of the blows.

Then it flung her away violently. She flew free of its arm and landed with a sickening thud. Sainte looked on in defeated silence, awaiting his own death.

▼▲▼

Aroc entered the cavern just in time to see Ellie's lifeless body hurled across the room. She searched frantically for Sainte and found him being held. Then she saw the grotesque creature at the center of all the chaos. She immediately knew what it was and that it was probably too late to defeat it. She should have left, but she could not bring herself to leave Sainte.

She spotted Sainte's dagger on the ground behind him. Aroc ran to it, unnoticed by the Malignin who were too caught up in their frenzy to see her. She picked it up in her ruined hands with pain.

Unhesitatingly, she stabbed the Malignin to the right that held Sainte in the leg. It was not a particularly strong attack, but the dagger was sharp enough to pierce it. Surprised, it let go of Sainte and swiped at her, not out of intent to kill, but like she was an annoying gnat.

She dodged the swipe, managing to keep a hold of the dagger. The other Malignin let Sainte go so it could join in the chaos with its brothers.

She ran to Sainte as he crumpled. "Sainte, it's me, Aroc. I have your dagger; take it." He turned to her, and she gasped at the sight of his eyes. He ignored her and felt for the dagger.

"Listen to me, Sainte. There is one more thing you must do," Aroc told him.

"Tell me when we're out of here," he said.

"No, it has to be done here, right now." She took a shaky breath. She was afraid. "You have to stab me in the stomach. You have to kill me. Ever since I lost my hands, the light has been building in me because I have no way to channel it out. With an open wound at the source of the light, I'll be able to channel it out one last time.

"It should be enough to clear out this cavern and then some and hopefully kill that abomination." Sainte shook his head futilely. "Do it, Sainte. You can still fix this. Everything you've done has accumulated to this point. This is your last chance to right your wrongs. You still have a chance to live."

"What about you? What will happen to you?"

"It doesn't matter anymore."

"Answer me."

"It will kill me. I will die." Saying the words made it real.

She was going to die.

Of course, it was always going to happen, but it had been just a thought then. Now it was out there, spoken, existed.

He stared at her pleadingly as she got on her knees. Sainte got on his as well. He placed the tip of the dagger on her stomach.

Aroc, now crying, nodded to him.

"Do it."

With a final breath, Sainte mustered up all his strength and pushed the blade through. She let out a choked sob, and he caught her as she fell sideways.

Light pulsed out of her and illuminated the entire cavern. The Malignin screamed in agony and crawled away, tearing at each other in the process. The closest ones to Aroc and Sainte dropped dead immediately. Two more pulses of light flashed out rapidly, and then the cavern was quiet. There were no more Malignin here.

Sainte cried now, no matter how much it burned his eyes. He rocked back and forth with her in his lap.

"Sainte, please... stay here," Aroc croaked through her mouth, slowly filling with blood. "Hold me," she said as her eyes slowly closed.

"I'll never let you go," he said through his blood and tears.

▼▲▼

Iris went in and out of consciousness. She remembered Sainte leaning over her at one point, his face was bloody, and his eyes were red, then she blacked out again.

When she regained consciousness, she was in a wagon. She groaned and the driver was by her side instantly, offering her water.

"You're going to be fine, Iris. You're lucky I found you when I did. I'm Jasmine, by the way," the woman said.

Iris said nothing. She just looked up at the sky. But something was different. The sky was blue. The sun was shining. She wanted to ask Jasmine some questions, but when she sat up, her vision quickly faded, and she passed out again.

Jasmine caught her so she did not hit hard when she fell back down. She went back up and grabbed the reins of her horse.

She brought Iris to the Shinta village outside of Munich. She did not want to bring Iris to Munich directly because it was too public there. She wanted to keep her a secret. For now.

When she got to the village, she found the healer, Laureen, and explained to her Iris' situation.

"I'll do what I can for her. What are you going to do now?" Laureen asked Jasmine.

"I'll stay a few days to make sure she is stable if that's alright with you?" she asked.

"Of course it is. I'll get a tent ready for you to sleep in."

"Thank you." She followed Laureen to another empty tent and, once alone, laid down on the cot exhausted.

Two days passed when Jasmine was awoken by Laureen one morning.

"Jasmine, are you up?" Laureen called from outside the tent.

"Yes, what is it? Come on in. Is Iris alright?" Jasmine said.

"Iris is fine. She would like to talk to you," she said.

"Is she strong enough for it?" Jasmine asked.

"Of course, I wouldn't have gotten you if she wasn't. You know where she is. One more thing, the cut in her arm was deep and cut through muscle, tendons, and broke a chunk of bone off. I'm afraid she will not regain any movement to it. I'm not sure if she has realized this yet, she's been rather... odd," Laureen said.

"I would think that would be expected of someone that has been through what she has," Jasmine said. Laureen nodded in agreement. "I'll go see her."

Jasmine walked quickly to Iris' tent and entered, feeling the comforting heat of the fire before she saw it. Iris was propped up on her back with a bowl of herbs on her lap.

"Hey, Jasmine," she said. Her left arm was bandaged with fresh gauze.

"Hey there, how're you holding up?" she asked.

"Fine, I guess. My arm was hurting a lot, but Laureen gave me these." She gestured at the bowl. "These herbs help with the pain."

"Laureen's good like that. She's seen many injuries and knows what's best."

"You got that right," Iris paused. "I have a question."

"What is it?"

"Why hasn't Sainte visited me? I saw him, I think... Is he all right?" She looked down and focused, trying to remember where and when she saw him last.

Jasmine sat down at the foot of her bed, sorry for the girl. "What do you remember, Iris?"

At the question Iris cried, but she tried to choke them back, "I remember it like a nightmare. I don't want to, but I do."

Jasmine found herself silently crying with Iris, sharing her pain. She did not know what to say, so she just said the first thing that came to her mind. "Everything's going to be alright."

Iris shook her head, still crying. "That's a lie. You can't know that. Nothing is alright. Nothing will ever be alright."

Jasmine just listened to Iris cry, troubled. She could not help but admit there was truth to Iris's words. Nothing she could have said would have been further from the truth.

She knew everything was not alright.

EPILOGUE

Jasmine rode by herself to the Council, mentally preparing the report that she was going to give them. She already decided to let them know about Iris, but she would not tell them all she knew about Sainte. She was prepared to lie. Expected to, even.

After what happened with Aroc, Isaac's letter was all but moot. The Council would have no choice but to initiate the Sever, and she could not blame them, but maybe she could delay it. The Barrier was dead, meaning there was now no possible means of a blooded heir. This was going to be an interesting conversation.

She arrived at the castle a day later and entered the converse chambers. All in attendance were seated around her, towering up in bleachers.

"Good morning Council," she began. All of the leaders of the White Wyverns were already gathered there. "I am Jasmine Shilda, and I bring you the report on Crearia. You know how everything began, so I will skip to the conclusion if that is acceptable to you."

"It is, continue," the Head Speaker said.

"Sainte Nore, upon discovering the location of Ellie, set off by himself to track her down. Aroc found this out a day later and set out to try to aid Sainte. I was to seek them out in five mornings if neither returned.

"I waited, and five mornings passed, so I left to search for them. Following the path north, I came across Miqel's body. He was dead. I continued to the cave, where I discovered Iris, alive but barely. By this time, it was morning, and it was the first time the sun was visible.

"I continued into the cave but found no trace of either Sainte nor Aroc. I left and did what I could for Iris, bringing her to the Shinta village. I figured Munich would not give her the privacy she needed to heal. When I was with her, she informed me of what happened.

"She said Ellie gave birth to a monster, the abomination. Sainte was forced to watch it all. When the abomination was complete, it killed Ellie. Aroc entered the cavern at this time and freed Sainte." Jasmine paused and looked at the members sitting above her.

"You are aware that Aroc lost both hands to searing?" she asked the Keepers.

"We are," the Head Leader replied.

"Then you will understand this. Aroc had Sainte stab her in the stomach. She used the wound as an opening and channeled all the light she had been storing. It effectively cleansed the chamber, if not the entirety of the cave, of Malignin. She gave her life to save what she could.

"This is all that Iris remembers. I know there are still Malignin around, but they are few in number. As for the abomination, I know not if it is still alive. The people that joined Ellie and the Malignin, I know not where they are, either. The same goes for Sainte and Aroc's bodies." She looked around expectantly.

"This concludes my report."

At that, the Council all began talking amongst themselves, filling the room with a buzz.

After a few minutes, they all quieted down, and the Head Speaker turned to Jasmine again.

"Do you know if anyone knows about us? Knows what we are doing?" he asked her.

"None that I am aware of," she told him.

"I think we have some news for you, then. Some of our scouts have returned and told us the abomination is alive. It also seems that it has as clear a memory as we do of the past. It's telling all human followers of their captivity as well. It tells them a twisted version of what we did to them to skew their idea of us. And the Malignin's numbers were not as damaged as you seem to think.

"This news will undoubtedly spread like wildfire among humans. Soon we will have an uprising on our hands. It is safe to assume that most people will join the Malignin upon hearing this news.

"Aroc indeed dealt a heavy blow against the abomination, the shining sun is proof of that, but it will not last. The abomination, and Malignin, have retreated to lick their wounds, but they will be back. They will return with darkness as before since there is no longer a Barrier to hold it at bay.

"As I'm sure you've come to the same conclusion, we have reason to believe that the abomination is Zith. He is back, and we have no idea what he is capable of. What you have told us is not the ending of a problem, Jasmine, but the emergence of a million more. The Sever must be initiated." The Head Leader told her solemnly. "We cannot allow the Malignin and Zith to go unchecked."

The marble chamber was silent at this point. All the White Wyverns present were deep in troubled thoughts. Jasmine listened in disbelief. How could so many people have died in vain? They gave their lives for nothing. Aroc gave her life for nothing. She knew one thing that the Council did not know.

She knew where Sainte was and where he was going. Jasmine could only hope for Sainte to agree to aid her and accomplish his task before the Sever commenced.

Acknowledgments:

First off, I want to thank everyone that actually took the time to read my rough drafts and nudge me in the right direction. *Blades of the Night* would not have gotten here without you. Second, I would like to thank my wife, Stephanie, for sticking with me and offering her words of encouragement throughout this process.

I'd be remiss if I didn't mention all the beta readers and ARCs, your help is so much more appreciated than you know!

Finally, everyone else that is not specifically mentioned. If you helped me at all in anyway with *Blades of the Night*, you deserve my gratitude. Thank you all.

I almost forgot the readers. Thank you, sincerely, for reading my words.

Whether you enjoyed this book or not, please consider leaving a review!

-Daniel

About the Author:

Daniel Wiebe lives in central Texas with his wife, Stephanie. He works as a firefighter/paramedic. He was in the Marine Corps for five years before working as a firefighter. Daniel writes when he has time, which isn't much between work and home life, but he squeezes it in when he can. If you wish to contact him for anything, his email is: authordanielwiebe@gmail.com.

Made in the USA
Coppell, TX
23 February 2026

72120548R00204